This is a work of fiction. All names, characters, locations and incidents are the products of the author's imagination or used fictitiously.

Any resemblance to actual persons, living or dead, business establishments, events or locations is entirely coincidental.

Order this book online at www.trafford.com/07-1660
or email orders@trafford.com

Most Trafford titles are also available at major online book retailers.

© Copyright 2007 Harold J. Cole.

All rights reserved. No part of this publication may be reproduced, stored in a retrieval system, or transmitted, in any form or by any means, electronic, mechanical, photocopying, recording, or otherwise, without the written prior permission of the author.

Note for Librarians: A cataloguing record for this book is available from Library and Archives Canada at www.collectionscanada.ca/amicus/index-e.html

Printed in Victoria, BC, Canada.

ISBN: 978-1-4251-4059-5

We at Trafford believe that it is the responsibility of us all, as both individuals and corporations, to make choices that are environmentally and socially sound. You, in turn, are supporting this responsible conduct each time you purchase a Trafford book, or make use of our publishing services. To find out how you are helping, please visit www.trafford.com/responsiblepublishing.html

Our mission is to efficiently provide the world's finest, most comprehensive book publishing service, enabling every author to experience success. To find out how to publish your book, your way, and have it available worldwide, visit us online at www.trafford.com/10510

Trafford PUBLISHING

www.trafford.com

North America & international
toll-free: 1 888 232 4444 (USA & Canada)
phone: 250 383 6864 ♦ fax: 250 383 6804
email: info@trafford.com

The United Kingdom & Europe
phone: +44 (0)1865 722 113 ♦ local rate: 0845 230 9601
facsimile: +44 (0)1865 722 868 ♦ email: info.uk@trafford.com

10 9 8 7 6 5 4 3 2

To my wife, Marilyn

whose love and unwavering support
makes life a beautiful experience.

1

APRIL 30, 1945

BERLIN   **1845 GMT**

Hundreds of filthy vermin clamored after the escaping figures as they crawled through the darkened passageway. The creatures were unrelenting in the pursuit of their human prey, chasing the terrified party through the underground subway tunnel. The rats scurried around and under the feet of the terrified humans, screeching and squealing in anticipation of their next meal. The noise was deafening.

A woman tripped over the leg of a dead soldier and fell heavily onto the wet concrete. No one stopped to help as the disease carrying rodents swarmed over the fallen figure and immediately began nipping at the exposed flesh. Driven by fear and the desire to survive, the woman struggled to her feet, flailing blindly at the rats as she stumbled forward to catch up to the others.

The group followed the underground passageway below the Friedrichstrasse, until they had passed the subway station. On their left was a large air vent, laid open by the blast of a British bomb. They were just south of the river Spree, next to the Weidendammer Bridge. They climbed upwards through the air vent to reach the outside. As they emerged, they found themselves in a world that neither rats nor humans could recognize.

The sky was bright orange in colour from the thousands of fires burning throughout the city. The landscape was a jungle of smashed concrete, broken glass and twisted metal. Bright flashes of light appeared randomly on all sides, accompanied by the vociferous sounds of the explosions echoing from the deadly bombs that rained down around them.

The members of the group were dressed in dark clothing, torn and frayed from contact with the jagged remains of what was once the city of Berlin. They pushed forward, making their way over the ruins that only hours before was one of Germany's most historic buildings. Escape was a slow and arduous journey, but the singular thought of survival amidst the death and destruction that was consuming Berlin, motivated the group. Frightened and afraid for their lives, they pressed onwards.

Their planned rendezvous point was on the other side of the Weidendammer Bridge, but an anti-tank barricade and heavy Russian artillery forced them repeatedly to retreat.

They journeyed around, over and through a myriad of gutted buildings. There were few familiar landmarks left by which to navigate. Frustrated and disoriented, the party reached a clearing and paused. It took a moment before they recognized the location. It was the remains of the New Reich Chancellery, where Hitler's power had lived. They had wandered around in a circle.

Fires ignited as if by magic, and explosions occurred with eerie regularity. Everywhere they turned, shrapnel and noxious clouds of burning sulfurous gases filled the air. They had left the safety of the bunker and found Hell. It was worse than anything they could have ever imagined.

This night's relentless bombing of Berlin was the fiercest air battle ever fought over the Nazi capital. It was unequaled by any of the hundreds of previous daylight raids. Over one thousand Allied bombers fought their way more than five hundred miles across Europe, battling through a gauntlet of German fighters and bursts of anti-aircraft fire to reach their target.

The first of the Allied bombers arrived at twenty-five thousand feet above the Berlin at precisely twelve o'clock noon, and the devastation began. The continuous stream of aircraft continued, dropping a torrent of exploding steel and incendiaries on invasion weary Berlin. The onslaught of the deadly cargo of Grand Slam and Tallboy bombs from the Lancaster, Halifax and Liberator aircraft continued unabated. Violent firestorms erupted throughout the city, exposing Berliners to a symphony of light and fire of unimaginable proportions. The heavy smoke and lethal spray of shrapnel amplified well into the night, making any movement in open areas both difficult and extremely dangerous. Those still in the city were witnessing the real and terrible preliminaries to the inevitable invasion by the Allies. Berlin was disintegrating about them. The British and American air superiority had made it clear. The war was over.

Advancing Allied ground troops were poised to enter the city from the West. They were preparing the signal to advance as the Russian troops, filled with hatred so intense, were attacking from the East. The Russians would not wait for the Allies signal. With the fierce battles near Moscow and Leningrad still vividly embedded in their minds, they were anxious to enter Berlin and capture the spoils of war.

In the ruins of the Reich Chancellery Garden, a bizarre scene unfolded as a small group attempted to pour gasoline on what appeared to be a simple mound of garbage. The mayhem of the war enveloped them like a second skin. Shrapnel from an exploding bomb hit the leader as he poured liquid on the rubble, his body crumbling into a lifeless heap next to the mound. Another member emerged from behind the cover of fallen concrete. Ignoring his comrade, he picked up another container and resumed pouring gasoline over the mound, tossing the jerry can aside as it emptied. A momentary lull in the intense rain of death gave another time to run over to the mound. He struck a match and then dove for safety as another bomb exploded nearby, sending a shower of debris over the area. Again, he ventured back to the mound and lit another match. This time the match found its target and the pile of rubble erupted into a flaming inferno.

Across the wide street, in the middle of a pile of concrete and glass that was once a very prestigious jewelry store, the small group of five stood awestruck. Their leader motioned frantically to the others to keep moving forward.

Terrified, they reluctantly followed their leader along the tracks of the surface railway until they reached the Lehrter Station. The group turned towards the east and followed the Invalidienstrasse back towards the Weidendammer Bridge, finally reaching an iron footbridge that ran parallel to the overpass. They crossed the river Spree and found their rendezvous point. The street was barren. There was no sign of their contact. Alone, amidst the destruction of Berlin, fear and panic began to take hold.

No one heard the heavy bulletproof vehicle as it approached. The constant reverberation that was the destruction of Berlin smothered the sound of the large black 770 K Mercedes-Benz sedan clambering over the rock-strewn streets.

The twenty-foot long chassis, laden with two thousand pounds of half-inch thick armor plating and one and a quarter-inch thick bullet-proof glass weighed nearly ten thousand pounds when fully fueled with its maximum five hundred pounds of fuel.

The body of the massive car was in pristine condition, a strange juxtaposition to the surrounding scene. The only mark was a slight nick on one of the side windows, a blemish that had occurred when the Furher had personally tested the strength of the bulletproof glass, having fired his Luger at the window from pointblank range.

In the background, the blazing fires were slowly melding together as the insistent wailing of the air raid sirens continued to permeate the night air. Overhead the beams from the searchlights moved quickly across the dark sky, trying in vain to lock on to the bombers flying five miles above them. Flashes from the anti-aircraft fire that ringed the city continued to light up the sky, but the never-ending procession of aircraft and their deadly cargo persisted.

In the middle of the devastation that surrounded them, the headlights of Hitler's personal vehicle, masked with only the familiar blackout slits, seem to beckon them to a safe haven. The group of five quickly made their way towards the car parked amongst a huge pile of rubble. The leader opened the door and waited as the others hurried past. They were virtually climbing over each other in their quest to find sanctuary in the armored car. In a seemingly odd gesture, the last person paused for a moment and shook hands with the guide. As the last man turned and entered the car, the guide closed the door, stepped back and saluted.

The man who had led them to safety turned, casually walked back towards the rock-strewn area and stood under the doorway to the former jewelry store.

The sound of grinding gears from a hurried shift permeated the air as if the car rebelled against the driver's over-anxious commands. Seconds later, the single-overhead-cam straight eight, with dual carburetors and dual ignition, transferred its entire two hundred and thirty horsepower to the driveshaft. The massive vehicle slowly moved away from the rubble-strewn area with its human cargo. They had found refuge from the carnage of war.

The German manufacturers had designed the Mercedes 770K to handle such demanding tasks. As it reached a clear stretch of roadway, the superchargers kicked in and the vehicle immediately began to pick up speed. The independent four-wheel independent suspension with coil springs and hydraulic shock absorbers provided an unusually comfortable ride through the remains of the war torn city, but the road, strewn with abandoned vehicles and pieces of concrete, made it difficult to achieve any speed near its maximum one hundred miles per hour.

The guide stood in the doorway where the party had been only moments before. He watched, as the vehicle with its mysterious cargo of panic-stricken passengers disappeared into the hellfire of the night. His job was finished. He calmly removed his pistol from its side holster. "Niemand müssen wissen" he said quietly as he placed the revolver against the side of his head and pulled the trigger.

2

May 1, 1945

WICK, SCOTLAND   2035 GMT

Members of the base personnel from the RAF station at Wick exited the Breadalbane Cinema. They laughed and jostled each other, seemingly oblivious to ongoing war that was raging throughout Europe. The tides of war had turned. They were living for the moment.

The theatrical posters proudly announced the current movie fares as "The Perils of Pauline" and "Flash Gordon". Away from the rigors of their life and responsibilities at the airbase, the group was obviously enjoying themselves. Everyone seems to be talking at the same time, turning the conversation into a cacophony of words with each person compelled to get every thought out in the shortest possible time. It was wartime, and every second counted.

"Bloody good fun it was. Especially the newsreel movie that showed the Allied forces poised to enter Berlin. Fantastic!"

"I'll say. We should have a drink to celebrate."

"Brilliant idea, old boy, but it's early and there's no joy in dry old Wick town, How's about driving up to Thurso for a few pints?"

"Either that or we go up to the Church of Scotland Canteen and get some cakes, scones and a cup of tea."

"A wad and a cuppa tea? Sounds good to me. Besides,

Thurso is almost an hour away. We've got an early flight tomorrow."

"Hey, why not head over to the harbour area to 'Hell's Kitchen'. Old Bill will be frying up those succulent fish & chips until at least eleven. There is no better food anywhere around here."

"And he never runs out of supplies."

"Yeah, and his girls are pretty nice too. I'd sure fancy one of them, all right."

"You would fancy anything, as long as it wore a skirt."

"Aye. I'm a very healthy nineteen-year-old and I do have my ration of weaknesses."

"Right, but you had better be careful of Old Bill. He always watches out for his girls. Besides Scotty, your crew is on patrol tomorrow morning. We wouldn't want you to be overly tired".

"Yeah, right. Tomorrow is probably another of those bloody practice bombing runs, or worse, a local test flight again."

"When are we going to get some real action? The war will be over before we even get to see a Jerry."

"Don't worry, you've got lots of time."
The young flying officer laughed and nodded affirmatively.

"Right, then. Hell's Kitchen it is. Off we go, then."

The members of the group continue down the road, holding on to each other, their arms entwined, weaving back and forth to the music of their conversation. They were intoxicated with the feeling of being alive. This was wartime. They had no way of knowing what tomorrow would bring. They had seized this special moment for themselves.

3

MAY 2, 1945

HAMBURG, GERMANY   **0334 GMT**

The bombing raid had ended several hours earlier. The deadly Allied aircraft had emptied their lethal cargo over the city were returned to their bases, leaving Hamburg in chaos, a mass of burning buildings, death and destruction. The beautiful black car that was once Hitler's pride and joy was no longer in pristine condition. Flying debris had hit the left rear fender soon after they left Berlin, smashing it inwards to the point the tire constantly rubbed against the metal. The hood and right fender had also suffered damage when the driver was forced to use the car as a battering ram to move abandoned vehicles out of the way, an event that occurred more times than they could remember. Despite the incredible punishment, the car continued onward, a testament to the skill of its German builders.

The light from the hundreds of fires surrounding Hamburg made it easy for the driver of the black sedan as he maneuvered the vehicle along the heavily damaged coastal road towards the docks. Several ships were ablaze and the entire area appeared in ruins. The driver drove black car alongside the remaining half wall of a bombed out factory that bordered the main dock. He exited the vehicle, scanning the area for his contact. The smell of death hung in the air like a bad dream.

A sudden flash from a nearby exploding incendiary device lit up the dock area allowing the driver to see his target off to the right. In the water, amidst the remains of what was one of Germany's most efficient boatyards waited a black submarine with a large swastika prominently displayed on the conning tower.

A temporary walkway had been fashioned from materials that once were part of a shipbuilding factory. It was the only link between the dock and the submarine. The captain of the U-Boat skillfully used its engines to maintain contact with the makeshift gangplank.

The driver turned and opened the rear door allowing the four passengers to disembark. They did not hesitate and immediately darted towards the dock, leaving the driver standing alone beside the car.

The last man paused, spun around on his heel, walked back towards the sedan and spoke to the driver.

"Niemand müssen wissen."

As the driver saluted, the passenger pulled a revolver from inside his heavy Great Coat and fired a single shot into the driver's head. He turned and walked briskly back towards the submarine, catching up with the other three passengers as they navigated the flimsy gangplank and boarded the vessel.

Within minutes, the submarine had eased away from the war torn dock, sending the makeshift gangplank crashing into the harbour. The crew secured the hatch as the U-Boat slipped silently into the River Elbe and made its way out towards the North Sea.

4

MAY 4, 1945

RAF BASE, WICK, SCOTLAND   **0700 GMT**

The airbase at Wick, in Northern Scotland was one of the most remote bases in the RAF. Bordering on the edge of the North Sea, it was a perfect spot to station Squadron 962, a group of flying Catalina aircraft specializing in Submarine Detection.

While a few roads provide access to the town of Wick in the summer months, they remained virtually impassable during the long months of winter's siege.

The main access to the town of Wick was by train or air, and neither was a particularly good option, especially in wartime. The train trip from London took thirty-six hours, and although quicker, with the airbase constantly harassed by the Germans, the option of flying personnel into the area proved to be far too dangerous.

The base was the standard Air Force design. The position of the runways was in the classic triangle shape with the longest facing the relentless winds that continually blasted in from the northwest.

Each of the wooden buildings was of the same design with little or no imagination given to the overall appearance of the area. Appearance meant little to those who posted to the airbase. There was a war going on, and if they managed to have any time off, they would be going into the little town of Wick.

The residents of Wick were most hospitable and greeted the

influx of RAF personnel with enthusiasm. The town itself, however, was completely devoid of beer and liquor. The nearest pub was in the town of Thurso, twenty-one miles to the north.

The weather at the base was, in a single word, grim. The prevailing winds were usually cold and quite strong. The combined effects of the winds and heat in the summer produced a predictable early morning fog that usually burned off by mid-morning.

Icing in the carburetors was a hazard at all times of the year. Flying low over the wave tops at night to obtain sea level readings when the weather turned rough made it extremely bumpy, rendering visibility often to zero. Landing at the base with fog or a very low cloud base over the airfield was a demanding task that became even more difficult after long and tiring sorties.

The squadron flew seventy to eighty sorties a month from the Wick base. Most were convoy escorts, which was fortunate, considering the weather was often more deadly than the Luftwaffe.

The normally patrol was up to six hours duration at about fifteen hundred above sea level, regardless of the weather conditions. However, spotters could easily see the coastlines and mountains with a naked eye up to one hundred and twenty miles away on those exceptional days when the weather cooperated. There was no radar available at the Wick base. The crew spent the entire flight scanning the sea. The work was monotonous and very tiring. They flew at five knots above the aircraft's stalling speed to give the spotters adequate time to locate the elusive German submarines. The U-Boats countered by prowling at periscope depth, hiding amongst the white breakers of the North Sea.

The crews did however, have a device, affectionately known as "George", which enabled them to fly without having to put their hands on the control column, permitting them to concentrate on scanning the open seas in search of the enemy.

The secret to a successful patrol was to stay high enough to survey the area, and low enough to permit a quick attack. While their objective was to hunt down and attack the submarines, their very presence in the skies forced the enemy to remain submerged, slowing their progress and disrupting their deadly missions. It was a reoccurring scene, and it would be the same again today.

The early morning fog hung over the airfield like a protective blanket, shielding the warriors from unseen dangers above. It was nine o'clock before the wet mist dissipated and the crews swung into action to get the day's sorties airborne.

Planes began to taxi to their take off positions as the crew members of Squadron 962's Catalina Flying Boat assembled at their aircraft in preparation for their next mission.

Built by Boeing in Canada, the Catalina aircraft was aptly nicknamed "Canso" by the crews of the Royal Canadian Air Force. It was a bulky craft with a wide body at the front and a high tail. With the two engines on top, it looked like a pregnant duck having a bad hair day. It was not a pretty aircraft, but it was effective in its role as a submarine hunter.

The wheels that permitted landing on regular runways folded up into the undercarriage when water landings were required. Two huge side blisters stuck out like sidecars. These plastic bubbles were where the wireless gunners would operate their .5-inch Browning machine guns to protect the aircraft when attacked. Two powerful Pratt & Whitney R-1830 twin Wasp fourteen-cylinder, radials engines were mounted on the top of the high winged aircraft above the crew cabin. Each produced twelve hundred horsepower, which provided for the quick climbs so often required for strafing and bombing runs once an enemy submarine was located.

"C'mon boys, let's get the lead out. We've got to get on patrol today," shouted Captain Neil Evans as he led his crew of eight towards the ungainly aircraft.

A soft-spoken teacher from Winnipeg, Manitoba, Flight Lieutenant Evan's slender build and quiet demeanor masked his fierce desire for combat. He was married with two children. The youngest, a girl, was born after he left for active duty. Evans had never seen her.

He had met his wife through his church and the very thought of war never entered his life, until the death of an older brother during the failed Dunkirk invasion. He had volunteered for duty with the RCAF immediately after learning about his brother's fate.

The war was taking its toll and there was an acute shortage of qualified pilots. Evans received his commission as Captain only three months after enlisting. He would fly the Canso, a submarine hunter. He immediately named his aircraft "Irene" after his wife.

"Ron, what's the latest on this wind?" asked Evans as he tossed his survival pack up into the belly of the plane.

"Should drop off some this afternoon, but will most likely pick up again by dark," answered his co-pilot.

Flight Officer Ron Grimley was from Vancouver and as was the case with Captain Evans, he too, went quickly through Flight School and directly to the war front.

A 24-year-old single who was studying to become an architect, he enlisted along with his friends from the University of British Columbia.

"What's the course this morning, Professor?" asked Grimley, as he climbed into the plane.

The Navigator was Flight Officer Gary Brand who hailed from Toronto. A brilliant mathematician, Brand was at the top of his

class and appropriately named "The Professor".

"Ops want us to do Quadrant J-3 again. Apparently, there was some activity up there yesterday. Two submarines were spotted, but managed to dive out of sight before our boys could engage."

"Hey, maybe we'll get lucky and find us one today," replied Grimley settling into the co-pilots seat.

Evans joined him in the cockpit and climbed into the pilot's spot. "Let's keep a good eye on things out there today. Things are getting quite hot in Berlin. The Germans are going to be throwing everything they have at us."

"Right, they are in a desperate situation and desperate people do desperate things," confirmed Brand putting his radio communications headset, "How are you gunners back there? You read me okay?"

Once inside the aircraft, each crewmember had his own position and all communications with others was by radio, a system that brought them together as a crew. They operated as a unit.

"Everything is shipshape back here," called #1 Wireless Gunner Flight Sergeant Scott Nelson, a twenty-year-old lad from Prince Edward Island. Young and good looking, Scott was dedicated to his role in the war effort, but he still found time to chase the girls. "Williams, you hooked up?"

"Yeah, I'm here." Wireless Gunner #2 was Flight Sergeant Sid Williams and despite being married, had signed on for a second tour of duty. His calm disposition was reassuring and gave a lift to the rest of the crew. Evans knew this and appreciated it.

"Everything's fine down here in the hole, Captain," responded the third Wireless Gunner, Bob Hartman. "Hell, if I had a couple extra inches, I could get my lunch in here too," he added with a touch of sarcasm.

"Know what you mean Bob, we all have the same problem," answered Brand, "I still haven't figured out how to get my lunch and the charts in here".

"Hopefully the charts take precedent." replied Grimley.

"Yeah, this crate may float, but I don't want to spend the night out there," offered Nelson, "I've got a forty-eight-hour pass and a date with one of the girls from 'Hell's Kitchen'."

"Which girl?" asked Hartman with feigned interest.

"The cute little blonde. Leslie. You remember the one that dropped the chips in my lap last week."

"How did you get a date with her?" questioned Brand, "I thought Old Bill was protecting her from all you bad boys."

"Just have to be patient, my friend."

"And eat a lot of Old Bill's cooking" offered Grimley.

"Or wear it," laughed Williams.

The radio crackled again. It was Flight Engineer Don Edwards. "Number one here. We're set to go."

"Ditto here for number two. Let's get this baby up there and find us something to shoot at. I promised my Kitty we would find us a sub today," answered Flight Engineer, Sergeant Joe Stojik.

"You bring your pussy with you, Joe?" asked Brand.

"Nah, she was far more interested in sleeping," replied Joe, suppressing a yawn. "Something I wouldn't mind doing either."

It was a glib remark, but down deep, Joe was concerned. On most every flight, Stojik carried the little kitten tucked inside the top of his flying overalls. He had befriended it at the barracks. It was bending the rules, but it was also wartime and he considered the kitten was his good luck charm. The kitten had brought him good luck on other missions, and he had an uneasy feeling that they would need all the luck they could get today.

Captain Evans fired up the first of the two Pratt & Whitney engines and brought it up to normal idle. He then proceeded to the second, which gave out a loud backfire before catching and building up its revolutions to normal idle.

The takeoff for a wartime plane is always stressful. They carried maximum fuel and, in addition to the ammunition for the three Browning machine guns, they would have four one hundred pound depth charges on board as well. A failure of one of the engines after the pilot committed to their take-off would often prove fatal. However, "Irene's" engines performed beautifully, taking the Canso down the runway and, with the help of a twenty-five knot headwind wind, lifted off before they hit the two-thirds marker.

The climb quickly turned bumpy as they made their way out over the cold, white capped waves of the North Sea. Evans executed a two-minute turn to line up on Brand's plotted track of two hundred and ninety degrees True. Quadrant "J-3" was just over two hundred and fifty miles away, but the members of Evan's crew had already begun the scanning of the surface, looking for the telltale signs that would identify a German submarine.

5

MAY 4, 1945

ABOARD GERMAN U-BOAT   **1142 GMT**

The submarine was a Type IXC/40, built at the Deutsche Weft AG, in Hamburg, in April of 1942. One of the first of its type, it had been relegated to duties in and around the North Sea with frequent runs to the port of Hamburg.

Its design gave it a look of a much larger submarine with an overall length of over two hundred and fifty-two feet and a beam of twenty-two and a half feet, although the actual hull itself was only one hundred and ninety-one feet long and fourteen and a half feet wide. Its total height was thirty-one and a half feet. The power plant of the submarine was a nine-cylinder diesel/electric with twin shafts that provided forty-four hundred horsepower on the surface and one thousand horsepower when submerged. Its top speed was nineteen knots on the surface, but reduced to only seven knots when submerged below its periscope depth.

The U-Boat pushed the envelope to complete its mission. Although it had a range of over thirteen thousand miles on top of the water, it was severely restricted when running under the surface.

Most of the credit for its new surface range was due to the complete refit the submarine underwent only a month earlier in Hamburg. Part of the refit involved reconfiguring the hull shape into a revolutionary streamlined design. The Germans changed the propulsion system to allow their U-Boats to cruise when submerged at periscope depth for longer periods at unprecedented speeds. It also possessed a new device the Germans called the "Schnorchel" which allowed the submarine to run its diesel engines while submerged at periscope depth, reducing the possibility of detection by the low flying Canso aircraft of the RCAF.

The shipyard had advised Captain Helmet Mohr that the Furher himself hastened the order to get his submarine back into service. They did not have time to test the ship's new configuration and suggested Mohr take extra care during the initial trials. Mohr had no alternative.

Running just below the surface at periscope depth, Mohr had just completed an amazing run to rendezvous with another submarine designated the U-112, one of the new "electric submarines" which was designed to run long distances underwater. The U-112 had an increased range of over twenty thousand miles.

"Captain, we are having some trouble with the Schnorchel. It is not permitting the exhaust gases to escape," reported First Officer, Lieutenant Gunter Werner. A twenty year-old from Munich, Werner transferred to the elite U-Boat service just a month ago. He showed great promise during his training and quickly advanced to fill the depleted ranks of the German submarine fleet. The Navy pushed him into action before he had even graduated.

Captain Helmet Mohr glanced at the gauges Werner was monitoring. He wasted no time shouting out his order.

"Cut the diesel engines. Switch to electric drive. Lieutenant Emmermann, use the periscope to check the exhaust portal."

"Yes, sir." replied Emmermann.

Mohr was an experienced Captain having served three years with his last ship. Although outfitted with a crew of fifty-two men and twenty-two torpedoes, the primary function of this U-Boat was to be reconnaissance duty in the North Sea between Germany and England.

Mohr disliked the reconnaissance missions, but his orders were direct from Admiral Dönitz. He knew better than to complain.

Lieutenant Gerhard Emmermann was Mohr's Executive Officer. He had been with Mohr for the last two years and longed to get into action against the enemy.

"Captain," reported an excited Emmermann, "I cannot find the Schnorchel. It has disappeared."

"We must have hit some floating debris. How much time do we have left on the batteries?" asked Mohr.

Werner turned from his console, "We less than fifteen percent left, Captain. We will have to surface soon to recharge."

"We will wait as long as possible," replied Mohr, checking his position on the chart. "It is still mid-day. We do not want to take unnecessary chances. We could be seen and that would jeopardize the outcome of our mission."

"But Captain," questioned Werner, "Have we not completed our mission by delivering our special cargo to the rendezvous point on Foula Island?"

The Captain spun and slapped the young officer hard across the face, knocking him off his chair, scattering charts and instruments across floor of the Bridge.

"You are never to speak of our missions again. Not to me, not to the crew, not to anyone. Do you understand?"

The officer slowly picked himself up and climbed back into his position at the console. "Yes, Herr Captain. I am sorry."

Captain Mohr continued to reprimand the young officer. "Admiral Dönitz has entrusted us with this mission and we must not fail to maintain total secrecy." Mohr looked at the young officer and closed his eyes. He knew that it was an innocent remark and he had over reacted, but he must show leadership. He did not have time to be nice.

"I have scanned the entire area, Captain," offered Emmermann. "There are no enemy ships in sight. This would be a good time to surface and run the diesels, even if only for a short time to recharge the batteries."

"We will surface in ten minutes," replied Mohr. "Have the deck crew standby for action." He paused for a moment and looked at Lieutenant Gunter Werner. "The breakdown of the Schnorchel has trapped some of the diesel fumes inside the ship. We could probably all do with a little fresh air as well. "

"Shall I recheck the surface again?" asked Emmermann.

"No," replied Mohr, "We must charge the batteries and clear these fumes. Take us up on top."

It was always a dangerous decision to surface during daylight, but he had no choice. Mohr looked at Emmermann and gave the order. "Surface!"

6

May 4, 1945

ONBOARD THE "IRENE"   **1159 GMT**

The Catalina was flying to the north of Foula Island, heading in a westerly direction. The crew was tired and looking forward to getting back to base. They had been using "George", the automatic pilot device to help steer the plane while they scanned the waters, but the hours of constant searching was beginning to take its toll on the crew's eyes.

"There's Foula Island," shouted Grimley over the constant drone of the Canso's engines.

Evans looked over to the port side, "Not much down there."

"Just a couple of fishing boats." acknowledged Grimley. "It is far too remote a place for me."

The lush green hills of Foula stuck out of the waters of the North Sea as if an afterthought to God's creation. Foula, whose name means 'Island West of the Sun', lies twenty-four miles due west of West Burra Island. With its high, almost four hundred metre cliffs, a dramatic little island that boasted a small but tenacious population made up of mostly fishing families who had been there for hundreds of years. The crew could see the small harbour of Ham in the distance. It was a very exposed area and would be an easy target for any submarine, but there was nothing in the harbour worth the cost of a torpedo.

The Canso droned on across the barren expanse of the choppy, frigid ocean surface. Occasionally a member of the crew would spot some movement on the surface and sound an alert, but it usually turned out to be the crest of a rouge wave or foam from the strong winds that brushed over the cold waters of the North Sea. Other times, the sighting would turn out to be debris from a ship that had fallen victim to a U-Boat. The crew had become weary of seeing such inordinate quantities of wreckage, but they were required to investigate and report each sighting.

After almost four hours of flying, the smallest of movements often played tricks on their eyes, but they pressed on, relentlessly scanning the waters in search for the elusive underwater killing machines.

It was now 1219 GMT and the Canso was flying at one hundred and five miles per hour, at an altitude of three thousand feet above sea level. The sky overhead had darkened, indicating the onslaught of rain.

"*A perfect cover for us*" thought Evans as he initiated a turn to the left to begin what would be their last sweep over Quadrant 'J-3'. "This pass should take care of the quadrant." Evans radioed to Grimley. "Let's take it to the end and then break back to the base. I have been watching the revs on number two engine. They seem to be oscillating slightly."

"Yeah, heat gauges are registering 'okay', but it wouldn't hurt to get it checked out when we get back to the base," replied Grimley.

"It could just be something in the fuel lines or maybe a faulty magneto."

As the Canso leveled out on a heading of one hundred and eighty-five degrees, #2 Wireless Gunner Sid Williams noticed a tiny flash on the water's surface. "Captain, I've got something on the port side, nine o'clock. There, on the water, do you see it?"

Evans scanned to his left. Off their port side, about three miles away, was a German U-Boat traveling on a parallel course. They had slowed their speed to pass through an area strewn with wreckage from a previously sunken ship.

"Got it," acknowledged Evans, "Okay boys; you know the drill, ready your stations. This might get a little bumpy."

The effects of the previous hours of boredom instantly disappeared as the crew sprang into action. The next few minutes would transform the young crew into a new dimension, filled with terror and heart stopping action. It was the same on every attack. Time would stand still. It would seem like an eternity.

Evans banked the aircraft and brought it around behind the submarine. He did not think the crew aboard the submarine had spotted them. The Canso would be over top of them in less than two minutes.

"Let's give this baby a few presents from home."

ONBOARD GERMAN U-BOAT   1221 GMT

The noise of the submarine's diesel engines drowned out the sounds of the approaching Canso. The lookout crew was busy examining the wreckage on the water. Captain Mohr turned away and quickly scanned the sky. He immediately spotted the approaching aircraft. It was three miles behind them and had begun its descent.

The German Captain knew it was too late to start a dive. He made his decision in an instant. He would stay on top of the water and fight it out with the aerial attacker.

Mohr radioed down from the conning tower, "Hard to starboard. Deck guns, enemy aircraft, bearing two-seven-zero degrees, commence firing."

The submarine's crew was fast to react. In only a few seconds the German crewmembers had removed the protective covers, loaded the guns and began firing at the approaching Canso, each shot reverberating throughout the submarine.

The U-Boat Captain looked up into the sky. The Canso had veered off to the left. He knew it would only be seconds before it turned on its final run towards the submarine. The situation was critical. Mohr radioed his first officer, "Emmermann, whatever happens, this submarine must not fall into the hands of the enemy. Notify Naval Command of our position! Longitude sixty degrees, zero minutes, twenty six seconds North, latitude seven degrees, three minutes and twenty seconds West."

Captain Mohr paused for a moment. "Gerhard," he continued, "put all the mission documents into an emergency recovery capsule and prepare to eject it into the sea on my order. Should we be damaged or sunk, it is imperative that those papers are recovered by Germany."

There is a short pause before Emmermann answered. "Yes, Captain, I understand."

Beads of sweat had formed across Mohr's forehead. *"I only pray it is Germany that finds them,"* he thought to himself, *"and not our enemy."*

The U-Boat turned again to its starboard making the Canso come at it from the side. The plane with its deadly cargo of depth charges was less than a mile from the submarine.

Mohr would wait until the last moment and maneuver a hard turn to the port to minimize the target for the Canso. It was their only hope. The submarine's two deck mounted guns, a 105-millimeter cannon and a smaller 45-millimeter anti-aircraft gun, continued firing their stream of lethal shells towards the approaching Canso.

ONBOARD THE CANSO   **1222 GMT**

Like a chameleon changing colours in preparation to attack, the crew had transformed themselves from a group of friends on a routine patrol, into the well-trained fighting machine. They were operating as a single unit in combat mode. Evans and Grimley had both hands on their columns, steering the Canso on its deadly path towards the sub.

"Grant, Joe, ready those depth charges." Evans called as he watched the submarine initiating another turn to the right, "They're changing direction. Two gun crews on deck. Hold on boys."

No sooner had Evans finished speaking when a shell from one of the submarines 105-millimeter guns hit just below the wing bear where the radio was located. The explosion ripped several holes in the side of the fuselage, smashing the aircraft's communications system. Pandemonium ensued as the Canso began to feel the effects of the hit.

Williams looked over towards Scott Nelson's station. His jaw dropped in disbelief. He could only see sky where the aircraft's main radio had been. Nelson was lying on the floor, blood covering his face and hands. "We've been hit! Port side," yelled Williams, "Scott is down."

Nelson was bleeding from the back of his head. Shrapnel from the exploding shell had torn through the radio equipment and hit him, but he was still alive.

"Didn't these guys read the script?" joked Stojik over the intercom, "We're the good guys; they're not suppose to hit us!"

The U-Boat continued firing its guns at the Canso, sending anti-aircraft fire towards them with uncanny accuracy, becoming increasingly fierce and more deadly as the seconds ticked away.

At a range of eight hundred meters, the front 0.30-inch gun of the Canso opened up, hitting in and around the large Swastika on the conning tower of the submarine. Moments later the two 0.5-inch side guns and a third 0.5 inch in the 'tunnel' underneath and behind the hull step opened up as well, spraying shots over the complete length of the submarines deck.

Evans ignored the enemy's fire and continued on his path towards the German U-Boat. He looked over to see Grimley slouched over in his seat, his headset askew. The concussion from an exploding shell had apparently knocked him out, but Evans had no time to take stock of his co-pilots condition. His eyes locked on the submarine. "Only five hundred meters to go," he told himself, praying inwardly that the aircraft would hold together long enough to make the bombing run.

Another round from the German guns hit the Starboard engine, shearing a portion of it from its mount and setting the wing on fire. Evans reached over to the panel above Grimley and flipped the switch for the automatic fire extinguisher.

The U-Boat was turning to its port, trying to become a smaller target, but the guns of the Canso crew continued to rake the deck and tower. A shower of 0.5-inch shells sprayed the submarines rear gunnery crew, silencing the big 105-millimeter gun.

"Get ready to drop the depth charges," Evans called out above the deafening noise caused of the wind roaring through the openings in the fuselage. "We will only have one pass at this."

"I'll drop all four at once," acknowledged Stojik.

The oil and fuel that poured from the twisted remains of the starboard engine, instantly ignited, the flames streaming out behind the wing. Evans continued his fight with the Canso's control stick as the vibrations increased. He knew the aircraft's fuel tanks were close to the source of the fire and could explode at any moment. The submarine's second gunnery crew continued to fire on the approaching Canso, hitting it repeatedly. The distance to the U-Boat was closing fast. They were committed. There could be no thought to turning aside. There was no thought given to saving themselves. It was victory or death, and it was only a hundred meters away.

Evans slipped the Canso to the starboard and lined up directly behind the submarine. He could see the faces of the men on the deck of the submarine as he brought his aircraft down low over the German U-Boat. In one quick motion, Stojik released all four of the three hundred and twenty-five pound depth charges in a perfect straddle of the submarine.

ONBOARD SUBMARINE 1223 GMT

Captain Mohr had stood transfixed, watching as the Canso approached, mesmerized by the skill and determination of his adversary. As the ungainly aircraft, with its torn and tattered fuselage engulfed in flames passed overhead, he saw the four depth charges release.

Mohr called down to Emmermann "Release the capsule." They were his last words. The depth charges hit on both sides of the submarine, erupting simultaneously in a deafening explosion.

The impact of the four detonations lifted the bow of the U-Boat out of the water with such destructive force; it snapped the hull just aft of the conning tower, the two pieces turning upwards to the sky in a grotesque salute to the burning Canso that passed overhead. The violent explosion tossed the deck gunnery crew and the officers from the conning tower into the boiling water like grains of sand. The two broken sections of the fatally wounded submarine dropped back down in a strange but eerie synchronized ballet, settling for a moment on top of the undulating surface, before finally sinking into the depths of the cold North Sea.

ABOARD THE CANSO   **1224 GMT**

A superhuman effort by Evans had brought the severely wounded Canso back up into the air as he past over the U-Boat, but the intensity of the fire increased, melting the starboard engine mounts, causing the burning mass to twist off and fall into the sea.

Wireless Gunner #2, Flight Sergeant Sid Williams was at the emergency radio, frantically tapping out an emergency SOS.

"Gary, what are the coordinates?" he yelled over the radio.

"Latitude sixty North, Longitude three West" replied the navigator calmly as the aircraft continued its turbulent flight path.

Evans applied full power to the remaining engine in order to bank the burning aircraft and turn into the wind. Then, ignoring the imminent dangers of explosions and death, he coolly set the craft down on top of a huge thirty-foot swell, bouncing off and sliding down the side of the next wave.

The hot tubes in the aircraft radio exploded in rapid succession as the North Sea poured in through the huge gaps in the fuselage, drowning everything in sight. The Canso remained upright as it slid to a stop on the icy waters.

The calm and serenity of floating on the ocean surface

seemed surreal in comparison with the intense battle that had raged only moments before.

They enjoyed, for the briefest of moments, the feeling of being safe. Then reality took over. They knew instinctively that the ordeal of battle with its anti-aircraft fire, the resulting inferno caused by the loss of the starboard engine and the death and destruction of the German submarine and its crew, had now became an ordeal of endurance in the frigid waters of the North Sea.

The crew immediately went into survival mode. The degree of devastation astounded them as they went towards the open port side blister in an attempt to evacuate the downed aircraft.

The ditching drill, practiced so many times before was paying off. The port side dingy had automatically inflated. Williams and Brand helped Stojik drag Nelson aboard the life raft. The starboard dingy was launched, but exploded as a large swell caused it to impact with a piece of twisted metal hanging from the starboard engine mount.

Grimley had recovered consciousness and held on tightly to Evans as they made their way out of the smoke filled cockpit, back into the belly of the aircraft. The co-pilot's leather bomber jacket snagged a piece of jagged steel on a bulkhead damaged by the submarine's 105mm shells.

"I'm stuck. I'm stuck!" yelled Grimley, his voice reaching almost panic levels.

Evans turned his head to see his co-pilot hanging from the side of the passageway.

The acrid smoke was getting worse and the water level inside the aircraft was beginning to rise. Evans knew they only had minutes to evacuate. He reached around Grimley, trying to locate the problem. Unable to free the man, Evans put one arm around his co-pilot, lifting and pushing him back towards the cockpit. With his free hand, he reached back and unhooked Grimley's flight jacket from the jagged metal and pulled his friend forward. Grimley passed out and the two men collapsed onto the floor of the aircraft.

"Irene" was sinking fast. Evans pulled himself up and hoisted Grimley onto his shoulder. He was getting out and Grimley was going with him. Evans half dragged and half carried his co-pilot through the devastated aircraft towards the starboard blister.

Hartman was the only other crewmember remaining on board the downed aircraft. He grabbed Evan's arm, spinning both him and Grimley around to face the port blister. "What about the radio?" shouted Hartman, "Do they know were we are?"

"Williams got a call out before we ditched," answered Evans as he tried to push Hartman out through the opening, "They will be coming for us. Go. Go."

Hartman was resisting.

"We only have one life raft, Captain," he shouted. "The other one blew up."

The smoke had dissipated, but the water was now waist high. Evans looked out the port side and spotted the single life raft with five men inside, still tethered to the aircraft. The cold North Sea water had begun to revive Grimley. He was almost semi conscious as Evans moved him towards the opening.

"Help me get Grim inside and then cut it loose. We'll have to swim for it."

"But it is suppose to hold only four," protested Hartman.

"We can put five in and three of us will hang on the outside," Evans declared, moving Grimley into position. "Unless you have some strange desire to stay with this ship or you can think of something better, let's get a move on."

Hartman looked at Evans in disbelief. "No way, Captain. The more the merrier, I always say."

The #3 wireless gunner grabbed Grimley's arm. "Let's get ol' Grim a front row seat."

Evans and Hartman struggled to push the Grimley through the open blister, toppling him out directly into the life raft where he landed on top of Williams. Hartman pulled his pocketknife, looked at Evans and with one swift motion, cut the life raft loose from the aircraft and dove out the window in pursuit, the cord grasped tightly in his hand.

Evans paused for a moment. He scanned the wreckage that was once an aircraft, his aircraft, then dove through the opening and swam towards his crew.

Within seconds of the crew clearing the downed Canso, "Irene" succumbed to her wounds and slowly sank into the chilling depths of the North Sea. The crew of eight was still together. They were sharing a single life raft designed to hold four people. They were cold and injured, but still alive.

7

May 4, 1945

RAF BASE, WICK   **1830 GMT**

The Canso "Irene" was overdue at the RAF base. Flight Operations had no way of knowing the Canso's battle with the submarine had ended over six hours ago or that the crew of 'Irene' had ditched in the cold North Sea. Commander Pete Richards was in control of Flight Operations at the base and his crew would remain on full alert until they could account for the missing plane.

"Have we heard anything from Evans yet?" asked Richards.

"No," answered the radio operator, "Not a sound."

"We've got to send out another Canso to J-3 quadrant. I know Evans. He is a good pilot. If they had to ditch, they would most likely be in the life rafts."

Richards turned to his assistant. "Jerry Smith just got back from patrol. If anyone can find Evans, he can."

"Right, I'll muster up his crew and get them airborne."

"We don't have much time," said Richards. "It's really rough out there on the North Sea. They'll be hanging on for their lives."

THE NORTH SEA   **2045 GMT**

Over eight hours had passed since the 'Irene' and her crew did battle with the U-Boat.

The only good thing, if one was to find a good thing in the midst of all the carnage and destruction that had befallen the crew, was that they were approaching the time of the summer solstice. The night sky was lighter and remained at a constant stage of twilight.

The sky was calm, but the seas were not. The dinghy had capsized three times since they evacuated the aircraft, throwing everyone into the freezing waters. The constant battle to stay together and afloat in the single life raft taxed their strength. The wind was still blowing at over forty knots tossing icy darts from the windswept crests, stinging their faces like needles fired from a shotgun. The icy North Sea waters accelerated the onslaught of Hyperthermia and it was not long before it started taking a deadly stranglehold on the beleaguered crew.

Though Evans was smaller than most of his men, he was adamant about staying in the water. Scott Nelson's head wounds were worse than anyone realized and he had passed into an unconscious state. Grimley was unable to hear. The effects of the exploding shell during the battle had given him a serious concussion causing him to pass in and out of consciousness. The others were simply cold, suffering from the shock of the cold water. Evans knew that Hypothermia, the silent killer, would soon take its toll.

The crew took stock of their situation, counting rations and securing the emergency flares. The situation was desperate but the uninjured did their best to build up the morale of the others..

The tiny life raft lifted up on the crest of a wave and slid down the backside, tossing Scott into the air. He landed on top of Hartman like a discarded doll. As the inflatable settled, Hartman tried to get Scott to roll over for better weight distribution. Scott did not respond. Hartman looked at Scott's face and placed his hand against his neck, searching for a pulse.

"Captain," Hartman chattered, "I think Scott is dead."

Evans was on the outside of the dinghy. Fighting the motion of the waves, he pulled himself around to the side where Scott Nelson was laying. He shook the crewmember's arm but there was no reaction. Stojik was checking for a pulse. There was none.

"Sorry Captain," said Stojik, "he's gone."

There were no words needed, but as the men rolled Scott's body over the side and let it slip down into the depths of the North Sea, Evans mumbled a few words he remembered from his Church prayers back in Winnipeg.

The fight for survival continued into the night. The wave height had diminished slightly and the crew managed to maintain a rotation of those able to spend time on the outside. Time was now the enemy and was affecting everyone. Twelve hours had passed since "Irene" crashed into the sea. The small yellow life raft repeatedly floated over the crest of a wave and careened down the other side, dragging the exhausted crewmembers along with it until the jumbled package of bodies smashed into the valley below. The men would barely have time to collect themselves before the raft raised up, starting the cycle all over again. The pain and resultant damage from the constant pounding of their bodies was escalating with every wave. Another hour of punishment passed before Grimley finally succumbed to the effects of Hypothermia, advanced by the concussion he had suffered during the attack. Once more, the Evan's watched as a member of his crew slipped silently into the cold, dark waters of the North Sea.

As Grimley's body slowly sunk into the depths, the crew heard the unmistakable sound of a Canso mixed in with the noise of the waves splashing against the dinghy.

"It is a Canso. They're coming," yelled Stojik.

"Fire a flare," yelled Hartman.

Brand fumbled with the flare but could not get his numb fingers to function anywhere near normal. With great difficulty, he finally managed to get the flare into the gun and fired the single shot projectile. The shot went off to the side. The crew watched as the flare ascended in a low arc two hundred feet to the side of the life raft and dropped into the water.

The remaining crewmembers sat silently as the Canso passed almost directly overhead. It did not alter its course.

"They didn't see us," screamed Williams, "they weren't even looking."

"They'll be back," whispered Evans, as he clung to the rope on the outside of the dinghy, "Keep the flares ready."

Another four agonizing hours passed. The crewmembers finally convinced Evans to climb into the dinghy, while Hartman and Edwards sat on the outer ring, their feet dangling in the water.

The morale of the six remaining crewmembers was at its lowest ebb when the crestfallen men heard the sound of a second Canso rescue craft.

"They've come back," yelled Williams. "Get the flare ready."

Everyone was scanning the eastern sky for the aircraft but they were amazed when the sounds of the rescue aircraft suddenly came from a westerly direction, opposite to where the first Canso disappeared. At first, they could not believe their senses, but the Canso came ever closer. Stojik was first to confirm the sighting. The beleaguered aviators felt a rush of adrenaline that gave them a shot of extra strength. They were on their knees, waving at the approaching aircraft in a futile attempt to make contact.

Their best chance of the rescue craft spotting the crew in the dinghy lay with Brand. He was in charge of the emergency flares and as Evans had ordered, he had had them ready for firing ever since the first Canso rescue plane passed overhead. He wanted to eliminate any chance that the next rescue craft would miss them, and to be very sure, this time Brand managed to fire off two flares in quick succession. The Canso spotted both flares and immediately executed a banked turn back towards the dingy and its exhausted occupants.

The cold waves in the North Sea had increased again to fifteen feet and the biting wind to over thirty-five miles per hour. Any safe landing of the Canso under these conditions was out of the question. The rescue craft circled the dinghy with its six fatigued crewmembers. Rescue was so close, and yet so far. The rescue craft realized the downed crew's dinghy was overloaded. They came in low and attempted to drop a second dinghy with survival supplies alongside. The dinghy landed within twenty yards of the downed crew, but the ferocious winds picked it up and carried it far to the east, out of their reach. Even with a drogue parachute streaming out behind as a sea anchor, the crew of Irene had no chance of capturing the prize. Stojik started to swim towards the dinghy but Hartman and Williams held him back. They quickly convinced him that in his condition, the wind and the sheer size of the waves made any recovery of the package impossible.

The Canso rescue craft had no way of communicating with the downed crew, but did contact the base to get a high-powered rescue launch immediately dispatched to pick up the survivors. The only thing the rescue aircraft could do was to lend moral support by continuing to fly in a tight circle around them until their fuel dictated they return to base.

Evans' health was quickly deteriorating. The extended time

he spent in the water had taken its toll. He was almost blind and starting to lapse into shock when the rescue launch appeared on the horizon. Although it was only twenty minutes later, it seemed like an eternity before the ship arrived.

Williams, Hartman and Stojik were able to climb up the Jacob's ladder with only a little assistance while both Grant and Edwards had to be hauled onboard the launch by two of the rescue crewmembers. Evans was in the worst condition. The salt water had almost blinded him and he fell into lapses of unconsciousness. The rescue launch had to construct a makeshift bosun's chair to hoist him onboard.

On board the rescue launch, the other surviving members of the crew of the downed Canso received emergency medical treatment, warm clothing and a large ration of brandy. They would survive, but Evans' condition was critical. It would be over six hours until they could reach the nearest port. The ship's doctor attended to the crew's captain with all the knowledge and medicines he had at his disposal, but it was not enough. One hour after the initial rescue, Captain Neil Evans lost his final battle and succumbed to the effects of hypothermia, passing away quietly without ever regaining consciousness.

It had been 21 hours since the "Irene" had ditched in the North Sea.

8

May 5, 1945

LONDON, ENGLAND   **2230 GMT**

In the War Room, an aide handed a message to Prime Minister Winston Churchill. The leader of Britain's war effort glanced at the writing.

"Well, the deed is done. The bastard is dead. It is indeed a glorious day for the Empire."

"What is it, Sir?" asked the aide.

"According to the Russians, the bodies of Hitler and Eva Braun were found outside the New Reich Chancellery, or what was left of it. The damn shame of it all is that the Russians got there first. They found most of Hitler's inner circle, with the exception of Bormann, dead in an underground bunker. Bormann was nowhere to be found."

9

JULY 26, 2007

Latitude 54° 17' 44.26" N **Longitude 8° 39' 35.21' W**

IRELAND **1140 GMT**

The sea was calm on this cool summer morning. The rolling swells gently rocked the "Puno", a 40-foot Lochin Sportfisher anchored just off the jagged cliffs of western Ireland. The majestic rock formations began far beneath the surface and etched their way upwards like jagged pieces of glass, cutting through the sky on their way to the clouds. The sheer magnitude of these cliffs, forged through the ages by the fierce winds and storms that rolled in off the Atlantic Ocean, was impressive.

To Jim Clark, a thirty-six-year-old financial wizard from Vancouver, Canada, they were an interesting study in contrast, considering the rolling green hills of the country they protected. Clark took in the breathtaking beauty of the cliffs that lined the dynamic coastline. He had extended his business trip so that he might enjoy one of his favorite pastimes, scuba diving; a sport he had taken up years earlier while attending the University of British Columbia. He was enthralled with the beauty of the inner sea and became very proficient in the sport, quickly achieving his certification for dives up to two hundred feet.

The waters off the coast of Ireland provided Clark with a

large number of wrecks, but the currents could be very hazardous, even deadly. For Clark, it was a means to escape the constant stress of the ruthless financial business world that enveloped his life.

Clark prepared his equipment for the dive. He was at the aft end of the Puno, checking the air regulators. The skipper inspected the international Diving Signal Flag attached to the floating ring that would signal others boaters that divers were below. Satisfied, he secured the line to the cleat on the port side and launched it over the side.

Clark paused before putting on his gear. He glanced up at the hills along the coast, admiring the beauty of County Sligo's rugged terrain. The scenery was an inspiration for Clark as it had been for Yeats, who lay buried at Drumcliffe Churchyard, under loaf-shaped Benbulben Mountain, not five miles from where their boat anchored. Clark had toured the area extensively admiring the strange juxtaposition of the spectacular lakes of Sligo, with their still waters and wooded islands, and the county's rugged uplands.

The imposing Neolithic cairn on the summit of Knocknarae, known locally as Queen Maeve's grave, was a striking landmark that had made an impression on Clark on his first trip to Ireland. Jim Clark enjoyed traveling the world. Aside from all the cutthroat dealings in the financial business world, being CEO of a large investment firm did have its rewards.

Success seemed to come easy for Clark, although those who really knew him were aware of how hard he had worked to obtain every goal. Working several jobs to make ends meet, he struggled to put himself through university, where he graduated with a Masters Degree in Business Administration. Many firms sought his services, but in the end, he decided to join Mercer & Company, a small brokerage firm specializing in Independent Prospectus Offerings.

The small firm gave him an opportunity to advance and it was not too long before he proceeded to carve out a name for himself with financial dealings that rocked the old establishment. Shortly after joining Mercer, Clark had married his high school sweetheart and his life seemed to take on storybook proportions. He had his girl, money, position, and power. Everything was starting to go his way.

In less than five years, Clark had reached the top of the corporate ladder at Mercer. It was not long before other companies took notice. The day after he celebrated his fifth anniversary with Mercer, he left the company and joined their nemesis and largest competitor, James T Walters & Company, taking on the position of CEO only three years later. He was only 32 years old.

However, success had a price and that price was time. Clark was working 24/7 and that left little time for other interests, including his wife Sheryl.

Sheryl faced constant loneliness when Clark was away on business, sometimes for days at a time. At first, it was not a problem. She had her workout club and the obligatory lunches at the club, and the parties with the other business wives, but it did not take long for the boredom to take over her life.

Clark failed to notice that Sheryl had begun to drink excessively. Her favourite nightly Vodka Martinis seemed to be ever-present and it was a common event for Clark to come home to find her drinking in front of a television screen with no sound. She always said she liked the quiet time. It gave her time to think. Clark missed the fact that his beautiful wife was married to a workaholic. He was not there for her. He never knew how desperate she had become.

Clark was away in Dallas on a meeting in February when she had made her decision. She would sit him down and tell him what was on her mind, while she still had one. Either he would change or she would leave. There was no other way. It would happen the day Jim returned from his trip. She wrote it all down so there could be no question. It would be their seventh wedding anniversary.

Sheryl had been on her way to pick him up at the airport when a group of young people joyriding in a stolen vehicle struck her broadside. She had died instantly.

After the funeral, Jim Clark retrieved her personal effects from the police and found the notes she had written to explain how their lives had gone wrong, and how she wanted to fix the situation.

He often thought about his wife and, in particular, one line from her notes that stuck in his mind. "We have to get away from what seems right, and find ourselves again."

After the accident, Clark had not gone into the office for almost four months. He was making a conscious decision to avoid his business affairs and, as Sheryl had said, *"to find himself"*.

Five months later, he was in Ireland, having completed his first business conference since her death. Now he was going to do what Sheryl had suggested, enjoy some time away from the stress associated with the financial world. He had contracted a private boat charter, just himself and the boat owner, for a day at sea off the West Coast of Ireland.

He missed Sheryl and was always looking for something unique that would help keep her memory alive. Today, it was a little scuba diving off the coast of Ireland.

The two men floated within ten feet of the bottom. The skipper motioned for Clark to follow him.

There were some fish in the area, although their numbers had been steadily declining over the years. This forces the Government to take a more proactive role in the interaction between the fisheries and the offshore oil and gas industries. Clark was pleased to see the different species swimming alongside. Most were Cod, a few Monkfish and some Whiting. The fish seemed to be completely indifferent about the two men in their rubber suits, with the big tanks on their backs.

The skipper led Clark down to an old wreck that was lying on its side. The Germans sank the cargo ship during the Second World War. The rusted hull, covered with an abundance of crustaceans was now home to thousands of fish.

Clark swam around the wreck, pausing for only a moment near a large opening on the starboard side of the hull. "Most likely a torpedo," he thought, staring deep into the cavernous wound. The years submerged in the cold waters had taken their toll, removing all traces of identification. It was difficult for Clark to envision the former beauty of the ship.

The skipper swam beside him as Clark explored the outer reaches of the ship, occasionally poking his light into the various nooks and crannies of the sunken wreck. Time passed quickly and the skipper tapped him on his arm. He pointed to his watch and then scribbled the single word "time" on the board. The air in the tanks was running low and their time down on the bottom was over. The skipper motioned to make their way back to the ship.

Clark gave the thumbs up and they turned away from the wreck, swimming along just a few feet above the sea floor. A twinkle of light on the sea floor caught Clark's eye. He turned to explore the source of the mysterious light and in that briefest of moments, veered off course. The skipper turned in time to see Clark disappearing into the dark waters to his right. Realizing his client was literally swimming off into the void, he quickly went after him. He continued kicking hard as he chased after his wayward diving partner. The pain increased exponentially with every kick until it felt as if two hot pokers had been jabbed into his legs. He was less than ten feet behind when Clark suddenly stopped, reached down and pulled at an object buried in the silt of the sea floor.

The skipper grabbed Clark by the arm and, again pointing to his watch, motioned to Clark that they both should surface. Clark pointed to the object, indicating that he wanted to retrieve it. The skipper stared at him for a moment and then, reluctantly gave a 'thumbs up' signal. The silt swirled around the two men as they plucked the object free of the sea's grasp. It looked like a small pipe about six inches in diameter and eighteen inches long.

The skipper immediately pointed towards the surface. Clark nodded and followed him upwards, his newly found prize cradled in his arms.

The two men continued on their way to the surface, pausing only as necessary to decompress, releasing the excess nitrogen stored up in their bodies to prevent them from catching a case of the crippling bends.

The Skipper was first to the surface. He climbed the swim grid ladder back onto the boat and grabbed the gaff, a menacing looking three-inch steel hook mounted on the end of a pole. As Clark came to the surface, the skipper reached out and hauled the mysterious object aboard the boat. It landed with a loud thump. Clark climbed the ladder and joined the skipper on deck.

"What the bloody hell were you thinking?" yelled the skipper.

"I don't know," Clark replied sheepishly. "I thought I saw a flicker of light and just went after it. Sorry about that."

"Well, you've certainly got something for your trouble, but I'm not sure it was worth the effort. Probably just a piece of the old wreck, I'm guessing." The Irish skipper laughed, "No worries." He looked at the rusted cylinder. "You want to keep it, or should we toss it back into the deep?"

Clark had taken off his diving tanks. He picked up the object and examined it closely. It looked like a miniature torpedo, covered with a thick layer of barnacles and other tiny crustaceans.

"I can't figure out what caused the flicker of light," he said pondering over the object. "This thing is covered in rust. There is no way it could have reflected any light."

"Probably the sea playing tricks on your eyes, me boy." said the skipper offered, picking up the air tanks and stowing them in the locker.

"No", replied Clark, rolling the object over in his hands, "I did see something."

"Well, whatever it was, it almost got you killed."

"I am really sorry about going off course down there, but, it did lead me to this," responded Clark holding up the strange looking object. "I think I will keep it for a bit. A souvenir, you might say."

"No problem, Mr. Clark." replied the skipper, shaking his head. "It's your call."

The skipper looked out to the sea. It was getting late in the afternoon. "Are we done out here now?"

"Yes, I think that's enough for today. Let's get out of these wet suits and enjoy a slow cruise back to the harbour."

Clark put on some warm, dry clothes as the skipper fired up the 420 horsepower Caterpillar engine to begin the ship's eight-mile trip back to Sligo.

As the boat ploughed through the water towards land, Jim Clark continued to inspect the cylindrical object. It weighed about twelve pounds, but Clark figured a lot of the weight was mostly barnacles and rust. He shook the tube but there was no indication of its contents.

The ship continued on its slow journey back to port. Clark grabbed a screwdriver lying near the ship's wheel and chipped some of the sea encrustations from the outer surface. The sea material split from the surface of the cylinder, revealing what appeared to be an emblem stamped into the surface of the metal. Clark continued scraping at the surface. The corroded mark seemed strangely familiar. He turned the cylinder over repeatedly in his hands. Aside from the unidentifiable printing stamped on the surface, the object had no other distinct markings. It seemed to be a solid one-piece object with no indication of where or how it opened.

"Interesting," mused Clark. "I bet this has been in the water for almost sixty years." He used the screwdriver to scrape the other end of the barnacle-encrusted tube. Another portion of the thick material that had built up during the many years immersed in seawater fell off. Clark was looking at a strange insignia stamped into the metal. It appeared to be similar to the one on the side of the cylinder. He stared at the symbol. The light seemed to be playing tricks on his eyes. He turned the cylinder to position it directly into the sunlight. Clark squinted a little, bringing the symbol into focus. There was no doubt as to the emblem. It was the familiar German Swastika of the Second World War. "Holy shit!" Clark exclaimed loudly, "If this is real, Sean would be ecstatic to get his hands on something like this."

Sean Dylan was Clark's best friend. A fellow graduate from the University of British Columbia, Dylan had become good friends with Clark from the moment they met during their inaugural year. Dylan was attending the university as part of his army education benefits, majoring in History. They continued their friendship ever since. When Sheryl died, Dylan was there to help Clark through the tough times.

Clark admired Dylan not only as a friend, but also as a man who had a seemingly uncluttered approach to life. At just over six feet, with a fit body and a quick mind, Dylan had made the university football team and beautiful women seemed drawn to him. When they graduated, Dylan went back to the army and Clark began his career in the world of high finance.

Five years later, Dylan left the army to explore other options. He loved visiting archeological sites and was always interested in any remnants of historical events, often getting involved in exploring the material in a search to discover answers to the age-old questions of "who" and "why".

Yes. Dylan would be excited and it made Clark feel good to do something to repay his friend for his support in the past. He wrapped up the cylindrical object in a towel, put it into his kit bag and stowed it inside the aft cabin.

"*Sean is going to love this*," he thought, smiling to himself as he made his way back onto the deck, "*This is right up his alley.*" Clark stood at the railing, enjoying the scenic beauty as the Puno continued on its way back to port.

10

JULY 29, 2007

DUBLIN 1110 GMT

Clark had called Dylan from Ireland and informed him about finding the strange relic with the peculiar markings. Dylan was definitely interested and instructed him to get it into a solution to stop any further deterioration of the object and to remove some of the foreign buildup on the surface.

At Dylan's insistence, Clark took the object to Stephen Saris, a member of an archeological group in Dublin that Sean Dylan had dealt with on an earlier project. While realizing that Clark's find might not be of any substance, Dylan still took the position that it could be significant and have some relevance in historical terms. Saris acknowledged that Dylan had called and asked that he look after whatever it was that Clark had found.

Without telling Saris, Dylan, the consummate security-minded person had also indicated to Clark that he should not let the package out of his sight. Clark watched as Saris deposited the cylinder in a special solution and began gently cleaning the object.

Restoration of old artifacts was a science. After determining the cylinder was made of brass, Saris wasted no time in moving the object into a more caustic solution. Within minutes, the solution had worked to remove the majority of the residue that had built up during its exposure in the ocean waters. Once the caustic acid had done its work, Saris put the cylinder into an acid neutralizer to stop any further erosion. This was followed by a soaking in a milder Tataric acid to bring the surface back to as near to original condition as he could, given the age of the object.

When Saris had finished, he had rejuvenated the surface to the point where it was possible to confirm without doubt that the marking on the one end was indeed a German Swastika. Saris found some additional writing stamped into the surface of the body of the cylinder, but it was not entirely readable.

There were a couple of small bumps on the surface at one end of the cylinder, and two others at the opposite end, but Clark could not determine their significance. Saris thought they might be some sort of electrical connections, but the condition of the object made it impossible to make an accurate assessment.

The intercom system crackled. "Professor Saris, I have a Mr. Zimmerman on line two. Please contact reception."

Saris apologized as he left the laboratory to attend to the incoming call. Moments later, Saris' assistant, Wilhelm Heinrich, came in to the room to photograph the mysterious cylinder. The young assistant's attention to detail impressed Clark. Heinrich paid particular attention to the markings on the object, photographing the object from all angles.

Professor Saris returned shortly afterwards and assisted Clark in packaging his mysterious prize for shipment to Canada as per the arrangements through his office. They had just finished the packaging of the object when the Federal Express representative arrived at Sardis' office.

Clark was excited and pleased with his find. What was inside the cylinder, if indeed there was anything inside, would remain a mystery until he got the package to his friend, Sean Dylan.

11

AUGUST 1, 2007

BERLIN   **1044 GMT**

The lighting in the offices of the underground Neo-Nazi Democratic Party's office cast dark shadows across the walls. The strange patterns were the result of a mixture of incandescent bulbs and natural sunlight. The effect of the strange combination of light sources in the office projected a sinister, almost evil setting.

Although the room was rich with dark oak paneling, it was, other than the huge boardroom table and some heavy antique leather-covered chairs, completely devoid of any other furnishings. On the end wall hung a picture of Adolph Hitler. Two large flags bearing the Nazi Swastika flanked each side of the picture. Three men sat at the huge conference table.

Hans Lüdden, the leader of the underground Neo-Nazi Democratic Party sat at the end of the large table, directly under the picture of Hitler. Lüdden wholeheartedly believed in Hitler's plans for a master race. He was a radical whose mindset made this group a very dangerous factor in German politics. Lüdden was bold, but still careful about revealing his connection to the German Neo-Nazis. The Nazi Swastika was still illegal in Germany, but the party was not. He was determined to build the party back to its former glory by spreading their ideology among a subculture of young Germans who were disillusioned and dissatisfied with the state of the country. The party used the power of the Internet to exchange encrypted messages about meetings, demonstrations and other activities with newly subscripted followers, mostly from the cities with high unemployment. This new medium allowed them to offer a forum for rightist intellectuals to propagate the ideology of a 'New Right' that embraced exclusivist, radical thinking without evoking the harshness of Nazism.

The party was a powder keg, ready to explode. Lüdden was waiting to light the fuse. The telephone rang. The call would prove to be the match.

Hans Lüdden answered the telephone, listened and then gently placed the receiver in its cradle. He turned to look at the picture of the Hitler. "It is confirmed," he said turning to the others. "I did not think it was possible that something, whose very existence has been a rumor for over sixty years, would ever be found. The telephone range again. "It is a facsimile transmission," Lüdden said matter-of-factly.

The ringing stopped and the fax machine began to print out a copy of the incoming message.

"This find will be of tremendous value to our party. It will help us bring the Nazi regime back to its rightful place as the only real power in Germany," he announced with great flair.

Lüdden got up, went over to the fax machine and retrieved the printed copy. He scanned the incoming message quickly and then began reading aloud. "Mr. Saris from the Archeological Society of Dublin has done a preliminary restoration of the cylinder. It will be taken to Canada where it is to be opened." Lüdden looked up at his associates. "Gentlemen, I am almost positive that this cylinder contains the missing Schliemann Papers, the very key to finding the hidden gold taken from the Great Priam Treasure."

12

AUGUST 3, 2007

VANCOUVER AIRPORT   **1610 PDT**

Dylan met Jim Clark on his return to Canada. It pleased him to see his friend appeared relaxed and more like his old self. It was the biggest change in the Clark's demeanor since Sheryl's death. As was his custom, he greeted his friend with a big bear hug.

"You're looking good, Jim. Your new approach to business looks good on you."

"I never knew how much good a few days rest could do," replied Clark, picking up his luggage. "Did you get my message about the cylinder?"

"Yes. When will it arrive?"

"It should be here by now. The arrival of the shipment was to coincide with my return to the office. Fed Ex should have it there by now."

The two men left the airport baggage area and made their way to Sean's Land Rover SUV, stopping only briefly so Dylan could pay what he considered an outrageous parking fee.

As they exited the airport parking lot, Dylan stopped to insert his ticket into the little green machine beside the exit ramp. The plastic yellow and black security arm retracted and Dylan pushed down on the accelerator pedal to join the throng of impatient motorists leaving the congestion of the airport.

The two men had much to talk about during the twenty-five minute trip from the airport to Clark's office. Their conversation was very animated and glossed over many topics. The two men were engrossed in their conversation and Dylan failed to notice the grey Chevrolet sedan that was following him out of the airport parking lot, a hundred feet or so behind. It was still a hundred feet behind the SUV when Dylan past the folding security gate and disappeared into the cavernous underground parking lot at James T Walters & Company. Although it was seven-thirty in the evening, there were still a number of employees working. The world of high finance never stopped.

Clark's corner office was located on the prestigious 33rd floor. His secretary, Ronnie Patterson was still working at her desk. Her serious look belied her age. Ronnie's eyes lit up when Clark and Dylan exited the elevator.

"Mr. Clark. It is so good to see you. Did you have a good trip?"

"Yes, Ronnie. It was very good," he responded motioning towards Dylan. "You know Sean, of course." Clark turned to his friend, "She always calls me Mr. Clark when I bring someone to the office."

"Yes. Hello Sean," she said cordially.

"The girl is efficient," said Dylan, smiling.

Ronnie and Sean had become friends after he had completed a special project for one of Clark's clients. They had an on and off again relationship that never seemed to find enough time to take root. She liked Sean, but he was always off on some adventure somewhere. He never seemed to want to stay in one place and Ronnie was firmly rooted in Vancouver. She could have had any man she wanted, but something about Sean made him a little bit more appealing than the others. She was not in a hurry. She would wait for the right one.

Ronnie looked at both men, giving Dylan a little more than a cursory glance. "May I get you two gentlemen some refreshments?"

"I'll have my usual Scotch on the rocks," replied Clark reaching into his attaché case, "Sean will, I'm sure, enjoy some of this." He placed a bottle of Midleton's Irish Whisky from John Jameson & Sons distillery in County Cork, Ireland on his secretary's desk. "This is bottle number 004882. It has been aged to perfection my friend." beamed Clark giving Dylan a pat on the back, "I hope you like it." Turning to Ronnie, "Did my shipment arrive from Ireland?"

"Yes, it did. We had a devil of a time getting customs clearance, but Jeffrey, down in the shipping department, got it done. It is on the side desk in your office."

Clark motioned for Dylan to follow him.

The office was a study of the man. Everything in the room reflected the image of Jim Clark. The huge and well-organized office featuring an oversized antique oak desk with its large leather chair was definitely the office of a man who was in control. Two of the walls were floor to ceiling windows, while the larger of the other two featured a library, which moved electronically to reveal a complete entertainment system.

On the opposite wall were two original paintings by the French impressionist Claude Monet. One was a Paris scene from the 1870's and the other from the Lillies period in the early 1900's. Both were beautiful idyllic scenes that represented the painter regarded as the archetypal Impressionist, one whose devotion to the ideals of the movement was unwavering throughout his long career. Much like Jim Clark was, until the death of his wife.

Dylan stopped just inside the door and absorbed the extravagant decor of the office. "So this is what the other side looks like. Very impressive."

"Came with the territory," answered Clark offhandedly as he moved towards the side desk, "but, believe me, it really isn't all that great, if you don't have the right person to share it with." For a moment, Clark looked somewhat despondent. An awkward silence followed as Clark stood next to a picture on his desk. It was a picture of Sheryl. Dylan moved towards a large Federal Express package on the side desk. "Is this it?" he asked, breaking the silence.

The sound of his friend's voice caught Clark's attention. "Yes," he answered, pushing the thoughts about his late wife aside, "That's our mysterious cylinder."

Clark's secretary came in quietly, almost unnoticed by the two men examining the package. "Your drinks, Gentlemen," she said, placing the glasses on the sideboard.

As she turned to leave the room, she paused for an instant and smiled at Dylan. "Good to see you again, Sean."

Dylan looked up and noticed the smile.

"It's been awhile. Are you still living down here in the big city?"

Ronnie nodded affirmatively, "Are you still living like a hermit somewhere out in the sticks?"

"Touché." Dylan laughed. He watched as Ronnie turned and walked out of the room. "Umm, she is one nice lady."

Clark turned and moved over beside the package. "Here's to whatever the cylinder is. I hope you enjoy its contents as much as the Midleton's."

Dylan lifted the glass of Irish whisky and held it high to make a toast.

"Cheers, Jim. Here is to your great find. May it prove to be a worthwhile project." As Dylan tasted the whisky, he looked past the package to where Ronnie was sitting. "Man, now that is nice."

Clark noted his friend's comment and smiled as he set his glass down and returned to the package. "You want to have a look at the cylinder?"

"I would, but not yet," said Dylan. "We do not have the proper tools and no telling what is inside. Even if we could open it, it could make a hell of a mess of your office."

"You're probably right. Look, why don't we go out and grab something to eat. Tomorrow, I can have our security firm deliver this to your place where you can work on it at your leisure."

"Sure, make a mess at my place," joked Dylan.

"There's a great little restaurant across the street, Antonio's. It is good Italian food and fine wines, and we don't have to drive."

"That would be fine for me," noted Dylan.

Clark walked over to the door and spoke to his secretary. "Ronnie, we're going to ship the package over to Sean's place in the morning. Right now, we are heading across the street to Antonio's for a bite. Would you care to join us?"

She looked over at Sean and smiled. "Love to. Just give me a minute to call security and informed them about the shipment."

Clark nodded and the two men made their way towards the elevator.

"So, do you have any idea as to what the cylinder might be?" asked Clark.

"I'm not sure, but from what you described and my conversations with Stephen Saris in Dublin, it sounds like it might have come from a German ship during the War," said Dylan. "What intrigues me is what might be inside."

"There were a number of markings on the outside of the cylinder. One was definitely a Swastika, but the others did not mean anything to me."

"Nor I. But it will be fun finding out," offered Dylan.

"I called Security," Ronnie confirmed as she joined the two men at the elevator. "They will pick up the package first thing in the morning and arrange the shipment."

Ronnie had also managed a quick restyle of her hair and added some makeup. He had forgotten just how beautiful she was.

As the trio exited through the large revolving front doors of the building, Dylan glanced over at the grey Chevrolet parked facing the entrance to the parking lot, only twenty yards from the main doors to the building. There were two men sitting in the front seat.

Out of habit, Dylan made a mental note of the license plate number "068KTS", breaking it into sections for easy remembering. "068, the year I was born, and KTS – Killing Time Slowly".

Dylan had no reason to suspect anything was amiss. It was just an old routine he had used in the past in his Special Forces training to sharpen his mind.

The trio crossed the street unnoticed.

The restaurant was smallish, but most definitely Italian. The distinct aroma from the kitchen greeted them as they entered. A gathering of small tables interspersed with comfortable chairs maximized the available space without loss of intimacy. The absence of empty tables confirmed the success of the establishment.

The Maitre'd, was also the owner of Antonio's, and greeted them as they came through the door.

"Welcome to Antonio's Mr. Clark. You are here for dinner?"

"Yes, Roberto. A table for three, please."

"Of course."

The Maitre'd escorted them to the centre of the restaurant and seated them at one of the larger corner tables.

"Enjoy."

A wonderful meal, complimented with a good Italian wine, capped off a great day for Clark and Dylan. Ronnie was thoroughly enjoying the company of the two men, although Dylan was the focus of her attention. She would never have permitted herself any thought of becoming involved with her boss, but Sean Dylan was another story. Ronnie was definitely attracted to her boss' rugged, good-looking friend, but in her mind, Dylan seemed to have too many other interests in his life to settle down.

Clark finished the last of his after-dinner espresso and excused himself from the table. "I have to go back to the office. I have a meeting scheduled with Bob Emerson. I am sure you two can talk over old times, or find something to do to pass the time."

"I'm sorry, Jim, I didn't know about the meeting. Do you want me there?" asked Ronnie.

"No, it's not necessary. I have a few personal things on which I want Bob's legal opinion. It shouldn't take very long."

"I will call you once I have some news about the cylinder," offered Dylan.

"Please. Let's hope we find something of interest. Although I'm betting it will be another disappointing Al Capone 'empty-vault' story."

"Maybe we should call Geraldo Rivera," offered Dylan, "he could to do a television special on the great mysterious cylinder from the deep."

The three burst into laughter.

"Call me tomorrow, Sean, and thanks." Clark looked over to Ronnie. "Now, don't let him keep you here all night."

Clark turned and walked out of the restaurant, pausing only for a moment to speak to the Maitre'd. He paid the bill, waved to his friends and left.

Dylan and Ronnie resumed their conversation. Time passed quickly and before long, they were the only customers still left in the restaurant.

"Well, I can't keep you here all night. Your boss' orders."

"We could go for a little midnight stroll in downtown Vancouver," Ronnie said, breaking into a mischievous grin, "I know a little place that has some Irish whisky. It is probably not as nice as what Jim gave you, but the ambience might be a more interesting."

"Sounds like a good plan. Après vous, my lovely lady."

Ronnie and Dylan made their way out of the restaurant. As they turned left along Howe Street, Dylan noticed the same Grey Chevrolet in front of Clark's office building. He gave the car a closer look as they walked past. He glanced at his watch. *"They have been parked there for over three hours,"* he commented to himself.

Dylan noticed the small pile of cigarette butts on the ground below the driver's window. The two occupants slouched in the front seat appeared to be sleeping. *"If they are doing surveillance, somebody had better get them some 'Bennies' to keep them awake,"* thought Dylan. He dismissed the idea as bizarre and turned his attention back to his interesting and far more beautiful companion.

The Italian wine consumed at dinner was having a pleasant effect on Ronnie. She was obviously enjoying Dylan's company as they walked along the now deserted street. A much younger, happier face had replaced the serious look of the professional secretary that had greeted him when he first arrived at Clark's office. Dylan was pleased with the transformation.

Four blocks from the office tower, Ronnie stopped.

They were standing in front of the entrance to a modern high-rise. "We're here," she exclaimed with a flourish.

"Is this the place with the infamous Irish whisky?"

"Aye, this be the place," replied Ronnie with a terrible Irish accent.

Dylan chuckled at her linguistic attempt as a doorman approached the couple. The efficient attendant opened the door and nodded politely as Ronnie led Dylan inside.

"Evening, Miss Patterson,"

"Good evening, David."

"Nice digs," whispered a smiling Dylan "And close to the office, too. That must be convenient."

"James T Walters and Company is a busy office. It is much easier for me to be downtown than to have to drive long distances every time something comes up."

Dylan followed Ronnie towards the elevator. "So, do you bring a lot of your friends here for Irish whiskey?"

"No. You are the first," she answered. "Most of the others drink wine. Now behave yourself or you won't get any," she paused for effect, "Irish whisky, that is."

"Yes Ma'am."

The couple made their way into the elevator and ascended to the sixteenth floor.

13

AUGUST 4, 2007

VANCOUVER 0845 PDT

The following morning Dylan was a little groggy as he slowly woke from a deep sleep. He shook his head, blinking his eyes a few times to bring his world into focus. For a brief moment, he did not recognize his surroundings. Then it all came back to him. It was like a dream. "Those long legs. That smooth, firm body. Yes she was definitely good enough to be dream material."

Dylan climbed out of the bed and found a note on the night table.

"Sorry I had to leave so early. I have many things to do today. Shower is straight ahead. Everything you need should be there. Thanks for a great evening. Ronnie."

Dylan smiled. It definitely was not a dream. He made his way to the shower and, as Ronnie had written, everything he needed was there.

Freshly showered and dressed, Dylan left the apartment and made his way back to the underground parking beneath the James T Walters and Company offices. He followed the curved parking ramp down to the second level. As he approached the Land Rover, he went through this usual routine of checking the mental notes he made when he had parked. Nothing about the vehicle seemed amiss. He unlocked the SUV and climbed in.

Dylan paused for a moment and thought about Ronnie. The more he thought, the more he realized how much he had enjoyed seeing her again. He started up the 4.4 litre V-8 engine, waited as the driver's seat automatically adjusted to the preset position, put the vehicle into gear, backed out of the parking stall and glided up the ramp onto Robson Street.

The morning rush hour in Vancouver usually lasted about four hours. It took Dylan almost an hour to maneuver through the streets and make his way out of town to the Tsawwassen Ferry Terminal. His timing was good, arriving only five minutes ahead of the boarding time. He was heading to Mayne Island, one of the Gulf Islands located between the Mainland and Vancouver Island. It was here, amongst the Gulf Islands where Dylan was at his most relaxed. Here he could get away from the daily grind and weight of the world's problems. At least, he thought so.

The ferry was quite full for this time of year and Dylan was lucky to make the fifty-five minute sailing over to Galiano Island, followed by the twenty-five minute trip to Mayne Island. He was always amazed at the increasing number of people that were traveling to and from the islands each year. When he bought the cottage eight years ago, the seven-room home, situated high on a hill overlooking the Strait of Georgia, the expanse of water that ran between Vancouver Island and the mainland, was the only building within two miles. Each year he noticed the number of houses and cottages seemed to increase. It seemed the city was following him and his quiet spot of solitude was quickly vanishing.

Dylan was an avid sailor, often boating in the Strait of Georgia and around the Gulf Islands. There was no other place with such diverse waters than the West Coast of British Columbia. It was a sailor's dream. He had constructed a dock in a little cove located just southeast of the cottage. It was a perfect place to shelter the 'Alcor', his forty-one foot Morgan Islander Ketch, from the local winds.

The ferry finally reached the dock at the end of Village Bay on Mayne Island and Dylan began his twenty-minute trip to his sanctuary. He picked up his cell phone as he past the Georgina Lighthouse, about two miles from the cottage. He punched in a preset number sequence. The phone rang once and an automated voice came on the line.

"Hello boss. Glad to see you have come back so quickly." The voice, although female, had the same inflections and tone as that of Hal, from the movie, 2001 A Space Odyssey. It sounded so much alike that Dylan had felt obliged to give a similar name to his system. He chose Helen. "You have three telephone messages and there was one visitor," droned Helen in her monotone voice. "There were no entries into the premises during your absence."

"You did well, Helen. Thank you." Dylan flipped the cell phone to the closed position as he made a left turn into the driveway.

It felt good to be home again, even if he had only been away for two days. There was something almost magical about living on the island. Maybe it was being far from the hustle and bustle of the big city life, or maybe just closer to nature. Whatever it was, here on Mayne Island, Dylan was much more at ease then he ever was on the mainland.

The computerized voice greeted him as he entered.

"Please enter your security code. You have fifteen seconds to disarm the alarm system or extreme force will be used to eradicate you from the premises."

"It's Okay, Helen. It's just me." Dylan punched in his security code prompting Helen to respond. "Thank you, Boss."

Dylan went to the console that controlled the electronic functions of the cottage. He hit another series of buttons and Helen dutifully played back the three telephone messages.

The first call came in at 0700, from Jim Clark stating the package was on its way. *"Geez, that boy does put in a lot of hours,"* thought Dylan.

The second was from his neighbour, Ray Tilley. He listened as Ray explained that some security firm had delivered a package and that he should pick it up soon because it was probably important. Ray would not want to be responsible for its contents. The thought of a security person asking Ray to sign for the delivery brought a smile to Dylan's face.

The third was a non-call. Whoever called had hung up when they heard Helen's voice. "The call was made from Vancouver. The number is 604-555-0178. It is a cell phone number, registered to a James Bell at 3201 West 16th Avenue. It is a fake address. The City files do not show a house at that address."

"Interesting," he replied to his security system. "I will be back in a moment." Dylan exited the front door and made his way to his neighbour's house to pick up the package.

He was pleased with himself as he carried the box back over the three hundred foot distance from Ray Tilley's home. Dylan had been able to get the package and get away before his neighbour had a chance to ask his usual myriad of questions that seemed to accompany every meeting. Helen's sensors picked him up as he entered his cottage.

"You had another telephone call. Shall I play the message?"

"Yes, please."

The message was from Ronnie. She had called to confirm that he had received the package. He picked up the telephone, hesitated and then replaced the receiver. He did want to speak with her, but the mystery of the package won out.

Dylan took the package down into his private workshop below the main living quarters. It was time to get some answers to the many questions posed by the intriguing cylinder with its Swastika markings.

Saris had done a good job cleaning most of the barnacles and tiny crustaceans that had clung to the outside of the brass object. The markings on both ends of the cylinder were definitely those of the German Swastika. The writings on the body of the object were in German. Some of the letters were missing but Dylan painstakingly took the time to transcribe everything in detail. After three hours, he had completed the transcript of the writings.

The only part he understood was 'Unterseeboot', which related to submarines. He could see the number '122', which he interpreted as the German registration number for the submarine. Judging by the pitting on the surface of the cylinder, it appeared that the number could have originally been four digits.

Dylan spent the rest of the day completing his examination of the mysterious cylinder. It was two in the morning before he decided to quit.

"The U-122," thought Dylan. "That number sounds strangely familiar."

Dylan poured himself a glass of Pinot Noir, sat down and scanned his notes. His mind raced with thoughts at what secrets the brass cylinder might reveal.

He fell asleep in his chair, the wine barely touched.

14

AUGUST 6, 2007

BERLIN   **1418 GMT**

The mood of the underground Neo-Nazi Democratic Party was upbeat. Hans Lüdden held up a newspaper for his associates to see. There was a red circle around a small article at the bottom of the page.

"This article was spotted by a friend of the Party," Lüdden expounded. "If he had not seen this, we might have missed this glorious opportunity to elevate our Party and its mission." He passed the paper to the others as he continued. "Our research indicates that this cylinder may contain information on a submarine's final top secret missions, including the whereabouts of the missing gold taken from the Great Priam Treasure. If it is indeed that cylinder, then we must spare no expense or resources to recover it before anyone else discovers its contents."

"How can you tell from so little information, Herr Lüdden?" asked the smaller man to his right.

Otto von Schlippenbach was Lüdden's deputy. He was the second in command in the Party hierarchy.

"We were able to obtain some inside information from a member of our party. The pictures we received from Cadet Heinrich indicate that there is an extremely good possibility the cylinder is the same one a submarine crew is rumored to have dispatched during a battle in the North Sea. The papers in the cylinder were supposed to notify the Third Reich of the final location of the Priam Treasure gold."

"But why was the gold taken from Germany?"

"In May of 1945, our glorious leaders made a last ditch effort to save the Third Reich," Lüdden responded.

"And Karl, you are sure the cylinder that was found by the scuba diver Clark now resides with this Dylan person?" asked von Schlippenbach.

Karl-Heinz Müller, was head of the underground Neo-Nazi Democratic Party's security arm, a group that emulated the former SS regime of Adolph Hitler. "Yes. According to our contact the package was shipped to Sean Dylan, a friend of Clark's," he answered. "Apparently, this Dylan person is something of a history aficionado who deals with antiquities."

"Do we know where he works, where he lives?"

"No. We believe he works for Clark, the man who found the cylinder," von Schlippenbach interjected before Müller could answer. "Our people tried to follow him, but unfortunately, they lost contact when he took a smaller ferry boat to some remote island."

"The fools!" barked Lüdden.

"All is not lost. We have our people watching Clark's office. Dylan will certainly return there and when he does, we will be ready to follow him properly this time," von Schlippenbach said assuredly.

"We must find this Dylan person, and retrieve the cylinder before he opens it and discovers its secrets. We do not want him to start asking questions," Lüdden warned. "If the public should learn of the secret missions, it would compound the situation. We cannot afford to bring attention to this discovery until we are in full control."

"We understand Hans. We will not fail."

Hans Lüdden looked at both von Schlippenbach and Müller. "Have your men find Dylan, retrieve the cylinder and bring it back here directly to me."

Lüdden paused for a moment and his face took on an evil appearance. "If the container has been opened, your men are to retrieve all of its contents and kill anyone who has knowledge of it. There must not be any evidence to show it ever existed."

"Yes. It will be done, of course," replied Müller. "We have already taken steps to eliminate the laboratory technicians."

"Good. The successful recovery of the gold from the Great Priam Treasure would restore our party to its former glory as the leaders of Germany." Müller paused for a moment, and then turned to the others, "And for the sake of the Party, the world must never find out the truth about the final missions."

15

AUGUST 7, 2007

MAYNE ISLAND   **0920 PDT**

The morning sun filled the room with its summer light as Dylan finished scanning and emailing the transcript of the cylinder's exterior markings. He was sending them to Professor Gertrude Kingsmill, one of his old university lecturers on antiquities, with a request for a quick translation. He trusted Trudy Kingsmill. She had a reputation for reliability and integrity. As a professor, she was reputed to be quite feisty and outspoken. So much so, that Dylan made a point of reinforcing the need for confidentiality.

He returned to the mysterious brass cylinder. The handle was hanging from a single end attached to the side of the outer casing. He noticed the two other mysterious spots on the opposite end of the cylinder that Saris had indicated might be electrical connectors, but they had eroded too much for Dylan to confirm that theory. The object was so well manufactured Dylan was unable to determine exactly where it opened. After several hours, he noticed that one end of the cylinder appeared to screw perfectly into the outer casing. The effects of salt water and time had long since worn away the tiny raised lugs were used to turn and remove the end plug. Sean decided that the easiest way to open the object would be by a precision cut around its circumference. He would make a cut just one quarter of an inch below the area where the end appeared to screw into the body of the cylinder. This would permit entry without jeopardizing the contents, if any, that were inside.

It was not a difficult operation. Using a large pipe cutter, Dylan started to score the surface and, as he rotated the cutter, the incision into the soft brass deepened, until finally the small end piece separated from the body.

There comes a moment in every quest, just before the final victory, when the mind experiences the curious mixed sensation of success and failure. For the briefest of moments, as the cut end of the mysterious cylinder was falling to the floor, Dylan had that feeling. The feeling that what was inside, would be nothing, or possibly, everything. The severed end hit the floor and rolled across the room.

Dylan slowly moved around to look inside the cylinder that was now open for the first time in over sixty years. He felt his pulse rate increase as he peered inside. He was looking at some dark, stained and crumpled plastic type material.

"At least it isn't empty," he thought to himself. *"Now I am going to find out what was so important that someone had to release this cylinder from a submarine during war time."*

Using a pair of rubber-tipped forceps, he carefully reached into the brass tube and extracted the dark, time-stained plastic material with its mysterious contents.

Dylan recognized the material that covered the mysterious contents in the cylinder was a form of polyethylene, a new substance that was created by Karl Ziegler during the Second War World.

He carefully removed the crinkly wrapping to expose a roll of damp and musty documents. They were, surprisingly, very pliable and laid flat quite easily, making a pile almost a quarter inch thick. Dylan looked at the stack of papers, his eyes open wide in a mixture of excitement and trepidation. He wondered if the documents would yield any historical significance, or would they prove to be nothing but worthless paper.

Dylan gently flipped through the papers. Sixty years of dampness had affected some of the documents. While a few of the pages were faded, to Dylan's surprise, many were still in pristine condition. He turned his attention back to the cylinder and removed it from the cutting machine. As he placed it on his workbench, he heard a small 'ping' sound. He carefully tipped the brass tube forward and heard the sound of a strange object sliding along the inside. He cupped his hand under the open end of the cylinder just in time to receive the mysterious item. Dylan recognized the object immediately. It was Germany's highest military award, the Iron Cross, 1st Class, also known as the EKII. The recipients of the unique medals were limited to submarine Captains credited with sinking more than 50,000 tons of enemy ships.

Dylan looked at the decoration for some time, trying to visualize the man to whom it had belonged, and the ships he had sunk to earn such an infamous lethal decoration.

16

AUGUST 8, 2007

BERLIN   1622 GMT

Lüdden paced the floor, pounding his fist into the palm of his other hand. His two subordinates were sitting at the main conference table.

"Why have you not heard from these so-called surveillance experts?" he asked sharply.

"I do not understand it either, Herr Lüdden. We have had them watching Clark's office for over a week, but we have not had any reported sighting of the Dylan person," offer Müller.

"They originally reported some activity, but nothing of consequence," corrected von Schlippenbach. "We have instructed them to find the location of the cylinder and report as soon as they have information."

"Well, somebody had better find out what is happening soon, or heads will roll," screamed Lüdden, his face turning a bright red. "Do I make myself clear?"

His two associates nodded in unison. Müller had not seen Lüdden this angry before. Privately, Müller thought that the possibility that Germany might actually retrieve the gold from the Great Priam Treasure was transforming Lüdden into a man possessed, but he knew it was wise to keep these thoughts to himself.

17

August 8, 2007

MAYNE ISLAND   **1542 PDT**

Sean Dylan stood on the deck of his cottage and stared at the boats moving across the Strait. He was holding the EKII medal in his hand as he reflected on the possible content of the papers he found in the cylinder.

The ringing of the telephone snapped him back to reality. He reached for the portable receiver, "Sean Dylan".

"Sean, my boy, I got your email. This is fascinating! Do you know what this is?"

"No. I think that's why I sent it to you, professor." Dylan replied as he casually placed the Iron Cross medal around the neck of a small statuette sitting on a bookcase shelf next to the telephone.

Trudy Kingsmill began to explain her findings regarding the transcript Dylan had sent to her.

"Basically, my boy, you seem to have found a cylinder that the German U-Boats used for emergency communications during the later stages of the Second World War. It was a novel idea the Germans started to develop during the Great War and then modified for use during World War Two. They would put documents into the cylinders, inserted the cylinder into a torpedo tube and launched them at a predetermined rendezvous point. I do not think the system ever really worked too well. There were too many areas where things could, and apparently did, go wrong. The internal radios did not work properly and the signals did not last long enough to allow for recovery. There was just too much going on with the war, to spend time looking for such a small item floating somewhere on a big ocean. That sort of thing."

"Radio? Are you saying this thing had a radio?"

"Right! It was a very crude device. If I am correct, there should be a small radio beacon transmitter in one end of the cylinder. Anyway, like I said, it was a good idea, but didn't work worth a pinch."

Dylan put his phone on speaker mode and picked up the cylinder. He picked up a pair of long nosed pliers and reached deep into the cylinder. After a few tugs, he pulled out a small, corroded package of electronics. It was a crude radio transmitter packet.

"You were right, professor, as usual. It looks like a small transmitter," reported Dylan, turning the small electronic package over in his hand, "I didn't know they could make things that small back in the forties."

"The Germans were very smart, my friend. You know, not everything was discovered in the fifties," the Professor laughed. "I would venture that the cylinder that your friend found came from a German submarine in the U-1200 series. It looks like 'U-122 something'. The last number in the picture has eroded too much to identify properly. Not much else that I can tell you, the transcript is basically just a record of what ship it came from, not much else substantial to go on." The professor paused, and then added, "Except that almost every submarine in the U-1200 series was sunk during the war, over sixty years ago. Very strange, I must say."

"Well, yes, but not entirely an impossible situation. Would there be any records with the German Unterseeboot command?"

"That is possible. However, you would probably have to go to Berlin to access those records. What I would like to know is how did this cylinder come to surface after over sixty years? My dear boy, it could be a hoax, you know."

"That's possible, but the papers I found inside the cylinder are very real, and very convincing. Most of them seem to be in some sort of code, with a few notations that are written in German."

"You found papers inside the cylinder?" asked an excited Trudy Kingsmill.

Dylan explained to the Professor how he had opened the cylinder and described in detail, the three packets of documents he had discovered. Professor Kingsmill was very attentive, and offered to do any work necessary to assist him in discovering what she could about the documents.

A premonition had surfaced in Dylan's mind, a feeling that told him something about this whole issue of the cylinder was bad news. He could not pinpoint the reason why, he just knew there was something about having the U-Boat information that was dangerous. Despite his misgivings, he agreed to meet the Trudy Kingsmill the coming Friday, and bring her copies of the papers.

Dylan ended his conversation with the Professor and then immediately dialed Clark's private number and waited for him to answer.

"Clark here."

"Jim? Sean. You called?"

"Just wondering how you were making out with our little project."

"Fine. I got the cylinder open and found a package of old documents. They are all in German, of course, so I have no idea of what we are dealing with yet. I'm going over to visit Professor

Kingsmill later and see what she thinks."

"Great. Oh, by the way, I got a strange call earlier today. It was someone from a museum in Berlin. They wanted to know if I still had the cylinder and if I wanted to sell it. Seems they think it would have some historical value in Germany."

"Unfortunately, like I said earlier, I've already cut the end off. I'm afraid they are a little too late," replied Dylan. "However, I am curious to know how they found out about the cylinder and how they located you?"

"I think it must have been that archaeologist fellow you sent me to in Dublin to have the cylinder dipped. He must have given them my name. They are rather efficient people, aren't they?"

Dylan's mind was wandering as he listened to his friend. *"Too damned efficient."* he thought to himself.

"Yeah. They are very efficient," he acknowledged. "I'll call you after I've spoken to the Professor."

"Fine. Talk with you then."

Dylan hung up the telephone and spent the rest of the day going over the papers and making quality copies for Professor Kingsmill. He separated some of the papers from the Professor's pack and put them in a separate envelop which he deposited in his floor safe. Tomorrow, he would take the remaining papers, catch the early morning ferry to the Mainland and visit Trudy Kingsmill.

18

AUGUST 10, 2007

VANCOUVER   **1105 PDT**

The Professor's home was her office. She lived in a large heritage home near the university grounds, with Mrs. Mackenzie, her housekeeper, and a very large black Labrador dog named Maggie. Dylan arrived just past eleven. He knocked on the door and the housekeeper let him in, showing him into the Professor's study. The huge black Labrador followed him into the room, waddling more than walking.

"*A few too many doggie treats, for sure.*" thought Dylan as he waited for the Professor to arrive.

They say that people often mirror their pets but Trudy Kingsmill was the opposite. It had been almost five years since Dylan had last seen her. When the short, thin person entered the room, it was obvious that the Professor had not changed. She still had the bounce in her step that belied her eighty-one year existence on the planet. It seemed to Dylan that the dog resembled the housekeeper more than the Professor.

His meeting with Professor Kingsmill was interesting as always, but it only deepened the mystery surrounding the papers.

Although some had been ravaged by the effects of time and moisture, the Professor had determined that one small packet of papers was the German submarines official ID package. It listed the complete specifications of the U-Boat, from the date of manufacture of the sub itself, to every component aboard the ship. It also contained a detailed crew list, including all officers and general seamen, and lastly, the full details of its onboard armaments. Despite all of the information, Professor Kingsmill was unable to confirm the submarine's official registration number. It was not on a single document.

There were two additional packets. They appeared to be quite different from the first. Unfortunately, as with the bulk of the other papers, there was some water damage and time had erased much of the original copy, but the primary difference was the encryption. There were some very readable sections, but without the ability to decode the writings, the message would remain a mystery.

"As near as I can determine, my young Sean, the papers in this packet form part of some special orders the U-122 or whatever its number was, had on their last mission. What fascinates me is the encrypted information. Unfortunately, it is probably a version of the old Enigma code. You would have to break the code in order to determine exactly what they are all about and you are going to need a source code book to do that," said the Professor as she collected the papers on the desk. She sat back and sighed, "These packets definitely pose more questions than answers."

"Such as?" Dylan inquired.

"Well, my dear boy, packet number one with the copies of the submarines crew layout mentions some highly secret passenger compartments. On the back of this page, someone has written a different identification number, possibly that of another submarine, the U-112, and the date, May 3, 1945."

"Are you saying the U-122, may have carried passengers during the war?"

"I don't know. It does not make a whole lot of sense, but one never knows. There were a lot of high ranking Germans who were desperate to get out of the country at the end of the war."

"Do you think it's possible that this submarine was used to help them escape?"

"It's a possibility, but I think for starters, you might want to find the proper identification of the submarine these papers came from, and then do a little checking on this U-112 to see if there is any connection."

"Your right, of course, but the thought of the Germans transporting passengers at the end of the war is an interesting hypothesis. What about the coded papers?"

"The other two packets we know are in code. Unless you can break the code, you will never know what you have. On this page, you can see the numbers 1220 and 112. They look like they are part of registration numbers, but unfortunately the rest is in code. All I really know for sure is that at the time, there was a reason for the Germans to have put it in code."

"But they could be registration numbers."

"Yes, but you also have a problem because a lot of the papers have been damaged by moisture and that, unfortunately, is going to make it very difficult to break the code."

Dylan thought for a moment. "I've got a friend downtown who might be able to extract a little more of what is on these papers. He is a specialist who works closely with the FBI. They have some special machines that can read things that are not visible to the human eye. I will call him and see if he can get access to this high-tech equipment to identify more details about what is on the pages. In the meantime, let's keep this between us and your very ample companion here." Dylan patted the dog and turned towards the door.

"No problem, Sean." said the Professor. "Mums the word, and not to worry, old Maggie here doesn't talk too much these days."

Dylan left the house and made his way back to the parking area. His cell phone started to ring, or more aptly, started to play the theme from the motion picture, Mission Impossible. He pushed the answer button. "Sean Dylan."

"Sean, Jim here. I got your email about the papers. It sounds like it could be interesting, although I do not really understand the significance of the submarine number and I am not much help to you with the coded stuff. Never could figure out those things."

"We have come up with a couple of ideas on how we might decipher the code."

"What's your next step?"

"I just left Professor Kingsmill's house. She has suggested with a few possible scenarios, which, if they were true, would certainly shake up the establishment. Unfortunately, the only way we will find the answers is to break the code."

"Do you want to keep exploring the possibilities?"

"I'd like to," replied Dylan without hesitation, "but this thing is starting to take on a life of its own. It is beginning to tax my limited resources."

"I understand, Sean," said Clark. He paused for a moment. "I have thought about the papers you found in the cylinder. They really are a mystery and I feel that finding the answers to that mystery would be worth the investment. You never know, the papers might lead you to the definitive answer to some of those cloudy issues left over from the Second World War."

"Or they could just be old worthless documents," Dylan echoed skeptically.

"True. I don't think I ever told you Sean, but I lost my grandfather in the war. My mother told me she was born after he went to England. Her father died in the war without ever seeing her. If there are answers to be found, I am sure he would want me to assist in finding those answers."

"It is going to take some time to solve the codes, if it is even possible, and then find out if the papers really do supply any of those answers. The problem, as you know, is that time equates to money."

"That's my point. If you are interested in following up and trying to solve this ambiguous puzzle, I would be willing to fund this as a research project in my grandfather's memory."

"Are you serious?"

"Yes, of course. I have already taken the liberty of speaking to Bob Emerson and gave him instructions to set up a research fund that should cover your expenses. I hope there might be something left over to pay you something for your time. What do you say?"

Dylan thought for a moment. "Are you sure you want to do this?"

"Yes, I'm sure," laughed Clark, "This thing might be a way for me to give something back. Lord knows I've made enough."

"Okay, but it could get to be expensive."

"No problem. Stay in touch and let me know how you are doing. Bob will call you later today. Good Luck."

Dylan stood by his SUV and looked at the cell phone. "What the hell have I got myself into this time?"

19

AUGUST 12, 2007

BERLIN   **1310 GMT**

Von Schlippenbach knocked on the heavy office door and entered. "Herr Lüdden. I have received an update from Canada."

The leader of the underground Neo-Nazi Democratic Party looked up from the pile of newspaper clippings scattered across his desk. "You have news do you have of the cylinder?" he demanded.

"Not exactly,' replied von Schlippenbach. "They spotted Dylan leaving Clark's office. They followed him to several locations in Vancouver, but there was no sign of the cylinder."

"I hardly think he would be carrying the object with him," Lüdden replied sarcastically. "Did they follow him to his home?"

"Their report states that he lives somewhere on an island, but they did not have any other information."

Lüdden gave his second in command a look of disgust. "Otto, we cannot afford such shoddy work. The people you have hired are acting like amateurs. There is too much at stake. I want that cylinder, now." He paused to pick up an old faded newspaper clipping. "See here. It says 'The gold from the Great Priam Treasure was Germany's key to the future.'"

"We will not fail, Herr Lüdden."

The German leader looked at von Schlippenbach. "Failure would come at a very high price, Otto," he said ominously.

20

AUGUST 17, 2007

MAYNE ISLAND   0720 PDT

Relaxing on the deck at the cottage overlooking the tranquil waters of the Strait of Georgia and watching the world pass before him was, in Dylan's opinion, one of the most serene experiences available to man.

The location of the cottage was such that it was virtually unseen to the public, hidden by the tall majestic cedars that sprouted from the island rock like a thousand fingers reaching towards the sky. Dylan was careful to preserve the trees on the property in order to maintain his privacy. Anyone passing, by either land or the sea, would have a difficult time sighting the house. The private dock in the cove to the east of the cottage where he kept his forty-one foot ketch-rigged sailboat, was a great natural shelter from the elements, and kept the boat hidden from any curious eyes.

The sun had just risen over the mainland to the East. Dylan, as was his custom in the warm summer months, finished his workout and retired to the outside deck to plan his day. On the horizon, he could see the first of the regular scheduled British Columbia Ferries making its way west from the Mainland, across the Strait to Vancouver Island. Through his binoculars, Dylan could see the name of the ferry, the Spirit of British Columbia. At over five hundred and fifty feet long, it was the flagship of the BC Ferry system, capable of carrying up to four hundred and seventy cars and trucks, and over twenty one hundred passengers and crew. Most of the passengers today would be summer tourists, off to see the wonders of Butchart Gardens or visit Anne Hathaway's Cottage on Vancouver Island.

The massive ferry powered on. Driven by engines with over twenty-one thousand horsepower, the ferry maintained a crisp nineteen and a half knot speed to cover the thirty-seven mile journey from the Mainland to Vancouver Island in just over ninety minutes.

Through his binoculars, Dylan could see the tourists lined up as the ship entered Active Pass, their digital cameras clicking away madly. Dylan smiled at the spectacle and marveled at the new age of technology that permitted people to take hundreds of pictures on a single digital chip. *"What ever happened to old fashioned film cameras, when you carefully selected your subject and actually cared whether it turned out or not?"* thought Dylan.

Overhead an eagle was slowly circling, looking down at the dark waters for telltale signs that would bring its first meal of the day. Dylan watched the majestic bird for a few moments, mesmerized by the beauty and grace of the magnificent hunter. Suddenly, the bird stopped and immediately began a dive towards the waters of the Strait, hitting the surface like a lightning bolt. A short flurry of its wings on the surface and it was airborne again, with a large Chinook salmon firmly clasped in its claws. It was Dylan's private window on the world. He was seeing nature at her best.

The morning passed quickly. After completing a few long overdue maintenance chores at the cottage, Dylan headed to the ferry docks to begin his journey back to the Mainland, his mind a cacophony of wild thoughts about the contents of the papers, and

Clark's generous offer. *"Working with Jim, that's neat!"* He also thought about Ronnie and smiled. *"This could definitely be interesting."*

BERLIN   **1115 GMT**

The doors to the Federal Chancellor's offices at the Deutsche Bundestag in Berlin remained closed. The meeting inside had gone on for over an hour.

Chancellor Wolfgang Schmidt was reviewing some intelligence reports with his aides. "You feel this rumor that has surfaced within the underground Neo-Nazi Democratic Party has validity?" he asked.

"To them it does. However, we do not feel there is much to substantiate the claim," said Franz Jung, the head of the Special German Intelligence. SGI was responsible for German Security.

"Do you think they really have a lead on the missing gold from the Great Priam Treasure?"

"It is possible," replied Jung, shaking his head, "but highly unlikely. A rumor is circulating that suggests someone found one of the old communications cylinders of the type used by submarines during the Second World War. The story about one such cylinder that was launched by one of the Third Reich submarines during the final days of the war has existed for years."

"Yes," confirmed the Chancellor, "the mythical cylinder was supposed to contain documents dubbed the 'Schliemann Papers'. It is said these papers will show where the gold from the Great Priam Treasure was taken. However, we now know the Russians took it after they entered Berlin."

"They only found part of the treasure," countered Jung. "No

one has ever been able to account for a very substantial amount of gold artifacts. To date, the Russians have only shown some minor pieces of the treasure. No one has ever displayed the gold from the Great Priam Treasure."

"I understand," said Schmidt. "If I remember correctly, there is also an old story about Hitler escaping at the end of the war. It was quite believable at the time, but not so much today." The Chancellor paused for a moment. "As a courtesy, have the Minister of Foreign Affairs place a call and inform our allies." He looked at his aide. "We cannot afford the controversy such a find would create. Have SGI look into it and keep me informed of any developments. We must ensure that this is only a rumor."

VANCOUVER   **1445 PDT**

Leaving the ferry dock at Horseshoe Bay, Dylan followed the winding highway alongside the mountains. He took the Lion's Gate Bridge over the First Narrows through Stanley Park and into the heart of Vancouver.

Shortly after three thirty, he pulled into an underground parking lot that had a large sign posted at the entrance marking it as "PRIVATE". Dylan parked the vehicle, picked up an envelope and made his way towards the elevators, clicking the remote locking system for the SUV as he went. Dylan flipped open his cell phone as he exited the elevator and dialed a number. A female voice answered.

"Are you up to do a little research this weekend?" he asked.

Ronnie immediately recognized Sean's voice. "I was wondering if I would hear from you again. I thought maybe my Irish whisky didn't make the grade and you had abandoned me again."

"Not a chance, lady. The whisky was good, but the company was better. This will be my chance to return the favour."

"That would be nice, but I don't know if I would be much help to you with any research."

"I am going to work on that little project Jim brought back from Ireland. At least, that's my story and I'm sticking to it."

"And just where is this research to take place?"

"Over at the cottage on the island. It will not be too difficult. I'm sure we'll find something to do to keep you busy."

"That definitely sounds interesting. I've heard a lot about the infamous cottage, but I don't recall that I was ever lucky enough to be invited over to see it."

"Well, let's say this weekend I make up for that oversight."

"I would love to go, but the problem is, I don't finish here until seven and I'll need at least an hour to get to my place and pack a few things."

"Not a problem. It's quarter of four now, how about I pick you up at eight fifteen."

"It's a date."

Dylan closed the cell phone and reached for the handle on the door with the sign that read 'Ashley Imports Inc.' He turned the doorknob and entered the office.

The offices of Ashley Imports Inc were in complete disarray. It was a small operation with only a small reception office, littered with magazines and old newspapers, and two offices, both with closed doors and from all appearances, completely devoid of any windows, inside or out. *"Definitely would not be a fun place to work"*, thought Dylan.

On the reception desk was a buzzer marked 'FOR SERVICE PUSH ONCE'. Dylan pushed it twice.

In a matter of seconds, the door of the office on the right opened. A man of about forty came out and moved directly to Dylan.

"Hi Sean," said the man, offering his hand.

Dylan shook hands. "Stan. Good of you to see me on such short notice."

Stan Bennett was an old friend of Dylan's. They worked together during Dylan's stint in the Special Forces Commando Unit.

"Didn't take you long to come out. Not too busy these days?"

"I knew it was you before you got through the door," replied Bennett. Come on inside and we'll talk. I don't like doing business out here. Never know who will come through the door."

Bennett led Dylan into the office and closed the door. The interior of the office was just as messy as the reception area. An old worn desk occupied the centre of the room. The only chair was an old leather type with a small tear in the arm and a permanent lean to one side. There was a single picture on one wall, while in stark contrast a half-full bookcase covered the entire width of the opposite wall.

Without missing a stride, Bennett continued past the messy desk, pressing the centre of the single book on the shelf, and walked through an opening that had miraculously appeared at the centre of the bookcase.

Dylan followed. As he past through the opening he heard a series of beeps. *"Heavy security,"* he thought. He noticed the camera capturing his image as the section of the bookcase unit swung closed. He was now inside a much larger, cleaner area that comprised eight offices with a central meeting area. Each office had windows that opened up into the centre and Sean could see the individual members of the Vancouver office of Canada's premier spy agency, working at their computer stations.

"This place always amazes me, Stan. The good citizens of Vancouver would be shocked to know what goes on here."

"Yeah," said Bennett with a smile, "but as you know, there are many of us around."

"Yes, Big Brother is very alive and living right here in Vancouver."

Bennett chuckled at Dylan's reference. "So what do you have for me, Sean? I must admit, it did sound interesting on the phone."

"I'm not really sure. A friend of mine, Jim Clark, you know him, right," Dylan paused as Bennett nodded in the affirmative. "He was scuba diving off the coast of Ireland last month and found an object near an old sunken merchant marine ship. It was a brass cylinder with some interesting markings on it. Knowing that I like to chase old artifacts, Jim gave it to me to play with. It took some time, but I finally got it apart and found some papers inside." Sean placed the envelope containing the papers on the desk in front of Bennett. "Most were damaged by time and elements, but they turned out to be, and I think I'm right so far, ID papers from a German submarine, the U-122 something. There is an ID number on the cylinder, but the last digit has corroded to where it can't be positively identified."

"Given the number of years involved, it's amazing that there is anything left of the paper, let alone the writing. Anyway, it's not so strange for subs to have ID papers, so why do you need me?" asked Bennett.

"Well, there are three packets of papers in the cylinder."

"You said 'we'. Who else knows about this?"

"I took the papers to Professor Kingsmill at the University

and we were able to determine most of what I have told you so far regarding the first bit. Of course, Jim Clark knows about it, although he really was not able to shed any more light on what we already knew. So far we have more questions than answers."

"Do you have the other packets with you?"

"Right here," said Dylan, opening the small attaché case and taking out the other two packets, each individually protected in its own clear cellophane case.

Bennett examined the papers carefully.

"Not much here to go on, it's all in code," he said as he turned over a page and spotted the handwritten note. "But there are a few words. If my German is still working," Bennett continued, pointing to the pages from the first packet, "it refers to a 'passenger' or 'passengers', and 'Unterseeboot' which is 'submarine'. The number '112' is probably the submarine's registration number." He paused for a moment. "I thought you said it was the U-122 something."

"That's the number on the cylinder and on the ID packet. We think the U-112 is a reference to another submarine."

"That could be, although I'm not aware of any submarines with such a low designation that were actually put into service," said Bennett, flipping through the pages. "I see what you mean about more questions than answers."

"And then there are the other two packets which are encrypted. The second has six pages and the third packet has another four. Do you have any ideas on how we can break the code?"

"If it's Second World War codes, they were probably produced on the Enigma machine and your best bet would be to contact the British War Records office in London."

Bennett held up a single page from the third packet. "You

said 'four pages', where are the rest?"

"The other three are all quite legible and, no offense, but I don't want them seen by everyone just yet."

"No offense taken. I wouldn't want to give away too much either, until I knew what I was dealing with."

"If you could work some of your magic on these pages and retrieve some of the missing words that have been lost to the effects of Davy Jones Locker, we may be able to find out if these pages do actually contain anything important. Then we can determine what to do with them."

"That shouldn't be a problem."

"How long before you can get something back?"

"If there is anything there to be recovered, we should be able to get these back to you sometime on Monday."

"That would be fantastic. I am going to do a little research over the weekend, just so I can talk a little more confidently about the subject. You know my number, right?"

"Right," confirmed Bennett. "I'll call just as soon as I hear back from Seattle."

"Take care of those," said Dylan, pointing to the papers, "I have good copies, but I may be able to sell the originals to somebody if it turns out to be anything worthwhile."

"No problem, Sean."

Dylan returned to the Land Rover. The day was playing out perfectly. He had ample time to shop for some supplies for the weekend and still be on time to pick up Ronnie. With a little luck, they could catch the nine-thirty ferry and be drinking a nice glass of wine on the deck before eleven.

Dylan only had to make two stops to complete his shopping list. First was at Clancy's, his favourite meat shop, where he picked up some tasty New York Sirloin steaks for the Saturday barbeque. He would phone and order a fresh salmon for Sunday from one of his local contacts on the island. The second stop was at the Specialty Wine store. He remembered that Ronnie liked red wine. He picked up a couple of bottles of their preferred choice, a very smooth Pinot Noir.

He had completed his shopping and pulled up in front of Ronnie's building at precisely eight fifteen. As he got out of the SUV, David, the door attendant, greeted him.

"Good evening, sir. I believe you are here to see Ms. Patterson."

"Yes. David, could you buzz her and let her know I'm here?"

"It is my pleasure, sir."

The Doorman went inside the foyer, pressed a combination of numbers, waited, and then spoke into the intercom and returned to the SUV. "Ms. Patterson said she will be down in a moment. She asked me to tell you that she was packing some Irish Whisky."

Dylan smiled, "She's quite the lady."

"Yes sir." David replied, "She is."

Ronnie arrived at the front door and greeted Dylan with a smile. She handed the Doorman her small travel bag as Dylan opened the door of the SUV for her.

"Good to see chivalry isn't completely dead."

"Only the best for the lady." he quipped. "But, beware, I sometimes forget."

"Oh, don't worry, I will remind you."

Dylan laughed as he climbed into the SUV and fastened his seat belt. He started up the Land Rover and pulled away from the building.

As the SUV started down the street, an old gray Chevy

pulled out of the shadows and began to follow.

The trip to the ferry docks was slow. The evening traffic had not yet dissipated, and they reached the departure point with only minutes to spare. The cars had begun to board onto the ferry.

"Just made it," said Dylan with a sigh of relief."

"So where is this mysterious cottage that we are going to?" asked Ronnie, "I forgot to ask so I packed a little of everything."

"It's not far. Only a fifty-five minute ferry ride to Sturgies Bay, and then a twenty-five minute run to Village Bay on Mayne Island. After that, a short 20 minutes by road and you are there." Dylan smiled at Ronnie's reaction. "It is a bit of a trip, but not to worry, there's running water and we have most of the amenities of the big city."

Dylan followed a blue Honda up the ramp and onto the ship and parked the Land Rover. He got out, motioning for Ronnie to join him at the side railing. "I'm sorry, I rushed you off this evening and you haven't had a chance to eat. Worse, there's not much in the way of an eatery on board this tub."

"It's alright. I am not really hungry." She paused and then confessed, "I cheated and had a light snack before you arrived."

He smiled at her. "Thank goodness. I wouldn't want you to starve on the first day."

Dylan looked down as the last few vehicles were making their way onto the ferry. There seemed to be a little confusion at the loading area. He looked over to see the cause of the commotion but the brightness of the summer sun was too much. He squinted to get a better look. The driver of a gray car was frantically waving his arms. "Seems we have another disgruntled car and driver," he said casually, turning back towards his beautiful companion. "It is always hard to be the one that just missed getting onboard."

Ronnie laughed. "Oh well, he will be first on the next ferry."

Dylan smiled at first, but then suddenly became quite pensive. He looked back towards the vehicle ramp. The gray car started to move, but not up the ramp. Instead, it made a u-turn and drove out of the loading area, heading back towards the city. Dylan was sure he had spotted the same gray Chevy earlier outside Clark's office. *"Somebody is trying to follow us,"* he thought to himself. *"Who the hell are they?"* he wondered.

Ronnie squeezed his hand and brought him back to reality. It was a warm summer's eve and the sun was just beginning to set as the ferry pulled away from the slip and gently moved out into the waters that led to the Strait of Georgia.

The ferry that made the run between Vancouver and Mayne Island was the appropriately named the Mayne Queen. Built in 1965, this 278-foot ship made a respectable fourteen knots on its route.

Ronnie had not been across the Strait for many years and was enjoying the beauty and serenity of the crossing. The rugged coast seemed to challenge visitors to find a welcoming landing site. As the ship neared the halfway point crossing the Strait, Ronnie looked back toward the city. It was a breathtaking sight. The mixture of commerce and the beauty of the land made an interesting combination as the picturesque mountain peaks with vestiges of snow still clinging to the tops, overshadowed Vancouver's concrete towers. Ronnie flipped her hair back in the gentle breeze. *"Truly, this was one of the most beautiful places on earth,"* she thought to herself with a smile.

Twenty minutes later, the ship began a turn to starboard and headed slowly into Sturgies Bay. The sun was dropping fast as the ship slowly proceeded into the arms of the hauntingly beautiful cove, finally coming to rest at the government dock. Dylan explained that the stop would only be long enough to permit some passengers and vehicles to leave, while others would board, venturing off for their weekend pleasures amongst the other islands.

It was dark as the ferry began the second leg of its journey to Mayne Island, but that did not diminish Ronnie's appreciation of the beauty of nature. The ferry seemed to float across the channel under a blanket of stars as she picked out the few lights from the small cottages on the shoreline.

"Which one is yours?" she asked.

"You can't see it from here. It's around the East side, and a little higher up."

"I can see why you want to live over here. It is so beautiful."

"We're almost there. That's Village Bay to the left. We better get back to the Rover and get ready for the next part of the journey."

They were back in the SUV when they felt the slight bump that signaled the Mayne Queen had docked. Dylan started the vehicle and followed the others off the ferry. They immediately vanished under the cloak of the dark island forest.

MAYNE ISLAND   **2225 PDT**

It was only twenty minutes from the docks to the cottage and Ronnie enjoyed the drive immensely as Dylan followed the winding ribbon of asphalt towards the cottage. His experience and knowledge of the area were fully evident, as the SUV seemed to develop a rhythm totally in tune with the surrounding topography.

At the same point as always, Dylan flipped open his cell phone and called his security system. "How are things at the cottage,

Helen?" Dylan listened to the computer's reply, and then flipped the cellular telephone shut, ending the call.

Ronnie was intrigued and suddenly became very serious. "You didn't tell me you had another woman at the cottage. What's going on, Sean?"

Dylan laughed, "Oh, that's only Helen. You'll like her."

Ronnie looked at Dylan. She started to protest as Dylan pulled into the winding driveway. "I'm not prudish, but three people alone in the wilderness was definitely not in my weekend plans."

Dylan parked the SUV and looked over at her. He was still smiling at Ronnie's reaction to the call. "It's not what you think. Let's go in and meet Helen before you get your knickers in a twist."

Ronnie looked at him, giving him her best look of disapproval.

"Okay, but if there is any funny business going on, I'm out of here and back to the mainland on the next ferry."

Dylan laughed. "You don't have to worry about Helen. Besides, the next ferry doesn't leave until seven in the morning," he said, leading the way to the cottage. The automatic exterior lights came on as they neared the building. Dylan inserted a key into the lock and quickly opened the door.

Helen's monotone voice greeted him immediately.

"Please enter your security code. You have fifteen seconds to disarm the alarm system or extreme force will be used to eradicate you from the premises."

"It's Okay, Helen. It's me." Dylan punched in his security code prompting Helen to respond. "Thank you, Boss. I detect a visitor with you. Please introduce."

"Yes, this is Ronnie Patterson. Ronnie, say hello to Helen."

"Helen is your security system?" asked a surprised Ronnie.

"I am a state of the art CS 1400 Security System," answered Helen. "Please use my name if you require any assistance."

"She is very good at looking after the cottage, and me too," offered Dylan. "Helen, Ronnie will be staying for the weekend. She has a level two clearance. Thank You."

"Right, Boss. Welcome, Ms. Ronnie Patterson."

A somewhat relived Ronnie replied, "Call me Ronnie."

"Thank you, Ronnie."

"I never spoke with a security system before."

"Helen's very good. She is the latest and greatest. If you ever have a question, she is always there to assist. Right, Helen?"

"Right, Boss."

"Good night, Helen."

"Good night, Boss."

Ronnie looked at Sean and whispered, "Does she hear everything we say?

"Yes, but she is very discreet. She looks after all the operations here at the cottage but doesn't talk to anyone other than those with a level two clearance, and then only when you activate a response by mentioning her by name."

Ronnie chided Dylan, "How come I only get level two clearance? Is there something wrong with me?" she pouted.

Dylan laughed. "No. Level Two is the highest level for anyone other than the system administrator, the person who programs Helen's functions, and that would be me. You would have to know all her programs to get to level one. Far too much work. Besides, if I told you all her secrets, you wouldn't be able to leave."

"She seems to be quite the lady."

"Helen can do far more than you can imagine," said Dylan sporting a mischievous smile.

Ronnie scanned the large open Great Room of the cottage. She was impressed.

"This is gorgeous. I was expecting something a lot more of the rugged outdoorsy type."

Dylan was pleased. "Make yourself at home and have a look around. I'm going to grab the bags from the car."

When he returned, he spotted Ronnie on the outside balcony, gazing out over the water. Dylan left her there enjoying the serenity of the night scene and returned to the kitchen to open a bottle of the Pinot Noir. He poured two glasses and joined her on the balcony.

"Like the view?"

"This is marvelous," she beamed. "Simply marvelous."

Dylan excused himself and went to the console that controlled the electronic functions of the cottage. He hit a series of buttons and Helen dutifully played back the single telephone message. It was from Bob Everson, Clark's lawyer.

"Hi Sean, just wanted to let you know that I sent a package on behalf of Jim Clark, via Fed Ex. It is self-explanatory. Call me if you have any questions. Bye."

Dylan punched the 'Off' button and rejoined Ronnie.

"Sorry about that. Have to stay on top of all my calls."

"All of your calls?" she replied with surprise. "My, how busy you are."

"Never mind," laughed Dylan, "I get my share." He picked up his wine glass and turned to Ronnie. "Here, a little toast to celebrate your first visit to the Island," he said, "to my little piece of heaven?"

. "My first visit?" exclaimed Ronnie with a laugh. "You are pretty sure of yourself, Mr. Dylan."

"Well, I can live in hope."

"Well," replied Ronnie with a somewhat devious grin, "chances are, if the wine is good, and you behave yourself, you could be right."

Dylan poured each another glass of wine. They spent the rest of the evening talking about their lives and those of people close to them. Ronnie's parents died in a car crash when she was only five. An older couple in the British Columbia's interior town of Kelowna adopted and raised both her and her sister. The girls had done very well in school and in winter, had become proficient skiers at the Big White Resort just outside town. They graduated one year apart. Ronnie had gone to Simon Fraser University and her sister to the University of Calgary. James T Walker & Company hired Ronnie after she graduated with a degree in Business Administration. Her first job was to assist a new hotshot financial wizard, Jim Clark. She had worked with Clark ever since.

The evening seemed to pass quickly. Dylan and Ronnie became very relaxed and had no problems sharing stories with each other. The soothing ambiance of the evening and the excellent wine cumulated in a slow and wonderful night of lovemaking.

21

AUGUST 18, 2007

MAYNE ISLAND   **0800 PDT**

The early morning sun filtered through the tall pine trees, performing an abstract dance that seemed to welcome Ronnie to the new day.

She had just awakened to find herself alone in the king sized bed. Ronnie sat up and rubbed her eyes, trying to focus on the interior of a room that she never really had an opportunity to view the night before.

"Well, the lady is finally awake," chided Dylan as he entered the bedroom and placed a large breakfast tray in front of her. "I thought you might enjoy a little nourishment."

"Is this because I missed dinner last night, or to replenish my system from all the extra late night activities?"

"A little of both, I imagine," said Dylan. He noticed a small golden cube hanging from the fine gold chain around her neck. "That's a very interesting charm," he said softly. "It is very unique."

Ronnie held the object in her fingers. Her eyes began to glisten. "There are not too many like this, that's for sure," she replied. "I got it from my sister. It has my initials on it. She has one just like it." Ronnie closed her eyes. "We made a pact that we would leave instructions in our wills that when we died, our executor would send the chain with the cube to the surviving sister. I know it sounds strange, but it's a sister thing."

"It's not so strange," replied Dylan. "Unless you are worried about my cooking," he added with a half smile.

Ronnie looked at the breakfast Dylan had set before her and laughed. "No." she laughed. "But what about you? Are you not going to eat?"

"Oh, I've already had a full breakfast," he replied. "Bacon, sausage, three eggs and hash browns, with toast and tea."

"You keep eating like that and you'll be the size of a house."

"As you said, we have to replenish the system. Besides, we have a lot of research to do today." Dylan replied as he turned to leave the room. "Don't stay there all day, now."

Dylan was in the Great Room, sitting at a desk looking over the coded papers when Ronnie appeared from the bedroom door. She was wearing loose fitting shorts and a short sleeved top that was opened just enough at the front to tantalize a little, and sandals. He had been deeply engrossed in the papers, but the sight of Ronnie entering the room completely disrupted his thought process. *"This is going to be harder than I imagined,"* he reflected to himself. He did not notice the sandals.

Ronnie moved behind him, wrapping her arms around his neck. Dylan showed Ronnie the papers from the cylinder, handling each of them carefully. He explained that they would be researching the Internet for all information on German submarines built during the Second World War.

"What are we looking for?"

Dylan picked up the cylinder and pointed to the corroded inscription on the outside of the casing.

"We need to locate the correct registration number for the submarine. Here, see this number, 'U-122'. We think there is a fourth digit. It has disappeared over the years due to surface corrosion. We have to find the submarine that ejected the cylinder to prove the papers are authentic. By the look of the corroded number on the brass cylinder, the missing digit should look somewhat similar, like a three, a five, six, eight, nine or a zero. I've eliminated the numbers one, two, four and seven as they wouldn't match what little there is remaining of the outline of the missing number."

Ronnie was excited about the project and immersed her self into the research. It took less than an hour for her to come up with information on the six possible submarines that fit the missing numbers. She was about to show Dylan when there was a knock at the door. It was the local angler delivering an order of fresh salmon. Dylan met his friend at the door and paid for the catch.

"Thanks, Joly, we're going to cook this on the barbeque tonight."

"Right you are, Sean. Enjoy."

Dylan placed the salmon in the refrigerator and rejoined Ronnie to continue the research.

The two went over the list and quickly eliminated two of the ships, both of which had seen service in the Atlantic. The allies had sunk both the U-1226 and U-1229 prior to May of 1945, which was the latest date listed on the papers retrieved from the cylinder.

They checked the remaining four, focusing on a process of elimination by date of service. Ronnie discovered an RCAF Catalina had sunk the U-1225 prior to 1945. Another struck it from the list.

That left only the U-1223, 1228 and U-1220. One of these ejected the cylinder into the ocean. Dylan was determined to find out who, and why.

Dylan and Ronnie spent the balance of the morning engrossed in their research. It was late afternoon and fatigue was setting in on both of them.

"We have gone as far as we can today," he declared, "let's take a break and enjoy some of this beautiful weather."

They spent an hour relaxing on the deck before Dylan began preparing the salmon dinner.

"Fresh Salmon with the Chef's special Pepper and Lemon sauce, fresh Asparagus with Ginger and Yams. That do it for you, ma'am?"

"It sounds positively delightful. Need some help?"

"No. You are the guest. Just sit back and enjoy."

Dinner was superb, followed by some wine and the most pleasant evening Dylan could remember in a long time. Ronnie was as good as she looked. "*In fact*," he thought, "*she may be even better*."

22

AUGUST 19, 2007

SEATTLE   **0700 PDT**

The telephone beside the bed of the FBI's Seattle office's Chief, Samuel O'Brien's telephone rang four times before he reluctantly rolled over to answer it. "O'Brien here. What's up?"

A monotone voice replied. "The man at the top has requested you contact your CSIS man in Vancouver and see if any other papers exist. The German SGI Department has expressed an interest in the contents of the cylinder. Apparently they actually might have some value."

"Do you realize this is Sunday?" asked O'Brien.

"The man wants this looked into. His office works 24/7. When he wants something done, we do it."

The monotone voice hung up. O'Brien looked at the receiver, its dial tone droning on incessantly. He replaced the receiver back on its base, yanked up the covers and went back to sleep.

MAYNE ISLAND   **0730 PDT**

Dylan and Ronnie awoke on this beautiful sunny Sunday to find themselves entwined in each other's arms. Words were not required as they enjoyed the pleasure of each other's bodies in the early morning light. They showered afterwards, had a healthy breakfast and then somewhat reluctantly, resumed work on the research project. After several intense hours, Ronnie had exhausted all the information she could find on the fate of the remaining three submarines.

She printed the data sheets, took them into the room where Dylan was working and spread them out across the desk. The detail of her work was impressive.

"The U-1228 was surrendered off the coast of New Hampshire, USA on May 17th, 1945," she stated.

"This doesn't eliminate it as a possible source."

"No, but it was apparently in that area for two weeks. While I do not know a great deal about submarines, I don't think they traveled fast enough to get from somewhere near Ireland to New Hampshire in less than four days."

"You've got a point there," he conceded.

Ronnie continued. "The U-1223 finished its last mission on April 15, 1945 and was scuttled somewhere near Norway on May 5th, but no records exist to prove where it was between the last mission and the time it was scuttled."

"Now, that's a possibility," suggested Dylan, "We will have to find more information on the U-1223."

The final submarine was the U-1220, but after her exhaustive checks into the available records on the Internet, Ronnie was unable to find any record of its service.

"Apparently, the U-1220 never existed, so we can forget that one," said Ronnie, scrunching up the final sheet into a crude ball and tossing it towards the wastebasket. "Two points!" she stated triumphantly, as the crumpled paper hit the side of the desk and ricocheted into the basket.

"I don't know. The number 1220 does appear in one of the coded messages. Let's not totally discard it just yet," he said pensively. "In the meantime, we should enjoy some of this day." He paused, flicked his head in the direction of the wastebasket and grinned. "Nice shot!"

Ronnie smiled and moved away from the computer desk, making her way over toward Dylan. As she past the bookcase, she spotted the Iron Cross medal he had casually hung around the neck of the small statuette.

"What's this?"

"It was in the cylinder. It fell out when I removed the papers. It's the Iron Cross, 1st Class, Germany's highest award for a submarine captain," Dylan explained. "Don't have a clue as to why it was in the cylinder."

She gave the medal a cursory look and then placed it back around the neck of the statuette. "It makes a neat souvenir," she said., looking over at Dylan. "So, what are we to do now, my captain?"

"Enjoy ourselves," he replied, taking her hand and leading her out onto the balcony.

The afternoon sun was still high in the sky and the one hundred and eighty degree view from the cottage balcony was spectacular. A myriad of small ships were plying the waters of the Strait, each with its own destination and purpose. A large ferry, loaded with its weekend passengers was making its scheduled crossing from the Mainland to Vancouver Island. It would meet its counterpart returning from the Island at the halfway point in Active Pass. Dylan waited for the sound of the horn as the large ship announced its presence in the pass. As the ferry disappeared from view, the horn sounded. Seconds later, a second horn answered. The two blasts melded together as one. Faint echoes of the sounds bounced off the hills of the neighbouring islands, rolled across the water. lingering in the warm evening air for several minutes.

In these idyllic conditions, all thoughts of the research had quickly faded from their minds. It was the perfect ending to the day. Dylan was enjoying Ronnie's company but he knew that tomorrow, he would have to take her back on the early ferry. He looked at Ronnie gazing out over the water, the sunlight shining on her hair, her smile soft and warm. She was the beauty that made the scene complete. Morning would come too soon.

23

AUGUST 20, 2007

BERLIN 1100 GMT

Both Müller and von Schlippenbach were waiting in Lüdden's office when he arrived. Müller was the first to speak. "Our contact reports that the elusive Mr. Dylan seems to have disappeared again."

Lüdden shot both men a look of disgust. "Is there never any good news from those incompetents?" he snarled.

Von Schlippenbach responded immediately. "They have successfully entered Clark's office and planted a listening device."

"We should be able to obtain more information very soon, Herr Lüdden." Müller echoed, not wanting to look uninformed.

"Is that all?" asked Lüdden expectantly.

Otto von Schlippenbach glanced at Müller, with a look that froze him in his place. "Yes, Herr Lüdden. That is all the news for now. Is that not right, Karl?"

Karl-Heinz Müller swallowed hard. "Yes. That is correct," he answered staring at the floor. He was the head of security, but he knew von Schlippenbach had more influence with Lüdden.

"Well, at least that is a move in the right direction," said Lüdden. "Keep me informed of all progress, no matter how small or insignificant you think it may be." He waved them unceremoniously out of the office.

MAYNE ISLAND   0610 PDT

Dylan rose early to fix breakfast so they could catch the first ferry across the Strait.

They had showered, made love again and then re-showered before finally getting dressed and rushing to the ferry. Dylan's local knowledge proved a bonus as they arrived at the ferry dock with five minutes to spare.

The trip back was almost as enjoyable as it was on the way over. It was obvious that although Ronnie knew she had to be at the office, she would have like to have stayed on the island a little longer.

They made their way back to their vehicle on the parking level as the Ferry made its approach to the Tsawwassen terminal.

"We could do this again next weekend, if you like." said Dylan as he unlocked the SUV.

"That would be nice," a smiling Ronnie replied. "Very nice."

VANCOUVER   0845 PDT

The drive from the ferry terminal to downtown Vancouver was always the worst part of the journey for Dylan. Commuter vehicles packed the road, most carrying only a single person. If Vancouver did have a downside, it was the lack of a viable road system. Everywhere a person wanted to travel involved crossing a river at one time or another. As Dylan and Ronnie made their way from the terminal towards downtown, they traversed four expanses of water by tunnel or bridge. At every crossing, the number of vehicles on the highway increased dramatically. The number of vehicles had clearly surpassed the capacity of the highway.

Dylan steered his vehicle into the High-Occupancy Vehicle lane and passed many of the single drivers in the other lanes.

"Don't understand why these people don't see the light." he said, "What is so hard about carpooling? That's why they build the HOV lanes."

"That comment coming from a man who lives his life his way, and drives by himself most everyday," Ronnie replied dryly.

Dylan knew she had him on that point and decided the best defense was to keep quiet. Both were silent for a moment, and then burst into laughter. The ring tone from Dylan's cell phone began to play the theme from 'Mission Impossible'. He picked up the cell phone and flipped the top open.

"Sean Dylan."

"Sean, Stan here. Do you have some time to meet with me this morning? We've managed to come up with a few more details from the papers that you might want to see."

"How about eleven o'clock?"

"That would work. Meet me at the outdoor restaurant on the second floor, overlooking the water."

"Right," replied Dylan. "See you there." He flipped the cell phone closed and turned to Ronnie.

"That was Stan Bennett, a friend of mine at CSIS. I gave him some of the papers to check out using some fancy equipment called a Laser Spectra Analyzer. He was able to use the equipment through his contacts at the FBI. Hopefully he has found additional information that will narrow down our search or at least tell us what the hell it is that we are searching for."

"It would help if they could tell us how to break the code," she reasoned.

The HOV lane was ending. Dylan had to move quickly to

merge with the other lanes. The balance of the trip was at Vancouver's usual stop-and-go rush hour pace. It took another forty minutes to reach Ronnie's apartment.

"Now you know why I live so close to the office." she said, "I couldn't do that everyday. Although I might consider it on occasion if I lived on the island."

"You have to give up some things in order to get others." Dylan replied as he pulled up in front of Ronnie's building. He scanned the area. "What, no David?"

"No, David is off in the mornings. Grant does the daytime shift, but I don't see him around anywhere. That is strange for him. He is usually very conscientious when it comes to his duties."

"You want me to come in with you?"

"No, I'll be alright." She glanced at her watch. "But, I do have to run. I was supposed to be in the office an hour ago. It has been a wonderful weekend, Sean. Thank you."

"Take care."

Ronnie gave Dylan a quick kiss on the cheek, exited the SUV and made her way into the apartment building.

Dylan watched her enter the building and then slipped the Land Rover into gear and melded back into the traffic. It was time to see what interesting information Stan Bennett had discovered.

BERLIN   **1850 GMT**

Karl-Heinz Müller, the Head of the Party's security section, handed the message to Hans Lüdden. "This just arrived from our Canadian surveillance team.

The leader read the message out load, "Intercepted phone communications. We can confirm that he has opened the cylinder.

Apparently the only contents were some worthless old papers, mostly in code."

"The idiots," shouted Lüdden. "The papers are everything. Why did they not acquire them?"

"Our people have not been able to locate Dylan's location. They are watching for him, but they have only been able to intercept telephone communications from Clark's office," von Schlippenbach responded.

"That is the second time these idiots have failed!" screamed Lüdden. "Why do you have such incompetents involved on the most important issue in our party's history?"

"They were highly recommended by our Canadian cell," offered Müller, looking directly at his leader, "They had worked for the cell in the past. Herr von Schlippenbach approved their mission."

Otto von Schlippenbach shot Müller an intense look. "On your recommendations, Herr Müller," he countered.

Lüdden was looking at a plastic folder containing a single sheet of paper. He did not appear to listen to the accusations of his two subordinates. "This," he said, motioning to the folder, "is the key to the very survival of our Party. However, to reap the benefits of its power, we must have those papers."

Von Schlippenbach and Müller were silent.

The leader of the underground Neo-Nazi Democratic Party stared icily at his two subordinates. "We must recover those papers at all costs. Do I make myself clear, gentlemen?"

Both men nodded affirmatively as Lüdden turned and exited the office.

Von Schlippenbach waited until the leader had disappeared from the room and then moved directly in front of Müller. "Be very careful, my dear Müller. If Herr Lüdden loses his temper and needs a scapegoat, you can be sure that it will be you who is sacrificed, and not his second in command. I will make certain of that."

Müller seemed to shrink in front of his immediate superior. He said nothing.

VANCOUVER   **1105 PDT**

Dylan arrived at the Harbour View restaurant just shortly after eleven. Stan Bennett was at a table near the window, sipping on his coffee.

"I was beginning to wonder if you were going to make it."

"The usual traffic again. You know this city. A bridge connects everything, and everyone wants to go over the same bridge at the same time," explained Dylan as he sat down. "So what's the news?"

"I sent the papers over to Angus MacDonald at the Bureau in Seattle. He called yesterday to give me the basic details, and then emailed his full report this morning. He was not able to decode the papers, of course. He said if you wanted to read the message, we would need an Enigma Encryption machine to break the code. Apparently all the encrypted papers that you found in the brass cylinder are a series of special orders that were issued by the German Navy."

"What exactly is an Enigma Encryption machine?"

"During the war, the Germans had a very sophisticated cryptography system called the Enigma which was a portable cipher machine used to encrypt and decrypt secret messages. The Enigma used a system that continually changed electrical paths within the machine to cause the rotors to rotate, which in turn caused the pin contacts to change with each letter typed, providing implementation of the polyalphabetic encryption. That was the basis for the success of the encryption system."

"Which means what, in plain English?"

"Using known Enigma settings codes and an Enigma machine, a person would be able to decode your messages."

"How do we get a hold of an Enigma machine, and where do I find the setting codes?"

"Not too many machines exist today. The only place you are likely to find one, is over in the War Office Museum in London, England. As for the code settings, Angus says they may be here somewhere in the coded messages, but he can't help you."

"Great," grumbled a disappointed Dylan.

"There was one thing he could confirm though. One of the pages was a special radio transmission between two German submarines, the U-1220 and the U-112."

"What do you mean, '1220'?" asked Dylan as a young waitress came by to take his order. "Just a cup of tea, black." he said. Dylan looked at his friend. "And you'd better give my friend here a refill, too. He can't function without his usual morning fix."

Bennett nodded to the server to confirm the order and continued. "We know the submarine had a four number designation. The laser analysis confirmed it. The number appeared in the coded messages and was also in the faded handwriting on the back of the papers."

"But we could not find any trace of a submarine designated the U-1220."

"The Germans never encrypted numbers, they just used them verbatim," responded Bennett. "If the U-1220 is in the message, then it probably did exist."

"I understand your logic," replied Dylan. "But we researched every German submarine used in the Second World War and according to all the records and information available, the U-1220 never existed."

"Sorry, but the facts don't lie. Unless the Germans made a mistake, but I don't think that's very likely in this case."

Dylan listened intently as Bennett continued to explain the details of the pages and expounded on his theory as to how it all related.

"All this happened around the time of Hitler's death near the end of the war. There could be a possible connection to missing members of Hitler's inner circle including Bormann. Hell, it might even give some credence to the stories about Hitler himself escaping, but that would be a long shot. The Russians arrived in Berlin first. They claim they found both the burned bodies of both Hitler's and Eva Braun outside the New Reich Chancellery. Funny thing is, though, the allies were never shown any proof."

"You don't think Hitler could have escaped from Berlin, do you?" asked a surprised Dylan.

"Well, the Laser Spectra analysis did reveal some other interesting details. They were hand written on the back of the original copies. There are notations about persons being picked up in Hamburg and taken to a rendezvous point at latitude sixty degrees, eight minutes north by longitude two degrees, 3 minutes west. I checked on Google Earth. The coordinates put the location up in the middle of the North Sea near the Shetland Islands. It is possible that there may have been a submarine-to-submarine exchange, but I cannot confirm that for sure. We simply do not have enough information. There are no other details as to who these people were or what happened to them. I would imagine there could be something in the coded messages that might tie it all together."

"But why would anyone meet in the middle of nowhere?"

"I agree that scenario would be strange, but there is also a stranger reference to the submarine U-112. We are not sure what to make of that connection. We do know the U-112 series was a Type IX, one of a series of exceptional submarines that the Germans thought about building just before the war. They had a much superior range over their actual wartime boats and could maintain underwater cruising far in excess of what was possible by the 1200 series of submarines. They were supposed to have a cruising speed of twenty-six knots on the water. But as far as anyone knows, they were never built."

Dylan had picked up on Bennett's thought process.

"But if they were built, the U-1220 could have met up and transferred their passengers to the larger submarine who then could have escaped to wherever." He paused in reflection, "Then it might be possible that Hitler, or at least his cronies, could have escaped from Germany."

"I admit it's a bizarre assumption based on bits and pieces of clues. However, that idea is not all that crazy. I think one should be careful not to jump to some wild conclusions without a lot more proof."

"What kind of proof do we need?"

"First, we would need confirmation that the U-1220 really did exist. Then you would have to decode these papers, find the right submarine and confirm its operations area. Then some of these strange clues might make sense. Until then, it is only conjecture. An interesting fantasy, but until we get that proof, only fantasy. As for the U-112, it is probably only fantasy."

The two men discussed details of Dylan's weekend research.

Dylan was careful to omit any reference to his research partner and their non-research related activities.

"So, we eliminated all but two of the submarines by virtue of the date they were sunk or where they were around May fourth. The U-1229 and the U-1220 were the only two possibilities and according to all the available records, the U-1220 apparently never existed. Therefore, that leaves the U-1229. Right?" Dylan declared.

"Theoretically, but the Germans didn't always put everything into the books. I wouldn't write off the U-1220 submarine just yet."

"Was there anything else on the papers?"

"No, just the coded messages. We managed to clean them up so you can at least read what you don't understand."

"Well, that will definitely help. Thanks."

"I must tell you," offered Bennett. "The papers did generate some interest at the Bureau. Seems a few of the fellows in their special codes section over there would like to get their hands on all the pages. I told them these copies were all I had. It was not a lie. It was all I had."

"Any indication why they're so excited?"

"I don't have any firm answer to that," Bennett replied, "but I would be very careful. These guys play for keeps." He handed Dylan a set of papers containing a clear detailed printout of the previously unintelligible pages, "Here it is, neat as you please." The page, in unbroken code, read:

MPC040545714

LPB 091002085

HPKA AZSP RDTP RTEH YZMV

AFJG NYCH DZPK MFTZ ADPJ ROSD

ILTT LAKE YDDS NLSI

"We didn't have any problem in recovering what was written, but we don't have the resources needed to attempt breaking the Enigma code, especially without the source codes. I guess, like everyone else, they want to find out more about what was going on back then."

"I've heard that the Allies were unable to crack some of the German codes." Dylan replied.

Yes, it had something to do with the introduction of a new code book and a more complex version of the Enigma machine, a new Naval Enigma cipher called Shark."

"I am heading over to Berlin next week. Maybe I can stop in London to see if I can find an Enigma machine and get some help in decoding these messages."

Bennett looked at Dylan. "Do you have the source codes?"

"No. I don't think so. Some papers are quite readable. They have a lot of numbers and letters on them, but I'm just not sure what they mean."

"You might want to keep them locked somewhere," said Bennett. "You know, besides our friends at the FBI, there are still a lot of people out there who have ties to World War Two and they have reasons not to be found. If you start asking questions in the wrong places, you could meet up with some nasty receptions."

"I am excited about what these papers might reveal and I realize there could be a certain amount of danger involved. I will be careful. My Berlin connection is looking into a few possibilities that could prove interesting. With a little bit of luck, I might be able to solve some of these mysteries."

"Be careful, my friend."

Dylan looked at his friend. "No problem, Stan. I will keep both eyes open." He paused for a moment. "Thanks."

24

AUGUST 22, 2007

VANCOUVER   **1642 PDT**

It was late Wednesday when Dylan arrived at the offices of James T Walters and Company. He spotted Ronnie standing by the filing cabinet behind her desk. She had her back to the entrance. Dylan moved silently around the desk and crept up behind her. He poked her on the arm, causing her to jump away from the cabinet.

"Anyone around here know where a guy can get a good shot of Irish Whisky?"

"Sean! You scared me half to death."

"Sorry, I just couldn't resist," he laughed. "Is the Big Guy in? I think he's expecting me."

"And I thought you came in to see me," she said, her lower lip curling in feigned sadness.

"Well, I did, but to keep up appearances, I have to use your boss as an excuse."

Ronnie turned her eyes up to the ceiling as she made her way past Dylan and into Clark's office to announce his arrival.

"Jim, there's some reprobate out here, says he has an appointment with you."

Clark smiled at Ronnie's description, "Sean's here. Good! Send him in."

Dylan made his way into the office and fell into the comfort of one of the large leather chairs in front of Clark's desk.

"I hear you are stealing my secretary away these days. Don't tell me Ronnie is finally going to make an honest man out of you?" Clark asked, smiling. "You know I can't afford to lose her."

"Ah, no," responded Dylan, "nothing like that. We were just doing a little research."

"Right!" Clark laughed.

"That's not a terrible thought, but you know me, I'm not one for settling down. Not just yet, anyway."

"You sure could do a lot worse. She won't wait forever."

Dylan looked out towards Ronnie's desk. "You never know where the ball will roll, my friend."

He turned back to Clark and began to describe Bennett's findings, and explain how they related to the research that he and Ronnie had done over the weekend.

"So, you actually did do some research. I am impressed."

"Me too, that girl does make concentrating a real challenge. It must be difficult for you, putting up with a sight like that on an everyday basis."

"It could be, my friend, except that I am far too busy and not really into dating my secretary, especially when she was such a good friend of Sheryl's. Having her here actually helps me keep everything in perspective." Clark paused for a moment, "Enough about that. What's our next move?"

Dylan realized he had struck a sensitive chord and appreciated that Clark had changed the subject.

"Well, if we can confirm the submarine the cylinder actually came from, and somehow decode the encrypted messages, we might be able to prove what they were up to and who was involved. It is a bit of a long shot, but Stan Bennett thinks there is a possibility that some very high-ranking members of Hitler's inner circle may have escaped from Berlin in that U-Boat. It could have been Bormann, or even Hitler himself."

"That sounds a little far fetched. Everyone knows the Russians found Hitler's body and those of his entourage when they reached Berlin. However, Bormann on the other hand, he could be a possibility. Several witnesses claimed they saw him killed by a Russian tank, while others said he took cyanide capsules on a Bridge in Berlin. Other rumors having him escaping to South America."

"Actually, the Germans claim to have found bones they identified as Borman's, but it wasn't through any DNA checks, so we still don't know for sure. As Stan said, this is all just conjecture."

"What are you going to do now?"

"I'm heading over to Berlin. An old friend from my Armed Forces days has done some preliminary investigation with the Head of Staff at the German war records office. He is trying to pin down the movements of U-1229 during its last month or so in service. If possible, he is going to try to locate additional information on the mysterious U-1220, which, as far as we know, doesn't really exist."

"Sounds interesting. When are you back?"

"I am going to stop in at the War Records Office in London on the way back to see what I can find out about the possibility of decoding the messages."

"What are the chances?"

"I don't know. The work of the British cryptanalysts literally changed the course of the Second World War, which incidentally led to the creation of the modern computer. If I can locate an Enigma encryption machine, and learn a bit about the codes the Germans used in the war, I might be able to get these messages deciphered. Time wise, I should be back in about ten days."

Clark got up from his desk and shook hands with his friend. "Call me if you have any news."

On the way out of the office, Dylan stopped by Ronnie's desk. She told him that Grant the door attendant was back on duty and had been asking questions about Dylan.

"He asked where you worked. I told him the question was quite inappropriate."

"Since I've never met the man, I don't understand why he would want to know about me. Maybe he spoke with David and he's worried about the strange man you have been seeing lately."

"It's not funny."

"Sorry." Dylan replied, laughing.

"Maybe he wants you."

"Ah, don't think so." He picked up a magazine and flipped through the pages. Then, in a more serious tone, "Ronnie, I know we said we might go over to the island this weekend, but something has come up. I am heading over to Berlin to meet with a friend who is checking out information on the U-1229 and a few other things."

Ronnie closed her eyes and shook her head.

"Seems like we've been here before." she replied in a disappointing tone, "Call me when you get back. If I am still in town, maybe I will talk to you. On the other hand, maybe I won't."

Dylan knew his spur of the moment plans had upset Ronnie but he had no choice. He had to go to Berlin to find the information on the submarines. He turned and walked out of the office.

"You're incorrigible, Sean Dylan." Ronnie called after him. Dylan opened the glass doors and walked out into the hall towards the elevator. He turned, smiled and blew her a kiss.

25

AUGUST 25, 2007

BERLIN 1630 GMT

Dylan looked out the window of the Boeing 767 as it banked to the left and lined up with the runway zero eight, in preparation for landing.

The sleek blue KLM jet glided effortlessly onto the tarmac of BBI with only the slightest of bumps. *"Not bad,"* thought Dylan.

The former Berlin-Schönefeld Airport was equipped with gates, runways and taxiways capable of handling the new A380 super jumbo jets and featured an integrated motorway connection and new rail infrastructure with a high-speed ICE train station directly underneath the airport to shorter traveling times to the city. Berlin had the distinction of being the European capital with the shortest distance to an international airport.

Dylan exited the Boeing jet, making his way through the new aircraft departure tunnel and into the terminal building. He was impressed with the new structure and marveled at its efficiency.

It only took ten minutes for Dylan to reach the Baggage Claim area. Luggage from his flight was already starting to appear on the revolving carousel. As he waited for his own bags to appear, Dylan scanned the arrivals area, catching sight of the tall, attractive woman standing near the exit doors.

"Nice," thought Dylan.

For an instant, he thought he recognized her, but dismissed the thought from his mind as he spotted his bag on the carousel. He reached between to other passengers to retrieve it. When he looked up again, the woman had disappeared. He casually looked around as he left the baggage area. *"I guess she wasn't looking at me after all,"* he said, feigning disappointment. Dylan proceeded to the Hertz Car Rental kiosk where he spoke to a clerk who quickly directed their Gold Card member to his waiting vehicle.

It was always a surprise for Dylan when he rented a vehicle. Being a preferred customer of the world's number one car rental company had its benefits. Today was no exception as the company upgraded him to one of their new prestige vehicles. As he approached the rental car area, he located his name on the Gold Card member's message board. *"Mr. Dylan – Stall #6".* He located the parking slot and found a new Jaguar XK waiting for his pleasure.

The XK´s extensive range of intelligent safety features including Jaguar's Adaptive Restraint Technology System (ARTS), a new Performance Braking System, Intelligent Lighting and Active Speed Limiter control. Designed to optimize driver control in difficult driving conditions, they also provided high levels of occupant protection.

It was the state-of-the-art engineering.

Dylan settled into the comfort of the XK and turned the key. The Driver Information Centre, a new and highly intuitive Touch Screen control system, latest generation Satellite Navigation and Adaptive Cruise Control was impressive. It was definitely sporting luxury that encompassed expressed spirit and elegance in equal measure. He quickly punched in the coordinates for the Grand Hyatt Hotel into the GPS navigation system and headed out of the airport.

Precisely balanced, the XK responded instantly to every touch. There was an instantaneous fusion between Dylan and this highly engineered machine. Sporting a powerful 300 horsepower 4.2 litre V8 engine with its sequential shift 6-speed transmission, the performance of the Jaguar was nothing short of invigorating.

The express route from the airport quickly took Dylan into the heart of the city. He marveled at the vibrancy of its people as he drove along the Berauer Strasse past the last visage of the Berlin Wall, the formidable structure that had hermetically separated the East and West sectors of Germany's largest city.

In 2007, Berlin had become a dynamic, cosmopolitan and creative metropolis allowing for every kind of lifestyle. *"East meets West at the heart of a changing Europe,"* Dylan thought to himself.

He drove past the Federal Central Record building that housed many of the documents and information of historical importance to the German Federal Republic. It was the Bundesarchiv Zentralnachweisstelle. Much of the information held there related to World War II. Dylan had contacted a friend who was working in Berlin and asked if he could go to the Bundesarchiv and dig up some information on the final days of U-1229.

Dylan drove along the infamous Strasse des 17 Juni, glancing at the Soviet War Memorial on the north side. The destroyed Reich Chancellery building, Hitler's former headquarters, had supplied the marble for its construction. The first two Russian tanks that entered Berlin at the end of the World War Two siege flanked each side of the monument.

The broad avenue led past the new Reichstag, the location of Germany's modern government and on to the famous Brandenburg Gate, which used to separate East and West Berlin. Dylan continued through the Brandenburg Gate directly on to the Unter den Linden

Linden. The strange name translated into 'Under the Lime Trees'. Unter den Linden Linden was Berlin's grand old boulevard, featuring a center pedestrian strip with two rows of the lime trees.

He turned to the South and noticed the strange paradox that marked this area that encompassed both East and West Berlin. West Berlin was awash in trees with large flowerpots decorating the streets. The section of East Berlin was barren. The entire area was mostly solid concrete.

It was only minutes before Dylan came to the Grand Hyatt Hotel on Marlene-Dietrich-Platz. He noticed a car pulling out of a parking stall in front of an old Mercedes. Dylan slowed a little and then carefully pulled into the newly vacated spot, taking care not to scratch the XK on the older Mercedes.

The Grand Hyatt, featuring minimalist styling with Bauhaus influences and state of the art communications facilities is arguably one of Europe's finest hotels, and a major presence on the Potsdamer Platz, in the heart of 'New Berlin'. It would be home to Sean Dylan for the next two days.

The lobby of the Grand Hyatt was striking, with its grey marble tiled floor and expansive reception area that featured a mezzanine level that overlooked the entrance. The high circular columns that rose from the floor to the ceiling with small intimate meeting areas, each with plush leather chairs and individual tables placed between, reminded Dylan of the Greek Parthenon. He stood admiring the architecture for a moment and then moved to the reception desk.

"Sean Dylan" he said, placing his credit card on the counter.

The clerk at the front desk greeted him, after a quick check on the computer screen, returned Dylan's credit card and handed him a computerized key.

"We have a beautiful suite for you. Number nine-twelve. It is on the ninth floor. The elevators are to your right," said the clerk with typical German efficiency. As Dylan turned to go, the desk clerk called after him. "Mr. Dylan, I am sorry, I almost forgot. Sir, there is a message here for you."

The clerk retrieved the written message from behind the desk and quickly handed it to Dylan. "I am very sorry, Sir." he said most apologetically.

"No problem," replied Dylan. "Thanks."

"Would there be anything else?" asked the clerk regaining his composure.

"Yes. Please inform your housekeeping staff that I do not wish to be disturbed. I will call for service if and when I require it," he replied handing the desk clerk a twenty Euro bill.

"Very good, Sir. Thank you."

Dylan turned and made his way to the elevators, surprisingly finding one waiting with open doors. He entered and pushed the ninth floor button.

As the elevator doors closed, he flipped open the message. *"Sean, meet me at Borchardt Restaurant Regensburgherstrasse 7, across from the museum. Dinner at Eight."* It was signed, Oz.

Dylan had known Ozzy during his time with the Special Forces Branch. His real name was Oscar Bauer. Both men were stationed at the base at Baden-Baden in the nineties and when their active service ended, Sean had returned to Canada to continue work in archeology, while Ozzy accepted a contract with a German security company and moved to Berlin.

The elevator stopped at the ninth floor. Dylan exited and followed the signs to room nine-twelve. He inserted his key card and entered a spacious room that was anything but a typical hotel room.

The Grand Suite included a plush king bed, living area with a large flat-screen TV and a cocktail and wine bar. To the right was an all inclusive work area with internet connections and kitchenette complete with amenities including fresh fruit and bottled water. Dylan whistled as he drew the sheer curtains back and looked at Marlene-Dietrich-Platz and the New Berlin. The view from the huge windows of the corner suite was impressive.

His placed his travel bag on the bed, opened it, took out the few clothes he brought for the trip and placed them in the large walk-in closet. A quick shower to wash off the drowsiness from the long flight and he would leave to meet Ozzy.

The Borchardt Restaurant, one of Berlin's finest, was a favourite haunt of Berlin's power brokers, catering at times to ambassadors, presidents and prime ministers. The current restaurant was actually a re-creation of the original, which was located next door at No. 48. The original restaurant was a victim of the bombing during the Second World War. They reconstructed the present restaurant on the adjoining site, with an eye to authenticity done so well, one could not tell the structure was not bona fide 19th-century.

The owners' reputation for the presentation of traditional German and French dishes of the highest standard was stellar.

Dylan arrived at the restaurant to find his friend Ozzy pacing back and forth in front of the entrance. Ozzy's face brightened when he spotted Dylan. "I hate going in there alone." Ozzy declared. "They always make me feel like I'm in the wrong place."

"It's good to see you, Ozzy, my old friend," said Dylan, cheerfully shaking his hand. "Still tormented about the little things, I see. You will never change."

"Hello Sean. And yes, I still worry about things. Not so much anymore, but sometimes." Ozzy handed Sean a small gift-wrapped package. "Here's a little something that might come in handy while you are in town."

Sean accepted the package. "Smith and Wesson?" he asked in a low voice.

"What else? It was all you ever used."

Dylan put his arm around his friend as they entered the restaurant. The ever efficient staff met them inside the door and assisted the Maitre'd as he quickly escorted the two men to their waiting table. The establishment was the picture of elegance.

Dylan and Ozzy caught up on the happenings of the past nine years since they left the Armed Forces. The service was exceptionally good. Dylan ordered some of the oysters from the German North Sea island of Sylt, often said to be the best in the world, followed by the house special, a feather light Wiener Schnitzel that came with a delicious hot German potato salad. Ozzy was delighted with the choice of oysters, but opted for another of the restaurants fine offerings, perch in herb sauce.

The meals were as expected, a culinary experience made only greater with the addition of a fine Monchoff 2004 Urziger Wurzgarten Riesling.

"It's going to be difficult to concentrate on business after such a fine meal," said Ozzy, reaching into his jacket and extracting some papers.

"I agree, there is always something to take away the joy of a good meal, but it has to be done." Dylan answered. "And seeing as we can't enjoy the luxury of a good cigar anymore, let's get to it."

Ozzy started detailing the information he had acquired regarding the submarines when Dylan noticed the tall woman across the room. He looked at her with an instant sense of recognition. There was no mistake. It was the same woman he spotted earlier in the baggage claim area on his arrival at the BBI airport. She was sitting alone. *"That's a strange coincidence,"* he thought. His mind went into overdrive, racing with thoughts about the tall woman. Ozzy's mention of the submarine U-1229 instantly brought him back into the conversation.

"I've found conclusive details on the U-1229 which have eliminated it as a possibility." Ozzy continued, handing Dylan a folder full of documents. "The facts are all here. There is no way the U-1229 is the submarine you are looking for, and to make matters worse, the German Records Office checked out the registration for the U-1220. According to all the available German naval records, a submarine numbered U-1220 never existed."

A disappointed Dylan sat in quiet reflection. His search had apparently come to a screeching halt.

"The only thing I can suggest," Ozzy continued, "would be for you to visit the dockyards where the submarines were built to see if there are any records there that might prove otherwise."

"But if the submarine existed, why wouldn't the German War Records show it?"

"The war was moving at an extremely fast pace near the end and it may be that the records are not all complete. There could have been an oversight that occurred by accident," Ozzy paused, "or maybe on purpose."

"But why would they have an unmarked submarine?"

"It is hard to say what was going through the minds of the German leaders near the end."

"Yes, you're right. The final days were in a state of chaos, but how do you lose a submarine," Dylan asked, "unless, as you said, it was done on purpose."

"That would make it untraceable and," suggested Ozzy, "if a

person or persons were trying to escape persecution for war crimes, no one would ever know."

Dylan thought about the scenario for a moment.

"Where were the twelve hundred series submarines built?" he asked.

"In Hamburg. At the Deutsch-Werft boat building yard," Ozzy replied. "I did a little research and found a few interesting details." He reached into his jacket and retrieved a folded paper that he handed to Dylan, "There's a person on that list that you might want to look up while you're in Hamburg. A man named Horst Schneider. He was the supervisor of the yard during the last days of the war. Herr Schneider might be able to shed some light on the phantom U-1220 submarine."

"Is he still alive?" Dylan queried.

"According to my sources he is, and at ninety-one years of age, still has a good memory, especially when it comes to details of the ships he built during the war."

"I'll head up there tomorrow," said Dylan, beaming in anticipation of what he might learn from the former ship builder.

Ozzy looked at his friend with genuine concern. "You know there are still a lot of the 'old boys' around. You could be stirring up some history they may want forgotten. They could play rough."

"I'll be okay," answered Dylan, picking up the gift Ozzy had given him earlier. "Besides, I've got a little helper."

"Just be careful."

"You've done a great job, Ozzy. I owe you one."

Dylan scanned the room and noted that the tall woman had left. He picked up his glass. "Here's to the many mysteries of the U-1220. May all its secrets be revealed."

The two longtime friends clinked glasses, drained their wine and rose to leave. It was past midnight, but despite the hour, the restaurant was full with the glamorous after-theatre crowd.

The traffic had diminished, allowing Dylan to enjoy the exquisite performance of the Jaguar XP. Passing the Brandenburg gate, he used his free hand to open the gift from Ozzy. In the box was a Smith and Wesson Model 6906, nine-millimeter semi automatic handgun. This compact unit weighed only twenty-three and a half ounces and fired twelve shots from its deadly three and a half inch barrel. Like the Jaguar, the Smith and Wesson was an exceptional piece of workmanship. It was as beautiful as it was deadly. He checked the clip. It was full.

"A little newer than what I had in the old days," he thought to himself. *"But very nice."*
He slid the gun inside his jacket as he entered the Hyatt parking lot.

Dylan exited from the elevator on the ninth floor. He did his usual scan of the hallways and then proceeded to his room. Reaching the door to room nine twelve, he noticed the 'Do Not Disturb' sign on the handle was still in place. He bent down and slipped his key card up between the door and the doorframe. The card slid easily. The Canadian coin he had placed there when he left was gone. Someone had been, or possibly still was, in the room.

His Special Forces training had prepared him for every type of situation. Dylan automatically slid his right hand inside his jacket and grasped the handle of the Smith and Wesson. With his left hand, he placed the magnetic key into the locking mechanism, pulled it out. He dropped to one knee as the light flashed green, and pushed the door open.

The room appeared empty. Dylan reached back with his foot, to close the door. The television set was still on, exactly as he had left it. He scanned the room, checking in the mirrors and the glass in the pictures for reflections. Nothing. The bedroom was to his left. Dylan followed the same methodical procedure, with the same results. Whoever had entered was long gone. He replaced the Smith and Wesson back inside his jacket and surveyed of the room.

Although nothing was amiss, Dylan was sure someone had entered the suite. He proceeded with a systematic check of the rooms and its contents. It took only fifteen minutes to find the 'bug'. It was inside the lining of his overnight travel bag. It was an older type "MD41", about the size of a package of matches, but capable of sending a radio signal up to a mile away. Someone in Berlin desperately wanted to track his whereabouts.

Dylan carefully removed the 'bug' and put it in his pocket.

"So someone wants to know where I am. That's fine by me," he thought. *"At least for now."*

Dylan stowed the bag, took a shower and went to bed.

The next morning before heading down to breakfast, he would call Ozzy.

26

AUGUST 26, 2007

BERLIN 0810 GMT

Dylan was up early. He showered, shaved and dressed before telephoning Ozzy.

"Oz, do you remember Operation Sand Dunes back in '89?"

"Yes."

"Do you recall the bug the Iranians planted in our vehicle?"

"Yeah, it was an MD41 type. Why?"

"Last night I found one hidden in my overnight travel bag. Someone must have put it there while we were at dinner."

"Geez, Sean, who even knows you're here?" questioned Ozzy. "And why should they want to tail you anyway?"

"I don't know. The only people, other than yourself who know I am here are Jim and Ronnie, and I doubt they would have been talking to anyone. I did talk with Stan at CSIS. He mentioned some of his FBI contacts were interested in seeing the coded papers. I think maybe they might be more interested in the contents of that little cylinder than they let on."

"The German Records Office might be a possibility," said Ozzy. "I mentioned that some of your papers were in code, but they didn't seem to have much interest or even cared about the project at all." Ozzy paused for a moment. "There is a so called Neo-Nazi Democratic Party, but they would have no way of knowing about the cylinder. Besides, they are all talk and not much substance."

"Well, I can't worry about it. I am heading off to Hamburg after breakfast to find the ship builders supervisor. After that, I will be heading to London for a couple of days. Apparently, they have all the German Enigma codebooks on file. I am going to do a little research. Who knows? Maybe I will get lucky and crack the code."

"Hopefully you can at least find out what the hell you're dealing with, anyway."

"Yeah, that would be different."

"Take care, buddy."

"Always," echoed Dylan. "I'll be in touch."

He hung up the phone, grabbed his jacket and went down to the hotel restaurant for breakfast.

BERLIN   **1135 GMT**

Hans Lüdden was sitting behind the desk at the underground Neo-Nazi Democratic Party headquarters. His second in command, Otto von Schlippenbach was standing beside him. Spread out on the desk was a sequence of photographs showing Dylan and Ozzy during their meeting at the Borchardt Restaurant.

Schlippenbach spoke. "The wire tap on Clark's office alerted us that Dylan was coming to Berlin. We had him under surveillance from the moment he landed. We followed him to the restaurant where he met with a man named Oscar Bauer. We checked his background. He works for a German security company here in Berlin, specializing in corporate alarm systems. We do not know why they met."

Lüdden held up one photo. "What do we know about this package Dylan is holding?"

"It was given to him by Bauer. It is a gift of some kind. Apparently they are old friends."

"Dylan must be up to something. Stay with them both."

"Do you want us to eliminate Bauer?"

"Not yet. Let us see what their next move is. We do not want to bring any undue attention to Dylan. It might interfere with an opportunity to retrieve the contents of the cylinder."

Karl-Heinz Müller entered the office. He looked pleased as he approached Lüdden's desk. "We have managed to put a bugging device in Mr. Dylan's overnight travel bag. We will now know his whereabouts when he leaves the hotel."

"Very good, Karl," said Lüdden. "Make sure you keep a close watch Dylan's activities. We must be sure that he has the papers with him before we strike take any action."

BERLIN   **1235 GMT**

Dylan unlocked the Jaguar and tossed his overnight bag into its spacious trunk. He settled into the driver's seat, switched on the seven-inch high-resolution, touch-screen navigation system, and programmed his trip. The roads to Hamburg were modern highways and the onboard navigation system had already determined that, without any construction delays, the entire trip would take only three hours and fourteen minutes. With a short twist of the ignition key, the XK's powerful four-point-two litre V8 engine roared to life and Dylan, following the computerized female voice of the navigation system, which he had quickly named "Katarina" after the famous German ice skater, headed out of the Hyatt parking lot and turned right onto the Knobelsdorffstrasse.

He immediately checked the XK's mirrors. There was only

the regular traffic passing the hotel entrance Every thing appeared normal. He checked the mirror one more time and then pulled out onto the Strasse. There was a small blue German van at the exit of a gas station to his right. The van was waiting to merge into the traffic. He slowed down a bit to allow the van to pull out, but the van waited until Dylan passed by and then pulled out abruptly, just missing the front of a dark green Mercedes sedan that was bearing down on him.

Dylan thought to himself, *"Either he is very stupid or he's not the one I'm looking for."* He proceeded along the Strasse, keeping a close watch on the vehicles in the rearview mirror.

As he approached the entrance to the A10 ramp that lead to Hamburg, Katarina advised Dylan to turn right. Dylan ignored the instructions of the computerized voice and continued past the exit. He would double back once he was sure no one was following him.

He stayed on the Knobelsdorffstrasse for four kilometers, keeping an eye on the blue van as he drove. At this distance, most of the traffic behind him had disappeared. Only the blue van and the dark green Mercedes behind it were still in the same positions. Katarina, the voice of the navigation system was busily informing Dylan that he had missed his turn and that she was recalculating his route.

"Take the next left turn, in one-point-three kilometers," intoned Katarina.

Dylan ignored her again. He picked the entrance to a small shopping area about three hundred metres ahead on the right. He pulled into the parking area and then making an immediate 'U' turn to come back facing the main road. The van did not follow him. He watched as it went by the parking area and continued on, disappearing in the maze of traffic.

The Mercedes following the van had signaled for a left turn, which it made at the next street. Dylan was satisfied. Although he had no reason to suspect the dark green vehicle, his training instincts took over and he glanced up to check the license plate of the sedan as it made its turn. He managed to catch the final three digits as he pulled back onto the Knobelsdorffstrasse. '714'.

The change in direction caused Katarina to inform him that he was going the wrong way. Again, the computerized voice advised him she would recalculate the route. Two minutes later, Katarina announced, "Take the second exit to the left and proceed onto the A10 ramp. Smiling to himself, Dylan followed her instructions and took the exit marked Hamburg/Schwante. Nine minutes later, Katarina's instructions had successfully placed him on the main autobahn leading to Hamburg.

As he drove along the highway, Dylan glanced periodically into his rearview mirror. It was twenty minutes later when he spotted a dark green vehicle some distance behind him. He slowed the Jaguar slightly to draw the car closer. As the vehicle slowly crept up on the Jaguar, he could make out the shapes of the two people inside. There was a short bulky figure driving and another very tall person in the passenger seat. Moments later, the dark green Mercedes had drawn close enough to allow Dylan to read the license plate. It ended with the numbers '714'.

After finding the 'bug' planted in his overnight bag, Dylan was sure there would be some sort of surveillance unit on him when he left the hotel. He started to plot his move to lose the tail. Spotting a sign indicating a work yard ahead, he signaled and quickly pulled off onto the side road. The Mercedes continued on the highway. Dylan waited a full ten minutes before making his way back onto the highway. He had only traveled six miles when he noticed the dark green sedan had once again appeared in his rearview mirror.

"Once might be a coincidence, twice is definitely a tail," Dylan murmured to himself. He quickly put his plan into place to shake his unwanted followers.

Using the Satellite Navigation system's touch screen, Dylan pulled up the list of gas stations on the 2-D map display. The first one was a small station just two miles up the road. The second one was a full Service Centre twelve miles further. He punched in the request for directions to the Service Center. Katarina quickly confirmed the selection with a new ETA.

The Service Center was on the opposite side of the road. This would require him to take an exit and cross over the highway. A move that was well suited to Dylan's plan.

He kept the dark green sedan in view as he approached the exit for the Service Centre, only slowing as necessary to negotiate the overhead pass to the opposite side of the freeway.

Parking the XK facing outwards towards the highway, Dylan exited and locked the vehicle, prior to making his way into the entrance to the restaurant area that formed part of the Service Center. From his vantage point, he could easily see the Mercedes and its two passengers as they pulled into the parking area.

The dark green car parked near the back of the lot. The driver, a short stocky man wearing dark glasses exited the vehicle and made his way towards the restaurant entrance. Dylan feigned interest at the newspaper display outside the eating area and watched as the man entered. He looked like an old boxer whose face had been the recipient of far too many blows. He walked through the entrance and made his way into the restroom. Dylan waited until the door closed before following. As he approached the door, another customer exited the lavatory. Dylan spotted an 'Out Of Order' sign on a cleaning trolley, picked it up and hung it over the outside door handle as he entered the washroom.

The man from the green sedan was standing at the centre urinal, his back to the door. He did not take any notice of Dylan as he approached him from behind, his right hand nestled firmly around the grip of the Smith and Wesson inside his jacket. The man had finished relieving himself and was looking down, closing the zipper on his pants. Dylan stepped up behind him, grabbed the back of the man's head with his left hand and in one continuous motion rammed it downward onto the top of the urinal. An ugly bone crunching sound resonated throughout the washroom as the man's face made contact with the rock hard white porcelain receptacle. As the unconscious man's knees buckled, he sank to the floor, his head falling forward into the urinal.

Dylan pushed the man sideways with his foot. The man's body fell to the floor. Blood oozed from his nose, ran down his face and formed a small pool on the white tiles. He reached inside the man's jacket and removed a snub-nosed gun. "I'll bet you don't have a license for this, my friend," he said offhandedly. "Best I get rid of it for you before you get in trouble."

Dylan removed the clip and dropped the gun into the trashcan. He reached inside the unconscious man's jacket and withdrew his wallet. Flipping through the wallet, Dylan pulled out a driver's license. He held it up, comparing the picture to the face on the floor. "Eric Faust," Dylan said reading the name on the document. "I am afraid, Eric, you are going to need a new picture."

He stuffed the clip of nine-millimeter bullets and Faust's license into his pocket, turned and immediately left the washroom, pausing only to ensure the 'Out Of Order' sign was still in place. He stationed himself near the main exit doors, making sure that no one entered the washroom as he waited for the other occupant of the green Mercedes. Minutes later, the second man exited the car and made his way towards the restaurant area.

"*Shit, he certainly is a tall one,*" Dylan thought to himself as the man approached. "*He has to be at least six foot eight. A real 'TallOne' for sure.*" 'TallOne' was a nickname Dylan gave a friend he played basketball against in high school. The man making his way towards Dylan was much taller. "*Okay, TallOne, I'm out of here.*"

Dylan slipped into the small convenience store next to the restaurant where he watched as TallOne entered the restaurant. The man paused by the counter, reached up and selected a magazine from the stand. He flipped through the pages, pausing only briefly to admire the pictures. Dylan noticed a tattoo on the back of his right hand. The man stood quietly, occasionally looking over the top of the magazine to scan the area. Dylan withdrew, exiting by the side door into the parking area. He made his way quickly over to the dark green Mercedes. He gave a quick check of the parking area for any sign of TallOne returning. Confirming there was no one in sight, Dylan extracted his favourite Swiss army knife and in one quick motion, cut the stem from the front wheel, releasing all the air from the tire. He repeated the action on the rear tire of the car.

"*Two flat tires and one big headache should hold them for awhile,*" he said to himself with satisfaction.

Dylan hurriedly made his way to the Jaguar, pausing only to let a huge truck pass on its way back towards the highway. The truck was hauling a huge canvas covered trailer and heading in the direction of Berlin, the opposite direction to the route Dylan would take. He reached into his pocket and withdrew the clip of nine-millimeter bullets along with the small MD-41 bug. As the trailer went by, he reached up under the end tarp and tossed the items inside. "That should keep them busy for awhile."

He moved quickly to the XK, got in and started the engine. Before the computerized voice of Katarina spoke, Dylan was over the bridge and back on the highway heading to Hamburg.

The balance of the hundred and seventy nine-mile trip to Hamburg took just under three hours. Dylan thoroughly enjoyed the ride, in particular, the hundred-mile stretch on the A24/E26 highway where he had a chance to experience the essence of the unbridled power and superior handling capabilities of the potent Jaguar XK.

Katarina was apparently pleased that Dylan was back on his preprogrammed route and lapsed into a quiet mode. She would speak again until he was within ten kilometers of his final destination.

27

AUGUST 26, 2007

HAMBURG   **1600 GMT**

It was four o'clock when Dylan arrived in the city of Hamburg.

With a total population of almost two million, Hamburg is Germany's second largest city. Situated between Baltic and the North Seas, the city has a direct link to the sea by way of the river Elbe, which also gave Hamburg the second largest harbour in Europe.

Most of the old Deutsche Werft construction yard in Hamburg had been reduce to rubble during the Allied bombing of Germany. Rebuilt over the past sixty years, it was now one of the largest shipbuilding firms in the world. He had come here to find the man who built the German U-Boats, and get information about the phantom U-1220 submarine.

Dylan checked the paper Ozzy had given him for the address of Horst Schneider, the former supervisor of the German submarine building division during the war.

Schneider lived on the second floor of a building near the wharfs. It was one of the oldest areas in all of Hamburg. Fortunately, this particular stretch of buildings had somehow managed to avoid destruction during the bombing raids.

Dylan parked on the street, climbed the stairs and knocked on the door at number 105A.

Moments later, a wizened old hand drew the curtain covering the side window back to reveal the face of a small elderly man. The face peered at Dylan for several seconds before disappearing again behind the curtain. A moment later, the door opened slightly.

At first, the ninety-one-year-old former submarine builder seemed reluctant to welcome his visitor. Dylan slipped a picture of the cylinder through the small opening in the door. The photo seemed to stimulate the old man's interest. Schneider opened the door and invited him in.

The two men carried on an animated conversation for over two hours. Dylan was doing his best to speak German and Schneider was attempting to answer in his broken English. They spoke of ships and submarines, and of wasted lives and the devastation of war. Schneider brought out an old scrapbook, filled with photographs taken at the Deutsche Werft shipyard during the war years.

The pictures depicted many of the submarines during various stages of construction and Schneider was in the forefront of most of the photos. Horst Schneider was a very proud man and Dylan could sense the pride the man had for his beloved submarines. As their conversation continued, the old man's fascination with the picture of the cylinder grew. He wanted to know more about the object.

Dylan explained how Clark had snagged the object and how he came to be involved with the recovery of the papers inside.

"Do you know where it came from?" asked Schneider.

"No. There is a marking on the exterior of the casing. The number U-122 is readable. However, there appears to be a fourth digit. Unfortunately, the surface has eroded to the point that it is impossible to confirm the actual number. I have checked all the possible numbers of the submarines with numbers in the series from 1220 to 1229. U-1220 never existed, and the date recorded on the papers found in the cylinder, eliminated the rest. It doesn't make sense."

The old man looked at the picture again and smiled. "Perhaps." he said.

"What do you mean?" asked Dylan.

Schneider had a serious look. "The war was a terrible thing. Near the end, the German command was frantic. They told us to prepare a submarine for a secret mission. The only submarine we had for this project was a prototype model built to carry cargo. It had never been properly tested or officially commissioned. The workers dubbed it the "Phantom". The refit was completed in late April and we were under secret orders to have it on standby and available at a moments notice."

"Why?"

"The rumor was that the submarine was needed to transport some mysterious cargo and persons coming from Berlin."

"Do you know what the cargo was, or who the people were?" asked Dylan.

"We were never told. Our orders were only to refit the submarine with certain special equipment and have it ready."

"Did it ever leave?"

"Twice. Once, when it took some cargo and the last time when it disappeared on May the First during the bombing raids."

"Disappeared? Where did it go?"

"I do not know. It was during the heavy bombing. I remember there was much secrecy." The old man gave a small laugh. "Of course, we knew better than to ask questions. Besides, at that time, we were more concerned with saving ourselves."

Dylan looked over at the old man, trying to imagine the horror of what he had gone through during the war. "I understand," he said quietly.

"You mentioned the phantom submarine took some cargo. When was that?"

The old man thought for a moment. "In April of 1945."

"How long was it gone?"

"About eight days, as I remember."

"Do you know where it went?"

"No. The Gestapo was in control and they did not allow anyone to go near the submarine before it left. We would have been shot if we dared to speak to the crew."

"Do you have any idea of what the cargo may have been?"

"If I knew, I probably would not be alive today," the old man laughed. "It was loaded at night and left before the morning light."

"Could this have been the submarine that launched the cylinder?"

The old man's eyes seemed to brighten. He looked directly at Dylan as if trying to get inside his mind..

"Have you ever heard of the Schliemann Papers?" he asked.

"No." answered Dylan.

Horst Schneider smiled. He had the look of a man who was pleased that he had finally unraveled a long unsolved puzzle.

"Apparently there were some documents called the Schliemann Papers, named after German archaeologist Heinrich Schliemann. Schliemann was a pioneer in the field of archaeology. He lived from 1822 to 1890 and was famous for his excavations of a number of sites in Greece and Turkey, where he found objects made of gold, bronze, and silver which he mistakenly dubbed the 'Great Priam Treasure' in reference to the king of the ancient city of Troy."

"Yes, he was the one who excavated the ancient city of Mycanae, and the fabled city of Troy," offered Dylan, showing his knowledge of archeology. "He claimed to have found the golden Death Mask of Mycenae."

"Yes, but Herr Schliemann was a very greedy man," continued Schneider. "On the morning of the original discovery, he was watching his Turkish workers when he saw a flicker of sunlight reflecting off a piece of gold. He quickly made up some very elaborate excuse in order to send his workers home, so he could complete the recovery himself. Once he had it secured, he took a circular route away from the ancient site and under the cloak of darkness, moved the treasure out of the country."

"What happened to the treasure?"

"He tried to sell it to museums and brokers but without proof of authenticity, it was impossible. After many years of frustration at not being able to sell the artifacts, and shortly before his death in 1890, he donated it to the National Museum in Berlin where it sat in a vault until World War II."

"What was the treasure worth?" Sean asked.

"There has never been an official value placed on the treasure, but it was rumored that the gold alone was worth over a hundred million dollars. I am sure it would be worth much more today."

"So what happened to the treasure?"

Schneider looked at Dylan, deciding if he should continue. He smiled at his new friend. "It supposedly remained in the vault in Berlin until the end of the war in 1945. But," the old man's eyes seemed to twinkle, "this is where things become interesting. Within three days, all the Great Priam Treasure vanished without a trace."

"How could it simply vanish?" inquired Dylan.

"There are many theories. In 1993, the Russians admitted having found what they referred to as a most valuable treasure. The treasure they found was in an underground bunker with eight-foot thick walls below the Berlin Zoo. That was most likely the remains of the Great Priam Treasure. It is rumored the real Priam Treasure, the gold, had already disappeared."

"You think the gold was taken before the Russians arrived?"

"It is possible. In 1996, when the Pushkin Museum displayed the artifacts they called the Priam Treasure, the published manifest did not match the German's original accounting of the complete Priam Treasure. The Russians have steadfastly refused to return the treasure they took from Germany and they will not allow anyone to inspect or verify what they claim is to be the Great Priam Treasure."

"How are these Schliemann Papers connected to the Priam Treasure?" asked Dylan.

"There was talk of the gold from the Great Priam Treasure being taken out of its vault in early 1945 and transferred to a secret location by submarine. The RAF sunk the U-Boat on its return from its final mission, but before it went down, it was supposed to have released a cylinder rumored to contain documents that record the actual location of the gold. The contents of the cylinder, dubbed 'The Schliemann Papers', have never been found."

Dylan held up the photograph of the cylinder and asked, "Do you think this could be the cylinder?"

"It would be a most interesting find," sighed Schneider, "but not very likely."

"If it was, would the papers not show where the gold was taken?"

"Perhaps. However, if a submarine was used to move the gold and it was sunk before it managed to reach its final destination; the gold may still be there in the submarine, at the bottom of the ocean."

"If this was the cylinder, the papers I found inside might reveal the location of the gold."

"I do not know," sighed the old man. "You will have to decode your papers in order to find your answer." Schneider paused for a moment. The tone of his voice became serious. "You must be careful. Some people out there would not want the world to know about the treasure. There are also others would kill to get the Priam gold. If your find is indeed related to the Schliemann Papers, and it becomes known to these madmen, you will not be safe."

Schneider's eyes closed as he yielded to a large yawn. It was apparent that the long conversation was wearing on the old man.

"You must go now. I am quite tired. I have talked too much."

Dylan still had many questions he wanted to ask. He hesitated for a second, but then realizing the old man was exhausted, stood up to leave. Dylan extended his hand to thank Horst Schneider. The old man was motionless for a moment. He opened his eyes and looked up at Dylan. "Wait a moment," he said. His frail hands opened the worn photo album and slowly flipped through the sheets, stopping at a page with pictures of several submarines. He carefully extracted an old black and white photo from the four black corner holders that secured it in place. He examined the photo again before handing it to Dylan.

"This is for you," said Schneider with a sense of pride.

Dylan accepted the picture. It was a picture of Horst Schneider standing next to the conning tower on a German submarine. There is a large Swastika painted on the conning tower.

"Thank you," said Dylan, reaching out to shake the old man's hand. "I will treasure this always."

The old man looked at him and said, "That is good." He closed his eyes, nodded his head and fell into a deep sleep.

Dylan placed the picture inside his jacket pocket and made his way to the door. He paused for a moment and looked back at the old man. He was sleeping. There was a trace of a smile on his face. Dylan exited the apartment and made his way back to the Jaguar.

Dylan sat in the car, going over his conversation with Horst Schneider. He pulled the picture out of his jacket and looked at it again. He looked at the image of Schneider standing beside the conning tower of the submarine. The menacing symbol of Nazism, the large Swastika dwarfed the shipyard supervisor. Dylan studied the photo. He thought about the man, his love for the ship's he built, and the futility of war. He appreciated Schneider selecting a picture to give to him. He began to put the photo back into his jacket pocket, and then stopped. Dylan squinted at the photograph once more, trying to get a better look. Then he saw it. There, in the picture, directly below the large Swastika in small black letters, was the submarine's registration number, 'U-1220'. He had found the missing submarine. He thought about the old man and smiled. Horst Schneider knew the picture was the 'U-1220' and had given it to him willingly. Dylan would return later to thank him.

It had been an exhausting day. He was relieved to know that the U-1220 had existed, but he had much more work to do. The night sky was darkening and a light rain fell as Dylan pulled the XK onto the highway and headed towards the city. He would spend the night at a local hotel in Hamburg and return to Berlin the following morning.

VANCOUVER 1450 PDT

Ronnie was alone in the Clark's office, working on some files when the telephone rang. She made her way back to her desk and picked up the receiver.

"Jim Clark's office. How may I help you?"

The caller spoke in a cold, monotone voice, thick with a German accent.

"Please connect me with Mr. Dylan."

"I'm sorry, Mr. Dylan is not here," replied Ronnie.

The voice continued, "It is very important that we reach Mr. Dylan. We understand Mr. Jim Clark has engaged him on a special project. Mr. Dylan has certain documents that hold much interest for another party. Please to give me the contact number for Mr. Dylan."

Ronnie hesitated for a moment, and then lied "I don't have any number for Mr. Dylan. He does not work here. You must have the wrong information."

"Please tell him we must have the papers. Tell him it is better that he works with us, or he will regret to have interfered."

Ronnie was suddenly both afraid and defiant. "I do not know where this Mr. Dylan is, and I don't like threats." She hung up the telephone and then quickly picked it up again to place a long distance call to the Grand Hyatt in Berlin. The front desk was efficient as usual, but they did not know where Mr. Dylan was and could not contact him. Ronnie left an urgent message for him to return her call.

28

AUGUST 27, 2007

BERLIN   **1106 GMT**

It was just past eleven when Dylan finally arrived back at the Grand Hyatt. After the interesting events of the previous day, he was not in the mood to be taking any unnecessary chances. He parked the Jaguar in the huge circular driveway, in front of the main hotel entrance. As he exited the vehicle, he pushed the button to open the trunk. The parking Valet was already beside the car.

Dylan gave the Valet a quick look. "Keep an eye on the car." Dylan gave the keys to him along with a fifty Euro bill to ensure the car received special attention.

The Valet smiled and nodded. "Yes, thank you, Sir. It will be the sole object of my attention," he stated briskly, stuffing the note into his pocket.

After retrieving his bag, Dylan made his way into the Hyatt, stopping only to check for messages at the front desk. There were calls from Ozzy and Ronnie, along with a third message that was signed simply, *"Bridgette"*. He turned and made his way towards the waiting elevator, and pushed the button for the eighth floor. He would take the centre stairs to the ninth floor.

Dylan paused at the stairwell door to the ninth floor. With his right hand comfortably on the grip of the Smith and Wesson, he reached for the handle and slowly opened the door. The view from the centre stairway gave him a direct view of the entrance to his hotel room. The 'Do Not Disturb' sign was still in place. Everything appeared normal. He exited the stairway and cautiously proceeded towards his room.

Dylan checked for the Canadian coin he had inserted in the doorjamb and found it was still in its correct position. He slid the magnetic key into the locking mechanism, opened the door and entered.

He tossed his bag on the bed as he pulled the messages from his jacket pocket. He would call Ozzy now. *"Might even get a free lunch today,"* he thought to himself, smiling.

He looked at the message from Ronnie. It was marked *'Urgent'*. He quickly glanced at his watch and calculated the time in her part of the world. The nine hours differential would put her current time at past two in the morning. While he did want to talk to her, he decided to wait until morning when she was at the office so he could make contact with Jim Clark as well.

The third message contained only a name and number.

'Bridgette, 345 555 9022'

Dylan looked at the message for a moment and then decided to call Ozzy. Bridgette, whoever she was, could wait.

It was not hard to convince Ozzy to meet him, but the free lunch idea would have to wait. His friend had sounded anxious and had selected what Dylan thought was a somewhat strange but intriguing rendezvous point, the New Synagogue Museum in Oranienburgerstrasse, once the site of the largest and most beautiful synagogue in Germany.

Dylan grabbed a fast shower, changed and was on his way within the hour. It was a twenty-minute drive from the hotel to the Oranienburgerstrasse.

Located in what was East Berlin, Oranienburgerstrasse was emerging as a new center of Jewish life. The Third Reich had ransacked the "New Synagogue", which was constructed in 1866, and left it in ruins. To add insult to injury, it became victim to the Allied bombing of Berlin.

The reunification of Germany had begun after the infamous Berlin Wall came down following the collapse of Communism. They rebuilt the entrance tower of the original Synagogue using much of the original building materials they had found amongst the ruins. The renovations had only recently been completed with the building's gold dome and towers restored to their pre-war condition. Rather than being restored to its original purpose, the huge main sanctuary now housed a memorial and museum to the Jewish community and its leaders who were so much a part of Germany and Berlin before World War II.

Dylan arrived at the appointed time and was surprised to find armed guards patrolling the grounds as he entered the Synagogue.

Ozzy was already waiting inside the building. He watched as his friend submitted to a thorough security check far more stringent than any airport security system. Ozzy greeted Dylan once he had successfully completed the rigid security screening process.

"It's sad, my friend, but necessary." said Ozzy. "This is true for all spots of Jewish interests in Berlin. Those who caused the Jews to suffer in the last century are still very much a presence in the community today."

"So that's why you told me to leave the Smith and Wesson in the car."

"Yes. This is probably the safest place in all of Germany, my friend. Besides, it would have taken months to get you out of detention if they found that little gem on your person."

The two friends began to walk through the interior of the massive synagogue. Dylan marveled at the amount of detail that had been required to bring the structure back to its previous glory. The beauty of the surroundings made it difficult to get back to business, but he knew he must.

"So, Oz, what have you found out?" Dylan asked as he scanned the area.

"Well, it seems we have sparked some interest from several groups. There has been someone tailing me since I left the Borchardt Restaurant the other night. It is not the most efficient surveillance I've seen, but he was there nonetheless."

"Have they made any moves?"

"No. They just followed me to my office. I had no difficulty shaking him when I left. He picked me up again yesterday, but I lost him quite easily. It kind of reminded me of the old days," he said with a laugh.

Dylan related the story of the two men who had followed him when he left for Hamburg.

"Did you get a good look at them?" Ozzy asked.

"The driver was a tall guy. He had a tattoo on his right hand and an evil smile that exposed a missing tooth. I would not have a problem recognizing him again. The guy in the washroom, on the other hand, probably doesn't look exactly the same anymore after his face had a run-in with the urinal."

"Ouch. That must have hurt."

"Nothing that a few months of dental work and a new nose won't fix."

Ozzy laughed. "Do you have any idea as to who they were?"

"No, but I would know them if I saw either of them again." Dylan reached into his pocket and produced the driver's license he took from the short man. "And I do have this," he said handing the card to Ozzy. "It is probably a phony, but the before picture is real. Check it out for me anyway."

"Why the hell would these guys want to follow you?"

"Not sure, but after my conversation with Horst Schneider, I have a few thoughts," replied Dylan. "For starters, I would like you to check on the activities of an underground Neo-Nazi Democratic Party."

"Do you think the idiots in that Party are interested in your papers?"

"Schneider brought a new wrinkle into the picture. Apparently there was a huge treasure that disappeared from Germany at the end of the war."

"The Great Priam Treasure?" he volunteered.

"So, you've heard about it too?"

"That was big news after the war. Apparently, it's rumored that the Russians got the treasure as spoils of the war, but no one has ever actually confirmed it."

"Schneider feels a large portion of the gold may have been spirited away by the Germans before the Russians got there."

"Now, that would be an interesting find. It would be worth millions."

"Over a hundred million," Dylan offered. "He thinks it may have been sent by submarine to some secret location. Schneider thinks something called the Schliemann Papers holds the secret."

Ozzy looked at his friend. "Do you think your cylinder might have something to do with these Schliemann Papers?" he asked.

"I don't know for sure, but if the rumor about the gold from Great Priam Treasure is true, and these Schliemann Papers really did exist, we might have stumbled on to something very big."

"Geez-us," exclaimed Ozzy. "So what are you going to do?"

"Again, I am not sure, yet. Something Schneider said about *'There are those out there who would not want the world to know about the treasure. They would kill to get ownership.'* that makes me think we should increase our own security on this little operation."

"Well, there are always some crazies around, but how would they even know about the papers?"

"Who knows, Oz, but there is definitely somebody out there who is interested. It could be the German government, the Neo-Nazi group, or maybe just some mafia types. Whoever they are, they are serious players and we are going to have to be a lot more careful."

"I'll check around to see what I can come up with. I am not sure about the German government, but we do have some contacts in security that have had contact with the underground Neo-Nazi Democratic Party. We should be able to get some information on what they have been up to."

"Good."

Dylan and Ozzy left the synagogue and made their way past the armed guards to the Jaguar. The presence of the guards made Dylan feel both quite secure and a little apprehensive. He noticed a tall blonde standing by the doorway.

"By the way," Dylan asked nonchalantly, "do you have a friend named Bridgette?"

"No, why?" asked Ozzy.

"I had a call at the hotel from someone named Bridgette. I thought maybe you were trying to palm off one of your old flames."

"Sorry, Sean, not this time. What did she want?"

"Don't know. I haven't called her back yet."

"Are you going to call her?"

"Later. Right now, how about we go somewhere and get

some lunch."

"How hungry are you?" asked Ozzy.

"I'm starved."

"Great, I know a perfect place for a great lunch. The Grossbeeren Keller, but one does not even think of going to this famous cellar without a big appetite. The pride of this joyful, generous, old-fashioned restaurant is in its abundance."

"It sounds great. What's the specialty?"

"Hoppelpoppel" Ozzy responded. "It's an artery-stopping omelet like a dish of smoked and pickled pork, eggs, sautéed potatoes, onions, and herbs. It is a famous hangover cure and makes for great winter eating on the slopes."

"Interesting," replied Dylan with a half smile, "Just what I need to stay in shape."

SEATTLE   **0750 PDT**

The early morning rain pelted against the side window of FBI Chief Samuel O'Brien's office, running down the panes in a series of small rivulets. The Chief was looking out over the waters of Puget Sound. Most days it was a beautiful view. Today it was simply dark and overcast. "Bloody winter is on its way already," protested O'Brien in reference to Seattle's lengthy rainy season. "The stuff just keeps coming. No wonder everything is so damned green."

"Don't fret boss," replied the stocky man sitting at his desk. "We still have a couple of good months before the crappy weather sets in. There will still be lots of time this fall to get out on your Bayliner."

O'Brien grunted at the mention of his forty-two-foot yacht

and returned to his desk. "So, what do you make of these ridiculous papers everyone seems to be chasing? Is there anything to this?"

"We have our people looking at the situation. There are a few different scenarios. One: The papers are a hoax or just plain worthless. The majority of the players already favour that theory. Two: The papers actually did come from a Nazi submarine, but are still worthless. Three: The papers are real and could lead to the recovery of the gold from the Great Priam Treasure or even shed light on the events at the end of the war. Bottom line: The war was almost seventy years ago. Whatever they find, except for maybe the Priam Treasure gold, which we think the Ruskies stole the day they entered Berlin in '45, probably will not be worth much. The Big Guy is worried about someone finding out about some of the unexplained events relating to the end of the war. Personally, I do not think anyone gives a damn. However, it is your call, Chief. We can stay on top of Dylan and the others until they land their fish, or we can save the Agency a whole pile of money. What do you want to do?"

"I hate wasting resources. We will give it another week. If we do not see something worth chasing by then, you can pull your people off and cancel the file. Just let me know and I will notify Washington and the SGI in Germany."

A sheet of rain blew hard against the glass windows. "It's your call, Sam," said the man. "In the meantime, why don't you get out on that yacht of yours and enjoy the weather."

O'Brien instinctively looked out the window as another sheet of rain slapped against the glass. He turned abruptly to face the man but only caught sight of the agent's back as he disappeared through the door. O'Brien raised his hand and extended his middle finger to the sky. "Asshole."

BERLIN   **1325 GMT**

The trip to the Grossbeeren Keller Restaurant took fifteen minutes. The lunchtime crowd had started to dissipate and they found a table immediately.

The 1862 vintage basement dining room with the wrought-iron sphinx door handle had an atmosphere so unselfconsciously comfortable, it would not have surprised Dylan if the Kaiser himself stopped by for beer. This was the place to come for the kind of old-fashioned delicious German cooking, the kind that predated the new found affluence that resulted in the Mediterranean becoming Germany's favorite sea. Despite the lumberjack portions, Dylan found himself enjoying the plate full of Zwiebelrostbraten mit bratkart, a meal of roasted beef with onion gravy, while Ozzy was devoured his favourite dish of wild boar cutlets with cranberry relish.

The two men continued their conversation over their very ample lunches.

"So what's our next step, Sherlock?" asked Ozzy.

"Schneider did help me identify the submarine, and it is the U-1220. It really did exist. He thinks the gold, if it was taken by submarine, might still be onboard the sunken sub at the bottom of the North Sea. We should be able to confirm it once we decode the papers."

"So, how do we decode the papers?"

"I am going to visit Bletchley Park, just outside London to see if anyone there can help me figure out how to decipher the messages. Hopefully we can find some clues as to what we've got."

"What happens if you don't get the message decoded?"

"Schneider figures the treasure was worth several hundred

million in 1950's dollars. That would be a whole lot more in today's market. I was thinking that if we can find the U-1220 and if you're game, maybe we could get into the salvage business together."

"Now that would definitely be something new for us."

"It would be different, that's for sure."

"But how are we going to find the U-1220? It's a big ocean out there."

"I think I already know where it is."

Ozzy looked incredulously at his friend. "How?"

"We'll use the process of elimination, my dear Watson. Can't be too many subs sunk around the date on the messages."

"And what about the cost? This isn't going to be any cheap vacation to Florida, you know."

"I am going to speak with Jim Clark later today and fill him in. He is the man behind this project, and he has the money. If he agrees, we can go after the right people to locate the submarine. Right now, Oz," Sean said, putting his hand on his bulging stomach, "I've had it."

Dylan sat and watched as Ozzy enthusiastically polished off the last of his cutlets.

"Ozzy, I've eaten enough here to do me for the next week. How do you manage to put so much away and not look like a three hundred pound lineman?"

"Practice my friend. Lots and lots of practice."

It was late afternoon when Dylan returned to the hotel. He parked the Jaguar near the entrance, dropped the keys off with the Valet and proceeded to the front desk.

"Any messages?" he asked.

"No sir," replied the desk clerk, "But that lady over there has been waiting for you for over an hour."

The desk clerk nodded his head in the direction of the piano bar in the lobby. Dylan looked over and saw the woman. There was no doubt in his mind. She was the same tall blonde-haired woman that he had spotted in the airport and then again at the Borchardt Restaurant. He walked over to where she was sitting.

"Bridgette. I presume?"

The woman stood up. She was tall. Dylan gave her a quick look. She was quite beautiful. Even with her blonde hair, which appeared to be short, she was still an inch taller than he was. Her taste in clothes was impeccable. Dylan thought his mind was playing tricks on him. For a brief moment, he felt that he knew her.

"Yes. Bridgette Appleby. I've been waiting for you."

Dylan tilted his head to one side. "I must say, I am not used to having beautiful women waiting for me in strange hotels. Do I know you from somewhere?"

"No. However, I believe we do have a mutual friend. My superior arranged for me to meet you after he received a call from someone in Canada."

"Really?" questioned Dylan. "I don't recall anyone mentioning a meeting with someone over here, especially someone as beautiful as you."

"Thank you, but I understand this was a last minute assignment. I have been asked to assist you whenever possible."

"Well," Dylan shrugged, "other than having you follow me to one of Berlin's nicer restaurants I really don't know what you could do."

"Yes, at the Borchardt, and I did see you arrive at the airport as well. Perhaps I should explain."

"Yes, please do."

"Shall we have a drink?"

Dylan motioned to the waiter. He ordered a Dry Martini, straight up, for Bridgette and an Irish Whisky for himself.

The woman seemed quite at ease and gave Dylan details about her superior, Horst Jager, the head of Bremer-Wilhelm, one of Germany's largest shipping companies, receiving a call from Canada. She related details about his leaving Berlin by car, including the circumstances of how he eluded the two men who had followed him. She did not mention his visit with Schneider in Hamburg, or the hotel where he stayed.

"I see you have been busy."

"My job was to follow and observe. Unless, of course, you need some help. Apparently you are quite proficient at looking after yourself which makes my job very easy."

Dylan's mind was racing. *"This woman is obviously well informed,"* he thought, *"But by whom?"* He was amazed that she was aware of the events that occurred the previous day, although he was not certain as to how much detail. He had to find out how she was connected and who was responsible for having her shadow him. Dylan did not like surprises, and this woman was full of surprises. He decided not to mention his meeting in Hamburg.

"I thought it would be best to let you know the details, Mr. Dylan. I understand that you are very good at what you do and it would only have been a matter of time before you noticed me."

"Well, you are very attractive and it would be difficult for me not to notice," he answered with a smile. "Now, please do not take this the wrong way, but you really don't appear to be someone I would look to as a backup if I got into a bit of trouble."

"No offense taken, but you can't always judge a book by its cover. I am quite capable of taking very good care of myself."

"Um," Dylan muttered to himself as he again inspected the

tall blonde-haired woman. "In the meantime, perhaps you and I could have dinner tonight. You would not have to waste time following me, and you could bring me up to date on what is happening in Berlin."

"I'm not sure what I can tell you about what is going on in Berlin, but dinner would be wonderful. Would you like to pick me up around eight o'clock?"

"Can do," replied Dylan with a smile. "Where?"

"I live on the Klausener Platz. Number one-forty-nine. It is right near Berlin's famous organic food shop, the 'Brotgarten', about twenty minutes from here. I will see you around eight then?"

"I'll be there."

Bridgette got up and left the table, giving Dylan a little smile. He sat at the table and watched the woman as she disappeared through the hotel doors leading to the parking area.

"Well, this should be interesting," he thought, *"Very interesting indeed."*

Dylan gave Bridgette a few minutes to clear the parking area before making his way up to his room. The elevator ride seemed to be in slow motion as he replayed his meeting with the attractive woman. He wondered how she knew so many details about his activities in Berlin. Her display of confidence made Dylan wonder if she really was that good. Did she know about his visit to Schneider? If so, was the old man in danger? Once again, he had more questions than answers.

Dylan took his usual route to his room. He took a quick look to ensure his security coin was still in the doorjamb, slipped his computer key into the slot and entered the room.

It was 1750 GMT. Dylan immediately placed a telephone call to Clark's private line. Ronnie answered the call before the second ring had finished. She sounded distraught.

"Sean, I'm so glad you called. Jim hasn't been in the office since last Thursday and he hasn't called either."

"Did he have any private business meetings that you might not have known about?"

"No. We were working on the Carter account and he was supposed to have been here today to complete the analysis for a meeting on Wednesday. Jim never goes anywhere without calling to let me know," said Ronnie in a terse voice. "It's not the way he does business. And another thing, Jim told me last Thursday that he thought someone was following him."

Dylan shook his head, "Seems to be a lot of that going around," he replied offhandedly. The remark did not register with Ronnie.

"He said he could feel their eyes watching him," she continued. "I have never seen him so nervous."

"Okay, okay," Dylan interrupted, "Calm down. Let's not get too excited. There has to be a logical explanation for all of this."

"Right!" exclaimed a frustrated Ronnie. "When you figure that out, then maybe can you explain the weird telephone calls that I have been receiving."

"Weird telephone calls?" echoed Dylan. "What weird telephone calls?"

"Some man called three times. Twice last Friday and then again today. First, he wanted to a number where he could call you. When I told him that you did not work here, he wanted to know where you were and if you had the contents with you. I told him I had no idea on either count."

"Did he leave a name or say who he was with?"

"He didn't leave a name. I tried to trace the number he called from but it was unavailable. That is why I called you yesterday. Something about this whole deal is not right. I don't like it."

The whole situation was starting to get confusing. There were too many people involved. Clark was not available and there was no way he would be able to shed any light on Bridgette's story. He briefly considered asking Ronnie to investigate, but dismissed the idea just as fast. She was obviously upset about Clark not being in the office and Dylan did not want to create more anxiety for her. He would get the information from Clark later. "I'm not sure what to make of the calls, Ronnie," he offered, "It's probably some kind of mix up. I'm sure it's nothing to panic about."

Dylan's words did not calm Ronnie. "Sean, Jim said you were due back last Saturday. This is Monday. What is going on over there?"

"I've been busy getting some clarification on some questions we had on the submarines. It has definitely been an interesting trip, to say the least. It was a good move coming over here."

"Right now, I could really use you back here," Ronnie declared softly.

"I should be back around the end of the week," he said reassuringly. "I have a meeting in London regarding the encrypted papers. I will be back right after that."

Knowing that Dylan was returning seemed to relax Ronnie.

"Did you find out anything about the missing submarine?"

Dylan thought it best to keep most of what was happening to himself for the time being. There was no sense getting Ronnie and Jim Clark involved. He gave a cursory description about the meetings he had in Germany. He left out most of the details involving the two men who tailed him on his trip to Hamburg, and all the details about Bridgette. Dylan did give her a brief report on his meeting with Schneider, without mentioning either the city or the old man by name. He was not going to take any chances.

"It was a very good meeting and I think we've found our missing boat," he said, referring to the submarine U-1220.

"You might still be chasing a phantom ship," she offered. "What are the chances of breaking the code?"

Dylan smiled at the reference to the 'phantom ship'. "I will know soon. My plan is to go over to London tomorrow to meet with some people at the War Office to see if there is any possibility of decoding the messages. I should be finished there by Wednesday and back in Vancouver on Friday at the latest."

"I'll let Jim know as soon as I hear from him," she replied, adding, "That is, if he ever calls."

"He is probably OK, just doing some big last minute business deal. Look, I have to go. Call you when I finish in London. In the meantime, you call Security and let them know about Jim and that you are concerned."

"Be careful, Sean."

"Funny, everyone seems to be saying the same thing. Thanks, I will. You take care, too."

Dylan hung up and walked over to the desk. He picked up the one of the papers he had taken from the cylinder and examined the encrypted document closely. *"Just what the hell are you all about?"* he asked aloud.

VANCOUVER   0850 PDT

Ronnie replaced the telephone receiver in its cradle and then immediately picked it up again. She punched in the number for Security. The Chief of Security was unavailable, prompting Ronnie to leave a message requesting a meeting upon his return. After she hung up from Security, Ronnie dialed the private number for Bob Everson, Jim Clark's lawyer.

BERLIN   **2005 GMT**

It was 8:05 when Dylan knocked on the door of number one forty-nine Klausener Platz. The door opened to reveal a much different looking Bridgette Appleby. She was wearing beige slacks and a fawn coloured top. Her hair was down and appeared much longer than he had remembered. Her makeup accented her features and she looked even younger. Dylan caught himself staring at the woman, admiring the obvious transformation from business to a captivating beauty.

"Fix your self a drink," she said, pointing to a bar in the living room, "I'll just be a moment."

Dylan went into the living room and found a sideboard with a well stocked bar. He was surprised to find a bottle of Irish Whisky sitting front and centre on the bar. He poured himself a short drink and sat down on the oversized sofa, taking in the ambience of Bridgette's home.

The house itself was a brick structure that had recently been totally renovated. Inside the entrance was a small den that housed a computer with internet and telephone. Small by North American standards, the décor of the house was a modern theme with good furnishings that created an atmosphere of comfort and intimacy.

Bridgette returned looking even more radiant than before. Dylan was impressed.

"There seem to be quite a few nice restaurants and some artistic cafés along the Klausener Platz. Do you have a favourite?"

"Yes, but not here. I know a little place that is not too far and their food is quite wonderful. Well, that is if you like Italian food."

"Italian would be fine."

"It's called Ristorante Fellini. It is at the Berlin Hilton, but it is not your usual hotel restaurant. They serve wonderful Tuscany styled dinners. You'll love it," she said smiling. Bridgette grabbed a sweater from the back of the chair and moved towards the door. She was looking anything but a well-trained security person.

Dylan followed her out the door, closing it firmly as he went.

The restaurant was located in what was once the hotel's old wine cellar. It had a magnificent chandelier near the entrance that was as impressive as it was large. The Maitre'd greeted them at the door and immediately seated them at Bridgette's reserved table.

The dinner was everything Bridgette said it would be and more. They dined on Milanese-styled Osso Buco, an Italian staple dish made with Veal, followed with a fine white wine. They rounded off the dinner experience with Zabaglione, a warm Italian dessert made of egg yolks, sugar and Marsala wine.

Dylan found their conversation warm and friendly. Although he repeatedly tried to change the conversation to determine exactly whom she worked for and what her job actually involved, Bridgette managed to dodge all attempts, steering the conversation to more general subjects. They spoke about a diverse number of issues, ranging from world commerce, including the transformation of Berlin after the fall of Communism, to the war in Iraq. They covered subjects from the serious to the amusing. Bridgette told a story about her first trip to the French Riviera and how she felt embarrassed going topless. Dylan pictured this in his mind and he knew she would not have to worry about being embarrassed. Then he wondered to himself why he had never been to the Riviera.

Dinner had ended without Dylan having learned anything more about Bridgette. He would speak to Clark to find out what, if anything, he knew about the connection.

Dylan drove Bridgette back to her home, parked the Jaguar and escorted her to the house. As they reached the door, she turned around to face him.

"I understand you are off to London and I've got much to catch up on at my office tomorrow," she said. "It was very enjoyable. Maybe some day you will come back to Berlin."

Bridgette's mention of his plans for London caught Dylan off guard. He resisted the temptation to ask her how she knew. "You are full of surprises, Ms. Appleby, but as for my returning to Berlin, I really don't think that will be happening soon."

"That is too bad." Bridgette said seductively. She leaned over and gave him a quick kiss on the cheek. "Good Night," she said, turning to unlock the door. "Have fun in London." She opened the door and went inside, leaving Dylan standing alone on the steps.

Dylan smiled to himself as he turned to make his way back to the Jaguar. He marveled at the woman's style. He could not remember ever having such a beautiful woman dismiss him so easily and yet so effectively.

He returned to the Jaguar, started the engine and pulled out onto the Klausener Platz, heading back to the Grand Hyatt.

Dylan checked at the front desk. There was a single message from Ozzy. He had made contact with a mutual friend at the War Office who referred Ozzy to Bletchley Park, the home of the Enigma Code Breakers of the Second World War. Ozzy had set up an appointment for Dylan.

29

AUGUST 28, 2007

BERLIN 0910 GMT

The big German sat with his back to the others. Hans Lüdden was trying to control his anger.

"You can't even execute a simple order without letting this Canadian get the best of you. What kind of fools did you hire, Herr Schlippenbach?"

"They were taken by surprise, Hans. It is not entirely their fault."

TallOne and Faust were off to one side of the room. TallOne looked awkward as he stood in front of Faust, shielding his shorter, more heavily set partner. The smaller man, his swollen head heavily bandaged above his obviously badly broken nose, was quietly staring at the floor. His eyes looked like two bloodstained eggs floating on a sea of bruises. Dylan had not been gentle.

"The recovery of the contents of the cylinder is paramount. If the Schliemann Papers were in that cylinder, we must retrieve them at all costs." Hans Lüdden turned to the head of the Party's Security force. "Müller, you will take these two inept idiots von Schlippenbach hired and find this Dylan person."

"Yes, Herr Lüdden."

Lüdden looked at his Security Chief. "Our intelligence has reported that Dylan is presently in London with the papers. Find him and retrieve the documents. Then kill him."

"We will not fail, Herr Lüdden."

"You and von Schlippenbach have said that before, Müller. If you fail again, people will start to question my leadership and that would not be good. Am I making myself perfectly clear?"

"Yes, Herr Lüdden," replied Müller, stepping back slightly.

"The success of our party, and the very future of Germany itself, could hang in the balance."

Von Schlippenbach mumbled in the affirmatively. TallOne and Faust nodded in agreement. TallOne put his arm around the shorter man and gave a sinister smile. He was looking forward to his next meeting with Sean Dylan.

LUTON AIRPORT 1145 GMT

The flight to London's Luton Airport was only an hour and a half. Dylan used his Irish passport to avoid the long lineup at British Customs for non-European Union citizens. Once he picked up his bag and cleared the area, he made his way directly to the taxi stand.

Although London was one of his favourite cities, he had decided not to hire a car. The problems of driving in and around the city, which was insane at the best of times, having to find accommodation for parking, and the restrictions regarding travel within the 'Congestion' area of the city far outweighed the luxury of having a car. Taxis and the 'Tube' would have to suffice this time.

The drive in from Luton was quick by London standards, only ninety minutes down the M-1 motorway from the airport to his accommodations at Dolphin Square, on Grosvenor Street.

Dolphin Square, set in three and a half acres of private landscaped gardens, was the largest development of apartments to let in the heart of London. Close to the River Thames at Pimlico, Sir Richard and Sir Albert Costain built Dolphin Square in the nineteen thirties. Over the years, it had been home to some of the nation's most celebrated people.

Dylan had contacted a friend from his army days who was now involved in British politics. The friend had one of the small apartments permanently reserved at the Square. *"It pays to have friends,"* he thought to himself as the taxi pulled up in front of the unadorned entrance to the Square. As he handed the driver a one hundred pound British note, Dylan noticed one of London's finest supervising the removal of a vehicle from one of the many 'No Parking' areas.

"The area around the Square is a 'no tolerance' zone. The police and private security personnel do not offer any leniency to anyone," said the driver. giving Dylan his change. "You've got a good place to stay."

"That's good to know," said Dylan. He tipped the taxi driver a ten-pound British note, grabbed his bag and made his way through the double doors into the Reception area where three very attentive staff members greeted him with great flourish.

The desk clerk processed Dylan's information into the registry, pausing only to point out that within the Square itself were a number of convenience shops just off the reception area, plus a bar and brasserie, as well as a health and fitness spa within the main building. Dylan picked up his bag and entered the old styled elevator that would take him to the well-appointed apartment on the fourth floor.

Dylan opened the door and entered. He had a feeling that he had stepped back in time. *"If the walls could talk,"* he said scanning the ancient architecture of the unit.

He immediately picked up the telephone to place a call to his friend Saris in Dublin.

"Good afternoon. Institute of Archeological Studies." the receptionist answered.

"Yes, could you put me through to Mr. Stephen Saris, please?"

"I'm sorry," the voice replied, "Mr. Saris is no longer at the Institute."

"Do you know where I can reach him? He's an old friend."

The receptionist sounded surprised. "You don't know?"

"Know? Know what?"

"I'm sorry, sir, but Mr. Saris was killed in a motorway accident last month. He was driving at night and his car went off the roadway. I'm very sorry."

The news stunned Dylan. He mumbled a *'Thank You'* to the receptionist and replaced the receiver. He thought about his friend Saris. He had lived alone for the last forty years and had no close relatives. His work was his only passion. It was then that Dylan remembered.

He immediately picked up the telephone and hit the 'Redial' button.

"Good afternoon. Institute of Archeological Studies."

"Yes, I just spoke with you a few minutes ago. Did I understand you to say that Mr. Saris was killed while driving on the Motorway?"

"Oh, yes sir. That is correct. It happened on the evening of the twenty-fourth of August. The police said that it was raining that night and he lost control of his car. I'm terribly sorry."

"Thank you" replied Dylan. He hung up the telephone.

The news of Saris' death had shocked him, but what was

even more incredible was that he knew Saris never owned a car. In fact, Saris was one of the few persons he had ever met that had never driven in his life. Dylan had a feeling that Saris' death was not accidental. His inner sense told him that somehow, Sardis' death and the cylinder were connected. The rusted object Clark found in the ocean off the coast of Ireland was attracting an unusual amount of attention, and most of it was the bad kind.

In preparation for his meeting, Dylan checked on the internet for directions to the Bletchley Park Museum where he was to meet his contact regarding the encrypted papers. The museum was about forty miles outside London, and the trip would take almost two hours in the afternoon traffic.

Dylan took a cab to Harrods to pick up a package Ozzy had arranged for him.. He noticed that his adrenalin was starting to flow. The strange events surrounding the cylinder's and its contents, coupled with the reconnection with his partner, brought back memories, both good and bad, of the many clandestine missions they had shared during their stint in the Special Forces.

The instructions from Ozzy for the Harrods pick up were, as usual, simple and to the point. He was to go to the souvenir stand on the second floor near the escalator, where an Asian male member of Harrods staff would greet him. Ozzy always liked to complicate matters. The contact would recognize Dylan from a picture Ozzy had forwarded by email. The code phrase was, 'Would you like to purchase some tea?' His return password would be, 'Do you have any Special Pekoe?' It was vintage Ozzy.

When he arrived on the second floor, he quickly found the large display of Harrods souvenirs. He quickly scanned the area for his contact but there was no one in the department that even remotely appeared to be of Asian descent.

Dylan continued to move around the shopping area, acting as an interested customer, picking up a few items, examining and then replacing them as he went along. He turned the corner of the aisle, almost knocking over a man who was rearranging the Harrods tea kiosk. Dylan excused himself. The man turned and looked at him. He was Asian.

"No problem Sir. I am finished here," said the man giving Dylan a closer look. "Would you like to purchase some tea?"

"Do you have any Special Pekoe?"

The Asian man smiled while making a scene of showing several different options. Dylan chose one and handed it to the man. The Asian led him to the cashier's desk and rang up the purchase. He reached under the counter to retrieve a Harrods bag. Although Dylan was watching carefully, he could not determine when or how the man made the switch. He placed the box of tea into the bag, and handed it to him.

"I hope you enjoy your 'special' tea, Sir."

Dylan handed the man a twenty-pound note and received his change. He thanked the Asian man and made his way back to the street where he caught a cab to keep his appointment at the Bletchley Park museum.

During the long taxi ride, he opened the bag and retrieved the box of tea. He opened it carefully, revealing the newest Glock .45 ACP G36 semi automatic. Ozzy had done it again. Dylan checked the ammunition clip and quickly slid the Glock into the inside pocket of his jacket. There were four additional clips in the box.

30

AUGUST 28, 2007

BLETCHLEY PARK   **1615 GMT**

The drive was quick by London standards. The taxi arrived almost twenty minutes before his appointed time. He paid the driver and exited the taxi. After removing the four clips of ammunition and putting them into his jacket pocket, Dylan deposited the Harrods bag in a container by the arched entranceway. He paused for a moment to admire the beauty of the Mansion at Bletchley Park, and then entered.

Dylan met his contact, William Hill at the office of the Director of the Museum, which was located next to the reception area. He had introduced himself over the telephone, as a person with a great interest in cryptography. After the obligatory greetings, Dylan showed Hill several of the papers he had retrieved from the cylinder.

Hill, the bespectacled custodian of the museum, was an amicable person and quickly examined the papers through his very thick glasses. He handed them back to Dylan.

"I'm afraid you've come a long way for the proverbial goose egg, Mr. Dylan. There is absolutely nothing I can do with these papers."

Dylan was surprised at the quick retort. "What's the problem?" he asked, incredulously.

"Well, for starters, it's not a real message. Not complete. Here, let me take you around the Park so you can understand what I mean. It is a long trip up here from London, and you should at least get a bit of a tour for your trouble."

Hill exited the office with Dylan in tow. The two men left the building and started to walk around the perimeter of the complex. Hill was acting as a private tour guide.

"The Government Communication Headquarters during the Second World War was located here in Bletchley Park. It was a massive secret operation employing almost 10,000 people by the end of the war, including two famous mathematicians, Alan Turing and Gordon Welchman, the leaders of the group.

The code breakers were equipped with electromechanical devices, called Bombes, a nickname for a mechanical device used during WWII at Bletchley Park. They were actually the forerunner of the computers of today. The use of the 'Bombes" permitted Allied Forces to break the Kriegsmarine message traffic within twenty four hours, thus playing a huge part in changing the course of history."

Dylan stopped to take in the sight. Several of the large buildings were in need of a good paint job. There were many lesser buildings scattered throughout the area. The whole complex looked a bit dilapidated.

"Today, Bletchley Park remains much as it was, still flanked by the huts which housed the code breakers," said Hill. "Of course, after sixty plus years, things are a bit worn."

Hill continued his tour of the Mansion at Bletchley Park, explaining the workings of the encryption system that was its 'raison d'existence'. He took Dylan inside one of the larger buildings that contained many displays relating to the war effort.

"The Enigma code was the most complex cipher system of its age with numerous settings and virtually foolproof," Hill expounded. "It was used by the Nazis as early as 1938 to encrypt top-secret messages between their forces. The original machine was developed by the German intelligence service. It was known as an Abwehr Enigma G312, an eccentric typewriter-like assembly with keys and lights. It worked with a complex series of spinning rotors which could come up with seemingly infinite permutations."

"Were they hard to move around?"

"Yes, at first. The Germans quickly improved the design and they became quite portable. By the time the war started, the German U-boats had one on board their submarines and their shore based Commanders had another. Germany used the Enigma to issue orders to its "wolf packs" of U-boats in the Atlantic which resulted in the sinking of many of the merchant ships that were supplying Britain's war effort."

Hill explained to Dylan how the Prime Minister, Winston Churchill, responded to the magnitude of the threat posed by the German U-Boats by recruiting the greatest minds of the day to work at Bletchley Park in a massive effort to decipher the Enigma codes in order to protect Britain's supply chain.

"The Bletchley Park code breakers were in a perpetual race against time to get ships into position to protect convoys from the German submarines. They were dubbed by Churchill as his "Golden Geese" and worked around the clock, systematically typing possible code combinations that were extracted from messages, using Signal Intelligence, cryptanalysis and cribs, pieces of plain text that were guessed by traffic analysis, to reduce the key settings, before feeding the messages into their 'Bombes'. Once the red code was broken, the race was then on to decipher the yellow and green codes."

Dylan shook his head in amazement, "When did they first crack the code?"

"Britain got lucky when an Enigma machine was snatched from a sinking U-boat early in the war, but the German naval high command regularly changed the codes each day in order to foil British intelligence. To combat the changes in codes, the battle to crack the latest red code would restart each night on the stroke of midnight. It took the first few years to get the system right. A short time later, the deciphering of the Enigma code was so good that the Golden Geese were being credited with providing the British government information on where German troops were moving to, often before the soldiers themselves were aware of their destination."

"This must have been a wild place to work at the time."

"Well, you didn't exactly have to be mad to work at Bletchley Park during the War," laughed Hill, "but it probably helped. The eccentric mix of cryptographers, mathematicians and linguists, even some chess masters, was unusual to say the least. They worked night and day within 'Station X', as the Buckinghamshire code breaking centre was known. It was never easy. However, the amalgamation of these sometimes alarmingly individualistic intellects did result in the deciphering of the German military codes, and in doing so, I'd say they shortened the Second World War by a good couple of years."

"The free world owes them a huge debt," Dylan acknowledged.

"True, but much of the credit for breaking the code must be given to a group of accomplished Polish mathematicians who actually started the process prior to Hitler's invasion of their country. They got out prior to the invasion and joined up with the

Allies to create 'Station X' here at Bletchley Park. The overall process benefited greatly from the knowledge acquired by the Polish efforts"

"What happened to all the Enigma machines?"

"At the end of the war," Hill continued, "most of the Enigmas were destroyed. Less than a half dozen working models still exist in the world today. It is interesting to note that of all the coded transmissions sent during the war, only one of the original Kriegsmarine messages still remains a mystery today.

"Why weren't they able to decipher that message?"

"Simple. They didn't have access to the proper settings."

"So, besides the Enigma machine and a code book, you need settings to break an encrypted message?" asked Dylan.

"To break a coded transmission that was sent on an Enigma machine from a Kriegsmarine U-boat, you would need the code book with its source codes, the ring settings which were the starting positions for the rotors, and the Steckerboard connections for the Enigma machine. And, of course, you need the Enigma machine itself. Without all of these ingredients, it would be virtually impossible to decode the message."

Hill pointed to a display containing an encrypted message.

"See those letters. They were the settings needed to be able to match one Enigma machine to another in order to decode the message. If one did not have these settings and a code book to verify them, they would never break the code."

Dylan thanked his host for the tour and the information relating to the Enigma machine. As he turned to leave, he asked, "Do you ever give demonstrations of the Enigma machine?"

"Oh yes, on occasion. Would you like to see how it works?"

"Most definitely," Dylan replied.

Hill opened a drawer and pulled out a sheet of paper with a coded imprint similar to the page Dylan had shown him.

"See, here on the top. These are the settings," explained Hill. "One just sets the proper settings, adjusts the Enigma machine accordingly and types in the coded message. The machine does the rest."

Dylan watched as Hill typed the code settings into the Enigma machine. The museum director then typed in some fully coded text. Dylan watched as the deciphered message magically appeared. Hill pulled the finished copy from the machine and handed it to him.

"Here you go. A perfect sample of how it works. Keep it. It is your souvenir, a little something to remember us by."

"Thank you," replied Dylan, placing the sample in his folder. "Just how would a person go about buying an Enigma machine?"

"I don't think there are too many left these days," replied Hill. "Most are owned by museums or collectors."

"Not really advertised too much I suspect."

"Surprisingly, there was one in the news just last week. Apparently, a small museum in Berlin reported an Enigma machine stolen during a break-in. Odd that someone would steal something they would have no use for, isn't it?" ventured Hill.

The mention of the theft of an Enigma machine in Berlin was not lost on Dylan.

"Perhaps if I can get the setting numbers for my message, you could run it for me someday."

"Not a problem. However, remember that you must have the correct settings and the Steckerboard connections."

Dylan's mind was racing as he struggled with the problem. How could he find the rotor settings for a message sent over sixty years ago? For the second time in as many days, his quest had seemingly come to a dead end. "If I can get those settings, may I come back and visit you again?" he asked.

"Yes, by all means. Call ahead the next time you are over this way and I will make it happen. Jolly good."

On his return to London, Dylan began to replay the events from the time Clark had found the cylinder, to the present. He was searching for answers to questions as complex as the Enigma machine.

LONDON 2038 GMT

When he arrived back at the Dolphin Hotel, Dylan made a few calls in an attempt to find more information regarding the death of his friend, Saris. The police accident report was much as the receptionist had said. The only new information he did manage to discover involved the release of Saris' body to a relative for burial.

Dylan was thankful that someone had come forward to look after the funeral arrangements, although the fact that the director described the person as a relative had surprised him. In all the years he knew the man, Saris had never mentioned any relatives. Again, the hair on the back of Dylan's neck seemed to rise as he sensed something was not right. He would visit the mysterious relative to pay his respects and dispel his suspicions.

VANCOUVER 1318 PDT

Stan Bennett was sitting at his desk at CSIS, directly across from two men dressed in the standard FBI issued black suits. The taller of the two handed his card to the agent.

"Gary Anderson. FBI Foreign Relations."

The other man also pulled out a card and handed it to Bennett, "Mike Gerrard, also from Foreign Relations."

"What can I do for you, gentlemen?"

"You recently had some papers scanned by a member of the FBI. These papers have created a little more than cursory interest at the Department."

"I take it you are referring to the four pages I sent down last week?"

"Yes," said Gerrard. "We would like to see them again," he paused, "and all the other missing pages."

"Do you want to tell me what's going on?"

"Based on the nature of those papers, Foreign Relations is interested in a few of the possibilities that might be applicable to certain events surrounding the end of the Second World War."

"Are you saying those papers have a significant historical value in relation to the events of the day?"

"We're not sure, but they could be of some relevance," said Anderson. "Our sources tell us that it could be possible that some high ranking German officials might have escaped."

"Like Hitler, for example?" asked Bennett.

Gerrard looked up at the agent. "We are not at liberty to discuss details."

"Hell, even if Hitler did escape, he was born in 1889 and I'm sure is long dead by now," Bennett replied. "What possible interest would the FBI have in pursuing a dead person?"

"There are a lot of issues still to be answered," Anderson stated brusquely.

"There have been a series of events recently that have generated much interest in the actions of the Third Reich leaders at the end of the Second World War," Gerrard chimed in. "Events that our government would like to know a whole lot more about."

"So why follow Sean Dylan?" asked Bennett. "He's not a German and I doubt he has any more knowledge of Hitler's actions at the end of the war than you."

Bennett leaned back. The tall FBI man looked at his partner and then back at the CSIS agent.

"He has been at the center of some recent actions that might have a connection to this theory. We think he may know details about the documents that would be of interest to our superiors."

"Why don't you just ask him? Why do you FBI guys always have to do the cloak and dagger routine?"

Anderson did not react to Bennett's question. "I believe you are aware that Mr. Dylan is in possession of these documents of interest. We think those documents might shed light on the situation. We want those papers."

"What do you need from me?"

"We are here to request formal assistance from CSIS in observing Mr. Dylan's movements."

"I don't know that I can help you. I believe Mr. Dylan is out of the country at present."

"Yes, we know. We have someone in place to take care of that situation. Our request here only relates to his movements on Canadian soil. We wish to meet with Mr. Dylan when he returns. Knowing his whereabouts would assist us greatly. The Bureau would appreciate anything you can tell us about Mr. Dylan."

Bennett looked up at the FBI men. "Sean Dylan likes his independence and his privacy, so it will be difficult to keep tabs on him. I sure don't have the budget to put men out trying to tail him."

"We would prefer he not leave the area until we resolve the

location of the papers."

"You mean you want me to keep him contained until you get what you want."

"We do want to recover those papers through legal means. We are hoping Mr. Dylan will cooperate with us."

Bennett looked at the FBI agent. "You realize that Dylan isn't obliged to surrender them to foreign parties. What if he doesn't want to give up the papers?"

The FBI man locked eyes with Bennett. "Then we will get them by whatever other means we deem necessary."

"That could touch off an international incident."

"I am sure my superiors will be able to handle the situation."

Bennett checked his impulse to tell Anderson to put his request somewhere where the sun did not shine, but checked his emotions and simple responded, "A little heavy handed, isn't it?"

"Can we count on your support?" asked Anderson, ignoring the comment.

"I'll run it by my superiors," replied Bennett. "If they approve it, no problem. I will let you know."

31

AUGUST 29, 2007

LONDON   **1012 GMT**

Dylan telephoned and obtained the address of the funeral home from the duty officer in London. His next stop was at the car rental shop where he hired a car for the day. Dylan was hoping for another upgrade but the rental agent had only one car left. It was a Ford Fiesta Zetec S.

"It's a fun car to drive, sir," said the agent. "Very responsive and it has the auto-start feature as well." The agent held up the keychain to demonstrate how it worked. "Just press this button and it unlocks the car and starts it for you, all in one simple move." The agent was beaming. "The car is brand new, less than two hundred miles on the odometer. You get the pleasure of breaking her in."

Dylan thanked the agent and made his way to the car.

"Auto-start. What gimmick will they think up with next?" he murmured to himself. As he got into the car, Dylan took off his jacket and placed it on the passenger's seat. As he settled in, he noticed the extra ammunition clips had slid out of the side pocket of the jacket and onto the seat. He scooped them up and dropped them into the glove box.

The Zetec proved to be a spirited little car and he soon cleared the city on his way out to the M25. In less than forty minutes, he was heading west on the A3 towards Guildford.

Dylan took the slip road for the town and made his way around the traffic circle to the A25, and turned left onto Woodbridge Road, the main street into the town. The City of Guildford's claim to fame, other than the fact that Lewis Carroll, who wrote Alice in Wonderland, once resided there, is that it is home of the University of Surrey. The City boasted an inherently large number of pubs in relation to the normal population contained within its small boundaries. Each year, the influx of students into the small city fills the pubs to their limits. Dylan was quite happy that the University was not in session at this time of year.

The funeral home that handled Saris' body was at the edge of Guildford. Dylan entered the building and introduced himself to the director as an old friend of the family.

"Well, it's nice that someone showed up," stated the man dressed in the worn black suit, "although you are little late, mind you."

"I just came in from overseas and heard the news." Dylan replied. "What do you mean, about someone showing up?"

The funeral director proved to be a fountain of information. He explained that a relative of Saris had paid all of the fees for the funeral service in advance. The body arrived at the Funeral Home, but no one attended the actual service. Dylan looked at the director, "Did you meet the relative who arranged the service?"

"Yes, he came in the day after the accident and paid for everything up front. Strange fellow, he was. I think he may have been German."

"Did you get an address to forward the ashes?"

"Yes, of course. They were sent out last week."

"Would you mind giving me the address? I would like to meet the family members, to pay my respects."

"No problem, Sir. Let me get that for you."

Dylan was amazed at the ease of obtaining the address information for Sardis' relative. In Canada, he would have had to produce a myriad of identification to prove who he was, before ever getting someone's private address.

The funeral director returned moments later and handed Dylan a sheet of letterhead from the funeral home with the address of Saris' mysterious relative handwritten above a hastily drawn map.

"Here you go. Hans Everton, Auston House, Bradford," the funeral director said. "I've drawn a sketch of the area to help you find the location. It should not take you more than a half hour to get there. Driving carefully, of course."

"Of course," Dylan echoed with a smile. He folded the paper and put it into his jacket pocket, thanked the director and left.

The map was rough but the directions were quite simple. Dylan compared it to the map he had of the area. He would take the A281 down to Bradford. The relative's home was the first farm past the Shalford train station. Dylan started the car and the spirited Ford Fiesta Zetec S shot forward.

Dylan enjoyed driving on the roads in southern England. The Zetec S had plenty of power for its size, and handled well. He kept his speed down, ensuring he would not draw any unwanted attention, while allowing himself ample time to maintain a close watch on the road signs. The roads in the UK were well marked, but as he had found out on more than one occasion, a wrong guess at any of the many roundabouts could easily lead a person miles off course. The A281 was a smaller road with high hedges on both sides that effectively blocked him from seeing the countryside. Dylan glanced through the occasional opening in the seemingly endless shrubbery, looking for any sign of life.

Fifteen minutes later, the hedges gave way to the beginnings of the town of Bradford. The Shalford train station was just two miles further.

He proceeded through the town past the train station. Dylan noticed a small group of buildings a hundred yards off to the right hand side of the roadway. An old barn, with its doors slightly ajar, was about thirty yards from the house. Two horses were grazing in a penned area alongside the barn.

Dylan spotted the sign at the entrance to the driveway. *'Auston House'*. He pulled the Fiesta Zetec S into the well-worn driveway and drove along the rough surface until he had reached the house. He parked with the car facing towards the barn, turned off the ignition and waited. No one came to the door.

He retrieved his jacket as he slowly exited the vehicle, made his way up the steps of the house and knocked on the door. The door was unlocked and swung opened to reveal a darkened hallway with a small table holding an old styled telephone, surrounded by a bunch of curios. Beside the telephone was a small packet of letters. Dylan stepped inside and called out. There was no answer. He glanced at the letters and noticed the name on the envelope 'James Milner, Auston House'. A sense of uneasiness came over him, his mind immediately stepping up to a higher state of alert. The location was definitely the right house, but the name on the envelope did not match the name that the funeral director quoted as Sardis' relative. The date on the envelope was over three weeks old. Dylan noticed a small spot of dried blood at the base of the table.

He reached inside his jacket, gently wrapping his fingers around the plastic handle of the Glock. He kept the gun hidden, but ready for action. Dylan treated the house as a crime scene, taking care not to disturb any potential evidence. Moving forward with catlike agility, he inspected each room in the house in a matter of minutes. The house was empty.

Dylan started towards the front door and then stopped. While there was no one in the house, there was a cup sitting on the kitchen counter. The coffee inside was still warm. Someone was on the property, somewhere. Dylan moved to the front door. He would check the barn next.

The expanse of open area between the house and the old barn did not look inviting to Sean. *"An easy target"* his instincts advised.

He assessed his options and quickly settled on the safety of the little Ford Fiesta. He would drive the car over next to the barn and park it under the second-story loading window.

Dylan strode over to the little Ford with a casual flair. In less than a minute, he was standing outside the huge barn doors, putting the keys to the car into his pocket with his left hand, while firmly grasping the Glock with his right.

He moved slowly towards the open door, every single sense working in overtime mode. In one quick move, Dylan slipped around the left door, pulling it shut behind him. He darted inside the darkened barn, dropping to one knee and sliding off to the side. There was no reaction from inside the structure. He waited a moment before attempting to move around inside the barn, giving his eyes time to become accustomed to the low light level. Dylan scanned the lower floor. There were a couple of empty stalls, a feeding trough and some farm machinery over to one side, but no sign of human presence. The only sound he could hear was the squeaking of the hinges on the swinging door of loading window.

Dylan looked up at the second level. A crude ladder built into one of the support beams, led up to where a number of hay bales were stacked. He moved slowly towards the ladder.

The steps creaked under his weight as he slowly climbed the fifteen-foot distance to the second level. He was only three steps from the second story landing when he heard the noise. Dylan's ears instantly recognized the distinctive click of a small arm safety clip.

In one lightning fast move, he hurtled himself up the last of the steps and rolled across the floor as several muffled shots rang out from the unseen gun below. Dylan could hear the bullets slam into the roof above his head. He crouched behind the support beam, pulled out the Glock and answered with a quick burst of three shots.

"*Shit*" Dylan exclaimed to himself. He had not fired this new version of the Glock. It did not have the same safety mechanism as the older models. When he eased the trigger back, it automatically released its new built in safety, and the hairline trigger had fired before Dylan realized its sensitivity. "*Well, three shots gone, three to go.*" He thought as he viewed his surroundings in an attempt to find a way out of his predicament. He checked the remaining shells in the Glock. "*I left the ammunition clips in the car,*" he cursed to himself. "*Bloody Hell!*"

The only opening was the loading window the owner used to hoist up the hay bales. The block and tackle was still in place. Dylan considered his options. He was safe for the moment, but was pinned to the spot and would have to cross an open area to get to the window. Even if he made it, they would be on him before he got to ground level.

A voice echoed from below, "Mr. Dylan, we could have killed you easily. We chose not to. We only want what you took from the cylinder."

Dylan listened but was not ready to reply.

"You are not able to escape, Mr. Dylan. Give us the papers and we will leave you here," offered a second voice from below.

"I'll bet you would." Dylan thought to himself. *"You would leave me here alright, but quite dead."*

Dylan's eyes darted around the room, searching for an escape. He did not see his adversaries, but he could hear their voices below. They were speaking in German. He picked up some of the words. Dylan recognized 'feuer' and 'brand'. They were discussing a plan to burn the barn in order to flush him out.

Dylan scanned the upper level for anything that would help him out of his predicament. There was a small board lying on the floor. He reached out with his right foot and dragged it over to his position. If he could distract his adversaries, he could make it over to the window and slide down the rope. Dylan picked up the small piece of wood. *"This used to work in the movies,"* he thought to himself. He hesitated and quickly revised the plan as he recalled the hay bales stacked in rows close to the edge of the opening below. The men who wanted to kill him were behind the machinery directly below. Dylan would have to get behind the hay bales.

"Who are you? Who are you working for?" Dylan called out.

"That is of no concern to you," a voice answered in a thick German accent. "Just give us the papers and we will leave."

In rapid succession, Dylan tossed the wood at the wall behind the machinery and simultaneously fired off the final three rounds from the Glock. He was not aiming at anything in particular, just wanting to let them know he was still there, and armed. The shock attack worked, giving him the precious seconds he needed to move behind the hay bales. He slipped the Glock back into his jacket pocket and put his back against the stack, pushing them over the edge, down onto his enemy below.

Several shots, muffled by silencers, greeted the first bales as they crashed downwards. As Dylan continued to push the remaining bales of hay over the side, he pressed the auto start on the Zetec's electronic keypad.

The cascading sea of hay bales caused a short respite from the gunshots. Dylan did not hesitate. He sprang across the floor and dove through the window, grabbing the hanging rope as he went. The rope burned his hands as he slid down to the ground level. He landed with a resounding thud. The little Ford Fiesta Zetec S was waiting, its engine running. Dylan pushed himself up and limped the short distance to the car. In one motion, he got in, hit the clutch, dropped the transmission into gear, and floored the accelerator.

The Ford surged forward, its front wheels spinning in the loose dirt and gravel as it tore away from the barn. The little 1.6 litre engine was screaming well beyond its maximum revolutions, the tachometer redlining as Dylan jammed the transmission through each of its gears.

He had made it halfway down the driveway before he heard the unmistakable sound of a bullet ricocheting off the car's exterior. With his foot pressed firmly to the floorboard, Dylan kept the Ford moving at top speed. When he was only about twenty yards from the roadway, he slammed on the brakes and made a hard cut to the right. A quick downshift into a lower gear followed by immediate acceleration launched the tiny Ford into a right-hand slide. The tiny car screamed onto the southbound lane of the A281 roadway in a cacophony of squealing tires, grinding gears and the high-pitched sound of the engine. Dylan did not have time to notice that he had narrowly missed an oncoming car.

With the extra adrenaline pumping through his body, Dylan navigated the Ford Zetec along the winding road, driving with one hand as he attempted to reload the Glock with the other. It was not long before he noticed the large black Mercedes in his rearview mirror. As the vehicle got closer, the driver appeared to fill the windshield. His passenger seemed to be somewhat smaller. There was a third person in the rear of the vehicle but Dylan could not make out any distinguishing features.

"*Don't these guys drive anything but Mercedes?*" he mused.

Dylan took a quick glance at his map. Like most of the roads in England, it looked like a badly laid out maze of trails that seemed to go around in circles. He spotted a small side road ahead on his right and quickly downshifted, putting the car in another right hand slide as he made the corner. The black Mercedes was gaining. The side road was too small and not built for fast driving. The road was coming to a sudden end at an intersection to the A3100. He braced for a turn, downshifting quickly, and putting the car into a perfect corner slide to the left, onto the A3100. The more powerful Mercedes was in close pursuit, but the small road preventing it from overtaking the tiny Ford. A brief glance in his rearview mirror and Dylan confirmed the driver was TallOne and his passenger, the shorter pug-nosed man named Faust. A third man was in the back.

Dylan looked ahead. He spotted a road sign indicating a route to the main highway. "*B3000 to A3.*"

"*The Mercedes doesn't like small roads. I will have a better chance on the B3000.*" he muttered to himself.

The little Ford, engine howled in protest as Dylan again put it into yet another right hand slide as he approached the next intersection, driving hard onto the B3000. The high hedge on both sides of the roadway made it appear so narrow that passing another car would be next to impossible.

Racing along the B3000, Dylan had both hands on the leather-wrapped steering wheel alternately checking between the road ahead and the black Mercedes following closely behind.

Ahead, a small narrow bridge suddenly appeared.

Dylan was fortunate to line up the Ford on the center of the bridge, becoming airborne as he crossed over between the cement pillars. The Zetec landed relatively easily on its stiffened sports suspension.

Although the black Mercedes had closed the gap, it had to slow down quickly to negotiate the bridge.

Dylan floored the accelerator, increasing the distance between the vehicles. The Mercedes crossed the bridge and increased its speed. The road continued to weave through the English countryside, heading towards the town of Compton. Dylan checked his mirror. Now less than fifty metres distance separated the two vehicles. Fortunately, the Ford, despite its small size, kicked up enough dust to block the view of those in the black Mercedes, forcing them to stay well back of the Ford.

Dylan looked ahead and spotted the lorry coming from the opposite direction. His earlier concerns about passing almost became pure panic as he picked out the shape of another narrow bridge between himself and the lorry.

"This is going to be close, very close."

The gap between the Ford with the black Mercedes in close pursuit and the oncoming Lorry was quickly diminishing. Dylan knew he would have only one chance to pull off his move. They were less than fifty metres apart and he could see the expression of disbelief on the lorry driver's face. Dylan planted the accelerator on the floor and the engine in the little Ford screamed. He waited until the last possible second before quickly applying, and then releasing the brakes and hitting the gas pedal again. The first part of his plan worked as the black Mercedes saw the taillights through the cloud of dust and hit his brakes.

Dylan was close enough to see the lorry driver's eyes, wide open in fear of the impending crash. He had both hands pushing down hard on the truck's horn. Dylan shifted gears and the little Ford surged over the bridge, veered to the left and passed between the end of the bridge and the front of the oncoming lorry. *"Sorry,"* he exclaimed. In one quick motion, he cut the wheel back hard causing the tiny Ford to fishtail back onto the road, safely behind the lorry.

The driver of the black Mercedes did not notice the Ford's sudden move until it was too late. Dylan's action left the Mercedes staring directly at the front end of the lorry as it came over the bridge, heading directly at them. The lorry driver was equally as shocked and again, stood on the brakes, his horn blasting at the black car. The driver of the Mercedes had no options. He took the only evasive action possible and steered the large black car off the road into the slough to the side of the bridge, landing in a huge shower of water and debris.

Dylan let out a sign of relief as he watched the event unfold in his rearview mirror. He continued on the B3000 until it connected with the A3 motorway. He slowed to a stop and then turned onto the highway that took him back to his room at the Dolphin.

32

AUGUST 30, 2007

LONDON 0730 GMT

The call from Ozzy came at 7:30 in the morning. Dylan had just dragged himself out from the comfort of a warm bed. His body was still sore and a little stiff from the previous day's episode.

"Hello Sean, how are things going over there?"

"Much like the old days," he replied with a laugh that caused him to wince with pain.

"What happened?" asked Ozzy.

Dylan relayed the events of the previous day, including the incident with the Germans.

"Did you get a look at any of them?"

"Just while I was driving. Things were happening too fast and I didn't exactly have a whole lot of time for introductions, but I am sure it was TallOne and Faust, the two guys who followed me in Germany, plus one other guy who I didn't recognize."

"It sounds like they definitely knew who you were."

"Seems that way. What I cannot figure is, what the hell they are after? The papers are useless without the proper rotor settings and code numbers. And Saris. Granted, he was not the most active person I ever knew, but far too young to have died already. Can you see if your sources can dig up anything about what really happened to Saris?"

"No problem," responded Ozzy, knowing Dylan felt some responsibility in the death of his friend. "I'll get back to you tomorrow."

"I would like to know how these things are connected."

Ozzy could hear the hurt in Dylan's voice and moved to change the subject. "Sean, you said the Mercedes ended up in the slough. Can you get any info from the towing company who hauled the vehicle out? It could give us a lead on where they got the car and who the hell they are."

"I would imagine they have covered that trail by now, but it is worth a try."

"Hey, you never know."

"I'll put a call into my friend at Scotland Yard and see what he can find out about them."

"Touch base with me before you leave for Vancouver. Oh, and by the way, don't forget to drop the Glock off before you leave," Ozzy reminded him.

"Right, Thanks. In the meantime, put together a crew and equipment for a deep-sea salvage operation. I think we might change our course and see if we can get some answers from another angle."

"What do you mean?"

"Hypothetically, what would we have if we found the Enigma machine that was on board the U-1220?"

Ozzy sounded puzzled, "A rusted piece of junk?"

"Well, not exactly. We would have the Enigma machine that sent the original messages. We would also have the exact settings of the rotors on that machine and would be able to replicate those settings on a working machine and decipher the coded messages."

"Shit!" exclaimed Ozzy. "That would work, wouldn't it?"

"It would," Dylan confirmed. "The only problem of course,

is finding the Enigma machine onboard a submarine that was sunk sixty-odd years ago. However, the salvage companies have some sophisticated equipment these days and I think it is worth a try. Remember, if we solve the riddle of the coded messages, this little project could lead us to the gold from the Great Priam Treasure."

Ozzy's eyes lit up at Dylan's statement. "I'll get on the salvage possibilities today and have an answer by tomorrow."

"Good. Just don't give out too much information."

Dylan said goodbye, flipped the cell phone shut and headed for the shower.

SEATTLE   **0610 PDT**

Anderson was sitting at his desk reading a report from his contact in Berlin when Gerrard entered.

"Got a call from the London bureau. It seems our Mr. Dylan visited Harrods and the museum at Bletchley Park. He bought some tea at Harrods and toured of the museum with the curator, a Mr. Hill. They talked about the Enigma machines, but nothing of any real consequence."

"Stay with him, but at a discreet distance. We might as well let him do the work for us."

"What about his friend in Berlin?" asked Gerrard. "You still want to keep a man on him?"

"Hell, our man has lost him more times than I can count. The stupid son-of-a-bitch couldn't follow his nose without a map. Forget him."

Gerrard moved closer to Anderson. "Look, if Dylan does not have codes, why are we following him? He will never be able to break the code."

Anderson looked at his associate, "Ours is not to reason why. We were told to do it, so we do it."

"You're the boss. I think it is just a lot of unnecessary expense with no real object in sight. Maybe that CSIS guy was right. It's just a lot of supposition, no real substance."

"That's not your decision. You just do your job, Mike, and keep tabs on both of them until I tell you to stop. Understand?"

"Your call." replied Gerrard indifferently. Just trying to help.

"Don't bother," replied Anderson brusquely.

BERLIN　　　　　　　　　　　　　　　　　　**1112 GMT**

Hans Lüdden opened the file and read the dossier again, before setting it down on his desk. "You have done well, Karl. I am sure a man with such resources will be very helpful to our cause."

"Thank you, Herr Lüdden."

Lüdden flipped through the pictures in the file. "He certainly does enjoy his women, and his gambling debts are enormous." The leader of the underground Neo-Nazi Democratic Party was smiling. "Now that we have a contact that can get access to Clark's organization, it should not be long before he is able to secure the papers from Dylan's home. However, we do not want to take any chances. If he would deceive his friends and those he works for, he will betray anyone. Keep a very close eye on this man."

"Yes, Herr Lüdden," replied Müller as he watched the leader lock the incriminating photographs in his desk. "What do you want me to do about Dylan? He managed to escape von Schlippenbach's trap in the south of England."

"The fools!" bellowed Lüdden, slamming his fist onto the desk. "This Dylan fellow has more lives than a cat. Let us hope our new contact recovers what Dylan found in the cylinder. Once we have the papers, you can personally kill Mr. Dylan and the contact. We do not want any loose ends."

"Yes, Herr Lüdden. I understand. You can count on me."

YORKSHIRE   **1305 GMT**

Dylan reached the Five Crowns restaurant in the town of Reading at five minutes past one in the afternoon. The little Ford Fiesta Zetec S was looking somewhat the worse for wear after the previous day's events, but still seemed to have a little zip. He parked across the street from the restaurant, got out and pressed the auto-lock button to secure the car.

He had scheduled his meeting with Carol Janes for one o'clock, and he knew the ever-efficient former Operations Manager for Special Forces would be there on time. Dylan entered the restaurant and spotted the attractive brunette sitting alone at a table. Sidestepping the hostess, he went directly to her table.

"Carol. It has been a few years. You're looking great."

"Hello, Sean." she beamed, "Yes, it has been awhile. The peacekeeping mission in Nicaragua; back in 1989, wasn't it?"

Dylan sat down at the table. "Yes. We were helping to end the civil war and if I remember correctly, it got a little tense."

"But, as I recall, it was also a lot of fun."

Although she was only five foot, two inches tall, Carol Janes was a battle-hardened veteran who could hold her own against most men. It always amazed Dylan that someone so small could have so much energy and strength. He admired her resolve to be successful.

The waiter approached the table and took their orders for drinks.

Dylan ordered an Irish Whisky neat, and Carol ordered a glass of Merlot.

"So, you left the service and are in charge of the RAF Research Library. That is quite a switch from the field operations."

"I had had enough of the rigors of combat. Even if they only deemed our missions to be a peacekeeping role, it was a tough job. I left the service in ninety-eight and returned here to England. Not as much excitement, but I am getting used to it."

"Did you finally settle down and get married?"

"No, not yet. I have thought about it a few times, but there is still so much to do, especially with my new position and all."

"Speaking of the new position, were you able to find anything relating to my submarine?"

Carol flashed a quick smile. "That is quite the project you have got yourself involved with, Sean. Sounds very exciting."

"It could be. That is why I need the information. We have to be sure we are going after the right submarine. It has to be the one that sunk on May the fourth, back in 1945. We need positive identification before we commit to dropping a bundle of cash on a research dive. If we can't confirm the sub and its location, there is no way we could justify the cost."

"I'm not exactly sure what you are doing, but I was able to get some information that might help," replied Carol. "But isn't finding a submarine that sunk sixty years ago, like looking for the proverbial needle in a haystack?"

"That depends on what information you found for us. They managed to find the Titanic, so if you are able to get us close to our target, there is a good chance we can locate it."

Carol swirled her wine and took a sip. "You realize that even if you do find the sub, there won't be anything left of value."

"The object is for us to confirm the submarine is the U-1220. At this point," said Dylan, flipping through the menu, "we are only going after positive identification of the U-Boat."

The waiter returned. Dylan and Carol ordered their lunches and a refill on the drinks.

"Seems a hell of a waste of money, but it's your call." said Carol as the waiter departed.

"You mean the lunch, the whisky or the wine?"

Carol laughed as she pulled a file folder from her bag and passed it to Dylan. "Well, this should help to get you started."

A slow smile came over his face as he slowly picked through the pages.

"There were several submarines sunk on the day you specified," Carol continued. "One was near Greenland, the U-505, and two others in the North Sea above Scotland. I think the one off Foula Island in the North Sea is more likely your missing submarine."

"What makes you think so?" he inquired as he flipped through her report.

"This particular submarine was shot down by an RAF Canso patrol in the North Sea on the exact date you specified," she replied.

"But you said there were two others."

"Right, but you told me that your submarine did not have any identification other than the German Swastika. Correct?"

Dylan was reading her report as he listened, "Yes, but how could you know that?"

"I read the Canso crew's debriefing that was filed after the crew was rescued."

"Rescued?"

"Yes, they were shot down as they made their run to drop

their depth charges during the attack on the sub. Only five of the eight crewmembers survived. The report states that the submarine's only identification was a Swastika on the conning tower."

As he read the last page, Dylan shouted a loud "Yes!" with unbridled excitement. He looked at the page again, pointed to the last line and read, "May fourth, 1945, Latitude fifty-nine degrees, twenty-six minutes, twenty-nine seconds North, Longitude zero degrees, forty-four minutes, forty-three seconds West, Unregistered U-Boat." Dylan was ecstatic. He was sure this was the U-1220.

The waiter returned with their orders.

Dylan passed the wine to Carol and picked up his drink. "This calls for a toast. To the U-1220".

They clinked glasses and toasted the find.

"I hate to rain on your parade Sean, but knowing where the submarine went down and finding it again are poles apart."

"I know," replied an excited Dylan, "but we are one hell of lot closer now than we were when I got up this morning."

"You should also know that the U-boat was literally blown in half by the depth charges. You might not find much of it left."

"That could be a bad thing, depending on where it broke apart. The radio room was just forward of the conning tower. However, it might make it easier to explore the inside.

"I thought you just wanted to confirm the actual submarine."

"Well, if it turns out that we can get inside; we might be able to find some special items."

She looked at Dylan and shook her head. "If I was to bet on anyone finding interesting things, you would be my first choice," replied Carol with an impish grin. "Good Luck, Sean."

Dylan got up and helped Carol with her coat. "Do you want me to drop you off somewhere?"

"No, I have a car outside."

Dylan took the folder containing Carol's research papers and put it into a tight roll. "I owe you one, Carol," he said. "This is fantastic."

"You can buy me dinner some time. That would be fun." She paused and looked up at Dylan's face. "Then you can tell me what this is really all about."

"I promise."

The two friends made their way out of the restaurant. Dylan had offered to walk Carol to her car, but she would have no part of it. She laughed at his offer, "I am just down the street, for heaven's sake. Remember, I was on those missions with you. I can take care of myself, thank you very much."

Dylan watched as she made her way down the street, her fit body swaying just enough to make his eyes hold a little longer than normal. He finally turned away when she reached her car. With a low whistle, Dylan stepped off the curb to cross the street to his own vehicle. He pulled out the key chain to push the remote auto-start button. As his thumb hit the button, he noticed the man standing beside the car. Dylan could not stop the pressing motion of his thumb. As the button made contact, the little Ford Fiesta Zetec S erupted instantly in a ball of fire and smoke. The force of the explosion ripped the driver's door off the small vehicle, tearing the man's body apart. The little Zetec soared ten feet into the air, rolled over and landed on its roof. A shower of glass and debris rained over the parking area.

The strength of the detonation knocked Dylan to the curb. He rolled over to avoid the wall of intense heat that accompanied the explosion. A mixture of fine particles continued to fall as Dylan struggled to his feet.

Carol was already at his side. "Are you okay?"

Dylan shook his head. The force of the blast had knocked him down, but he was not injured. He looked over at the smoldering ruins of the car. "The rental agent did tell me to break it in," he said, dusting himself off, "But, I'm not sure that was quite what he had in mind."

"What the hell is that all about, Sean?"

"I'm not sure. Either that car had a serious flaw in its system, or whoever was standing there had just installed a very nasty package meant for me. It seems that I have picked up some very bad-tempered friends here in England."

"Well, it seems your friends don't like you very much."

Dylan looked at Carol as he dusted off the effects of the explosion. "You want to give me a lift?"

"Sure, but what are you going to do about the car?"

"Don't think I can do much here. Let us get back to my hotel. I will call my friend at Scotland Yard and explain what happened. They can check out the scene and identify whomever it was that was standing there. Right now, I think it would be wise if we made ourselves scarce."

Carol looked up at Dylan. "Sean Dylan, you haven't changed," she said, playfully poking him in the ribs. "Action and excitement just seem to follow you wherever you go. You are such a fun date."

Dylan shook his head and laughed. "I might have done a lot of things to get a date, but blowing up cars isn't in my repertoire. Let's go."

A crowd of curious onlookers was starting to form around the scene, checking out the carnage. Dylan hooked his arm in Carol's and walked to her car.

33

AUGUST 31, 2007

BERLIN 0745 GMT

Hans Lüdden was pacing back and forth in front of his desk as he read the English newspaper Karl Müller had purchased earlier. He was furious.

"What idiot gave the order to kill Dylan?" he screamed. "I said I wanted him alive until after we had the Schliemann Papers."

Von Schlippenbach looked down at his feet. "He was causing us too many problems," he offered almost glibly. "It does not matter. We have Müller's contact. We will still get the papers."

Lüdden looked at his second in command. "This article does not confirm the identity of the body, only that the car which exploded in Yorkshire was rented by a Canadian. Have you spoken to our contact yet to confirm it was Dylan?"

"Not yet, Herr Lüdden." answered von Schlippenbach.

Lüdden glared at von Schlippenbach, his eyes seemingly piercing the man's body. "We need confirmation before we can proceed. Find out for sure if it was Dylan."

"The car was set to detonate when he started the engine, Herr Lüdden. While the police have not confirmed the identity of the person who killed, I am sure it was him."

"And what about the papers, Karl," Lüdden asked in an almost frantic voice. "Have you any news about the papers?"

"Our people have been located where Dylan was staying in London. I expect to hear from them later today about what they have found. They will also verify what happened in Yorkshire."

Lüdden took a deep breath and suddenly became calm. His voice lowered to a normal pitch as he addressed the two men. "First you tried to capture this man so he will give us the papers, and then you kill him before we have found the documents. These futile and ill-advised attempts have drawn much unwanted attention to our cause. That is not good for the Party."

"In spite of the ineffectiveness of Müller's men, there is some good news, Herr Lüdden," Otto von Schlippenbach offered, in a vain attempt to redeem himself. "The information we received from our wiretaps that our Canadian contact installed on Clark's telephone lines indicate that the original papers are most likely either at Clark's or Dylan's home."

"How confident are you about this person, Karl?"

Müller's face was bright red. Although he wanted to respond to von Schlippenbach's insinuation that he and his men had been incompetent, he suppressed his anger. "I think he has the best chance," he replied. "He has secured all of the necessary information to gain access to the homes of both Clark and Dylan. He is waiting for our orders."

"Are you sure we can trust this man?"

Von Schlippenbach seemed to enjoy deflecting the blame for the failures onto Müller. "Yes, Herr Lüdden. We can trust him. I made sure that we provided the right incentive to ensure that trust," he boasted with an air of superiority. "We will soon get the papers we need, whether they are with Clark or at Dylan's home."

Lüdden looked down at his desk. "I hope so." His eyes lifted and looked at the two men. "For both of your sakes."

LONDON 0710 GMT

The early rays of the morning sun streamed through the windows blinds as Dylan finished packing his bags. His mind bounced between the bizarre events surrounding the previous evening with Carol and finding the location of the U-1220. The night was full of memories they had shared over the years, replayed over dinner and late night drinks. Carol had delivered him to the Dolphin just after midnight. Dylan wished he could have spent more time, but his flight out of Luton Airport was at noon and it was imperative that he return to Vancouver.

He had called Ozzy as soon as he woke and arranged to meet him at the Frankfurt Airport so he could bring Ozzy up to date on the latest events including Carol's latest information on the location of what he was sure was the final resting place of the U-1220.

Dylan wanted to call Ronnie, but the time difference made it just past one in the morning. He decided to call her office and left a message to greet her in the morning.

He decided his next call would be to Detective Inspector Snow of Scotland Yard to explain what had happened in Yorkshire. Dylan had met Snow, a Colonel in the British regiment, during a joint British and Canadian Special Forces training exercise in Canada. During the initial phase of the exercise, Snow found himself trapped underwater when a bridge his jeep was crossing collapsed. Dylan had been first on the scene and was instrumental in rescuing Snow from raging waters. They had remained friends ever since.

When he finally reached the Inspector, Dylan gave Snow a full account of the events in Yorkshire and the car chase near Guildford. Snow asked him to keep in close touch while Scotland

Yard checked out the identity of the person who killed by the car explosion. He would also check on the black Mercedes. Dylan gave Snow his contact numbers and promised to be available as needed.

Dylan hung up and quickly scanned his room at the Dolphin as he packed his travel bag. He would head out to Luton to catch the connecting flight to Frankfurt. After the incidents of the past forty-eight hours, he would not be taking any chances. He put the Glock into the inside pocket of his jacket. He would meet Ozzy's contact at the airport and return the weapon. He called the concierge to request a cab, picked up the bag and left.

The drive to the airport was uneventful and the EasyJet flight was on schedule. Dylan checked in with ease, the petite check-in attendant's smile making the exercise almost enjoyable. He headed towards the entrance to the gates, bypassing the Duty Free shops that line the corridor, and ran into the end of the lineup waiting to enter the Security area.

Dylan picked up a copy of the morning newspaper and glanced at the headlines. Given that it was an airport in Britain, the line of passengers moved well. In less than ten minutes, Dylan found himself nearing the main entrance to the departure gates. He scanned the area, quickly spotted the Asian contact he met at Harrods. The man was now wearing an airport security badge as he stood outside the entrance, directing passengers to the various checkpoints. Dylan performed a little slight of hand as he approached the short Asian man. Dylan smiled to himself, *"This guy is good."*

The Asian man motioned him towards the end door.

"Would you like a newspaper?" Dylan asked as he passed through the doorway.

"Yes, if you are finished with it," replied the man reaching for the newspaper. "Thank you, Sir,"

Without missing a beat, Dylan had handed the Asian man a folded newspaper with the Glock wrapped neatly inside and passed through the doors into the Security area. He placed his bag on the conveyor belt that led to the scanner. He paused for a moment, turned and looked around. The Asian man with the security badge had disappeared.

Dylan smiled and continued through the passenger-screening portal, retrieved his bag. He proceeded to his assigned gate.

VANCOUVER   **0800 PDT**

"Gary Anderson, FBI Foreign Relations."

"Yeah, I remember you," answered the CSIS agent. "What can I do for you today?"

"We've been in touch with our Berlin associates and they tell me that Mr. Dylan and his friend are apparently causing all sorts of problems over in Europe."

Bennett smiled "Sean Dylan. Really? That's hard to believe," he said with a slight smile.

"My superiors are not amused. They are wondering if someone might have tipped them off that we were interested in the papers?"

"Firstly, I don't know the friend of Mr. Dylan that you are referring to, and secondly, I do not compromise any investigation, no matter who is involved, even the FBI."

The agent was unmoved by Bennett's declaration. "I hope not," he warned. "This matter is of major interest to our government and we will not tolerate interference from any source."

"Unless you have something new to add to the request you have already made, I have things to do," Bennett stated dryly. "I will call you if and when I have something. Good Day."

Anderson looked at the CSIS agent for a long moment, turned on his heel and made his way out of Bennett's office.

"Goddamned FBI agents. Think they own the fucking world."

FRANKFURT   1420 GMT

The Boeing 737 made a perfect landing at Frankfurt's Airport City. The transportation facility was massive, spread over more than twenty million square metres of space.

For Dylan, the process of changing airplanes and airlines was always an adventure. Frankfurt was no different, as he made his way through the maze of concourses, taking in two separate terminals on two levels.

He had just rounded the corner to Concourse 'A' and spotted the Airline Lounge. His flight was to depart at four-forty. He would relax with a couple of drinks while he waited for Ozzy to arrive. As he pulled open the door to the lounge, his cell phone rang.

"Sean, this is Ronnie."

Dylan could hear a sense of urgency. She did not sound like the cool, sophisticated woman he was with two weeks earlier. He checked his watch. "It's just after five in the morning over there, Ronnie. What's wrong?"

"It's Jim. No one has heard from him. He did not come in yesterday and he missed an important meeting with the Carter group this morning. This is not like Jim. Something is wrong. He always calls in to let me know where he is or if there is a change in plans."

"Ronnie, I've known Jim for a long time," said Dylan in an attempt to console her, "He's a big boy and he can take care of himself. Did you call the company Security?"

"Yes, they are checking all possible locations."

"What about that lawyer guy, Bob Emerson?" Dylan asked. "Have you checked with him?"

Ronnie paused for a moment, "Not yet, but I will."

Dylan's inner fears echoed her concerns. "Look, put a call through to Emerson and see what he has to say. Okay?" He did not wait for a reply. "My flight arrives in Vancouver this afternoon. I'll come directly to the office and we'll get this sorted out."

The confident sound of Dylan's voice seemed to reassure Ronnie and the urgency in her voice lessened. "I hope so. Have a good flight, Sean," she paused, "Thanks."

Dylan said goodbye, folded his cell phone and stuck it into his belt holster as he entered the lobby of the Lufthansa lounge.

The smiling attendant took his ticket and checked him in at the front desk. She returned Dylan's flight documents.

"You have very nice eyes," he said with a smile, but I suppose you hear that from every passenger."

"Enjoy yourself, Mr. Dylan," she gushed, a hint of a red appearing on her face. "I will inform you when your flight is boarding."

BERLIN   **1550 GMT**

"Are you sure? And the papers were not in the home?" asked Müller. I will inform Herr Lüdden of your progress. Stay on top of the situation and update me once you have any further news."

There was a pause in the conversation.

"What about my money?" the other party asked.

"I am sure Herr Lüdden will be advancing your fees as per our agreement. Just retrieve the contents of the cylinder."

VANCOUVER   0815 PDT

Ronnie gazed out the window of Clark's office. The sky was clear. It was a perfect day in Vancouver. Perfect, except for the strange events unfolding in her life. She had not slept at all the night before, but was more worried than tired.

The telephone rang. It was Bob Emerson.

"Hello, Ronnie. Is he there?"

"No. I haven't heard from him for over four days and I'm getting worried."

"I have some papers that require his signature. Why don't you drop by the office this afternoon and pick them up? In the meantime, I will make a few calls to find out what's happening."

"Sure,"" replied Ronnie. "Is two o'clock okay?"

"Fine. I will be waiting for you."

FRANKFURT   1622 GMT

Dylan sat in the lounge quietly sipping a glass of fine Irish Whisky. He was both exhausted and excited. He had repeatedly gone over the activities of the past few days, trying to connect the different events. He could not explain the sudden emergence of the other players or understand why someone found it necessary to kill his friend Saris.

The connection between the contents of the cylinder and the gold from the Great Priam Treasure was looking more possible each day. Was the gold still be onboard the sunken submarine? He wondered about the final mission of the phantom submarine. Who were the passengers? What happened to them? The thought that Hitler may have actually escaped Germany fueled a rage within him.

The questions continued to race through his mind as he sat watching the steady stream of aircraft, landing and taking off from the runways below. His flight was leaving in twenty-five minutes and Ozzy had not yet arrived.

He downed the last of the Irish Whisky, flipped open his cell phone and pushed the buttons. The cell phone did its magic and the voice of a young girl answered in German, "Hallo?"

Dylan refocused and spoke in his broken German, "Hallo, ist Herr Horst Schneider dort, bitte?

"Er steht still."

"Kann ich mit ihm sprechen?"

The girl realized Dylan spoke English and replied, "You may speak in English if you wish. I understand perfectly."

"Thank you," said a relieved Dylan. He continued, "I met with Mr. Schneider last week and I just wanted to thank him for his hospitality.

"I am sorry. My grandfather is sleeping," replied the girl. "He is a very an old man. He must get his rest. Perhaps you could call back tomorrow afternoon."

"Yes, of course. He is a fine man. Would you please let him know I called? My name is Sean Dylan."

"I will tell him when he wakes up."

"Danke. Auf Wiedersehen."

Dylan flipped his cell phone closed to end the call and ordered another Irish Whisky from a passing attendant, as Ozzy came into the lounge.

"Make that two," he called after the attendant. "Hi, Oz. What kept you?"

"Hi Sean, sorry I'm late. Got delayed. I had to shake some idiot who followed me to the airport." Ozzy sat down and continued,

"This guy was getting rather determined in his efforts. It took me almost an hour to lose him."

"You must be slowing down in your old age," Dylan replied with a grin.

"I gave him the old double airline shift. Bought a ticket to Finland, boarded the plane and then slipped into the forward washroom. I exited the washroom when they said they were about to close the main door for takeoff. He never saw me leave. Hell, he is probably halfway to Helsinki by now."

Dylan shook his head, "Same old Oz."

"It is still fun," he said with a laugh. "What do you have?"

"I have some good news. You?" he asked expectantly.

"Bad, I'm afraid. Who wants to go first?"

"Give me the bad first," said Dylan. "That way we can end things on a good note."

The attendant returned with their drinks and Ozzy downed his in one shot. "Okay," he said as the Irish Whisky filtered down his throat. "That's better. Remember you told me in Berlin that the only persons who knew about the cylinder, other than Clark and yourself, were Saris and his assistant, the one who took pictures at the Institute. Well, a young German lad named Wilhelm Heinrich died in freak accident last week."

Dylan gave a questioning look.

"Heinrich was Sardis' assistant."

"That is quite the coincidence," Dylan observed.

"The strangest part is that he died only three hours after Sardis had had his accident. The police did not connect the two accidents. They are treating both as non-homicide investigations."

"What do you think?"

"Well, it turns out that young Wilhelm did have connections

to the underground Neo-Nazi Party's youth movement in Germany. He was an active member at their rallies."

"That's too much of a coincidence for me. Somebody got to them. But, the question is who?"

"Even more puzzling, is why they were killed."

"I don't know the answers Oz. I wish I did," responded Dylan. He reached into his jacket and retrieved the papers Carol had given to him. "The good news. My contact in Yorkshire managed to access the RAF records and found what we think is our submarine."

"You're kidding, exclaimed Ozzy.

"Nope. We cross-referenced all the submarines. We checked all those that the Allies sunk the day before and the day after the date on the papers. We came up with only three possible winners."

Dylan pulled some papers from his packet. "Only one scored on every count. It was in the projected search area on the exact date, and it did not have any known identity."

Ozzy looked at his friend, "How do we find our exactly where it is?"

"She managed to get the exact Latitude and Longitude of the sinking from the RAF war records. Best part is that the depth of the sea at that location is only 122 meters," said Dylan.

"That depth is definitely within reach. It should make the sub easy to explore," offered Ozzy. "That is, of course, if the U-Boat is actually there, taking into consideration, the accuracy of a position that was taken during the heat of battle. They could easily be off a mile or forty."

"There's only one way to find out. We go there and make an exploratory dive."

Ozzy pulled a file from his attaché case and handed it to Dylan. "The crew and equipment is on standby. They can be operational within forty-eight hours. All it takes is money." Ozzy's face took on a serious expression as he looked at his friend. "One thing you should know, there are no guarantees. Even if we find the missing submarine, we might not be able to recover anything of importance from the wreck."

"I know. But finding it will at least prove it existed and give us reason to continue the search for the real answer to whether or not the German's did remove the gold from the Priam Treasure before the Russians took Berlin."

"Sean. There are no guarantees. You could come up empty."

"Yeah, I thought of that, but then again, the stories of the gold might be true. I get back to Vancouver tonight and will get together with Jim Clark to see how far he wants us to go with this."

"What's the chance that he will want to go forward?"

"I would say they are very good, but, as you said, there are no guarantees. I will speak with him and call you as soon as I have an answer."

"You know we don't have a lot of time left this year," stated Ozzy. The North Sea starts to kick up in late September. If we start too late, we might have to bring the search to a halt and wait until next May before we could get back at it."

"As soon as Jim gives the word, we will head out to the coordinates and start a grid search. With any luck, we should be able to pick up the wreck within a few days."

The petite hostess who greeted Dylan when he entered the Airline lounge approached with a card.

"Your flight has boarded and is waiting for you, Mr. Dylan. I forgot to let you know earlier," she said apologetically. "I'm afraid you have to leave immediately." She turned away and then paused. "Have a pleasant flight."

"Thank You." He turned to Ozzy who was watching the girl as she walked away. "One more thing I would like you to do for me," he said, zipping up his carry-on bag.

"Sure, if it involves her." he replied with a wide smile. "Only kidding. What can I do?"

"I have run out of time on this trip. Could you go to this address and first, make sure that Horst Schneider is okay. Secondly, tell him that we may have located the missing U-1220, and that he was right about some people wanting the information to remain hidden. He'll understand the message." Dylan paused for a moment. "Tell him I need to know the layout of the radio room onboard the submarine. Anything he could tell me would be helpful."

"You think the old man will remember anything?" asked Ozzy. "It's been over sixty years!"

"Oh, he'll remember alright," replied Dylan. There was a look of concern on his face, "And tell him to be very careful."

"Sure. No problem. I'll call you right after I've seen him."

"Thanks, Oz. I've got to run."

Dylan gave his friend a big bear hug, grabbed his carry-on bag and left the lounge. He paused at the elevator, called to Ozzy and with a large grin, "Have a glass of wine on the house. You never know, she might come back up."

He could hear Ozzy laughing after the elevator doors closed.

VANCOUVER   1405 PDT

Bob Emerson's office was located on the twenty-second floor of the Toronto Dominion tower.

Ronnie exited the elevator and made her way through the large glass double doors into the plush reception area of Emerson and Lane, Attorneys At Law.

"Hello Elle. I'm here to see Bob Emerson."

The receptionist pushed a button and advised Emerson that she had arrived.

"You can go right in, Miss Patterson."

Bob Emerson met her as she made her way down towards his office. They were a study in contrast. Emerson was in his mid forties, slightly overweight and a good six inches shorter than Ronnie. By all accounts, he was very happily married to the daughter of his partner in the law firm. They had twin sons who were just entering university and he stood in line to inherit the business from his father in law. His family was his life, but he still considered himself a bit of a ladies' man, a well-known fact that amongst the legal secretaries in the firm. Emerson admired his client's secretary, but he never had enough nerve to approach her. The thought of being caught cheating, and losing control of his father in law's firm kept him in check.

"Good to see you again."

"Nice to see you too, Bob."

Emerson ushered her into his office and closed the door.

"Did you find Jim?" Ronnie asked anxiously.

"No. Not yet. I called all the numbers I have, but no luck."

"It just doesn't make sense."

"I know, but Jim has a lot on the go. I am sure he's okay."

"But, he hasn't called for four days and you know it's not like him to take off without letting someone know."

"Yeah, I spoke to him last week about the Walton merger, but he didn't say anything about any travel plans."

"I think we should report this to the police," Ronnie said in a nervous voice. "Something is wrong."

"Slow down," Emerson cautioned. "We don't need any bad publicity. Even the perception of something wrong with Jim would have a negative impact on many of his clients. Give him until the end of the week. If he hasn't called in by then, we'll call in the reinforcements."

"Okay, but I don't really like waiting that long."

"I understand," said Emerson, picking up some papers and handing them to Ronnie. "Here are the documents for Jim's signature. Get them back to me next week."

"Sure, provided Jim gets back in time."

"He will," he replied assuredly. "What else is going on? Have you heard from Sean?"

Ronnie welcomed the change of subject. "Yes, He was followed by some Germans who apparently knew about the cylinder, and they are very serious about getting it and the papers."

Emerson appeared a little uncomfortable. He shifted in his chair, regaining his composure.

"Are we any closer to knowing the value of its contents?" asked Emerson.

"Sean called. He's made progress, but he didn't elaborate."

"Where are the papers Sean found in the cylinder?"

Ronnie looked surprised. "I don't know. Sean has them, I suppose."

"Are they at his cottage?"

"I don't know. I suppose he has the originals there somewhere. Why do you want to know?"

"Jim has approved a lot of expenses for Sean. I think that we should be keeping close tabs on what Jim is getting for his money. We do not want some cowboy out there running up bills unless we know what is going on. It's strictly good business practice."

Ronnie gave Emerson a questioning look. "Are you saying you don't trust Sean?"

"No," Emerson protested. "I just want to protect my client's investments, Ronnie. You know, due diligence and all that stuff."

Ronnie nodded to indicate she understood. Inwardly, she was surprised at Emerson's desire to know so many details about Dylan's activities. She stood up to leave. "I have to be going. I want to be in the office in case Jim calls."

"I understand. Look, Ronnie, you've been under a lot of pressure lately. Why don't you let me take you out for dinner tonight? I could pick you up around eight. Hopefully we will have heard from Jim by then."

"Thanks Bob, but I'm too worried about Jim to even think about dinner, and Sean is coming back into town tomorrow."

"Sure, I understand," replied Emerson, the disappointment emanating from each word.

Ronnie turned towards the door.

"Thanks for the time."

"Right. And remember to keep me up to date on Sean's whereabouts and any progress he makes on Jim's venture."

Ronnie exited the lawyer's office, her mind racing between thoughts about her missing boss and Emerson's strange request for information about Dylan's activities.

VANCOUVER   1745 PDT

Although flying in Business Class did have its advantages, Dylan's flight was as enjoyable as a ten-hour flight could be for someone cooped up in a metal tube flying at five hundred and forty miles an hour.

While his flight arrived a surprisingly fifteen minutes early at Vancouver International, the wait to get through customs was much longer than usual and it was almost six-thirty before he was able to collect his luggage, clear customs and make his way to the long term parking area to retrieve his vehicle.

The drive from the airport to Clark's office was slow and tedious as the evening rush hour continued to tie up traffic. As he approached the building, he noticed all the available parking spots were full. He saw a number of possible parking areas but each was clearly marked with a copious number of 'No Parking' signs. He pulled up in front of the building and parked. *"Never can find a parking spot when you need one,"* he grumbled to himself.

Dylan exited the Land Rover and made his way up the steps of the building. As he entered the building through the revolving doors, he caught a glimpse of a car in the reflection of the glass. He stayed inside the revolving door, continuing completely around and back out onto the street.

He was sure it was the same grey Chevy. Someone was watching the building. Dylan moved slowly towards the vehicle, searching his mind, trying to recall the license number. *"068 Killing Time Slowly. 068KTS."* He was about forty feet from the car when it suddenly pulled out of the parking spot and moved down the street, quickly disappearing in the busy rush hour traffic.

Dylan reentered the building and made his way to the express elevators that went exclusively from the sixteenth to the thirty-fifth floors.

Entering the elevator, he pressed the button to reach the offices of J. T. Walker & Company on thirty-third floor, followed by the 'Close Door' button. *"Nothing moves slower than an elevator when you are in a hurry,"* Dylan thought to himself.

A well-dressed man was striding towards the open elevator doors. Dylan pressed the 'Close Door' button, but the elevator doors seemed to be on their own agenda, oblivious to his impatient request. He looked up and made eye contact with the executive, in the hope of getting him to stop. The man hesitated for a moment, and then deliberately increased his stride in a determined effort to make it into the elevator. As the doors finally began to close, the man stuck his hand in between, breaking the safety beam, causing them to reopen. The man entered the elevator, a smug look of triumph on his face as the doors closed behind him.

Dylan stepped in front of him before the man could press the button for his floor, "Sorry, I have an emergency. I have to get to the thirty-third floor, now." Dylan's face is only inches from the executive. "You can stop at whatever floor you want on the way down." It was not a request.

For an instant, the executive thought of protesting, but when he saw the intensity in Dylan's eyes, he instinctively knew it would be in his best interests not to argue.

The lift stopped at the thirty-third floor and Dylan exited, leaving the executive standing alone in the elevator and looking somewhat perplexed by the experience. The doors closed as Dylan made his way through the impressive glass entrance into the offices of J. T. Walker & Company.

He waved at the receptionist as he past. "*Strange that she is still here after five,*" he thought.

Dylan continued without speaking, making his way down the hallway towards where Ronnie was pacing back and forth in front of her desk. One look and he knew something was wrong. Her normal warm complexion was ashen and she had been crying. When she spotted Dylan, she started to move towards him and then stopped.

She wanted him to comfort her, to hold her in his arms, but that would not be professional in the office. She slowed her pace to regained control of her emotions.

"Sean, I'm so glad you're here," she said, wiping a tear from her eye. "The firm just received a call about twenty-five minutes ago. Jim is in the hospital."

"What happened?"

"He was in a bad accident. I do not have all the details, but it apparently happened a few days ago when Jim was on his way home. Someone sideswiped the taxi in which he was traveling and it went over the embankment near Lion's Gate and crashed onto the rocks below. The police found the wreckage early this morning. Jim is alive but he is in bad shape. The driver was killed."

"What hospital is he in?"

"Vancouver General," she stated, her voice trembling.

"I'll go over there right now to find out the details. I will call you as soon as I have some news." Dylan turned to leave.

"Sean." Ronnie said, grabbing his arm, "What's going on?"

"I don't know, but I will find out. I'll call you soon." He saw the tears form again in her eyes. "Courage," he said in a gentle voice, "Jim will be fine."

Ronnie seemed to gather strength from Dylan's words and quickly regained her composure. Dylan gave her a reassuring hug, turned and made his way back to the elevators. Ronnie caught up with him as the doors opened.

"Jim signed this last week. I was supposed to give it to you when you got back."

Dylan nodded and took the envelope, putting it in the inside pocket of his jacket as he entered the elevator. "Thanks," he called out as the elevator doors closed.

In less than three minutes, Dylan had exited the building. He scanned the area for any sign of the Chevy, but found nothing. Six minutes later, he arrived at Vancouver General Hospital.

Like all major hospitals in large cities, Vancouver General was always in a constant state of change in its attempt to keep up with all the latest technologies in the medical industry. Compounding the problem was having to adapt to the various restrictions placed on them by the government regulators and various unions in their quest for their share of outrageous dollars paid by through the medical insurances of those unfortunate enough to require treatment.

Dylan parked the Land Rover in the Visitor's parking lot and jogged around to the main entrance.

He approached the Admittance Desk, noticing the plethora of people waiting for Emergency service.

Quietly sitting to one side of the desk was an older man looking, patiently waiting his turn. Dylan could not determine the nature of his problem, but he felt for the man. There were others sitting or standing all around the room. No one seemed to be paying them any attention. The processing system for dealing with these emergency cases, if the hospital indeed had one, didn't seem to be working, at least not today.

Dylan did his best not to interfere with those who were there to get some much-needed help, but this posed a challenge for him, as he desperately wanted to find out about Clark's injuries.

Finally, there was a break in the onslaught of patients streaming into the Emergency area. Dylan stepped up to the window and managed to get the attention of the Admitting Nurse.

"What's wrong with you, today?" she asked, thinking he was another patient.

"No. Not me," he said with a half smile. "I am here to see a friend. Jim Clark. He had an accident and was apparently admitted here early this morning."

The nurse at the Admissions Desk gave Dylan the once over. The sight the man standing in front of her instantly took her from a world of boredom caused by a never-ending stream of patients, into one of enthusiasm. She checked the screen on her computer and looked back up to Dylan.

"Well, I'm glad to see it wasn't you." she said, smiling, "Jim Clark, you say. Are you family?"

"No," he confessed, "But he is a very good friend."
The nurse looked at Dylan and smiled. "We're not supposed to give out information, but for you...," her voice trailed off as she looked up the information. "He is out of surgery and is in ICU, Intensive Care Unit, room four, forty-six. Just go down the hallway, second elevator on your left. Fourth floor, but I am not sure they will let you in the room. You had better check with the nurse's station." She looked up at Dylan and winked. "Tell them you're family."

"Thanks."

"No problem. Drop back if you need any more help."

Dylan waved and made his way to the elevators.

While the Intensive Care Units on the fourth floor of Vancouver General were quiet, almost low key, the attending doctors and nurses were ultra efficient.

Exiting the elevator, Dylan noticed the room signs immediately and made a right at the first hallway, taking him towards Clark's room. The duty nurse looked up but did not question his presence.

He made his way along the corridor to room number four forty-six, pausing briefly before pushing the door open and entering.

He was not ready for the sight that greeted him.

Clark was lying on the only bed in the room. His body attached to a myriad of equipment. Dylan recognized the heart monitor and the intravenous tubes in Clark's arm. There were breathing tubes inserted in his nose. Both legs were in traction and one arm, obviously broken, was attached to a bar above the bed.

My God, thought Dylan, *how did he survive?*

Dylan made his way over to the side of the bed. Clark was clearly in a drug-induced sleep. As he stood there watching, a doctor dressed in surgical hospital greens, came through the door.

Dylan turned.

"Excuse me, who are you?" asked the doctor as he went to the foot of the bed and began reading Clark's charts.

"Sean Dylan. Jim is one of my best friends."

"I'm sorry, but you really shouldn't be in here. He is in very critical condition and we don't need to traumatize him any more than necessary."

The doctor finished checking the charts and replaced them on their holder.

"I know. I will be out in a few minutes. Okay."

"Okay, but make it quick," answered the doctor.

The doctor left the room as Dylan turned to Clark. "Well, good buddy, this is one hell of way to get some rest."

Clark did not respond. Dylan stood for a few minutes looking at the broken and battered body of his friend. He was just about to leave when Clark began to whisper in a strangely garbled, almost incoherently manner. Dylan strained to listen.

"It was no accident," Clark said feebly. "They wanted the papers. Tell Sean, no accident. Get Bob," Clark mumbled, his voice trailing off as he relapsed back into a deep, drug-induced sleep.

"It's okay, friend," said Dylan knowing that Clark could not comprehend. "Get some rest. I'll take care of it."

Dylan left the hospital a few minutes later. On his way out, he gave a business card to the smiling duty nurse, asking her to call with updates on Clark's condition.

The effects of the jetlag were hitting Dylan hard. He made his way back to the Land Rover, flipped open his cell phone, pressed a series of numbers and waited.

"Hello?"

"Jane. It's Sean."

"Well, haven't heard from you for a long while," replied Jane. "What does our Sean want today?"

"Look, I'm sorry I haven't called lately, but I have been busy dealing with some new historical documents."

"So you're not calling to ask me out for a wild weekend of wine, song and whatever, then?"

"Not this time, sweetheart. I need a favour."

"Where have I heard that line before? What is it this time?"

"I need you to check out a plate for me. 068 Kilo, Tango Sierra. It is a gray Chevy, probably around a 1998."

"068 KTS. And what is in it for me?"

"Just be a good girl and get the information. Please."

"What number do I call if I get the information?"

"The number's the same. If I'm not there, leave a message with Helen."

"At least that's one girl I don't have to compete with."

"Love ya, Babe."

Dylan smiled as he flipped the cell phone closed and put it back into its holster. He knew Jane would come through. She and Dylan had been an item eight years before but, at that time, it was obvious that their lives were heading in different directions. Jane wanted to marry and settle down. He was the direct opposite. He was still involved in the Special Forces and could not afford to have any permanent ties. It was an amicable split and they remained friends. After Dylan left the Special Forces, he ran into Jane at a party. She had gotten married to one of the police officers at her precinct, but it had not worked out. She was now divorced, and while she and Dylan had dated a few times, Jane knew there would never be any long-term commitment. However, it was better than not seeing him at all.

As the Rover made its way through the heavy Vancouver traffic, Dylan flipped open his cell phone and spoke. "Jim Clark."

The cell phone voice recognition technology did its work and automatically placed the call.

"Jim Clark's Office, may I help you?"

"Hi, it's Sean."

"How's Jim?" she asked nervously.

"He's sedated right now. The accident was quite bad, but he should recover. How are you holding up?"

"Fine. I am just worried about him."

"He'll be fine. You just worry about yourself."

"What are you going to do?"

"I have some calls to make and a few things to check out. I will call you at your place later. OK?"

"Sure. Thanks, Sean."

Dylan headed to the Marriot Pinnacle Hotel on Hastings Street. He would stay there for the night.

34

SEPTEMBER 1, 2007

VANCOUVER 0545 PDT

A restless Dylan lay wide-awake in the king-sized bed. His internal clock was out of rhythm with the local time and there was no way he would find sleep this night. He rolled out of the bed and headed for the shower. The warm water had a positive effect, leaving him feeling refreshed. Despite not being completely over the effects of jetlag, he was anxious to get started on the day's activities.

It was nearly seven in the morning when Dylan flipped his cell phone open and spoke. "Helen."

The cell phone automatically completed the call.

"Dylan Residence," answered the computerized voice of the security system.

"Hello, Helen, it's me. Any calls?"

"Hello Boss. Do you wish me to play the messages?"

"Yes please, and then save them in the archive."

Dylan put the cell on speakerphone as Helen dutifully played back three messages. The first was from the Professor Kingsmill. He grabbed a pen and began writing notes.

"Sean, Please call soon regarding your project."

The second was from Detective Inspector Snow of Scotland Yard. Dylan listened intently to a most interesting message.

"Sean, I have some information on the individual who was

near the rental car at the time of the explosion. The person was well known to the local constabulary. He had been involved in a number of unpleasant events. The explosion had a definite signature that matched this man's known handiwork. We think he was planting the device when it went off. There is not much else to go on. Give me a call at your convenience if you wish to know more details. 011-44-140 719 4255." The Inspector paused for a moment. "*Oh, by the way, we came up empty on that black Mercedes that unfortunately left the road near Compton.*"

Dylan smiled to himself, "*Unfortunately be damned. That maneuver saved my ass.*"

The fact that Detective Inspector Snow had identified the person who was attempting to install a bomb in the Ford Zetec intrigued Dylan. He wondered if the Inspector would be able to connect the would-be bomber to those in the black Mercedes. He would wait for a few days before contacting Snow.

The third call was from Ozzy.

"Hi, Sean. Just want to let you know the deal with the salvage firm is complete and they are waiting for instructions. We pay them on a percentage basis against a small guarantee, or straight up. It is your choice. Let me know soon if you want to proceed. In addition, I also found some information on the Neo-Nazi Party. They have an underground faction that appears to be quite active these days. Not sure as to what they are up to, but they are making a lot of noise. I have some names for you and an address for their main headquarters. Oh, about that girl, Bridgette. She apparently does work at the shipping company. I could not get inside their records, but a couple of co-workers told me she's some sort of computer whiz. There is not much available on her personal life though, although I wouldn't mind trying again. She is quite the *good-looking lady."* Ozzy paused for a second as if waiting for Dylan to confirm the fact, and then continued. *"Oh, I managed to stop in to see Mr. Schneider. I passed on your message. He is a delightful old man. Very interested in what you were up to. Asked me to tell you, 'Best of Luck'. That's all for now. Give me a call when you can."*

When the messages had finished playing, Dylan flipped the cell phone shut. *"So, Ozzy has the salvage company organized. Good."* thought Dylan.

Then he thought about Ozzy's reference to Bridgette and smiled to himself. *"Yes, she is quite the good looking lady."*

Dylan decided to call the Professor. The scholarly old woman was just finishing breakfast and asked Dylan to meet her at ten o'clock. Realizing the time, and acknowledging that he had not seen a decent meal for over twelve hours, he quickly agreed and then set out to find a good restaurant to satisfy his cravings.

BERLIN   **1810 GMT**

The mood of the people at the underground Neo-Nazi Democratic Party headquarters was anything but congenial as Hans Lüdden was engaged in a marathon chastisement of the members of his inner circle.

"Müller you are the head of our security section, yet you have been unable to recover the documents from this seemingly indestructible Canadian, Dylan. The inability of your contacts to perform has compromised our situation."

"Herr Lüdden, I know this Canadian has given us trouble, but we have been successful with all of our other initiatives," protested Müller. "We have eliminated most of the others who had direct knowledge of the cylinder and its contents. We took care of Saris and virtually eliminated the man who found the cylinder. Clark is in the hospital and not expected to live through the day. Our man has gone to Clark's home to search for the papers."

"Your men have not been successful to date and now too many people have had contact with Dylan. Apparently, the FBI and SGI have also expressed an interest in the papers. It is impossible now to eliminate everyone. Don't you agree Otto?"

Otto von Schlippenbach, Lüdden's deputy and second in command looked first towards Müller and then at Lüdden.

"Yes. The actions of Herr Müller have indeed jeopardized our mission."

"The lack of leadership has put our entire party at risk. Hitler would have shot someone for such incompetence. What do you think we should do about this, Otto?" asked Lüdden.

Karl-Heinz Müller's eyes widened as Lüdden spoke.

"It would be an appropriate action, in light of his failures," von Schlippenbach acknowledged with a look of disdain. He moved around and positioned himself behind Müller.

Müller now found himself in a very uncomfortable and vulnerable position between his two superiors. Lüdden was facing him, with von Schlippenbach directly behind with his right hand resting firmly on his vintage P.08 German Luger.

Müller began to stammer. "Herr Lüdden, I have always followed orders. I have always done the best I could."

"Your best does not seem to be good enough," spat von Schlippenbach, "You should have done better."

Müller pleaded to his leader, "But Herr Lüdden, we have managed to secure a reliable contact and have wiretaps on Clark's office and even though Otto failed in his attempt to kill Dylan, we now know of Dylan's movements and will soon recover all the papers. It is only a matter of time."

Lüdden looked past Müller to von Schlippenbach. He saw his second in command's hand resting on the vintage Luger and reached out his hand. "Pass that to me, Otto," he said in a cold and insensitive voice. "It is my duty."

Müller watched as von Schlippenbach stepped past him and handed the deadly Luger pistol to Lüdden. Von Schlippenbach snapped his heels and spun around, taking his place to the right of Lüdden, a look of supremacy etched on his face.

"People in charge should be able to do better," said Lüdden, raising the pistol to eye level, "They should not think they are invincible. Above all, they should not have disappointed me."

Lüdden was pointing the Luger towards Müller, who froze like a deer caught in the headlights. The blood drained from his face. He was turning white with fear.

In a lightning fast move, Lüdden spun to his right and fired a single shot from the Luger. The 7.65mm shell separated from its casing the instant the firing pin hit. The bullet exited the muzzle of the Luger at 985 feet per second, hitting its target in less than 1/1000 of a second, causing a small, but distinct entry hole in the centre of von Schlippenbach's forehead. The exit wound was much larger as the small-nosed bullet tore through his former second in command's brain and exploded from the rear of his skull, spreading bone and gray matter across the room.

Müller was shocked. He stood there, unable to move, not believing what had just happened.

Lüdden turned back to Müller and handed him the Luger.

"You did as your superior directed. It was his responsibility to ensure you carried out your orders properly. Arrange for someone to clean up this mess and see me in my office in one hour. We must retrieve those papers." He motioned to von Schlippenbach's lifeless body. "I will not tolerate failure," warned Lüdden. "Do not end up like our dear departed friend, Otto."

Lüdden turned and exited the room, closing the door as he went. Müller sank to his knees, oblivious to the damp sensation between his legs.

VANCOUVER   **1000 PDT**

Dylan had enjoyed the best breakfast he had in years at Slickety Jim's on Main Street. The restaurant was well known for its exceptionally good food, and he was now feeling recharged in both body and mind. When he arrived at Professor Kingsmill's home at exactly ten o'clock, he was ready for action.

The Professor's housekeeper answered the door and showed Dylan into the Library. The old Professor entered the room with a great flourish, her oversized black Labrador dog close behind. Trudy Kingsmill was always glad to see Dylan. She had developed a great fondness for him over the years. Maggie, the Labrador, had apparently developed a great fondness for food over the same period.

"So, my young friend, what progress have you made on your quest to find the meaning of life?"

"Well, Professor, the game has become quite serious. There are a lot more players involved now then I would have believed possible."

"You are playing with some serious people, Sean. You will have to be very careful."

"I know Professor. I am sorry that I ever got you mixed up in this at all. I never imagined that the contents of the cylinder could command such international interest."

"Oh, nonsense, my boy, I am only too happy to be doing anything at my advanced age. Besides, there is a mystery incorporated in all this and I would like to be a part of the solution."

"No offence, Professor, but please don't do anything silly."

"No offence taken."

Dylan detailed his meeting with Schneider and related the old man's comments about the submarine and the Priam gold.

"The gold that was taken from the Great Priam Treasure," reflected Professor Kingsmill. "Now that would be a find. Of course, without the setting numbers required to decode the Enigma message, you are going to have a devil of a time finding its location."

"Let's take one crisis at a time, Professor," laughed Dylan. "The depth where the wreck is located is well within today's technology," he explained. "I think we have a good chance to locate the submarine using side sonar scanning equipment. With luck, we will be able to retrieve the original Enigma machine, and maybe some of the actual Priam gold."

"If the treasure is indeed on board," replied the professor.

"It is a bit of a gamble," Dylan acknowledged as he got up to leave, "but given what I know about the submarine involved, and judging by all the interest that has been generated by other parties, I think the risk will prove to be well worth the cost."

The Professor looked at her former pupil and paraphrased an old Chinese proverb, "We are living in interesting times, my boy. Take care you don't fall in with the wrong people."

Dylan smiled in agreement. "I will. Take care of yourself too, Professor. I don't want to lose my research team."

The Professor gave a hearty laugh as she got up to

accompany him to the door.

"Don't worry, my friend. I am not quite an invalid yet, and I do have old Maggie here. Mark my words; she may be a tad overweight, but she would give them a tussle for their efforts."

Dylan bid the Professor goodbye. As he drove back to the city, his cell phone began to play its unique ring tone.

"Sean Dylan." he answered six seconds into the music. It was Jane.

"Okay, you big lug, I have the information on that plate number."

"You're a darling. What's the scoop?" he replied.

"Not so fast, mister," she shot back. "What do I get in return? Remember, you still owe me a dinner from the last time."

"Okay, okay. We'll do a special dinner, as soon as I finish up with this project."

"You had better come through, Sean Dylan, or I will personally see that someone fixes your little Irish wagon real good," said Jane, trying her best to sound tough. "No dinner, no favours. That's the deal, Mister." She paused and then started to laugh. Dylan laughed with her as she continued. "The car is registered to a James Bell, 3201 West 16th Avenue in Vancouver. Hope that helps."

"It does. And thanks."

"You can thank me when we go out for dinner after you wrap up whatever it is that has got your attention for the moment."

"You've got a deal, Babe," replied Dylan.

"And don't call me Babe!" Jane stammered.

Dylan flipped his cell phone closed and headed back to the hotel a little after noon. It already seemed like a long day and he felt exhausted. He would get some sleep and then visit Clark at the hospital.

35

SEPTEMBER 2, 2007

BERLIN 0930 GMT

Müller met Lüdden in his office at the appointed time. He was wearing a new pair of pants.

"You will ensure that no one traces any information of either of von Schlippenbach's botched ambush of Dylan or that ridiculous car bombing in Yorkshire, can ever be tied to us." stated Lüdden, "We must not be found to be associated with any of that business." "

"Of course, Herr Lüdden," answered a nervous Müller.

"And you are still confident we have enough to keep your Canadian contact indebted to us?"

"Very sure," replied Müller placing an envelope on Lüdden's desk. "The man is very much a family man, but with expensive tastes that outweigh the benefits of his position. I am sure he would not want these photographs shown to his wife or his superiors."

"Very good, Müller. Very good indeed," said Lüdden as he continued to scan the photos.

VANCOUVER 0245 PDT

Dylan had slept on and off over the past fourteen hours. He usually enjoyed staying at the Marriot Pinnacle Hotel, but the lingering effects of jetlag and the thought of his friend lying in the hospital played on his mind. He got up, made a cup of tea and sat down to contemplate his next move. He decided to visit the hospital.

Visiting hours were long over and the nurses had completed their nightly rounds. A tall man dressed in scrubs, entered Clark's darkened room. Glancing at the chart hanging on the end of the bed, he reached into his pocket and extracted a syringe with a two-inch hypodermic needle attached. After a quick glance towards the door, he moved closer to the top of the bed. He looked at the sleeping form of Jim Clark. "You won't feel a thing, friend," he said in a matter-of-fact tone. The man inserted the needle into the intravenous bag that hung beside Clark's head. He pushed the plunger down, injecting the contents of the syringe into the bag.

Dylan walked through the door as the plunger hit bottom. The 'doctor' turned and was startled to see him standing in the doorway. Shielding the intravenous bag from Dylan's view, the man removed the syringe and dropped it to the floor. He turned and faced the door. "What are you doing in here at this time of night?" the man demanded in a stern voice.

Dylan thought he noticed a slight trace of an accent in the doctor's voice, but dismissed it just as quickly. "Just checking on my friend."

The 'doctor' turned and moved towards the door, while continuing to admonish Dylan for being in the room. "You shouldn't be in here at this time of night.

"I couldn't sleep. He is a very good friend."

"He's doing fine. He should be out of the coma tomorrow," stated the doctor, as he moved towards the hallway. "Don't stay too long. I'll be back to check on him in a few minutes."

Dylan was mulling over the doctor's comment. *"He should be out of the coma tomorrow."* The remark did not make any sense.

Clark was on medication, but he was not in a coma. Before he could question the doctor about his statement, the man had disappeared. Dylan's mind bolted into high speed. He had noticed the green hospital smock, but he also observed the unusual combination of dark suit pants and the heavy street shoes showing from beneath the gown. The strange mix of attire did not fit someone who was supposedly working a long night shift in a hospital extensive care unit. Dylan checked the hallway. The doctor was gone.

"He must have gone into one of the other patients' rooms," thought Dylan. He paused for a moment. *"I think I must be starting to get a little paranoid."*

Dylan turned back into the room and returned to Clark's bedside. His suspicions were confirmed the instant he spotted the hypodermic needle laying on the floor under one of the wheels of the intravenous stand. He quickly checked both of Clark's arms. There were no marks. He checked the feeding tube, but found nothing was amiss. Dylan followed the tube back to the source. He noticed a small drop of fluid on outside of the intravenous bag. In one lightning fast motion, Dylan spun around and tore the connecting tube from Clark's arm as he pushed the unit away from the bed. The intravenous assembly rolled off to the far side of the room and crashed into the wall.

Dylan reached back to the side of the bed for the emergency call button to alert the nurse's station. He ripped the cord from its position on Clark's pillow, repeatedly pushing button as he moved towards the window in an effort to scan the parking area below. The overhead moon gave enough light for Dylan to see the same gray Chevy stopping next to the parking entrance. It paused only long enough to pick up the 'doctor' then disappeared down the hospital exit road.

The night duty nurse arrived and spotted the intravenous unit on the other side of the room.

"Somebody was in here and injected something into the intravenous bag," Dylan explained. "He dropped the hypodermic needle on the floor." There was a marked change in the tempo of Clark's breathing. It had become a series of short erratic bursts.

The nurse spotted the needle where the intravenous unit had been. "Stay here, I will be back in a moment."

Dylan guarded over his friend and waited. It was only minutes before the nurse returned with a new system. She hooked Clark up as Dylan carefully retrieved the tainted intravenous unit for the police. He had no way of knowing what the 'doctor' had injected into the fluid, but he knew he had just saved Clark's life. Within minutes, his friend appeared to be breathing normally once again.

"It appears that not enough of whatever the person injected into the intravenous bag reached his blood system to do him any irreparable harm," said the nurse with audible relief. She looked at Dylan. "You realize that I do have to report this to the authorities."

"I understand," Dylan replied. "Please do."

The nurse left to place a call to the Police while Dylan remained at Clark's bedside.

"I think it would be better if I am here when the police arrive," she said nervously. "I know you didn't do anything, but they might not understand."

"No problem. I'm just thankful Jim is going to be okay."

The two sat by Clark's bed. Almost an hour passed and there was still no sign of the police.

Clark's eyes began to blink. Dylan was ecstatic as his friend opened his eyes and tried to speak.

"What's going on, Sean?" he asked in a tentative voice.

"You've had a bad accident. You're banged up pretty good."

"It was no accident," said Clark, picking his words slowly. "They held me hostage. They wanted the papers."

"Who?" Dylan asked.

"I saw their faces, but have no idea who they are. We had received some weird phone calls. Kept asking about the papers. We must really have hit on something worthwhile in that cylinder."

"I think so too, but I'm not exactly sure what. I did manage to get a lot of information while I was in Europe. Too much to talk about now, but you have to decide if you still want to pursue this thing. Aside from the danger, it is going to be expensive."

Jim Clark was trying to hang on but the drugs were slowly easing him back into a controlled sleep.

"Go to the wall on this one Sean. Find out who did this, and why. I signed the first advance. Contact Bob Emerson if you need more. I instructed him to advance whatever you need. Ronnie has a copy of the directive in case…." Clark's voice trailed off without finishing the sentence. He had succumbed to the effects of the drugs and dropped back into a deep sleep as two police officers entered the hospital room, followed by a slightly overweight Detective. The police officers stood guard; one by Clark's bed and the other at the doorway.

Detective Ian McCarthy was a fixture with the Vancouver Police Department. He had a habit of pushing too hard and usually got himself reprimanded by the Captain for being over zealous in his pursuit of the facts.

McCarthy was polite at the start. He grabbed a chair, sat down and asked Dylan to explain exactly what had transpired. Dylan cooperated without hesitation, giving all the details of event, using the hospital nurse to confirm the various facts. When he was done,

McCarthy got up from the chair and stood in front of Dylan.

"I think you had better come down to the station so we can write up the details."

Dylan was ambivalent about accompanying McCarthy. It was still very early in the morning and he had nowhere to go. "As you wish, Detective," he said wearily.

It was Sunday morning and the police station in Vancouver was hosting its usual eclectic mix of Saturday night arrests.

McCarthy looked at the bizarre collection of hookers, drunks, druggies and robbery suspects that filled the station's holding area. "Jeez, same old shit again this weekend."

Dylan scanned the booking area. *This looks like a scene out of a Star Wars movie,"* he mused.

A tall, bleached blonde with long legs and micro-mini skirt noticed Dylan following McCarthy through the booking area. She let out a loud whistle and yelled, "Hey, McCarthy. Who's your friend?"

"Relax, Vicki," piped in McCarthy, "He's not interested and definitely not your type."

The hooker smiled, "You get me outta here and I bet I could make him interested."

"If you stopped hustling, you wouldn't be in here in the first place," replied the Detective.

The Night Desk Sergeant looked up from the mountain of paperwork and spotted the Detective. "Yo, McCarthy. All the interview rooms are in use. The Captain said it would be okay to use his office."

"Right," replied McCarthy picking his way through the sea of misguided humanity like a fullback blocking on a touchdown run. He pushed his way between a drug addict and a hooker.

"Watch where you're going, you stupid cop," yelled the addict.

McCarthy looked at the thin man. He decided not to react to the comment. "This is worse than a WalMart store at Christmas," he mumbled as he continued towards the stairway, Dylan following the Detective's lead.

The Captain's office was on the third floor. McCarthy lumbered up the stairs with Dylan close behind.

McCarthy enjoyed having an opportunity to use the Captain's office.

The detective slid a box of files off a wooden chair, bouncing it onto the floor. He motioned for Dylan to sit. "So, you just happened to be in Clark's hospital room? That right?" asked McCarthy as he set about busily making himself comfortable behind the Captain's desk.

"Look, McCarthy, we have gone over this a dozen times. Jim Clark is one of my best friends. I was there to see him earlier in the afternoon. He was in a lot of pain. I couldn't sleep, so I just dropped by to check on his condition."

"And what were you doing with the hypodermic? Playing darts?"

"I told you. There was a doctor, or someone who looked like a doctor, in the room when I got there. He left when I arrived. I thought it was strange and went looking for him. He had disappeared. When I got back to Jim's bed, I spotted the needle on the floor and hit the panic button. You know the rest."

Another Detective entered the room, leaned over the desk and handed the Detective a sheet of paper. "His story checks out." he whispered, "The day nurse confirmed he was there yesterday afternoon. He's clean, no record of any kind."

Dylan watched McCarthy's face as the detective read the report. There was no emotion.

"Well, Mr. Dylan," droned McCarthy, "It seems your story checks out. You are free to go. However, don't go too far. We might need you to identify your doctor impersonator for us."

"Do you have him?" asked a sleepy Dylan. "

"No, not yet, but we do have a lead. We got a partial print from the plunger of the hypodermic." McCarthy laughed, "Some of these idiots are so stupid."

"But you know who he is?"

"Not yet, but we will soon. There is only a skeleton staff in on Sunday. Probably take an hour of so to run the prints."

"Would you let me know when you find out?"

"Sorry, we don't divulge that information to the public. Nonetheless, when we do find out, it will not be very long before we nab him." McCarthy had tired of the conversation. He flicked his head towards the door. "You're done here. Take off."

Dylan looked at the detective and shook his head. He was about to comment about his methods, but thought better of it and simply turned to leave.

As he reached the door, Dylan turned back and faced the detective. "You realize if they find out they failed, they will be back to finish the job," he warned.

"What are you talking about?" McCarthy replied harshly.

"That hit was done by a professional. You need to put a guard at the entrance to his hospital room."

"He's got a good point, McCarthy." It was the Captain Riley. Riley entered the office and walked around behind his desk. He motioned for McCarthy to remove himself from the chair as he approached. "Maybe we should post a guard."

Dylan looked at the Captain. He knew Riley understood the situation far better than McCarthy. He decided to push the envelope. "Better still, why don't you get the hospital to release the news that Clark died. If whoever did this thinks they did get to him," Dylan continued, "it would negate any second attempt."

The Captain looked at Dylan and smiled. "You're pretty sharp. That would keep them off guard until we can locate and pick up the Perp." Riley glanced over at his Detective. "Get on it McCarthy."

McCarthy looked at Dylan and then at his Captain. "Geez. I'm never going to get out of here."

BERLIN   **1758 GMT**

Müller entered the office of the leader of the underground Neo-Nazi Democratic Party.

"I have a communiqué from our contact in Canada. He confirms the Clark individual is dead. Our contact went to the hospital and made sure that the job was complete."

"Very good, Müller, very good indeed. Your man is extremely efficient.",", acknowledged Lüdden. "Now that Clark is dead, we must concentrate on recovering the papers."

The leader of Germany's Neo-Nazi Party picked up a plastic enclosed paper from the desk. Lüdden looked at the faded paper. Its message was in a code similar to Dylan's papers.

He gave a sinister smile and looked up at Müller. "Find whoever has the papers and persuade them to surrender the documents." Lüdden paused for a moment, "And then kill them," he said coldly, "including Mr. Dylan."

"Yes, Herr Lüdden."

VANCOUVER   **0720 PDT**

Two and a half hours had lapsed since Dylan left the hospital and went to the police station. He was upset at the detectives for wasting his time. The fact he had to take a cab back to retrieve the Land Rover pissed him off even more. When he arrived at the hospital, he thought about going up to see Clark again, but then remembered that Clark was technically, supposed to be dead. He decided to call the nurse's station instead and get a quick update from the night duty nurse.

The nurse recognized Dylan's voice. "They have put a police guard on his room," she reported. "And we have already released the story that he died in his sleep. It will be all over the morning news."

Dylan was pleased that the police Captain had decided to act on his suggestion. Clark would now be able to recover without fear of another attack.

"Do you know what the guy put into the IV bag?" he asked.

"I'm not supposed to tell anyone, but it was Morphine," the nurse replied. "It would have killed him if you hadn't come along at that exact moment."

"It's the Luck of the Irish," commented Dylan.

"I'm sure Mr. Clark will be thanking you, once he finds out."

"Do me a favour, Love. Do not tell him. He has enough on this mind. He doesn't need any more things to worry about. Let's just get him better."

Dylan thanked the nurse and hung up.

He started the Land Rover and headed downtown. As he drove, he picked up his cell phone, flipped it open and spoke. The cell phone did its magic, quickly making the connection to Ronnie's private number.

She was crying when she answered the telephone. "Bob Emerson just called. Jim is dead. He passed away during the night," she bawled uncontrollably.

Dylan could hear the anguish and pain in her voice. He paused for a second to assess the situation. He could not let her go through the suffering that went with the loss of someone so close.

"Ronnie, listen carefully and do not mention this to anyone," he said calmly. "Jim is still alive. He's going to be okay." Dylan thought he could hear her mouth drop. She immediately became silent. "Jim told me it was not an accident. He was held captive," continued Dylan. "We had to put out a story about his dying to stop people from finishing the job. There is a twenty four hour police guard on him until they can move him to a safe house."

The revelation that Clark was alive stunned Ronnie. "Are you serious?" she asked incredulously as she recovered from the shock.

"Yes, but you must keep this to yourself. Under no circumstance do you tell anyone about Jim. If they find out he is alive, they will come back to finish the job. Do you understand?"

"No. Not really, but okay," she replied with audible relief.

Dylan did not like giving out so much information. He knew that sharing sensitive information could put people in jeopardy, but the complexity of this whole issue dictated a different set of rules. Dylan thought for a moment and decided to change the subject. He asked, "Do you have a key to Jim's home?"

"No. Why would I have a key to his house? Why do you ask?"

"I would like to take a quick look around. If they held him there, I might be able to find some clues as to who they were and what they were after."

"I'm sure Jim wouldn't mind your looking, but don't you think you should go to the police"

"Let's just say I've been there."

Ronnie paused for a moment. "I think Jim has a spare set of keys in his office. Drop by and I'll have them ready for you."

"Thanks, Ronnie. By the way, Jim said you have a copy of a directive regarding the project. Get a copy for me, Okay?"

"Sure. I'll have it ready with the key."

"See you at the office in an hour."

BERLIN   **1940 GMT**

Lüdden and Müller listened intently to the voice on the speakerphone. "The morning news has confirmed the death of Jim Clark."

"Very good," Lüdden stated without a hint of emotion. "What about the papers?"

"I have not retrieved them as yet. I am checking and will let you know," the voice on the telephone intoned.

"Very good," repeated Lüdden..

"You are sure the death of Clark will stop the flow of funds to Dylan and that he will not receive any more money for his search," questioned Müller.

"The funding will stop with Clark's death," said the voice. There was an awkward silence before the voice spoke again. "But that has nothing to do with our deal. I arranged to take Clark out and provide you with information on the papers. Clark is dead and I have provided you with the information on the papers. It is time to pay your bill. When will I receive the rest of the money and the pictures?"

"You will receive the balance of your fee when we have recovered the papers," Lüdden answered bluntly, "and not before. Is there anything else?"

The voice was silent.

"Call us when you have confirmed the whereabouts of the papers," Lüdden said pushing the button to end the call.

The leader of the underground Neo-Nazi Democratic Party turned to Müller. "Watch this one. He is a very dangerous person. If he would betray his friends, he would not think twice about doing the same to us."

VANCOUVER   **1045 PDT**

Clark's home was located in a very high priced residential area in West Vancouver known as the British Properties. Originally owned by the Guinness family, Clark bought the property on the day it became available. It was his personal tribute to his Irish background.

It only took Dylan twenty minutes to reach the house. He parked the Land Rover in the driveway and made his way to the front door. He was about to insert the key in the lock but noticed the door was slightly ajar. A quick scan of the jamb revealed the telltale signs of a forced entry.

Dylan reached for his .38 revolver and pushed the door wide open, and slowly entered the house. He made his way from the hallway into each of the rooms of the house. Whoever had broken in was long gone. He scanned the rooms, realizing quickly that whoever had been there had done a thorough job of trashing the place. All drawers were open and their contents tossed everywhere. Each room looked as if a tornado had hit.

These people were bad news, serious bad news. Dylan knew the events of the past few days and the papers he took from the cylinder were connected. He also knew that Clark only had a few of the papers. He suddenly thought about Ronnie. *"If they didn't find what they were looking for here, they would probably go to Clark's office. Ronnie would be there early today, alone."*

Dylan secured the .38 in the shoulder holster inside his jacket and left the house, pulling the door shut behind him.

Dylan flipped open the cell phone and spoke Ronnie's name. She answered in a matter of seconds.

"Ronnie, this is Sean. I want you out of the building. Now!"

"But, why?"

"Don't ask questions. Just grab your purse and head down the elevator and out of the building."

"What's happened?"

"Someone trashed Jim's house. I am sure they did not find what they were looking for and will most probably be paying the office a visit. I don't want you to be there."

"Should I go to my place?"

"No. I'll pick you up across the street at Antonio's,"

"Should I call Security?"

"No. Do not waste time. Just get out of there."

Dylan flipped the phone shut as he merged into the final lane leading up over the Lion's Gate.

He picked up Ronnie eight minutes later and immediately headed west, out of the city. The different events and permutations were coursing through his mind as fast as he was negotiating the streets of Vancouver. He had a number of things to take care of, but his prime concern was Ronnie. He wanted to get her to a safe house until everything was back to normal.

"What are we going to do?" she asked hesitantly.

"I have arranged for my neighbour, Ray Tilley, to pick you up on the other side and take you to the cottage." He handed her a key. "Helen will remember you. When you get there, make yourself at home and wait for my call. Helen will look after locking the doors and setting security."

"Why do I have to go there?"

"There are some very nasty people who are after the papers we recovered from the cylinder. I don't want them coming around to visit you at the office, so it is best that you keep out of sight for a bit, until I can figure out who's who in the picture."

"Wouldn't it be better to be in my apartment?"

"No, whoever has been tailing Jim might be watching your place, too. They don't have any idea where I live. You will be safe there."

"You're making it sound like a bad movie. Are you sure you're not going overboard?"

"Look, an old friend of mine in Dublin was killed. I have been followed everywhere and now Jim is in the hospital after being kidnapped and beaten. All because of those damned papers."

Ronnie reacted at Dylan's news, "Somebody was killed?"

"Yes, an old archeologist friend in Ireland. He was the man I sent Jim to see when he found the cylinder."

"My God," exclaimed Ronnie, "Who are these people?"

"I'm not sure. However, I do intend to find out. You have to get going. You have to catch the next ferry."

"Okay," she murmured, still not fully grasping all of what was happening. She started to get up from the chair and remembered. "Bob Emerson told me to put a stop payment on your check."

"Why?"

"I guess he thinks Jim is dead, so why continue."

"Did you call the bank?"

"No. I was waiting to talk to you."

Dylan helped Ronnie up and they made their way back to the car. "Good," he said. "Just forget about it for now. I will deal with Emerson later, if I have to."

The traffic to the ferry terminal was moving well and Dylan made it with time to spare. He pulled up at the passenger drop off point and let Ronnie out of the Rover. Dylan leaned over and gave Ronnie a light kiss on the cheek.

"Don't worry about trying to reach me. I'll call you when I have a little more information."

"Okay, but what if I do need to reach you?"

"If you really have to reach me, ask Helen. She can send me a message and I will call. I don't think anything is going to happen, but it is better that we don't take any unnecessary chances."

He looked at Ronnie and tried to redirect the conversation to ease her fears, "Just treat this as a holiday and enjoy a few days off."

He knew well that it would be more than a few days. Once he had Clark moved to a secure place, Dylan had to find the people responsible and neutralize the situation.

Ronnie would be safe at the cottage until all the scenarios played out. He waited, watching her as she walked into the passenger area and purchased her ticket. Dylan pushed down the accelerator as Ronnie disappeared into a crowd of passengers.

36

SEPTEMBER 12, 2007

SCOTLAND   **0550 GMT**

Dylan was standing on the Bridge of the Wandering Star, looking out over the rolling sea. The early morning sun was starting to break through the fog that had engulfed shortly after leaving Thurso, on the North coast of Scotland, almost four hours ago. Powered by its four efficient turbo-charged engines that produced over 2,400 horsepower, the refurbished fifty-eight meter long British Navy survey vessel was making way at twelve knots, cutting through the gentle swells with ease.

Ozzy was working with the Captain Robert McLeod as he plotted the ship's course. McLeod looked over at Dylan, "At the present rate, we will make the location in about three hours."

"Great," Dylan responded. "We should have a full day to set up the sonar gear and get started on the search grid."

The Captain was an experienced sea-hand. Seemingly born to the sea, he had spent most of his life working a small fishing fleet off the North Coast of Scotland, until the early eighties when the fish stocks started to disappear. He moved into the salvage business a few years later, working with the many oil rigs that were springing up around Britain. He was definitely no stranger to the North Sea.

The grizzled old sailor smiled at the two men. "My crew is very experienced and we will not be wasting any time. We will set up the side scanning sonar and start our first pass before 1500."

Ozzy and Dylan exchanged glances.

"Just as long as we don't miss our target because of haste," cautioned Dylan.

"No. No," the Captain replied, "My crew has done this many times before and because of the size of the object you want to locate, your project is actually quite simple."

"Yes, it is a large object, but we are dealing with coordinates that are over sixty years old," countered Dylan. "We just don't want to screw up."

The Captain nodded. "Aye, we have calculated tides and currents to determine the most likely location of the wreck," he said, looking quickly at the ship's compass, "Course 320 degrees."

"Course 320 degrees," repeated the helmsman, punching the numbers into the ship's computer system, which instantly relayed the information to the ship's autopilot.

The Wandering Star veered slightly to starboard as the Captain rejoined Dylan and Ozzy. "I would not worry too much about the coordinates. I would trust the navigators of yesterday far more than these modern gadgets that we use now." McLeod glanced at his chart and then to the Global Positioning System's screen. "Although these things do make it a little easier," he said somewhat sheepishly.

"Probably a little more accurate than sightings made with a sextant during wartime," echoed Dylan.

McLeod reluctantly nodded in agreement. "Let me go over the procedure that we will use to find your submarine," he continued. "First, we will divide our initial search area of thirty-six square miles into a grid of nine quadrants, each covering 4 square miles. We are starting at the exact location Mr. Ozzy gave me.

Latitude 59 degrees, 26 minutes, 29 seconds North, by Longitude Zero degrees, forty-four minutes, forty-three seconds West. This will be the North West corner of quadrant number one. Quadrant number one will be our centre point. We will begin our run in an Easterly direction. Each pass will be two miles in length at a speed of three knots. We will double back and forth until we have covered the two-mile wide section, using the Differential Global Positioning System to confirm our position on each pass we make.

We will cover the same quadrant by a North-South scan. Once we are satisfied that our submarine is not in that quadrant, we will then move on to the next quadrant directly alongside number one. We will complete each quadrant in the same fashion, working outwards in a circle from quadrant number one, until we find the submarine."

"What is the size of the swath that the sonar covers on each pass?" asked Dylan.

"Typically, the side scan sonar covers a swath 60 to 160 feet wide at about 2 knots. However, we will vastly improve on those numbers because we are looking for a very large object at a reasonably shallow depth, as oceans go. Our side sonar scan should be able to cover a minimum of 500 feet per pass while maintaining a speed of about three knots."

"Will the sonar be able to identify objects at that speed and resolution?" asked Dylan.

McLeod continued his briefing. "The technology we're using was developed specifically for underwater topographic survey, which includes searching for lost objects. The side scan sonar system's transducer is housed in a special torpedo-like housing and is towed through the water a few feet above the bottom."

The Captain pointed to the rear of the ship, "That large hoist abaft of us has more than 1,000 feet of electro-mechanical cable for deploying the side sonar in deep water."

McLeod paused to look at the electronics mounted above and in front of the helmsman. It only took a few seconds for the Captain to scan the Wandering Star's mass of computer instruments and confirm that everything was working normally aboard his ship. He turned back to Dylan and Ozzy and continued his explanation of the system they would see employed in the search for the U-1220. "The reflected acoustic signals are processed into an image similar to an aerial photograph, which is viewed by Mark in real-time on a computer monitor in the ship's radio room." McLeod handed Dylan and Ozzy a computer printout showing some details of the ocean floor. "This is from a search we conducted last month. You can see the details of the sunken oil rig that we found."

Dylan looked at the printout. "Impressive."

Ozzy was calculating on his handheld computer, "So," he said looking at the small screen, "each quadrant will take about 22 passes, or about the same number of hours."

"Almost, Mr. Bauer," responded McLeod, "we have to turn around at each end and adjustments will have to be made, but twenty-four hours per quadrant is a good estimate."

Ozzy punched the numbers into his handheld and watched as the numbers appeared. "That means our entire twenty-four square mile search area could take a minimum of 144 hours, or about six continuous days. Correct?"

"Providing we don't run into any snags," cautioned McLeod, "and you don't want to stop the scanning process every time you think you see something that might be your target."

"How can we be sure what we see is not our submarine?" asked Dylan.

"Mr. Dylan, our side scanning sonar system has an incredible resolution and it can reach out 10 times further than the older sonar machines that were used to find the Titanic. It will cover a swath approximately 500 feet wide. The other part of the system, and the best part, is our computer specialist, Mark Embry and his cohort, Jerry Parks. Mark and Jerry have been on many searches and their eyes and ears will see things that you and I would miss. Trust me, Mr. Dylan, if we pass near your submarine, they will be letting us know. It is a long, time-consuming process, but it does work."

"So what happens when we find what we all believe is the submarine?" asked Dylan.

We will confirm location information using a differentially corrected global positioning system, DGPS for short. The towing vessel has the DGPS integrated into its computer. That not only allows us to plot predetermined search lines, but also identifies the location of any waypoint during the side scan. It records the information on the actual images. The stored GPS information will allow us to return to any point on the image at any time."

Ozzy was impressed with the Captain's explanation. "Not bad," he exclaimed with a tinge of excitement.

"Once we have our location marked, we will use a small unmanned robotic submersible vehicle, the RSV. It is onboard the ship and can be put over the side to investigate any probable sighting. The RSV is equipped with up to two removable video cameras, four high-intensity flood lamps, and sensors to measure depth, pressure and temperature."

"How do we control the robotic unit?" asked Dylan.

"The RSV explorer is controlled by a joystick attached to a laptop computer that communicates with a microprocessor, the RSV's command center, via an 820-foot-long fiber-optic cable.

Our onboard operator sees what the RSV sees through live streaming video and sensor readings. Four variable-speed motors provide the RSV with vertical, forward or reverse movement and turning maneuverability. The deep-sea unmanned vehicle can be used under water to a depth of 750 meters. It also is equipped with its own side scan sonar which makes finding the objects a less strenuous task."

Dylan paced back and forth across the Bridge deck. "What is the time frame to get the RSV into the water and operational?"

"A couple of hours, maximum," answered the Captain, "That's why we like to be sure there is really something there, before we stop our side scanning track. Changing from one system to another is a time consuming venture."

"And when we find the submarine," asked Ozzy, "How do we get down to see if it is possible to find the Enigma machine?"

"As I mentioned before, finding the submarine is going to be relatively easy compared to finding an Enigma machine. That, my friends, will be like finding the proverbial needle in the haystack compared with finding the actual submarine. I would not be betting on your chances of success. However, we do have a Deep Sea Explorer known as the DSE-1 available. The company is prepared to dispatch it to our site once we have confirmed the location of the submarine. This three man submersible is equipped with side-scan sonar and satellite imagery capabilities, and with its mechanical arms, it can extract items from the wreck."

"Everything depends on what condition the wreck is and where the hull actually broke during the sinking," acknowledged Dylan. "It may be small, but we do have a chance. All we need is to find the submarine."

"A little luck wouldn't hurt, either," chimed in Ozzy.

Captain McLeod was good to his word as the Wandering Star reached the exact coordinates at 1345 GMT and his crew went to work in preparation for the lowering of the side scanning sonar rig into the sea. Dylan and Ozzy were standing next to McLeod, watching with interest as the crew paid out the electro-mechanical cable from the large drum, sending the towed sonar system out behind the ship and down into the depths of the North Sea.

"We are over a fairly smooth sea bed," stated McLeod, "at about 165 meters deep. We should be able to begin our first pass in less than an hour." He noticed Dylan looking at one particular crewmember below. "Cute thing, isn't she? This is her first operation with us, but she came highly recommended. Sure has added a little life to the crew."

"I'm sure she would," offered Ozzy. "She not only looks good, but she seems to work quite well with the others."

"Aye, she's a good worker," acknowledged McLeod.

Dylan smiled, "I'm sure she will do her part," he commented as he ran his fingers over a three-day growth that darkened his face. He was pleased with the situation. Carol Janes was successful in her quest to infiltrate the crew. She would keep him apprised of the other events onboard the Wandering Star.

37

SEPTEMBER 15, 2007

THE NORTH SEA   **1415 GMT**

The Wandering Star continued along on its programmed course, following the grid pattern like a donkey chasing after the unreachable carrot. It had been four days since the crew put the side scanning sonar into the water. They had traveled almost three hundred miles of distance, double scanning twenty-eight square miles of the North Sea's floor, completing seven of the nine quadrants chosen by Captain McLeod. Only two more remained.

The crew was still in an upbeat mood, despite having found several shapes on the seabed that, to their eyes, resembled a submarine. Each time they had begun to cheer and slap each other on the back, until either Mark or Jerry brought them down to earth by explaining the pictures were only of rocks or other normal features of the North Sea's seascape.

Dylan stood by the port side railing. He was reading a note Carol had given him. *"Nothing unusual about the crew. All are old hands, except for the cook's helper and the radio operator who are filling in for sick crewmembers. Everything seems okay."* He stuffed the note in his pocket and checked his watch as Ozzy came out from the Bridge.

"I don't mind telling you that this back and forth on the open sea is not really my idea of a cruise."

"I hear you," replied Dylan. "We had better find something soon. We are running out of time." He paused for a moment. "The only good thing so far, has been the weather."

"Well, that might come to an end, too. I checked online for the long-range marine forecast and it looks like a big front is moving this way. It will probably hit this area next Wednesday," warned Ozzy.

"We should be alright." Dylan responded. "We have plenty of protection."

"Yeah, you have, with that week old beard to keep you warm."

Dylan laughed. "Its' rather becoming for an old nautical salt, don't you think?"

"If I didn't know better, I would think you were one of the boys in the crew."

"If we don't find our submarine in the next two days, we won't need the crew. We'll be heading home by then."

"You going to quit?" asked Ozzy.

"We can't stay out here indefinitely. I have to consider Jim Clark's interest in this venture."

Dylan turned and made his way down the ladder towards the Computer Room. Mark Embry and his crew were in their customary positions, viewing the images that the sonar sent topside from six hundred feet below. There was the hum of activity going on, with an occasional laugh mixed in with the chatter. The crew was holding up well in spite of the monotony of the work.

The Wandering Star began her familiar turn to head back into the Westerly run on Quadrant number eight. The old ship swayed slightly, pulling the door from Dylan's grasp as he entered the room.

"Close the door," someone yelled. "Too much light."

Dylan was about to apologize, but Embry held up his hand.

"Hold on," he interrupted, "we may have something here." Embry reached out and hit the GPS waypoint button.

The room suddenly became extremely quiet. When Embry spoke, everyone knew it was important. In seconds, the only sound heard was that of the ship's Lisster Blackstone engines.

"There on the right," said Embry. "Doesn't look like a submarine, more like a fat torpedo, but I think it is the prize you have been seeking."

Dylan made his way behind Embry and viewed the screen. The image was clear, but he could not distinguish the form of any submarine, although he could make out the torpedo shape.

Embry's eyes continued to follow the images on the screen. "Mr. Dylan, did you say the submarine was damaged amidships?" he asked.

"Yes, the report from the RAF crew said the four depth charges straddled the U-Boat near the Conning Tower."

"Then, that is one definitely part of your submarine," Embry stated matter-of-factly. "I would say the foreword section. It looks like about eighty feet long and maybe about thirty feet high. I can make out the leading edge of the conning tower."

The members of Embry's crew gave a loud cheer and the celebration continued for several minutes. As the noise subsided, Embry picked up the intercom phone and called the Bridge.

38

SEPTEMBER 16, 2007

THE NORTH SEA   **0820 GMT**

Captain McLeod had immediately switched into part two of his search plan, launching the small, unmanned robotic submersible vehicle, the RSV, over the side to investigate Embry's sighting. Everything seemed the same to the crew in the Computer Room, except Embry was communicating with a microprocessor onboard the RSV via the 820-foot-long fiber-optic cable through the joystick attached to the laptop computer,. Embry touch was masterful.

"You must have spent one hell of a lot of time with video games," Dylan said, acknowledging Embry's talent.

"It did help," answered the smiling technician.

The RSV continued its dive towards the spot where they had spotted the front section of the wreck. Embry gently maneuvered the controls while turning on the four high-intensity flood lamps. Dylan and Ozzy watched the video screen intently, but the live streaming video only showed the four beams of light shining into the dark void. Dylan was about to question Embry about the spot when the RSV glided directly into place behind the wreckage. There on the screen was the unmistaken shape of a submarine hull.

Embry immediately switched on the two removable video cameras to record, and using the four variable-speed motors began to tape the first tour around the submarine's hull in over sixty years.

Dylan and Ozzy gave each other high-fives.

"We are going to get a quick look at this section of the hull and then switch on the RSV's own side scanning sonar to locate the rest of the wreck," Embry stated. "We should be able to locate the other half fairly easy."

Dylan gentle grabbed Ozzy's arm and pulled him towards the door.

"Oz, I am going to head out for awhile. You will be in charge."

"What do you mean, going out?" asked a bewildered Ozzy. "We're in the middle of the North Sea. Where can you go?"

Dylan laughed. "There has been a small change in our plans."

"But why are you leaving? As if you could anyway," said Ozzy flippantly.

"The weather is going to deteriorate next week so I am going to take a bit of a gamble. We have half of our submarine, and I believe Mr. Embry is going to deliver the other half very soon. I have set up a helicopter pickup that will take me to the base in Wick, Scotland."

"What? What for?"

"I have to get to Hamburg, to visit Horst Schneider. We need the diagram of the interior of the U-1220. If we have indeed found the U-1220, we have to know where the Enigma machine would be located. There will not be a lot of time to go looking everywhere trying to find that needle in the haystack. Horst Schneider could put us within a few feet of its location."

"That's a great idea, but what makes you think Herr Schneider will remember, much less give you the information?"

"I think he wants to know as much as we do."

"Yeah, his eyes did light up when I told him we were going to search for the submarine." Ozzy looked at his friend, "Are you sure about this helicopter pickup routine?" he inquired. "It's been quite awhile since you've done that sort of thing."

"No problem, Oz. It's like riding a bicycle," responded Dylan. "As soon as Embry confirms the other section, have Captain McLeod call for the DSE-1 Deep Sea Explorer. I should be back with the Schneider's map of the submarine's interior by the time it arrives here."

"I'm on it," Ozzy confirmed. "By the way, you had better shave or you might just scare the memory right out of the old man."

"I'll give it some thought." Dylan looked at his friend. "Keep an eye on the crew. I don't want anyone getting any ideas about talking to anyone on the outside."

"So who can I trust?" asked Ozzy.

"Remember the female crewmember you were admiring a few days ago?"

"The cute little one?"

"They are all cute to you Oz, but yes," responded Dylan. "That's Carol Janes, formerly with the Special Forces."

Dylan left Ozzy standing by the railing. He was speechless. Dylan exited, made his way to the Radio Room and had the ship's operator call through to the base at Wick to arrange the pickup.

39

SEPTEMBER 17, 2007

HAMBURG 0830 GMT

The helicopter pickup at sea went smoothly. Dylan had climbed inside the cage lowered by the AS36N Dauphin helicopter at 2005 GMT and the skilled pilot and crew whisked him off the rolling deck without incident. The helicopter maintained a speed of one hundred and fifty miles per hour, making the trip to the base at Wick in just over an hour and a half. Two hours later, he was on a flight to Glasgow where, after a six-hour layover, he made a connection on a direct flight to Hamburg. He had worn the same old jeans for the past four days and he looked like he felt, tired and rumpled. It was 0834 GMT when he finally reached his rental car. Dylan scanned the interior of the car. *"This is certainly not a Jaguar,"* he yawned. There was an old bluish sailor's toque on the back seat. Dylan picked it up and shrugged, *"Probably belongs to some local dock worker,"* he mumbled as he prepared for his drive to the home of Horst Schneider.

The sky was overcast, almost slate gray in colour. The light drizzle that fell over the City of Hamburg made it appear even drearier as he drove along the exit road from the airport. Out of habit, he checked the rearview mirror. It was important to ensure he did not lead anyone to the home of Horst Schneider. The road behind was empty.

Ten minutes out of the airport, Dylan spotted a sign for a small local restaurant just off the next exit. Having not eaten since last evening, he decided to make a quick stop to ward off the effects of his unusual travel from the ship that were starting to dull his senses. He did not notice the small blue Fiat van that pulled off the highway at the same exit, only a few hundred metres behind.

Dylan parked the rental, grabbed the toque from the rear seat and pulled it over his head. He looked at himself in the rearview mirror. "*You look a little rough, friend,*" he mused. "*But if one fits in with the locals, it does save a lot of questions.*" He entered the restaurant as the Fiat made its way along the side road and pulled into the restaurant parking area.

There was no one else in the restaurant. Out of habit, Dylan picked a table where he could simultaneously watch both the main entrance and the parking area. A short pudgy woman came out of the kitchen, looked at the downtrodden figure sitting before her. "You have money?" she asked bluntly.

Dylan nodded, took out several bills and laid them on the table. He picked up the menu and ordered a cup of tea, sending the old woman waddling back towards the kitchen.

A large man dressed in coveralls entered the restaurant. He looked around the room for a moment, and then finally sat at the table beside Dylan.

"A dull day out there, friend." he bellowed as he sat his bulk into the small chair, almost opposite Dylan's table. Dylan nodded affirmatively as the man reached into his coveralls and pulled out a book.

Dylan studied him closely. He was dressed like a worker, but his hands were clean and his shoes were almost new. Dylan could feel the hair on the back of his neck rise in alarm. He did not take his eyes off the man who had opened his book. The man glanced at the page for a moment and then looked up at Dylan. He tilted his head for a second, smiled, then closed the book and replaced it back into his coveralls. As he pulled his hand out, Dylan spotted the small snub-nosed 9-mm revolver sitting firmly in his grip.

"I believe you are Mr. Dylan.," the man intoned in a cold voice. "You almost had me fooled."

"What the hell are you talking about?" asked Dylan, his eyes searching for an escape route.

"You should have minded your own business. You have apparently become quite a pain to my employer."

Dylan looked at the hit man's cold eyes. He tried to stall. "I don't understand. Who is this employer to whom I am causing such pain?"

"Herr Lüdden" the man answered coldly. "He wants me to bid you a Fond Farewell." The man's finger slowly contracted around the trigger. "Goodbye."

Dylan knew he was defenseless. He had no gun, no protection. His only chance was to attack. In one quick motion, he flipped the table in the direction of the gun and dove towards the kitchen door. Amidst the deafening noise of gunfire and splintering wood, he counted four distinct shots. The force of his dive took him across the floor to the kitchen doorway. Dylan rolled to a stop by the doorway. To his surprise, all four shots had missed him. He looked back from his position on the floor towards the big man. The hit man was still in his seat, his smoking gun still pointing where Dylan had been sitting. A small trickle of blood began to appear at the corner of the man's mouth. Dylan watched as the body of the big man slowly fell forward onto a table. The wall behind him was a mass of blood and bits of body parts. The hit man's body landed on the table with a thud, paused, and then rolled off to one side, falling from the chair and crashing onto the floor in a bloody heap.

The old woman appeared at the kitchen door and found herself standing over a stunned Dylan. She was holding a serving tray with a teapot and cup. She spotted the man lying on the floor. Her legs grew weak as she fainted and slumped to the floor, landing directly on top of Dylan's legs. The tray with the teapot bounced off Dylan's head and smashed onto the floor, the hot liquid splashing everywhere.

Dylan did not know exactly what happened, but he was still alive. He struggled out from under the old woman. In a catlike move, he dove across the floor, picked up the man's gun, rolled and came to a crouching position on one knee. "*What the hell?*" he exclaimed as he spotted the outline of another person standing at the front door, backlit by the sun. Dylan paused. He did not fire at the target. He knew instinctively that he recognized the familiar shape and lowered his weapon.

The figure moved towards him and stepped out of the sunlight. He could see the detailed features of the person's face. It was Bridgette. She was holding a .357 Magnum in her hands, a wisp of smoke slowly curling out of the barrel up towards the ceiling.

"Are you okay, Sean?" she asked, in a matter-of-fact tone.

Dylan was shocked. "Where the hell did you come from?"

"As I said, my job was to look out for you when you were here in Germany."

"How did you know?"

"We intercepted a message from someone we have been watching. Someone wanted you taken out of the picture after you arrived at the airport. It appears you have made some unsavory friends on your journey."

"You said we. Who is we?" he asked brusquely.

"I'm afraid I can't say," responded Bridgette. "Let's just say there are some other parties who have an interest your affairs."

"Well, I am not sure who you are talking about, but I must admit that I am very happy to see you again."

Bridgette laughed. "Not exactly as I would have liked, but all's well that ends well."

Dylan looked at the tall woman as she casually placed the .357 Magnum into her handbag. "Now what do we do?"

Bridgette looked at him and smiled, "If you are through being followed, you can get on with your trip. In any case, we should leave here quickly, before anyone else arrives."

"What about the old girl?" he asked, pointing to the woman who operated the restaurant.

"She just fainted. She will come to in a minute. We need her to call the police," she said, prompting Dylan to move towards the door.

"So you're not going to follow me now?"

Bridgette flipped her head back towards the dead body on the floor. "My instructions only related to the actions of that particular gentleman back there."

"Whose instructions?" Dylan shot back.

"Sorry," she smiled, "but that is classified information."

Dylan knew from past conversations that she was not about to divulge who had sent her. "Are you still going to follow me or not?" he asked again as they exited the restaurant.

Her face broke into a mischievous smile. "I don't have any reason to," she laughed. "That is, unless you really want me to."

"No," Dylan responded when they reached his rental car, "not this time."

"Okay, but do look me up next time you are in Berlin."

Dylan paused, turned and gave Bridgette a quick kiss on her cheek. "I owe you one."

"And I intend to collect." she replied coyly, watching Dylan get into the car.

Dylan started the vehicle and began backing up. He stopped and rolled the window down as he came alongside Bridgette. He looked up and questioned the tall woman, "How did you know where I was?"

Bridgette just smiled back at him, turned away and got into her car.

It took Dylan an hour to reach Horst Schneider's home. The incident at the restaurant played on his mind for the entire trip and he took extra care to ensure no one else had followed him since he left the restaurant. Dylan rubbed his eyes. *"Shit, I don't have time for all this cloak and dagger stuff right now,"* he cursed to himself. The rental car stopped a half block from Schneider's home. Dylan got out, walked the short distance, and made his way up the steps of the old ship builder's home. Seconds after his single knock, a pretty girl in her early twenties opened the big wooden door. She greeted him in perfect English, "You are Mr. Dylan, I believe. Please come in,"

Dylan was surprised that the girl knew his name. "You knew I was coming?" he asked.

"No, but my grandfather said it was you when he saw you coming up the steps. I think he is happy to see you."

"I hope so. Is he feeling better?"

"Yes. He seems to have much more energy these days, ever since your friend, Mr. Bauer was here. It has been an improvement."

The young girl led him into the old man's study.

Horst Schneider did look better than the last time Dylan had seen him. He was standing by the desk, looking at some papers. He looked up as the girl announced, "Grandfather, Mr. Dylan is here."

"Mr. Dylan, I was wondering when you would return."

"Oh?"

"Yes. Your friend Oscar came by and told me about the submarine. I hoped that you would come back. Did you find it?"

Dylan smiled. "We think so. At least we have part of it."

"Part of it?" he questioned. "What do you mean?"

"It appears the submarine was broken into two pieces during the battle."

Dylan could see the disappointment in the old man's eyes. Every submarine that left his shipyard was part of his family and he felt for every one. Schneider's face suddenly brightened. "You want to learn the secret of the messages? Is that not so?"

The question caught Dylan off guard, but he recovered and responded with a simple "Yes."

"Your friend Oscar said you required a drawing of the interior of the ship."

Again, he answered "Yes."

Schneider seemed driven, almost obsessed in his efforts to help Dylan solve the mystery of the U-1220. "I suppose what you really need the location of the Enigma machine."

Dylan was amazed at the old man's understanding of exactly what was happening and why he was there. "Yes, Herr Schneider. If we could locate the Enigma machine, we could get the settings of the rotors and hopefully be able to decipher the messages that were in the cylinder."

"I understand." Schneider moved around the desk and sat in his chair. "I have done these few renderings for you," he said, handling three drawings to Dylan. "They show the radio room, the Bridge area, and the location of the Enigma machine."

Dylan examined the drawings, marveling at the details the old man had managed to capture. It was as if he was looking at the original plans for the submarine. "You are still the Master, Herr Schneider. These drawings are exceptional."

"When you have worked on something all of your life, you tend to remember the details," acknowledged Schneider. The old man pondered over his next comment. "If, as you say, the submarine is in two pieces, you may have some luck with you."

"What do you mean?"

"The Radio Room is located just forward of the Bridge area, almost directly under the conning tower. If the ship broke at that point, you will be able to access the area rather easily. However, finding the Enigma machine might still be very difficult."

"Is there anything else you can tell me about the machine itself? Like its size and shape?" Dylan inquired.

"I thought you might ask," laughed the old man. "I found this picture of an installation made on another similar submarine. It has the same Enigma machine in basically the same configuration."

Dylan examined the picture. "May I borrow this?"

"You may have it, my friend. It is of no use to me," replied Schneider.

The young girl returned to the room with a tray containing a pot of tea, cups and some cakes that looked very appetizing.

The old shipbuilder enjoyed his tea, listening intently as Dylan explained how they had located what he thought was the submarine U-1220. He told Schneider the details from the original records of the sinking. Dylan's account of the events impressed the old man, but he seemed to become very sad.

Dylan watched as the old man bowed his head for a moment in silence.

"Are you alright, Herr Schneider?"

"Yes. I was just recalling some old memories."

Dylan wanted to find out more information on the last days of the U-1220, but did not want to offend Schneider. "Would it be rude of me to inquire about the final mission of the submarine?"

"No. Not at all. So much time has gone by. So many lives wasted. It is all different now. We do not harbour any ill feelings over these things. Life goes on."

Dylan did not completely understand what the old man was thinking, but he took the opportunity to ask, "What was the last refit of the U-1220? How was it changed?"

"The German hierarchy had completely redesigned the ship. They ordered us to remove most of the ship's torpedoes and other combat equipment in order to make enough room to accommodate a large shipment of goods, along with ten passengers. The only armaments left on the ship to defend against any attack, were the forward torpedo tubes and the two deck guns."

"So the submarine was basically a transport ship," said Dylan.

"Yes. As I told you during our first conversation, it only had two outings. The first was in late April. The ship took a large cargo shipment to an unknown destination, but that was all very secret. I have no idea what they carried, but they did return to the harbour only a fortnight later. The next time the U-1220 left the harbour, was its last voyage, only three days later, during the bombing of Berlin and Hamburg. It was rumored that she may have carried some passengers on that trip."

"Did you see any passengers board the ship?"

"No. They would have arrived just as the bombing in Berlin ended. It was the middle of the night and everyone was too busy trying to stay alive to worry about who or what sailed out of Hamburg. All I remember was that someone said that they were destined for a secret rendezvous with another submarine."

Dylan smiled at Schneider. "I am surprised that any ship managed to get out of the harbour, given all the bombing that occurred. It must have been a nightmare."

"Yes. It was a very surreal experience. I lost most of my family that night. They were victims of the bombings. Only my son and I escaped." Tears began to form in the old man's eyes.

"I'm sorry," said Dylan. "It must have been terrible."

"Yes, my friend. War is so futile," replied a tired Schneider. "It is all so wasteful."

The old man was getting tired. Dylan knew he had to get back to the Wandering Star to complete the search and hopefully, the recovery of the Enigma machine.

"Herr Schneider, you have been very helpful and I thank you. Your knowledge about the U-1220 is very extensive. I would not have been able to continue my quest to solve the mystery of the papers without you." Dylan looked at the old man. He was smiling. "How did you find out so much about the missions of the U-1220?"

Schneider pulled a picture from between the pages of the book on his lap, and handed it to Dylan. "This is a picture of my son."

Dylan looked at the picture. It was of a young naval officer. He was standing in front of the U-1220. He was holding a pocket watch. "This is the son who escaped?"

"Yes," answered Schneider as his eyes welled up with tears.

"He is a fine looking lad. The pocket watch indicates that he may have been a navigator."

"Yes," Schneider exclaimed proudly. He was a good navigator. I gave him that watch. It was my father's before me."

Dylan handed the picture back to the old man. "Is that how you learned about the missions? From your son?"

"Yes. You see, he was an officer in the German navy."

"Was he killed in the bombings?" asked Dylan.

"No. He escaped being killed by the bombs, but his escape was as an Officer onboard the last sailing of the U-1220."

Dylan was stunned at the old man's news. He fell silent for a moment. "I'm very sorry."

THE NORTH SEA   **1205 GMT**

Ozzy watched the monitor as the RSV made its way around the large object that Mark Embry had found. It was the missing half of the submarine. The pictures sent back from the RSV were incredibly clear. The images provided exceptional details of the second half of the submarine, from its rudder to the conning tower.

"For a wreck that has been in these waters for over sixty years, it is in remarkably good condition," said Embry.

Ozzy looked at the pictures. "Fantastic." He turned to the Captain. "Sean wanted me to get the DSE-1 Deep Sea Explorer on its way as soon as we found this section."

"No problem, Mr. Bauer, I will put the call in straight away."

The Captain scribbled a quick message on a pad and handed it to Carol Janes. "See that this gets out immediately."

Carol took the message and left the Computer Room, making the short trip to the Room situated on the opposite side of the ship in less than a minute. She did not see much of Radio Operator Gunter

Mach during the search, but that was normal for the techie-types. She turned the door handle and entered, stepping over the doorstep and slipping in behind the Radio Operator. The images on the computer had Mach's eyes riveted to the screen. He did not hear Carol approach.

"The Captain wants this sent out right away. It is very important," she announced, pushing a copy of the message towards the man.

Her voice startled the radio operator who jumped up from the console, knocking his coffee onto the floor. "What the bloody hell?" he exclaimed, grabbing some paper towel to wipe up the mess. "Don't ever come in here without knocking."

Carol's eyes immediately gravitated to the writing on the computer screen where Mach had been working. She started to apologize while she took in the writing. "I'm sorry. The Captain was in a hurry."

Gunter Mach looked up at her as he blotted the spilt coffee from the floor. "It is still polite to knock, lady." He noticed the woman's eyes locked on the computer screen. He immediately jumped up in a flash hit a key that immediately rendered the screen dark.

Carol moved back towards the door. "I thought we were not supposed to have any contact with the outside while on this search," she blurted out.

"That is not your business and nothing in this room is for your eyes," he said with contempt. He grabbed the message from her hand and quickly scanned the writing. "Tell the Captain that I will send the message." Mach stepped towards Carol, herding her towards the open door. "Goodbye!" he said, as he ushered her through the exit.

HAMBURG   1325 GMT

They had finished the tea and cakes the young Granddaughter had brought for the two men. Horst Schneider, his energy spent was starting to drift off into a quiet sleep.

"One last question Mr. Schneider, do you recall a submarine with the U-112 registration?"

Schneider opened his eyes and looked at Dylan. "The Black Knight. It was a type XI-B. There have been many rumors about these submarines. Some people believe that Germany built the submarines in 1939 at the Deschimag A.G. Weser shipyard in Bremen, but I never saw them. They were supposed to be the biggest and best in the German fleet." The old man's eyes closed again and he lapsed back into an even deeper sleep.

Dylan got up to leave. He made his way to the kitchen and found the old man's Granddaughter. "I am very sorry, but I must get back."

"I understand. My Grandfather has spoken a great deal about you. He is very interested in your project. He believes you will use whatever you find for the right reasons. I hope he will not be disappointed, Mr. Dylan."

"Horst Schneider is a very good man. I will make sure that I do not disappoint him, in any way. Take good care of him."

"He is my Grandfather. It brings me joy to look after him."

Dylan looked back into the study where Schneider was fast asleep. "Please express my thanks and say goodbye for me," he said. He turned to the girl and added, "Good Luck and God Bless."

"Good Luck to you as well, sir."

Dylan shook the girl's hand and left.

THE NORTH SEA   **2125 GMT**

The light in the evening sky was starting to fade into darkness as the private AS36N Dauphin helicopter approached the Wandering Star. The Captain turned on the huge floodlights that lit up the deck of the ship brighter than the Las Vegas strip.

The captain was communicating on the VHF radio, preparing the Wandering Star to receive the incoming passenger. He barked orders to the helmsman, quickly matching the speed and direction dictated by the pilot of the Dauphin helicopter. The helmsman kept his eyes glued to his gauges. One slip could mean disaster for the passenger, the helicopter and the ship. Captain McLeod confirmed the data and passed control of the drop to the Dauphin. The responsibility for a safe operation now rested with the pilot.

The helicopter slipped into position. It was hovering slightly to the starboard side over the aft deck. The downdraft from the helicopters rotors was severe and flattened the sea around the Wandering Star. The winch man gave the signal to the pilot and began to lower the weighted Hi-Line that would help reduce the swinging motion of the main cable and reduce the amount of time the helicopter would have to remain directly above the ship.

The ship's crew received the signal from the helicopter and quickly secured the Hi-Line. The winch man swung the basket containing Dylan, out from the side of the Dauphin and lowered it gently onto the deck of the Wandering Star.

Dylan climbed out, moved to the side of the deck and gave the all-clear sign to the helicopter. He watched as the Dauphin rose above the Wandering Star and disappeared into the black night sky.

"Welcome back." It was Ozzy. "We have a few things to talk about," he said, leading Dylan below decks to his cabin.

SEATTLE 1410 PDT

The fall weather around the City of Seattle was showing signs of an Indian summer. The waters of Lake Union were dotted with small craft plying back and forth in the bright sunshine. FBI agents Gary Anderson and Mike Gerrard were holding an impromptu meeting in the parking lot by the Hiram M. Chittenden Locks in Ballard. The locks were part of the Intercoastal Waterway and provided a link for boats between the saltwater of the Puget Sound and the fresh waters of the inner lakes.

Gerrard passed an overseas communiqué and two photos to his partner. "This came in from our FBI office in Berlin. What do you make of it?"

Anderson read the message, scrunched the paper into a ball, and shoved it into his jacket pocket. "So they think Dylan figures the location of the submarine is contained in the coded documents. Hell, our guys had that scenario detailed when they first saw the papers he found in the cylinder."

"Yeah, but Dylan is actively looking for the U-Boat."

"He still doesn't have much to go on and I doubt he will actually find anything, but it's our job to monitor the situation. So who is the guy in photos?" asked Anderson.

"Jeremy Meyers, a known contract killer from the U.K. Our Berlin office thinks he was going after Dylan, but they do not know for sure. Our agent was at the airport but Dylan never appeared."

"Then were did he go? We had confirmation from Glasgow that he boarded the flight to Hamburg."

"Or maybe our agent just screwed up the assignment," insinuated Anderson. "Shit! I knew we should have had our man in Scotland tail him on the flight."

"Calm down, Gary. The damn bureaucrats are always screwing up the system. That was a budgetary move. It was out of our control."

"If the hit was going after Dylan, then that opens up a whole set of new questions." Anderson held up a photo again. "But then, somebody had to be there. The report says somebody took out Meyers with a .357 Magnum. That is definitely not standard FBI firearms issue. Two slugs went right through him into the wall behind. Both slugs went in only two inches apart. It made a hell of a mess coming out of his body."

"Yeah," Gerrard chimed in, "a .357 usually does."

Anderson stared at the photo. "But the report says there were four shots fired. The other two came from a small caliber pistol, 9 mm. most likely. It looks like the dead guy was shooting at something, or someone, when he got whacked."

"Could be. Ballistics is running a check on the bullets to see if there are any matches on file."

"I wouldn't hold my breath," Anderson replied. "What about the old lady?"

"She doesn't remember what the other guy looked like. Thought he was some local dockworker. I sent a picture of Dylan off to the office in case she might be able to ID him."

"Was there any other blood at the crime scene, other than the hit man?"

"None. Seems like whoever the other shooter was, got away clean."

"Dylan still has that rig searching up on the North Sea. He has to come back soon. Contact our Glasgow man and have him latch onto Dylan when returns to dry land."

"For how long?" asked Gerrard.

"Until I say stop," Anderson shot back. "How many times do I have to tell you? We are going to keep at this until we nail this Dylan guy."

"What about the budget memo? Aren't we supposed to have that sort of thing approved by the top Brass?"

"Fuck the budget, and fuck the Brass," grumbled Anderson. "I want to know what Dylan is doing. All the time. That bastard is just a little too slick for his own good. If he does find anything relating to the gold from the Priam Treasure, it could set off a whole mess of international incidents. There are at least four countries I know of that could claim some form of ownership over it, at some time or another."

Gerrard looked at his partner with new interest. Anderson was not the usual cool FBI agent that Gerrard had known for the past eight years. "So what has that got to do with us?"

"The good old US Government would also like to get their hands on it, too. Apparently, the value is somewhere around a hundred million, not to mention a certain amount of prestige that would go with having part of a treasures the Russians claimed to have taken from Berlin."

"On the other hand," replied Gerrard, "this whole Priam Treasure charade just might be a colossal waste of the Bureaus time and resources."

THE NORTH SEA   2240 GMT

Dylan sat and listened as Ozzy related the circumstances surrounding Carol's visit to the Radio Room.

Ozzy spoke in a hushed voice. "She gave me this note last night," he said, passing the paper to his friend.

"Is she okay?" asked Dylan with a look of concern.

"Yeah, she's fine. We only spoke for a moment. Her cover is still secure."

Dylan read the note. *"Caught the Radio Operator sending info on Dylan's travel to unknown source. I suspect the Radio Op is working for wrong side."*

"That might explain my run in with some madman in Hamburg."

"What do you mean?"

Dylan thought about the incident and replied, "I will tell you later. Right now, we have to figure out what is happening onboard this ship. Carol told us that there were two other new crewmembers on this trip besides her, the cook's helper and the Radio Operator. See if you can find the name of the original Radio Operator. Check with his family and find out just how sick he really is."

"How am I going to do that without going through Gunter, the present Radio Operator, who we suspect is working for someone else?" asked Ozzy.

"Carol is in with the rest of the crew. She should be able to get you the name of the original Radio Operator. Ask the Captain for the use of his Global Satellite telephone. Tell him it is a very private call. If you need them to contact you with information, tell them to send the info as a personal message about your dog. I doubt our friend Gunter Mach would clue in."

"But I don't have a dog," joked Ozzy.

Dylan shook his head, "Just pretend," he said with a laugh.

"Seriously, I think we should keep a very close eye on what Mr. Gunter Mach sends out over the wire."

"You are right, of course," yawned Dylan, "but at this precise moment, I am going to get some sleep."

40

SEPTEMBER 18, 2007

THE NORTH SEA   **0700 GMT**

The morning sun was just clearing the horizon, its rays sparkling in the crests of the rolling sea. The Deep Sea Explorer had arrived during the night and tied up alongside the Wandering Star. The crew was hard at work, checking out the systems aboard the DSE-1. The weather report was not good and McLeod did not want to waste any time. His best calculations gave them a possibility of two attempts to find and recover the Enigma machine before they would have to suspend operations until the following year.

"Captain," called the first mate. "We've got a problem. There is a broken cable on the DSE-1."

James Ward was McLeod's First Officer. They had met while working with the fishing fleet over twenty years ago and remained friends since. The many years of sailing together had made them very comfortable in their roles. McLeod trusted Ward totally.

"What happened?" asked Captain McLeod.

"The crew was setting up the crane attachments in preparation of the lowering of the DSE-1. One of the cables snapped during the pre-dive check."

"Any other damage?" the Captain asked.

"When the submersible shifted, it nearly crushed our cable rigger."

McLeod was concerned. "Is he alright?"

"It just brushed up against him. Thanks to his good reflexes, he only suffered a minor scrape on one arm. He's back on the job."

"Good," the Captain stated with relief. "Can we replace the cable?"

"Yes, but it will take the best part of an hour."

"Make it right, James, and get me a full report on the damaged cable as soon as you can."

Ward left the Bridge, as Dylan and Ozzy arrived.

"How are the preparations for the dive going?" asked Dylan.

"A small hiccup, Sean," said McLeod. "It seems one of the cables on the DSE-1 suffered some damage. Nothing too serious. My first mate should have the problem rectified within the hour."

"What happened?"

"Don't know as yet. Mr. Ward just reported it minutes ago."

Dylan pondered the situation for a moment. "It seems strange that a company as reliable as McKinnon & Sons in Edinburgh would send up a piece of equipment as incredibly complex as the DSE-1 with a bad cable."

"Aye," replied the Captain, "I have been chewing on that thought too. I have asked for a report on the issue. In the meantime, let's have a look at those drawings you acquired." McLeod turned to the console, flipped a switch on the Bridge intercom system. "Mr. Embry, would you please join us on the Bridge?"

Dylan spread the papers across the chart table. There were three drawings detailing the construction of the U-1220.

"Whoever drew these has done a first rate job," the Captain declared enthusiastically.

The first was a full-length representation of the U-1220 submarine, showing the conning tower, deck lines, armaments, propellers and the snorkel. The second graphic was of the interior of the Bridge area. It detailed the complexity of the underwater ship's command area, showing the location of the controls, including the periscope.

Mark Embry entered the Bridge and joined the others at the chart table. His eyes went immediately to the illustrations. The third diagram had caught his attention. He moved in between McLeod and Dylan to pick up the drawing.

"Neat," he said, his eyes scanning the details of the sketch.

"The Radio area," confirmed Dylan in a matter of fact tone.

"This is great." Embry reached past McLeod to pick up the other two drawings. A trace of a smile came over his face. "If these are as good as they appear," he stated enthusiastically, "you just might be able to get your prize, Mr. Dylan."

"You think we can get into the Radio area?"

Embry picked up number one and pointed at the submarine's conning tower on the drawing. "You bet," he stated without hesitation. "The submarine is split right about here," he said, pointing to the diagram. "The Radio area," he paused to retrieve the third sketch, "is right about here, only a few feet from where the hull split. The Enigma should be about eight feet in from the fracture," he continued, pointing to the drawing. "If it didn't fall out when the ship hit the ocean floor, it should be within the grasp of the DSE-1's mechanical arm."

"What if it was permanently mounted in place?" asked Ozzy. "How do we get it out?"

Embry shook his head negatively. "That shouldn't be any big problem. After sixty years down there, the mounting is most likely quite fragile. If anything, we have to be careful not to crush the unit as we pull it out."

"I guess the first thing we have to do is find the prize, and then we can work on getting it topside," said Dylan. "Captain, how long will it be before we can take the DSE-1 Explorer down?"

McLeod checked his watch. "We will start preparations for insertion in thirty minutes."

"Good. Who is going with me?" asked Embry.

"Mr. Dylan here, to confirm we do get the right barnacle-covered package, and Carol Janes to monitor the onboard systems." The Captain turned to Dylan, "That okay with you?"

Dylan gave the thumbs up signal.

"Better you than me," said Ozzy. "I had a peek inside that thing. There's not a whole lot of room in there." He paused for a second as new thoughts began to form in his mind. "On the other hand, being down there with Ms. Janes might not necessarily be a bad thing."

The Captain placed a hand on Ozzy's shoulder as if to console him. "I have a feeling Mr. Dylan will get more work done," he grinned.

"Yeah, but I would have more fun."

BERLIN 0830 GMT

Müller entered the office of the leader of the underground Neo-Nazi Democratic Party. He did not pause as was his usual custom, and proceeded directly towards Lüdden's desk.

"I am sorry, Herr Lüdden, but this is extremely important," he stammered with excitement. "I just received a message from our contact in Canada. He has located the address to Dylan's private home through Clark's company telephone records. He is sure that both the papers Clark's secretary are there."

Lüdden pushed himself back from the desk. "How convenient," he grinned. The party leader got up and walked around beside his associate. "Well done, Herr Müller. If this is indeed true, then we no longer have need of anything that Dylan's operation in the North Sea might recover from the submarine."

"Do you want me to call off the surveillance of the search?"

"Not yet. We will stay in contact with our operative onboard the Wandering Star. It will not hurt to know what is going on. In the meantime, get the coordinates of Dylan's home from your contact. Send TallOne and Faust there to recover the papers. Have them transmit copies back to me as soon as they have them in their possession."

"Are you not concerned about others seeing the copies?"

"No," answered Lüdden, picking up the faded document from his desk, "This is the key to decoding the documents and it is the only copy."

"But that is in code too," protested Müller, "How can that help us?"

Lüdden looked at the puzzled man and smiled, "You will see, Herr Müller, you will see."

THE NORTH SEA   0845 GMT

James Ward joined the Captain on the Bridge. He was carrying a piece of the half-inch steel cable that had snapped earlier. It did not require an investigation to confirm that someone had tampered with the cable. Several strands of the tightly wound cable had obviously been cut. There were other signs of tampering.

"This was sabotage, James, pure and simple. Someone deliberately cut this cable."

"I agree Captain, but whom? I have known everyone of the crew for over ten years. I am sure it is not one of them."

"We have three new crew members on this trip," intoned McLeod. "There's Cookie's helper, the Radio Operator, and the girl, Carol Janes. We can eliminate the girl. She is going down with Dylan in the DSE-1. That would leave Cookie's helper and the Radio Operator, Gunter Mach."

"You want me to talk to them? See what I can find out?"

"No, not yet," replied McLeod. "Is the DSE-1 secure and operational?"

"The repair to the cable will be completed in about fifteen minutes."

The Captain looked out the forward windows and observed the weather. The sea currently offered gentle four-foot swells with little wind. The Wandering Star had settled into a smooth rocking motion. It was a perfect situation to start the DSE-1 exploration of the submarine sitting 665 feet below the surface.

"No telling how long this weather will hold up. Get Dylan and let him know we will be ready to deploy."

Ward gave the Captain a look of concern. "What about the other two crew members? Are you just going to let them run free?"

"I want to be sure we get the right one. Put people you trust on both of them from here on out. If either one of them so much as breathes in the direction of the operation, tell your men to lock him down below in the hold. We'll sort it out later."

Dylan was with McLeod on the aft deck when Embry and Carol arrived.

"The Captain figures it's now or never. The weather is holding, but the forecast is not looking good for later in the day."

"I'm ready if you are, Sean," beamed an enthusiast Carol.

Mark Embry looked at Dylan and Carol and smiled, "Okay by me."

The crane operator began the final preparations to lower the Deep Sea Explorer into the water, moving the large hoist on the port side out over the barge.

Ward returned to the Wandering Star. "I've checked and double-checked the submersible, Captain. Everything is A-Okay. You are cleared to dive."

Dylan, Embry and Carol looked at the huge white submersible perched on its cradle aboard the barge. It looked like a snub-nosed submarine set on skis. The large red air tanks mounted on each side of the craft and the folded hydraulic arms mounted on its front, gave the vessel a very bizarre look. The DSE-1 crew gingerly made their way around the various cables lying on the aft deck and stepped over the ship's low gunwale and onto the barge. In less than two minutes, they had ascended the ladder, entered the three-man submersible, and sealed the pressure-sealed hatch behind them.

"She handles much better than she looks," Embry said as he made himself comfortable in the control seat. He was in complete charge of the operation, having worked with the DSE-1 almost a dozen times before during other search missions. Embry felt good to be back at the controls again. It was more interesting than working inside the Computer Room, operating the little RSV remote unit.

Dylan sat to his left and slightly behind Embry. Both would have a bird's eye view of the target submarine through the forward-looking view ports that extended 180 degrees horizontally and 90 degrees vertically. Carol was behind her two companions, but still able to see outside through the large acrylic domed window.

Embry flipped the switches to turn on the radio and air

filters, carefully pointing out to Carol which gauges she was to monitor. The three-person crew had gelled quickly, efficiently completing the extensive pre-dive checklist without a problem. When the crew had completed the list, Embry gave the crane operator the thumbs up signal with the command, "Deploy."

It was less than two minutes before they heard the scrapping of the cable on the outside of the hull, as the winch slowly tightened its hold on the submersible. The crane operator eased the control back and the twelve-ton DSE-1 moved imperceptibly. It was just enough to test the cable. Sensing everything was in order, he pulled the control further and lifted the submersible from its cradle and swung it clear. With the agility and grace of a ballerina, the crane operator moved the DSE-1 out over the side of the barge and lowered it into the North Sea.

The submersible bobbed in the water like a cork. Embry hit the switch to open the ballast tank, instantly taking in water to stabilize the craft. While the crew worked on disconnecting the hoisting cable, Embry flipped through a further series of checks to ensure the forward and rear thrusters worked properly.

"Disconnect," he called.

The confirmation crackled over the radio, "Disconnected."

Embry looked at Dylan. "Let's go find our submarine."

As the DSE-1 descended into the dark waters of the North Sea, Embry flipped on the exterior lights. The luminous glow seemed to dissipate quickly as the craft sunk into the depths below.

"We're good for eight hours," said Embry, "but I expect we will be back on top well before then."

"Given that it will only take about fifteen minutes to get down, and another forty-five to get back up, that should give us a good seven hours of search time on the bottom," stated Dylan.

"I think I would prefer to get back early," Carol replied.

Embry switched on the ship's communications system and called up to the Wandering Star. "This is DSE-1. We are now descending through one hundred feet. Everything is A-Okay."

Dylan sensed Carol's uneasiness. "You alright back there?"

"Fine," Carol reported in a nervous tone. "It is just taking me a couple of minutes to get used to the motion. Now that we're descending, everything seems to be okay."

"Good. Maybe you could rustle up some lunch for us then."

"Thanks, Sean. However, I think I will wait until we get back up top before eating. Just in case."

The North Sea waters quickly turned into total blackness. Viewing was almost none existent. A sudden flurry of colour flashed in front of the submersible as it descended through a school of cod. The fish disappeared in seconds. Embry adjusted the controls to slow the decent. The submersible continued its gravity assisted descent into the murky waters of the North Sea. Time seemed to pass slowly as the crew waited to reach the bottom.

Carol checked the depth gauge again. "Four hundred feet. Everything looking normal," she announced in a slightly nervous voice..

"Watch the air temperature," suggested Embry. "You may have to turn on the fans soon."

The submersible continued downward, its descent slowing slightly as Embry played with the ballast control.

"Five hundred feet," reported Carol.

Embry confirmed the depth on his backup gauges, "We'll be approaching the bottom in about four minutes. I'm going to switch on the video cameras now so don't miss anything on our approach."

Dylan peered through the three six-inch windows that looked

down towards the ocean floor. "With the lights, the sight range down here will only be about twenty feet. You could be on top of something before you get a chance to see it coming."

Carol called out as they passed the next level, "Six hundred."

Embry flipped another switch that purged water from the ballast tank to increase the crafts buoyancy. Dylan could feel the rate of descent slow even more. The ship had achieved neutral buoyancy. Its descent to the bottom had seemingly stopped. The small thrusters began moving the submersible ever so slowly forward.

"We are now at the six hundred and twenty foot mark," Carol reported.

"Have an eye, Mr. Dylan. We are very close to the bottom."

Embry had no sooner finished than the silt-covered ocean floor slowly appeared in the viewing windows. He flipped on the communications switch. "Wandering Star, this is the DSE-1 Explorer. We have reached the sea floor." The radio crackled but there was no acknowledgment from the ship.

Dylan could see some small mounds glide by a few feet below the craft. "Nice job," he said, giving the operator a little clap on the back. "You are good with these controls," he complimented.

Embry laughed as he gently moved the submersible along the path to rendezvous with the wreck he hoped was the U-1220. "It gets easier with practice," he said. "The fun stuff begins when we get to the wreck."

Carol checked the gauges. "I see what you mean about the heat," she declared. "I am switching on the air circulation system."

Embry hit the communications switch again. "Wandering Star, this is the DSE-1 Explorer. We have reached the sea floor at six hundred and thirty-one feet. We are proceeding to first GPS waypoint. Do you read?"

"Roger that, Explorer, you have reached bottom at 631 and moving to first waypoint."

Embry's hands moved quickly as he adjusted the controls on the craft's four thrusters. "Our first GPS waypoint is the back end of the main section of the wreck. We will come up from behind and tour along side to the Conning tower. That is where the submarine broke in two. We will photograph the entire sub and see what we can see in the opening. Keep an eye open for any debris alongside the wreck. We don't know what may have fallen out during its drop to its final resting place."

The submersible continued along its path, occasionally stirring up a little cloud of grey silt as the skis on the craft gently grazed the ocean floor.

"There it is! Straight ahead," yelled Dylan, as the aft section of the submarine's dark, crustacean-covered hull appeared out of the black void. It was sitting almost upright, the bottom buried a few feet into the sea floor. In the murky darkness, Dylan could see the two big screws of the submarine half buried in the silt.

The DSE-1 moved like a cat, around the aft end of the ship past the rudder, the elevators and its half-buried props. Embry adjusted the ballast and the Explorer eased up along the sleek hull in the direction of the Conning tower. "Careful of the cable," Dylan called out, seeing a large cable that seemed to float above the deck.

"I see it," responded Embry, adding power to the thrusters.

The DSE-1 continued along just above the deck of the submarine. Twenty feet from the Conning tower, the damage to the submarine became instantly visible. "My God," exclaimed Dylan. "She must have taken a direct hit."

"More than one," replied Embry, slowing the DSE-1 to a

snails pace. "Look at the deck plates. They are buckled and split."

The two men watched as the full extent of the damage unfolded beneath them. "To the left," exclaimed Embry, "that's all that remains of the Conning tower. They never had a chance."

Dylan was looking at the base of the tower. "Can you get a little closer?"

Embry adjusted the thrusters and the DSE-1 responded, moving slightly left.

"Just a little more," implored Dylan.

Again, Embry applied the power to the side right thruster.

"There," shouted an excited Dylan. "There, at the base of the Conning tower." It's the submarine's registration number. He read it aloud. "U-1220."

"We've found it." Carol shouted enthusiastically.

A sound of metal hitting metal scraping on metal resounded throughout the DSE-1, instantly silencing the crew.

"Shit!" Embry yelled, applying full power to the left thruster. The DSE-1 hesitated for a moment and then slid nicely off to the right, away from the submarine. "Carol, check for any damage."

"Everything appears normal," answered Carol, the hint of nervousness returning to her voice.

Embry repositioned the DSE-1 opposite the wreck, just left of the Conning tower. The crew could see the full extent of the damage. "You can see where she broke apart."

"The depth charges hit simultaneously on both sides, caving in the hull and pushing the centre downwards," said Dylan. "She was literally torn in two."

"If you compare this to your drawings, Mr. Dylan, it appears the ship broke directly above the Radio Room. I am not sure you are going to be able to find anything in that mess."

"Let's go over and come at the wreck from another angle."

"Okay, but we have to be careful. There is a lot of loose wreckage. We could easily become snagged."

"That would not be a lot of fun," chimed in an anxious Carol.

Embry negotiated the DSE-1 around to the open end of the wreckage so the crew could see into the interior of the submarine. Dylan repositioned the four one thousand watt lights to shine deep into the wreck. The craft edged slowly forward towards the warped and twisted remains of what was once the U-1220.

Dylan had his copy of Schneider's drawing of the interior taped to the wall beside him. His head moved back and forth, comparing Schneider's drawing with the actual wreckage that sat at the bottom of the North Sea. He was looking right into the u-Boat's Bridge area. He felt as if he could reach out and touch the controls. Embry applied power to the thrusters and stopped the forward motion of the Explorer. "This is as close as we can get without getting ourselves caught up in that mess of cables and twisted metal."

"No problem," answered Dylan, "Our prize is in the other half of the structure. The split is right at the Conning tower. The Radio area was just in front on the split."

Embry hesitated for a second. "Do you see that small mound on the interior floor? Looks like a piece of equipment."

Dylan looked over at the DSE-1 operator. "You want me to try to reach it with the hydraulic arm?"

"Might as well. It will give you a little practice for later."

Embry held the Explorer steady on its spot as he flipped a switch to power up the mechanical arm. Dylan slipped his hand inside the gloved control and gently touched the button to move the arm out of its cradle. The crew watched as Dylan maneuvered the arm outwards, unfolding it to its full length as it reached out and grabbed the small mass of encrusted material. "Got it," declared Dylan. "Bringing it back and dropping it into the basket."

Embry congratulated his crewmember on a job well done, as he backed the DSE-1 away from the aft part of submarine wreckage and, after punching in the GPS coordinates, traversed the two hundred feet of sea floor to find the remains of the foreword section.

The wreckage of the forward portion was lying on its side. The bow was turned around and facing the rear section. Embry maneuvered the craft up over the bow and moved down the deck towards where the depth charges had ripped the submarine apart.

When they had reached the point where the submarine's 105mm gun should have been, the deck literally disappeared, leaving a large gaping hole through which Dylan could see down into the bowels of the ship. Less than fifteen feet later, the entire hull of the submarine disappeared in a mass of twisted metal.

Embry moved the Explorer around to face the wreckage from the open end. "This doesn't look quite as bad, but still no hell."

"Can we get a little nearer?" asked Dylan.

Embry looked at the wreckage. "We might be able to get in a little. Just keep a sharp eye for any obstacles. We have to remember that the DSE-1 is almost sixteen feet high and over eleven feet wide. This is like driving a bus in a telephone booth. We don't have a lot of ability to maneuver around."

Dylan nodded as he compared the view with the drawings.

Embry used the Explorer's thrusters and the DSE-1 moved forward towards the wreckage. The sides of the submarines hull were like two large hands, beckoning the smaller craft to enter its grasp. The sound of metal grinding against the DSE-1's outer hull made Carol gasp involuntarily.

Dylan suddenly pointed towards the wreck, "There, on the right, just above the floor."

"I see it. It looks like the sub imploded into the Radio area."

"According to Schneider's drawings, our prize, the Enigma machine, would be that mound at the far end of the middle section."

"It would have to be on the far end," Carol echoed.

The crew immediately went into action. Embry flipped on the hydraulic power to the mechanical appendage as Dylan prepared to stretch out the motorized arm towards the prize.

Dylan maneuvered the mechanical arm to its full length as Embry repositioned the DSE-1's powerful lights to shine on the end of the arm. The beam of light revealed the claw was still several inches from the object.

"We need to get about another foot closer," Dylan stated.

Embry applied power to the thrusters. There was no discernable forward movement. "We are up hard against the lower flooring already." The U-1220's Enigma machine was still four inches away from the end of the hydraulic arm.

"Any ideas," asked Dylan.

Embry turned and looked at his crew, "We have one option. We could back off a little, then go forward and give it a small nudge. The rusted floor should fold a bit under pressure. Of course, there is always the chance we might get stuck in here, too."

Dylan glanced at Carol, "You game?"

"As long as it's a small nudge," she replied nervously, "I don't want to be a permanent part of an old World War Two wreck."

He looked over at Embry, "Let's give it a shot."

Dylan retracted the mechanical arm as the DSE-1 eased back from the wreckage. "That was easy," he said with a grin. "Now, for the interesting part."

Embry moved the Explorer into a forty-five degree angle and applied full power to the forward thrusters. The craft moved slowly forward and jammed its skids on what was the wall of the Radio Room. Embry added ballast to increase its weight. The DSE-1 stopped, with its skids resting on the wall. Nothing moved.

Carol looked at Dylan, and then Embry. "Well, so much for that idea. What do you want to try next," asked Carol.

"Give it a minute," replied Embry, "Listen."

The crew waited in silence. It was a small creaking sound at first, but quickly grew much louder. Before the crew had a chance to comment on the noise, the rusted wall of the sunken submarine gave way under the weight of the twelve-ton Explorer, folding like a stack of cards. The DSE-1 slid forward in an exploding cloud of gray slit that completely obliterated their view of the submarine's interior.

"What the hell?" exclaimed Carol.

"Don't panic. It was not as violent as it seemed. We just churned up the slit on the bottom a bit." Embry said assuredly. He looked at Dylan. "Switch off the lights. There is no sense wasting the batteries."

Fifteen minutes later, they turned the lights back on to view the situation. The wall of the Radio Room had disappeared. The equipment previously attached to the wall, had ended up on the sea floor. Dylan spotted the Enigma machine and immediately extended the hydraulic arm to latch onto his prize. He twisted the control handle to capture, then lift and drag the Enigma machine towards the Explorer. To his amazement, the complete panel of equipment was still in tack with its wires still attached to a portion of the wall.

"Houston, we have a problem," said Dylan, mimicking the

line from the Apollo 13 space mission.

Embry looked at the gangling mess of radio equipment streaming out from the claw of the mechanical arm. "Try to pull it as close as you can. I'm going to use the second arm to cut the wires."

Dylan pulled the equipment towards the Explorer. A myriad of wires streamed out from each piece. Embry unfolded the second arm and moved towards the spaghetti-like mess, cutting as he went. The arm performed flawlessly and in less than ten minutes, he freed the equipment from the persistent grasp of the U-1220.

"I'm going to raise the DSE-1 up, and then back out of here," said Embry as he tucked the mechanical cutter away, "You should bring the equipment up tight against the hull and hold it there until we're clear." He flipped the switch for the ship's communications radio and called up to the Wandering Star. "This is DSE-1. We are starting our ascent."

"Roger that, DSE-1, we'll be waiting," came the reply.

Embry applied power to the thrusters as he blew the ballast tanks to extract the Explorer from within the wreckage of the U-1220. The DSE-1 moved imperceptibly at first, but then gained a little speed. The sound of cables scratching against the hull echoed throughout the Explorer. The submersible was almost clear of the wreckage when it abruptly stopped, throwing Carol forward into Embry. The string of radio equipment broke free of the mechanical arm's grasp and dropped back into the wreckage below.

"Shit!" cursed Dylan. "Our package has come loose."

"Unfortunately, we're not," replied Embry with a trace of concern in his voice. "Something's hooked on the outside of the hull,".

"It sounds like it's wrapped around the hatch," offered Carol.

"I'm going to rock us forward and down to try to release

whatever is caught up there."

Embry looked over to Dylan. "Retract the arm. We can pick up the package once we get ourselves out of this spot."

Dylan hesitated for a second. He looked down through the six-inch acrylic window at his prize only a few feet away and then maneuvered the arm back into position.

"Don't worry. We are not leaving without it. I just want to make sure that we are leaving."

The first two attempts by Embry did not have any effect. The DSE-1 was firmly snagged and the U-1220 wreckage was not about to let it go. He readied for the third attempt, and then paused. "Use the arm and get the best hold on the package that you can. We are going to attempt to pull out of the sub's grip on this pass and we might not be able to get back into this area afterwards."

Dylan did not ask for any explanation. He slid his hand into the operator's glove and pushed the buttons that sent the mechanical arm down to the Enigma machine, trapped with the string of other equipment. He picked a point at the back edge of the Enigma machine and applied pressure. Dylan tested his grip on the equipment. It appeared to hold fast. He gave Embry the thumbs-up signal.

"Okay, folks, hang on. This is going to be a ride."

Embry pushed the buttons to blow out the ballast tanks while applying full power to the reverse and left thrusters. The DSE-1 moved upwards a few feet before starting to pull to the right. The Explorer was starting to list to one side. The buoyancy continued to increase and the DSE-1 passed through a full forty-five degrees of list before finally breaking free from the wreckage of the U-1220. Embry immediately opened the ballast tanks to neutralize the Explorer. They were free of the remains of the submarine. Carol checked the gauges. Everything was stable.

The DSE-1 was sitting motionless above the wreck. "Where's the package?" asked Carol.

Dylan looked through the small port. "We've got a string of pearls hanging from the mechanical arm. We've got our prize."

All three cheered in unison, reaching around the cramped module, giving each other high-fives.

A half-hour later, the crew could see the dark shape of the Wandering Star slowly coming into focus as the DSE-1 neared the surface. One minute later, the DSE-1 broke through on top of the rolling waters of the North Sea.

Embry checked the view through the small window below to confirm the mechanical arm still held the prized Enigma package in its grasp. He called the Wandering Star, requesting they put a diver into the water to secure a floating collar around their prize.

Dylan looked at his crewmates and smiled. All three were drenched in sweat. He released the safety switch, unlocked the craft's pressure hatch and popped it open, starting the flow of cool, fresh, sea air into their cramped quarters.

"Now that was exciting," he declared with audible relief.

The crew of the Wandering Star helped the three exhausted members of the DSC-1 crew disembarked from the Explorer. Ozzy pitched in, taking control of the Enigma machine and other items the crew had retrieved from the U-1220 submarine, stowing them securely in the ships hold.

The Captain issued the order to secure the DSC-1 Explorer onto its cradle aboard the barge and placed the call for the tugboat to arrive early the following morning to tow it back Thurso.

Tonight, the entire crew would celebrate.

41

SEPTEMBER 19, 2007

NORTH SEA   **0630 GMT**

The Captain was on the Bridge when Dylan entered. "Aye, I hear you had quite the adventure down there," offered McLeod.

There was a grin etched in Dylan's face that seemed to stretch from ear to ear. "It was fantastic!" he exclaimed cheerfully. "We had a couple of minor snags, but Mark did a marvelous job. It was fantastic."

The Captain smiled at Dylan's excitement. "It's a very dangerous game down there. You were lucky to retrieve the Enigma machine without getting yourself trapped in the wreckage."

"I understand."

McLeod picked his hat off and scratched at his balding head. "So what is your game plan from this point onwards?"

Dylan was like a child with a new toy. He could not wait to play with it. "I'm going down to Glasgow University to restore the Enigma machine. It will take the best part of a day to establish and verify the rotors and settings. After that, it's off to London to see a man about a little code work."

"I wish you the best of luck, Mr. Dylan. I hope they are able to decipher your papers."

"I have a friend in London who is quite qualified." Dylan

paused, "I just hope what we have found will allow him to work his magic. What time are we due in Thurso?"

"I should imagine we will be there by 1510, baring any unforeseen delays. Why?"

"I was working out my schedule. I sent Carol to the Radio Room to forward a message to advise my friend that I will be there on Saturday, that is, provided I have the settings."

McLeod bristled at the mention of the Radio Room. "Mr. Dylan, I think you had better check on Ms. Janes. I am not one hundred percent certain that our replacement radio operator, Mr. Mach is truly trustworthy. Nothing out of the ordinary, but we have had him under observation for some time."

"To tell you the truth, Captain, I have a few misgivings about him as well."

The door flew open as Ozzy appeared on the Bridge. He was panting, trying to catch his breath. "I just received a call on the satellite phone. The local police have found your regular radio operator - in a dumpster. He has been dead for some time."

Dylan bolted from the Bridge and headed for the radio room.

There was no reply to her knock on the Radio Room door, so Carol pushed it open and entered. Gunter Mach was not there. She scanned the room. The computer screen was blank, except for a single line of copy at the top. It read, "*...we will be back in port tomorrow.*" Carol looked around again and then moved to the keyboard. She was just about to scroll up to see the rest of the message when Mach entered the room.

"Reading other people's private mail, are we?" Mach asked positioning himself between Carol and the door. "You should have minded your own business, lady."

"A little touchy today, are we?" Carol replied with a laugh.

There was a menacing grin on Mach's face as he pulled a knife out from under his jacket, "This will wipe that smirk off your face, you meddling fool," he barked.

Carol immediately went into a defensive stance. Mach lunged towards her and she caught the knife hand and twisted his arm around, forcing Mach to drop the knife as he smashed against the wall. Mach felt a surge of strength race through his body as he pushed himself off the wall towards Carol. His sudden move caused Carol to trip over the leg of a chair and their two bodies crashed to the floor. The hard landing stunned Carol.

Mach retrieved his knife and spun around to face Carol. "Now, bitch, it's time you learned your lesson," he sneered as he approached the fallen woman. Carol shook her head, trying in vain to clear the dizziness. She saw the dark silhouette of Mach against the bright light that streamed in through the open door. She watched in horror as sun reflected off the razor sharp edge of the knife. As if in slow motion, Mach's hand moved forward, intent on its deadly mission. She passed out before Dylan grabbed the German's arm and flipped him over on to his back, saving her life.

Dylan's sudden appearance surprised Mach. An attempted kick to the groin glanced off Dylan's leg, but moved him back far enough to permit Mach to get to his feet. Dylan lunged forward, knocking the Radio Operator back against the computer desk, scattering the keyboard and monitor across the room. He had the man pinned to the desk, but a sharp head butt by Mach sent Dylan reeling backwards towards the open door. Mach again retrieved the knife and charged. Dylan sidestepped the lethal force of the oncoming blade, grabbing Mach's knife hand, pulling him towards the door. The two men crashed together, the force of the impact carrying them through the open doorway onto the outer deck.

Mach again kicked at Dylan to gain some separation.

A sweeping motion of the knife missed Dylan's arm and cut through the lanyard of the top safety rail. Dylan hit Mach solidly in the gut with all his force. The man winced, but did not fall down. Mach struggled upright and came at Dylan with the deadly knife. The Special Forces had thoroughly trained Dylan in the art of disarming a knife-wielding enemy. Dylan grabbed Mach's arm, the knife slicing through the air and stopping only inches from his face. Using all his force, he pushed the knife downwards, away from his body. Mach was quicker, but he could not match Dylan's strength. The knife moved lower and then with a sudden move, Dylan twisted Mach's arm, pointing the blade back towards the man's midsection. The faces of the two combatants were only inches apart. Dylan looked into the dark eyes of the radio operator and saw only hate. He relaxed his arms for a split second. The move surprised Mach. Dylan used the man's own weight against him and thrust the knife upwards, deep into his gut. Mach stumbled backwards like a drunken sailor on shore leave. The radio operator's eyes began to glaze over as he staggered towards the safety rail. He put his hand out to steady himself but the top lanyard of the safety railing was missing. Mach stumbled forward, tripping over the lower lanyard and flipped into the North Sea. Dylan peered down at the water as the lifeless body disappeared beneath the surface.

Seven hours later, the Wandering Star arrived at Thurso harbour. The Captain radioed ahead to inform officials that he had lost a man overboard. There was no mention of Dylan's involvement in Mach's disappearance.

Dylan bade the Captain and Embry goodbye and proceeded down the gangplank to meet Carol and Ozzy. It had been seven long days at sea, but he knew the hardest part still lie ahead.

GLASGOW   2130 GMT

The blending of the long shadows cast by the sun as it slowly set behind the hills and the antique lights along the main street in Thurso, produced an eerie scene. Dylan had decided to drive from the port, down the old roads to Glasgow.

Dylan carefully packed the heavily encrusted Enigma machine into the trunk of the rental car along with the other smaller items retrieved from the U-1220 and the trio's travel bags.

The drive down the A9 highway in Northern Scotland was a pleasant break from the days aboard the Wandering Star. The road narrow road had little traffic and they were able to make good speed.

Six hours after leaving Thurso, Dylan pulled into the Glasgow International Airport. It was three o'clock in the morning.

Carol and Ozzy exited at the departure terminal. Ozzy would accompany Carol on the first flight down to London, before returning to Berlin.

Dylan headed out of the airport to stay at a small local hotel near Helensburgh in Dunbartonshire. Dylan had called the proprietor before he left and told him that he would be arriving in the middle of the night. The man did not mind. "Just knock on the door and come in. Your key will be waiting on the desk. Breakfast is at eight."

He found the hotel at Sinclair Road and Clyde Street. Despite the owner's obvious abundance of trust, he locked the vehicle before going inside.

As he lay in the comfortable bed, Dylan wondered at the strange set of events that occurred. Through fate or coincidence, events were taking him on an exotic journey to a strange rendezvous with destiny. He did not know exactly where he was going, or why, but he knew he would keep the scheduled appointment.

42

SEPTEMBER 20, 2007

GLASGOW　　　　　　　　　　　　　　　　**0840 GMT**

It was a pleasant Scottish morning when he arrived at Glasgow University. The first traces of the oncoming fall season were beginning to appear in the hills around the City. The early morning mist hung in the air, giving Dylan a sense of renewal. He proceeded directly to The Centre for Battlefield Archaeology where, upon entering the large brownstone building, Dylan was awestruck by the samples of battlefield armor displayed in the halls. Dylan instantly felt a strange bond with the Centre.

He had received John Stewart's name from Professor Kingsmill. She had assured him that Stewart would be able to assist him in the cleaning of the Enigma machine.

Dylan was fascinated with the concept of the Centre for Battlefield Archaeology and meeting Professor Stewart proved to be a delightful experience. Archaeology was Dylan's main interest and he found it easy to get lost in Stewart's fascinating world of yesterday.

A half-hour into their meeting, Dylan knew he would have to return later to study with Professor Stewart. However, today, his mind was on the Enigma machine. He explained his needs to the Professor who arranged for the use of a work area in the restoration room where Dylan could clean the Enigma machine and the other items retrieved from the submarine.

Dylan entered the room at 0930 on Thursday to clean the Enigma machine. He had decided to put the small-encrusted item he dubbed as "Embry's package" into a chemical bath, where he let it sit while he worked on the encryption apparatus. Time passed slowly as he continually soaked and picked at the sixty years of sea growth and crustaceans that covered the machine. Dylan was exhausted, but overjoyed when he finally had the Enigma machine cleaned well enough to recognize the numbers on the rotors. He took pictures and wrote down the settings. It was ten past five on Friday morning. He had worked almost twenty hours without straight.

His appointment with William Hill was set for two in the afternoon, at Bletchley Park. He had less than seven hours to reach London. Dylan wiped down the Enigma machine and placed it into a cardboard box for the trip to London. He gathered his jacket and then paused, as he remembered that Embry's package was still sitting in the chemical bath. Dylan quickly returned to the sink, reached into the cloudy water with a set of wooden prongs, and lifted out a brass sextant. It was in pristine condition. Attached to the sextant was a small chain that hung down into the murky water. Dylan picked up the chain and lifted it out of the water. On its other end was a small pocket watch. The sight of the watch caused a smile to appear on his face. He knew it would also give Horst Schneider a reason to smile.

Dylan quickly rinsed the chemical from the two items and placed them inside the box with the Enigma machine, grabbed his coat and headed to his rental car.

43

SEPTEMBER 21, 2007

M-6 MOTORWAY   **0745 GMT**

    The trip down from Glasgow was uneventful. Dylan stopped at a roadside service station on the M6 motorway for fuel and some breakfast. He took the small pocket watch from his jacket pocket and wrapped it in tissue paper, which he placed in a padded postal envelope. Dylan wrote the address on the outside of the stamped envelop, sealed it and dropped it into the Royal Mail box. It would reach Horst Schneider within a few days. Dylan thought about the old man and smiled. Moments later, he was again heading towards London on the motorway.

    The speed of the cars traveling on the M6 amazed him. He was not a slow driver, maintaining an average of almost eighty-five miles per hour, yet the local drivers were passing him with regularity. Dylan passed a large Bowers Garage Tow truck towing a demolished Mercedes. The sight instantly reminded Dylan that speed and fatigue were a deadly combination. It also reminded him that he was very tired. He had not shaved or changed since the day before. However, at this point in his journey, time did not allow for the niceties of everyday life and he could not miss his appointment at Bletchley Park. He drove on, wondering if the rotor settings he found in the Enigma machine he recovered would permit him to decipher the coded papers, and learn the secrets of the U-1220.

MAYNE ISLAND   0710 PDT

The warm rays of the late summer sun began to filter into the bedroom, casting dancing shadows on the walls as the wind gently swayed the treetops. The weather was slowly changing and the early morning temperatures hovered near zero degrees Celsius. Ronnie looked at the clock. It was seven-fifteen. Ronnie grudgingly pushed back the sheets and she left the warmth of her cozy bed. She hoped a nice warm shower would help start her day off on the right note.

Three weeks had passed since Dylan left her at the Ferry terminal. The novelty of cottage life had virtually disappeared. She found she did not enjoy being alone at the cottage, sequestered away from the outside world. The effects from the lack of human contact were beginning to wear hard on Ronnie. She was rapidly growing tired of the loneliness on the island. Each day seemed to be worse than the day before. Ronnie had only spoken to Dylan once since she arrived. To complicate matters, she had not received any news about her boss, Jim Clark. She was feeling agitated and very alone. She knew she had promised Dylan that she would not call anyone, but she was lonely and becoming impatient. She needed to talk to someone.

She had made up her mind. If Dylan did not call today, she would ask Helen contact him.

BLETCHLEY PARK   1415 GMT

An unusually sprite William Hill looked up through his heavy rimmed spectacles as Dylan entered his office carrying his attaché case and the large cardboard box. He bounced to his feet and extended his hand, "Mr. Dylan. It is so good to see you again."

"It is good to be back," he replied.

"I understand you have been a busy fellow since our last talk."

"Yes, quite," Dylan acknowledged, placing the box on Hill's desk. "I think I have something you might like to see."

Dylan opened the box and removed the protective foam covering, exposing the Enigma machine from the U-1220.

"My word," exclaimed Hill. "Where did you get this?"

"It was retrieved from the U-1220, a submarine that was sunk in the North Sea on May 4, 1945."

The Director of the Museum was stunned. "Unbelievable."

Dylan lifted the Enigma out of the box and set it on the desk. "You said that if I could find the settings, you would run my coded message again. This is the very machine that sent the original message on May 4, 1945. The Steckerboard connections are still set in the same position as they were on that date."

Hill looked at the machine. "You have done well to clean up the machine but, it still may not be enough."

The possibility that he might not be able to decipher the coded pages shook Dylan's confidence to the core. "What do you mean?" he asked hesitantly.

"I dare say the Steckerboard and rotor settings are correct, and that is a huge step forward. One would even say it is fantastic. However, we need the proper code line in order to complete the process."

The news deflated Dylan. He stood motionless, looking at the Enigma machine. He could not think of anything to say.

Hill pondered the situation for a moment, and then asked, "Did you say you had other papers from the same date?"

"Yes, several. Why?"

"Were any of them sent to the U-1220?"

Dylan understood where the Director of the Museum was heading. "If the U-1220 received a message, the code line would be included. Correct?"

"Correct," echoed Hill.

Dylan quickly opened his attaché case and pulled out a sheaf of papers, flipping through them as he went. He stopped on a single sheet. "Here. Is this what we need?"

Hill's eyes lit up. He studied the page for a moment. "Yes, this line right here," he announced, pointing to a portion near the top of the page. "This is the code line."

"Halleluiah," shouted Dylan.

The Director of the Museum motioned for Dylan to follow him. "Let's see if we can finally read your mysterious papers."

It took Hill less than an hour to set the rotors on his working Enigma machine to match those of the unit Dylan recovered from the U-1220. The two men started to decipher the pages. It was a slow procedure at the beginning, but Dylan soon caught onto the process. It took Hill twenty minutes to decode the first page. The two men continued the process and were more than halfway through the second page when Hill's assistant entered the room.

"I have someone here to see you Mr. Hill. I told them you were busy, but they insisted that I let you know." The assistant passed a written message to her boss.

Hill read the message and turned to Dylan. "Sorry, old chap, but I must see this individual. I shall be back as soon as possible. Do continue on, Mr. Dylan. You are doing fine."

"No problem." he replied as Hill followed his assistant out of the room.

A full hour passed before a visibly upset William Hill

returned to the Enigma room. Dylan had processed all of the coded pages, inserting the translated copies into his attaché case. He was in the process of translating the final page.

"I am so sorry, Mr. Dylan. It was the new Chief Supervisor from London. He was here on a spot inspection. They usually do not undertake such inspections on Fridays, but he was a new man and had so many questions. I do apologize."

"Not a problem, Mr. Hill. I have run the pages through the Enigma and it worked perfectly," replied Dylan with excitement in his voice. "I was just translating some of the text, but my German is not as good as it used to be, so it has taken me some time."

"Your German is probably a far cry better than mine, I would venture," the Director laughed. "I'm afraid I really can't help you with any of that."

Dylan smiled at Hill's response, as he slowly read each of the messages. "The bulk of the deciphered messages are only standard U-Boat reports from the submarine sent as part of their daily routine," he announced to Hill. "Of all the papers, only these three pages are noticeably different. Each one includes the German heading "Dringlichkeit", which is German for 'emergency'."

Dylan separated the messages and placed three of them on the desk. "The U-1220 sent the first message just prior to the surfacing," he said, reading the text. "*Snorkel not operational. Batteries are low, we are surfacing to recharge.*"

"Not exactly an earth-shattering discovery," offered Hill with a slight tinge of sarcasm. "It was hardly worth your effort."

Dylan ignored the remark and picked up the second communication. "This message appears to have been sent moments later. He read the message. "*We have been spotted by enemy aircraft. We are under attack.*"

Hill involuntarily shrugged his shoulders again showing his disappointment.

The third message was the most interesting to Dylan. He gave Hill a rough translation.

"First cargo secured 4.30.45 Second cargo delivered 5.2.45 Coordinates awarded for first on east west wings. Destination of second is unknown."

Dylan read and reread the communication. "It makes no sense," he declared.

"The numbers look like dates," offered Hill, "but the rest is bloody gibberish."

"There must be some meaning. We are just not seeing it."

"Or maybe we just want to think there is, my friend. Who knows what someone meant if he wrote it during the heat of battle."

"But," reasoned Dylan, "it seems so illogical to have gone to the trouble to encrypt a message and send it out during the heat of battle, if it were not serious."

"True," said Hill pensively, "but if the sender did not want the whole world to know, sending the communication as a riddle in a coded message would surely have limited the number of persons who could understand the content."

"I understand, but I am not sure what it all means. There must be a code word or number in this message that means something to someone."

"I wish you luck, Mr. Dylan," replied Hill. "You've been on quite the journey. It would be a shame if it has all come down to such silliness."

"Yes, somebody seems to have had a weird sense of humor," said Dylan, scooping up the deciphered pages and placing them into his case.

BERLIN   **1722 GMT**

Lüdden was pacing back and forth in front of his desk like an expectant father waiting for the news. Müller entered the office and handed him a copy of an email.

"It seems Mr. Dylan has gone to London to visit the museum at Bletchley Park again."

"Do you think he has the information he needs to decipher the coded papers," asked Müller.

"He is grabbing at straws. It is impossible for him to decipher the encrypted messages without the code line and rotor settings. A sinister smile appeared on Lüdden's face. He opened the top drawer of his desk and pulled out a plastic wrapped sheet of paper. "This document, Herr Müller, is the original copy of the first message the U-1220 sent on the day it was sunk." Lüdden's voice gaining intensity as he continued, "It has the Enigma settings we need to decipher the coded papers that Dylan found in the cylinder. This," he exclaimed, holding up the paper, "is the very key to our success, to the success of our party."

"But where and how did you get it?"

"My father was the radio operator at the naval station in Hamburg," Lüdden said proudly, "He kept this copy of the final transmission for years. He told me that one day this piece of paper would save the Nazi Party. This document is the key to restoring power to the Nazi Party. When TallOne and Faust acquire the papers from Mr. Dylan's home, we will have the means to recover the gold that was taken from the Great Priam Treasure."

Müller watched in fascination as Lüdden continued his story. The German leader appeared possessed by thoughts of recovering the lost treasure.

SEATTLE   **1415 PDT**

Agent Gary Anderson and his partner Mike Gerrard were standing in front of Richard O'Brien, the Chief of the Bureau's Seattle office. They were not happy.

"What the hell have you been chasing?" demanded O'Brien. "You've spent thousands of Bureau funds following a guy with some useless papers he found in some tin can at the bottom of the ocean. Did anyone ever think to look at the dollars this little epic was costing? Washington is all over me, asking for justification."

"But," interjected Anderson, "our people saw some of the documents Dylan had and we understood that these papers could be of value to our government."

"And who made that decision?" questioned O'Brien.

Anderson shuffled uneasily. "Ultimately, I guess it was made in my department," he answered hesitantly.

"Your department?" the Chief questioned brusquely. "The last time I checked, you were still working for the Bureau. Since when were you assigned your own private department?"

Anderson shifted nervously from one foot to the other. "Our intelligence told us these papers could be proof of the existence of the Black Knight. They also were concerned that the decoding of the papers might confirm undesirable facts regarding a proposed treaty with Germany during World War II."

"The assertion that the U.S. was negotiating with the Germans has never been taken seriously. Our London office has confirmed that Dylan has decoded and translated the papers. The results show nothing but daily reports from the submarine and a childlike riddle. They have deemed them worthless. Your efforts have been an incredible waste of the Bureau's time and resources."

Gerrard wanted nothing to do with the conversation. He kept his eyes glued to the floor in an attempt to avoid O'Brien, but the Chief of the Bureau's Seattle office was not going to let him escape unscathed. "And you, Mike. What the hell were you thinking? You should have advised your partner long ago that he was off base."

"I did mention that the costs were piling up, sir," he said sheepishly, glancing over towards Anderson. Anderson glared back at him with an ice-cold stare. "However, in the end, we still thought we were dealing with something big."

"Big?" screamed O'Brien. "You two spent thousands of dollars of the Bureau's money chasing a goddamned riddle sent by some crazed submarine Captain over sixty years ago. This is big? You guys are as smart as a sack full of hammers." He paused for a moment. "As of today, this file is closed. There will be no more surveillance. No more expenditure of any FBI funds whatsoever." O'Brien was sweating profusely. "Gentlemen, have I made myself clear?"

Anderson and Gerrard both nodded affirmatively, uttering a quiet 'Yes' in unison.

"I want both of you to write up a full report on every aspect of this escapade, right down to the penny spent. If you are lucky, the Bureau will not want to recover the money you wasted on this useless caper." O'Brien paused for a moment before continuing. "If you are real lucky, they might even let you keep you jobs."

Gerrard was about to make a comment, but then thought better of it and joined Anderson as he exited the office. "Jeez, I've never seem the Chief so worked up about a dead end case," he whispered to his partner.

"This is not over yet," Anderson said with a determined grin. "Not by a long shot."

BERLIN   **2312 GMT**

Ozzy was sitting in front of his computer screen, talking to Dylan on the Skype network's voice-over-internet-protocol system. "I'm sure," he confirmed, looking at Dylan's face on his screen. "We traced the email address through the Internet Registry and it took us right to his office."

"So, just where in the German government does this Mr. Lüdden work?" asked Dylan.

"He's a junior minister in the environment department. Not a big player, but apparently he's a player with some big plans."

"Let's keep this information under wraps for the time being. I want to find out more about him and his relationship with the underground Neo-Nazi Democratic Party. It sounds like he is double-dipping in his choice of politics."

Ozzy laughed. "By the way, did you get everything done on the Enigma machine at Bletchley Park?"

"Went as smooth as silk," answered Dylan. "I got all eleven pages done before Hill came back complaining about the Chief Supervisor from London doing a spot inspection of his museum, and on Saturday yet."

"He was quite the funny guy. I thought he might catch on, but he was too concerned about having everything approved. Typical British approach."

"You did a fine job, '*Inspector*' Bauer. My compliments on a fine performance." praised Dylan. "I felt a little bad not telling him all that I learned, but he doesn't need to know all the gory details. In the meantime, see what else you can dig up on our friend Lüdden. And put a tail on him. Find out where he does his Nazi routine."

"I'm on it, mon Capitan," acknowledged Ozzy.

VANCOUVER   1642 PDT

Trudy Kingsmill stared at the computer screen, reading Dylan's translation of the message several times over. *"Sean was right. It does not make a whole lot of sense,"* she mumbled.

The elderly woman used her index finger to poke at the keys, bringing up the original copy of the deciphered message Dylan had sent to her. It was in German. *"Erste Ladung sicherte 4.30.45 auf Ostwestkreuzarmen. Zweite Ladung lieferte an das schwarze Bestimmungsortunbekannte des Ritter-5.2.45."*

Professor Kingsmill slowly translated the entire message, writing down the words as she went. When she had finished, she looked at the communiqué again, comparing it to Dylan's translated copy. *"I wonder,"* she said looking at the strange message, *"could we be missing a few words?"* Again, she checked both translations against each other. *"First cargo secured 4.30.45 on east west cross arms. Second cargo delivered to the Black Knight 5.2.45 Destination unknown."* They were the same, word for word.

Professor Kingsmill was sure the original German radio operator, caught up in the heat of battle, had used as few words as possible when he sent the message. The second half of the communiqué was self-explanatory. It was the first portion of the message that was the problem. She experimented with the text, adding a word here and there in an attempt to complete the sentence structure. The Professor had written a dozen lines when she suddenly stopped. She circled the last scribbled version It read, *"east west arms of the cross"*. A smile slowly appeared on her face. "I must get hold of Sean."

The Professor picked up the telephone to call Dylan.

44

SEPTEMBER 22, 2007

BERLIN 0855 GMT

Lüdden and Müller waited while two young members of the underground Neo-Nazi Democratic Party went about setting up the Enigma machine in Lüdden's office.

"This is the item we picked up last month from the Berlin museum. When TallOne sends the papers, we will be able to set the rotors, type in the correct code and decipher the communiqués. We are close, Herr Müller. I trust your contact will not let us down."

"Our contact has confirmed the original papers are still at Dylan's home, as is Clark's secretary."

"That is unfortunate for her," said Lüdden. "TallOne does not like to leave anything or anyone behind that could connect him to a mission."

Müller thought for a moment. "But, would it not be better to keep her as a hostage until we are sure we have exactly what we want?"

"You are sometimes much smarter than I give you credit for, Karl," replied Lüdden, smiling. "Contact TallOne and instruct him to keep the girl alive, for now."

45

SEPTEMBER 23, 2007

LONDON   **0110 GMT**

Dylan made his way through the streets of London, carefully avoiding the Control Zone on his way back to Dolphin Square. He had had a late dinner with Inspector Snow of Scotland Yard. Their discussion was primarily about the would-be bomber and the black Mercedes that landed in the slough during the chase from Auston House in Bradford. The inspector was able to identify the man who died in the explosion, but was not able to connect that incident to the black Mercedes. He did manage to trace the ownership of the vehicle, and the police had visited the address of record, a flat in central London, to speak to the owners. The elderly couple was adamant that their car was still in storage in a garage near Guildford. The Inspector explained what had happened, and advised them that their car, which had been in mint condition, was now severely damaged and located in the police pound. Dylan agreed with the Inspector that these people were not involved in the car chase. His lead had vanished, along with the Germans. It was after one o'clock in the morning when he finally made it back to his apartment. He was exhausted.

Dylan quickly checked the coin he had stuck in the doorjamb. It was still there. He opened the door and entered the room just as the telephone rang. It was Professor Kingsmill.

"Hello Sean, my boy. Hope I didn't wake you."

Dylan stifled a yawn and answered, "No, haven't found time to get to bed yet. How are you Professor?"

"I am fine. Fine," Kingsmill answered with a slight tinge of excitement. "I have come up with a theory on your riddle."

Dylan was instantly awake. "What?" he asked.

"Well, the German radio operators always shortened messages whenever possible. It saved them time decoding the documents. I am sure that applies here as well. Also, due to the ongoing battle, the original message was garbled a little when it was sent," the Professor stated matter of fact. "I think the radio operator may have dropped a few words and got a couple of the others mixed up. I have restructured the message and I believe it should have read, *"The first cargo was secured 4.30.45, co-ordinates are on the east west arms of the cross. The second cargo was delivered to the Black Knight 5.2.45. Final destination is unknown."*

"That sounds better, but it still doesn't make any sense to me," replied Dylan wearily.

The Professor paused for a moment. "Remember the Iron Cross you found in the cylinder?"

"Yes, but what of it?"

"The arms of the cross," Trudy Kingsmill declared excitedly. "That is where the coordinates are for the first cargo, whatever it is."

"Are you saying there is information on the arms of the Iron Cross medal I found with the papers?" Dylan asked incredulously.

The Professor ignored the rhetorical question and answered with a question of her own. "Where is the medal now?"

"At my cottage," replied Dylan. "But I don't remember seeing any markings on it. In fact it looked to be in quite good shape."

"Can you get it to me?" asked Professor Kingsmill.

Dylan's mind was racing, trying to process the information he had just received from the Professor while solving the dilemma of getting the medal from the cottage on Mayne Island, to Vancouver. "I will call Ronnie," he said. "She's staying at the cottage. I will have her send it to you via courier. It should be there within 24 hours. Call me as soon as you get it."

"There is one more thing, Sean. The 'Black Knight' that is mentioned in the communiqué. That is the submarine that both the Allies and Germany claim never existed."

"Professor, I think the Black Knight was real, but I don't know why no one wants the world to know. However, for the moment, let us keep that to ourselves. Okay?"

"Right you are." Trudy Kingsmill replied.

Dylan hung up the telephone for a moment, picked it up again and placed a call to the cottage.

The telephone only rang twice before Ronnie picked it up. It was good to hear the sound of her voice again. A few minutes into their conversation, Dylan could hear her frustration.

"Ronnie, I know it's not easy being shut off from the outside world," he said, trying to preempt the complaint he knew was coming, "but this little operation has taken some pretty scary twists, and I don't want you caught in the middle."

"The cottage is a beautiful place, Sean, but not when I'm alone."

"I will finish my work here tomorrow, and will be back in Vancouver on Thursday."

"That's great news," cried Ronnie. "Have you heard any news about Jim?"

"I spoke to the hospital and the police have moved him to a

secret location to complete his convalescence. He should be as good as new in a couple of weeks."

The news instantly changed Ronnie's mood. She seemed more upbeat and livelier. "Will you be coming straight here on Thursday?" she asked.

"I should be there in time for dinner," he replied. "In the meantime, I need you to package up that German medal, the Iron Cross, and give it to Ray next door. Ask him to ship it to Professor Kingsmill by courier. Tell him that it has to be delivered at once."

After almost a month of inaction, Ronnie was happy to have any form of responsibility back into her life. "I will wrap it in some bubble wrap and take it over right away. Where do I find the Professor's address?"

Dylan read the address from his Palm. Ronnie repeat it back to him.

"Keep the doors locked and advise Helen that security should be raised to the next level. See you on Thursday."

He hung up the telephone and pulled the deciphered messages out of his attaché case. He knew there were still many unanswered questions contained within the pages. What he did not know, was where or how he was going to find all of the answers. Dylan poured himself a glass of Irish Whisky, sat down and flipped through the pages in search of a clue.

MAYNE ISLAND   **1834 PDT**

Ronnie used a small piece of bubble wrap to protect the Iron Cross, stuffed it inside the shipping envelope and made her way across the three hundred foot distance to the home of Dylan's neighbour.

Ray Tilley was outside in the driveway, working on an old beat up pickup truck.

"Mr. Tilley," Ronnie called, "How are you today?"

"Just fine, Ms. Patterson. What brings you over to see this old man, today?"

Ronnie grinned at Tilley. He was only installing a new battery in the truck, but he was covered from head to toe with grease and grim. "Sean asked me to see if you could get this package sent by courier today. It has to be in Vancouver as soon as possible."

"Today is Sunday. There is no courier service on Sundays, unless Mr. Dylan is prepared to pay a little extra." Tilley explained.

"Oh," replied Ronnie. "I suppose he would. Could call your courier service and see when they could have it delivered?"

Tilley pondered the situation. "Let me see. If I get this battery installed by seven, I could have the package on the 7:30 Ferry. If I call my cousin James in Tsawwassen, he could pick it up at the Ferry Terminal and have it delivered before noon tomorrow."

Ronnie was surprised and delighted. "Are you also the courier service?" she asked, straining to keep from laughing.

"I am the only one on Mayne Island. I send and receive all courier packages for everybody on this rock."

She smiled at the old man. "That would be very good service, Mr. Tilley. I am sure Sean will be very pleased."

Dylan's neighbour looked at Ronnie. His eyes drifted to the package and then to his hands. "If I could ask you to put your envelope on the front seat," he said holding up his grease covered hands, "I will get on it as soon as I finish here and clean up."

Having successfully completed her mission, Ronnie thanked the old man and meandered back to the cottage. She was feeling better than she had in weeks. Today was a good day.

46

SEPTEMBER 24, 2007

MAYNE ISLAND   **1019 PDT**

The morning Ferry snuggled up to the Village Bay dock one minute ahead of schedule. There were only a dozen cars and four walk-on passengers onboard. A crewmember dropped the safety chain and when the last passenger stepped off the roadway into the secure area, he motioned for the lead vehicle to drive off the ramp.

Like a line of sheep, the cars followed in single file until the last vehicle, a black Mercedes, had disembarked.

The Mercedes immediately pulled over to the curb. The driver, TallOne, was waiting as his passenger studied the map.

"Which way do we go, Faust?"

Faust was scanning back and forth between the map and a handwritten note. "The instructions from Müller's contact said we were to go left and follow the perimeter road for eight miles. The house will be on the left side just after a sharp right turn." He pointed to the road. "Turn left at the top of the hill and follow the perimeter road."

"Do you ever know what you are doing?" TallOne mumbled aloud as he negotiated up the small hill, turned left, and headed towards Dylan's cottage.

Faust shrugged his shoulders. He knew it would not be wise to challenge TallOne's remark.

VANCOUVER   1148 PDT

The Professor greeted the courier driver at the door. Maggie, the friendly over-size Labrador, stood at her side.

"Thank you," she said, taking the package from the man. Trudy Kingsmill tipped the driver a dollar and closed the door. "Well, Maggie, let us see if this sheds any light on the mysterious messages." The dog waddled behind the Professor as she entered the study, opening the envelope and extracting the EKII Iron Cross medal as she went. She looked at the decoration. *"This is very nice. Very nice, indeed,"* she said gleefully.

The Professor turned the medal over in her hands, looking at the four arms of the cross. She could not see any signs of writing or etched letters or numbers. *"I think maybe someone has put something over on our dear Sean,"* she mumbled to herself. *"There is nothing here."*

Mrs. MacKenzie popped her head into the study to announce that lunch was ready. Trudy Kingsmill unceremoniously put the medal down on her desk. She was hungry. She would think about what to do about the Iron Cross after she had enjoyed her lunch.

LONDON   2024 GMT

Dylan was in his apartment at the Dolphin, translating the remaining pages that he had deciphered at Bletchley Park, when his private cell phone rang. It was Ray Tilley. From the instant Tilley said 'Hello', Dylan knew his neighbour was worried.

"Ray, it is good to hear from you. What's up?"

Tilley took a deep breath, as was his custom before he spoke about anything he thought was important. "Mr. Dylan, Sean, there were some very strange looking men around here today. They showed up about an hour ago, asking where you lived. I didn't tell them anything, Mr. Dylan."

"Whoa, slow down, Ray." Dylan interjected. "Who was around? What did they say?"

"The two men in the Mercedes. They were looking for your house," his excited neighbour explained. "It was as if they already knew you were not here. I got a bad feeling about them, I do."

Dylan stayed calm. He wanted to get as much information as possible but could not let on to his neighbour that he was also very concerned about these men. "What did they look like," he asked.

"That's easy," replied Tilley. "One was the tallest man I've ever seen. He must have been nearly seven feet tall. The other was the opposite. He was short and stocky, looked like a boxer."

Dylan knew it was TallOne and Faust. He also knew Ronnie was in trouble. "Ray, don't do anything yet. I will look after it. Just keep an eye out to see if anyone leaves. I will be there tomorrow."

"Okay, Mr. Dylan, I'll stand watch."

Dylan knew he could count on his neighbour. "Stay cool, Ray. Everything is going to be okay. Do not go out until I get there. Okay."

"Okay."

Dylan was worried about Ronnie. He immediately picked up the telephone and placed a call to the cottage. An automated operator came on the line and announced that the line was not in service. Dylan had a private number to access Helen's security system without using the home telephone. He tried the number but the result was the same. The recording stated the number was *'out of order'*. Somehow, TallOne and Faust had managed to sever all of the communication links to the cottage. He thought about calling the police detachment on the island, but opted to wait. Having the police arrive at the cottage would surely get Ronnie killed. He would have to wait until he was there before he could do anything. His only hope was that Ronnie was okay.

Dylan called the airline and booked the next flight back to Vancouver.

MAYNE ISLAND   **1325 PDT**

Ronnie had just finished her lunch when TallOne and Faust knocked on the door and walked in. They did not waste time with small talk. Faust gave Ronnie a quick backhand that knocked her hard against the wall. As she staggered to regain her balance, he hit her again, sending her crashing to the floor.

"We want the papers," Faust sneered. "Where are they?"

Ronnie was terrified. "I don't know what you are talking about," she lied.

Faust took two quick steps towards her. She cringed, expecting another blow from the ugly little man. She did not expect the vicious kick he delivered to her mid-section that knocked the wind from her lungs. She was gasping for air as Faust hauled her up by her hair and tossed her like a rag doll across the room. Ronnie landed against the chairs and fell to the floor. Faust was sweating, his face even more grotesque than usual. He was enjoying himself.

TallOne stepped between Faust and Ronnie. He reached down, picked up the frightened woman by her left arm, and callously dropped her onto a chair.

"Tie her up and gag her," said TallOne. "I don't want you to kill her," he growled, "not just yet. We must find the papers and get them to Lüdden. When he says so, then you can have your fun."

The smaller man grunted, but obeyed. He grabbed hold of the electrical cord that extended from a toaster and ripped it from the wall. He snapped the wire, tearing it from the appliance. The toaster crashed onto the floor. Faust used the electrical cord to tie Ronnie's arms behind the chair.

"Where are the papers?" Faust asked in a menacing voice.

"I don't know what you're talking about, you moron," Ronnie blurted out with instant regret.

Faust's fat hand smashed against the side of her face, knocking her and the chair to the floor. She was out cold.

"I told you not to do that, asshole," yelled TallOne. "Now she's unconscious and we don't have the papers."

TallOne reached down and pulled Ronnie, still tied to the chair, to an upright position. "Don't touch her again unless I tell you. Now find those damned papers."

The two men set out and systematically trashed the cottage in their search for the hidden papers. Twenty minutes later, Faust found a package on a shelf in the living room, stuffed between the copies of boating magazines.

"I have them. There are six coded pages, correct?" he asked, looking at TallOne for confirmation.

"I don't know the number of pages, but they are all coded and there should be a Swastika somewhere on the papers." Faust quickly checked the pages and located the Nazi symbol on the pages. "The symbol is here," he said proudly. "I found them."

TallOne looked at the smaller man. "I am going to call Herr Lüdden for instructions." He looked at his shorter companion. "Yes," he smiled, "I will also tell him that you found the papers." His face turned serious as he pointed towards Ronnie. "Finish gagging her. We don't want any noise when she comes around."

Faust watched as TallOne went out onto the balcony to make his call. He looked at the unconscious woman and hissed. He rummaged through the kitchen drawers looking for anything to gag the woman. He found a roll of gray duct tape in a side drawer. Faust grabbed a damp dishcloth from the sink, stuffed it into her open mouth and quickly wound the tape around her head. The fact that she could hardly breathe did not concern him.

TallOne flipped his cellular telephone closed as he returned to the room.

"Lüdden wants me to find a fax machine and send the papers through to him at once. We are to keep the woman alive until he is sure he has what he needs. TallOne gathered up the papers. As he prepared to exit the cottage, he turned to Faust, "We are going to wait for Mr. Dylan to show up. I think you will enjoy having your way with him even more that this woman."

Faust's eyes seemed to light up. "Yes, I owe Mr. Dylan a good time," he said with an evil sneer. "Dylan will soon learn what pain is really like."

TallOne laughed aloud as he left the cottage.

VANCOUVER   1412 PDT

The Professor always felt that she worked better after a good meal and today was no exception. She picked up the Iron Cross medal, took a large magnifying glass from the drawer and closely examined every millimeter of the German World War II decoration. *"Strange,"* she muttered to herself, *"not a mark on it anywhere."*

The Professor was disheartened. Her theory on the meaning of the riddle appeared to be wrong. *"Not sure Sean will be impressed,"* she mumbled.

Mrs. Mackenzie entered the study and placed a cup of tea on the Professor's desk. "My, my, Professor Kingsmill. Why so glum?"

The Professor explained her dilemma concerning the medal.

"Well, don't you be asking me to solve the problem," she said with a little laugh, "It seems I can't see well enough to find anything these days. It might as well be invisible."

Trudy Kingsmill looked up at the woman. "Pardon me?"

The housekeeper paused for a moment. "I just said that I couldn't see. Whatever you are looking for might just as well be invisible to me."

Professor jumped up from her desk and went over to the small cupboard next to the window. The housekeeper had not seen her move that fast in years. Mrs. MacKenzie left the study, shaking her head. "Thank you, dear." Professor Kingsmill called after the departing housekeeper, "I think you have solved my predicament." She turned away from the cupboard and quickly made her way back to the desk, a portable black light unit held firmly in her hand.

Trudy Kingsmill flicked on the switch as she picked up the Iron Cross medal from the desk. Holding the old war decoration in her left hand, she slowly scanned the black light over the four arms of the military award. The near-ultraviolet radiant energy was just outside the visible spectrum. The Professor knew that when the invisible black light hit the Iron Cross, materials on the surface of the medal would absorb and then re-radiate light at longer wavelengths within the visibility range of the human eye. Professor Kingsmill watched as the conversion of energy from the invisible black light caused the surface of the medal to fluoresce and emit visible light. As the black light passed over the arms of the Iron Cross, she was able to read the message someone had written on the medal over sixty years ago. *"Helmut Mohr 099893"*. Adrenalin coursed through her body as she anxiously flipped the medal over to scan the other side. Again, the black light reflected off the surface, revealing the hidden message. *"Latitude 60 degrees, 8 minutes, 27.3 seconds North, Longitude 2 degrees, 3 minutes, 42 seconds West".*

The professor had found the missing piece of Dylan's puzzle on the arms of the Iron Cross.

Buoyed by her discovery, Professor Trudy Kingsmill went to her library of books and selected a large dog-eared Atlas. After several minutes of searching, she was looking at the spot the coordinates written on the Iron Cross represented. Whatever it was that Dylan was looking for; it was located in an obscure place known as The Devil's Finger, on the western side of Foula Island.

The Professor picked up the telephone to call Dylan.

BERLIN **2348 GMT**

Lüdden stood waiting by the fax machine. He had a telephone receiver in his hand. "Why is the machine not ringing?"

"Patience, Herr Lüdden. It is coming," replied Müller.

A moment later, the facsimile machine rang twice before recognizing the signal from the sender and responding with its own electronic signature. Instantly the device began receiving incoming messages. Lüdden smiled as the first of the six pages TallOne sent slowly emerged from the machine. As each successive page appeared, the smile on the face of the Neo-Nazi Democratic Party leader grew larger.

"We have the papers, Herr Müller," said an excited Lüdden. "This is a great day for our party. We must run these through our Enigma machine to decipher the codes. At long last, we will have the means to regain power in Germany."

The last page had not left the grip of the fax machine before the telephone rang. It was TallOne. "Herr Lüdden, I am calling to confirm you have received the papers."

"Yes, TallOne, I have them. You have done well."

"Do you wish me to dispose of the girl?" he asked.

Lüdden thought for a moment and replied, "No, not yet. Dylan will come looking for her. When he does, kill them both."

TallOne acknowledged the order, "Of course."

"Be careful of Dylan. He is very clever," cautioned Lüdden. "Have our associates in Vancouver meet you at Dylan's home. They may be of some help to you when he arrives. I do not want any loose ends."

"Yes, Herr Lüdden, I understand," replied TallOne.

SEATTLE   1455 PDT

Chief Samuel O'Brien of the FBI was waiting in his office when Mike Gerrard arrived. The head of the Seattle arm of the FBI operations sat in his high backed chair. The thoughts he was processing in his mind were causing the furrows on his forehead to appear as if etched in stone.

"Something is not right," he said as Gerrard sat himself down in the large leather chair facing O'Brien.

"Not right?" questioned Gerrard. "What's not right?"

O'Brien leaned forward, as if he was going to tell a secret. "I'm not sure, Mike, but I have a feeling that your partner is not totally committed to his job these days."

"I'm not sure what you mean, Chief."

"This little episode about some papers allegedly from a German submarine. The Gary Anderson I knew would not have been so intent on chasing such a bogus lead. I read both your reports. It still seems that Anderson thinks there is some legitimacy to this preposterous claim."

"With all due respect, sir, I believe the order to pursue this issue came down from upstairs. Gary did not take this matter on of his own volition."

"I understand that, Mike. However, he should have realized that it was just burning up FBI funds and recommended that we stop. We train you people to realize when a lead is false."

"I understand and I agree that we should have stopped," offered Gerrard. "I tried to tell Gary a couple of times, but he was really into this case. Actually, I've never seen him so intense."

O'Brien leaned closer. "Do me a favour, Mike, keep an eye on Gary and let me know if you see anything I should know about."

Gerrard gave the Chief a look of concern. "Gary is my partner, and a good friend of mine. Are you asking me to ...."

O'Brien stopped him short. "No, I just want to be sure he's okay and that we get him to understand that all the business about coded papers and missing submarines is over. He is a good agent and I don't want to lose him."

The agent relaxed. "Sure, Chief. No problem."

"I am going to put in for a transfer for both of you."

Gerrard knew the decision was final. There was nothing left to say. He turned and left the office.

O'Brien watched as the agent moved down the corridor between the rows of agent's cubicles. He reached down, picked up the telephone, punched a series of numbers and waited. The other party picked up the receiver on the second ring and spoke a single word, "Report".

"This is Chief O'Brien from the FBI, Seattle office.

According to William Hill at Bletchley Park, the papers Dylan found appear to be worthless. I spoke to agents Gerrard and Anderson. There was no mention of the actual mission of the U-112 anywhere in either of their reports. As far as the Bureau is concerned, Dylan is chasing a phantom ship and a non-existent treasure. As of today, the file is officially closed."

The Chief waited for a response. There was only silence, followed by the sound of a click, as the other party hung up.

LONDON   **2355 GMT**

"Sorry to call so late, Sean," said Ozzy in an apologetic tone, "but I have some news you might be interested in,"

"No problem, Oz. What's up?"

"According to the official documents, Lüdden is a lower minister in the German government," he stated, "but there have been persistent rumors that he has ties to the underground Neo-Nazi Democratic Party here in Berlin."

"I thought the Nazi Party was illegal in Germany."

"That's why it's underground. They are a bunch of die-hard Nazis trying to keep the Third Reich ideology alive until it is has grown big enough to bring it out into the open."

"Keep a tab on him. If he is behind all this crap that has been going on, we could do the world a favour by turning him over to the authorities."

"Yeah," laughed Ozzy, "provided the authorities aren't part of his little underground movement." He paused for a moment. "What's happening on your front?"

Dylan confirmed that the Professor had solved the riddle relating to the first delivery of the U-1220. "I just tried to reach of

Ronnie to tell her, but I couldn't get through. She's at my cottage, but there seems to be some problem with the telephone service."

"Why don't you have your neighbour go check it out?"

"It was my neighbour who alerted me to the problem. Apparently there were some strangers poking around earlier and from Ray's description, it sounds like TallOne and his partner."

"Aren't those the guys you had the run-in with in Germany?"

"Yes. They are two very mean bastards and not the type of people Ronnie should have to deal with."

"Can't you call the cops?" asked Ozzy.

"I thought about that, but the island doesn't have any real cops, and sending in a couple of well-intentioned locals could get everyone killed. Helen's security system has a backup so Ronnie should be okay. I will be back home tomorrow, so I can check it out myself. Once I get everything straightened away, I will come back over and we can visit the treasure site. I should be back in about a week."

"Mind if I bring Carol?"

"Are you and Carol still hanging out together?"

Ozzy hesitated for a moment. "Yeah, she is quite the lady. She is also a good person to have on your side in a fight. All that and she is smart, too."

Dylan laughed. "You are right there." He paused for a second to consider the options. "Sure, bring her along; we could use an extra pair of hands."

"See you next week," replied Ozzy as he hung up the phone

The first direct flight back to Vancouver was at 0950. Dylan called the airline and made the booking. He would be there by noon, local time. Getting to the cottage would probably take another three and a half hours.

47

SEPTEMBER 25, 2007

BERLIN   **0912 GMT**

Hans Lüdden and Müller were huddled over the Enigma machine, reading the decoded papers.

"It could mean only one thing," said Hans Lüdden. "The coordinates for the delivery of the first cargo are written on the wings of the Captain's Iron Cross."

"But how would you know that, Herr Lüdden?"

"Every German submarine commander was awarded the EKII Iron Cross. The government presented the award so freely at the end of the war it became a joke. It was said that the only use for the medal on a submarine was as a compass to show which way was down."

"What about the riddle?" asked Müller.

"The riddle is a version of an old German school yard rhyme for telling directions," answered Lüdden as he reread the papers. "The Iron Cross must have been with the papers."

"It must still be at Dylan's home."

"That would make sense. Get hold of TallOne and tell him to go through the house and find it."

Müller dialed the telephone number for TallOne but a recording said the number was not available.

Hans Lüdden was becoming frustrated. "Call your contact

and have him go to the cottage and tell TallOne to find that medal. We must have it to guarantee our success. Tell him there is more money. Tell him anything. Just find that Iron Cross."

VANCOUVER   **1620 PDT**

Dylan arrived at the Vancouver International Airport over two hours behind schedule. He knew there was no way he was going to clear customs, pick up his luggage and get to Mayne Island in less than four hours. He placed a call through to an old friend.

It was less than an hour before Tim Wilson picked him up at the terminal door. Dylan tossed his bag behind the seat as he got into Wilson's beat up sports car.

"So, let me get this straight," Wilson said. "You want me to fly you over to Mayne Island and drop you at nine thousand feet and you'll return my parachute back to me in a couple of days. Right?"

Dylan looked at his friend. "Just trust me on this one, Tim. There's a lot at stake."

"The same goes for me, too," exclaimed Wilson. "If Transport Canada catches me, I could lose my plane and my whole Sport Parachuting business."

"Look, we can turn off the transponder and just climb out and over, you can drop me and head down to water level and come back across the Strait."

"Shit. You always were getting me into some wild and crazy adventure."

Dylan knew he could count on Tim. "Where is the plane?" he asked with a grin.

"At the Delta airport. It's a Pilatus Porter. We can be up in the air in about an hour and you will be down on Mayne Island forty-five minutes later."

"What rig am I jumping?"

"It's a Quasar II rig with a Stellar main and reserve. It is similar to the one you used with the Special Forces Demo Team. It handles a little quicker on the turns, and it is very soft on the openings. You should feel right at home."

"Thanks Tim, I owe you a big one."

"Hell, just bring the rig back to the DropZone and buy me a beer. Then you can tell me what this was all about."

"Not a problem." Dylan flipped open his cell phone and punched in a number.

MAYNE ISLAND   1635 PDT

The knock on the cottage door startled Faust who immediately extracted his gun from inside his jacket. He peered out the side window to see who was there. *"Goddamned salesman,"* he mumbled to himself.

Ronnie lifted her head. She still had a throbbing headache and two large bruises on her face were turning a dark bluish colour. She tried to move her hands but the electrical cord only seemed to tighten.

Faust holstered his weapon and opened the door a few inches, peering out at the unwanted intruder. "We don't want any. Go away," he yelled, waving his fat hand in front of Anderson's face. "Get outta here before I get pissed off and throw your sorry butt into the water."

Anderson looked at the short pug-nosed Faust. *"This guy wouldn't last fifteen minutes in the city,"* he thought to himself. "Hans Müller sent me. I've got a message for Mr. TallOne."

Faust stepped back. He did not know anything about someone coming to visit TallOne, but the mention of Müller's name got his attention. He opened the door and motioned for Anderson to enter. Faust withdrew his gun as Anderson passed. "Turn around and put your hands on the wall. Don't move until I tell you to."

"What is this all about?" asked Anderson.

Faust said nothing. He stepped behind his visitor and patted him down. He seemed relieved to find the man was not carrying a weapon. He had missed the tiny single shot .22 pistol Anderson had in an ankle holster.

"Sit down over there. TallOne will be back shortly."

Faust sat down opposite Anderson. "What is the message?"

"I told you, I was supposed to see a Mr. TallOne. If that isn't you, and judging by your obvious membership in the world of the vertically challenged, I would say you are not him, so I can't give you his message, can I?"

Faust was furious at Anderson's comment. "TallOne and I work as partners," he boasted, "Whatever you have to tell him, you can tell to me."

Anderson was sure Faust was just a little man who felt a need for power to compensate for his shortcomings. He decided to play with the man's mind. "Our friends need something from here. They want us to find it."

"They already have what they want," Faust shot back with a know-it-all sneer.

"No my little friend, they need something more." Anderson was trying to decide if he could chance telling Faust what they needed. For an instant, he thought of trying to make a deal with him to find the Iron Cross and then resell it to Müller. Anderson looked closely at Faust. It was a dumb idea. This piece of overused muscle was not capable of making a deal, much less being trusted. He looked over at Ronnie. "Who is she?"

"None of your business," Faust replied tersely.

The door to the cottage swung open as TallOne and two other men entered the cottage.

Faust jumped up and moved near TallOne. "This guy arrived a few minutes ago. He says he has a message for you."

TallOne walked over and stood in front of Anderson. "So, what is this message that you have for me, my friend?"

The FBI man looked up at the imposing figure standing over him. Anderson had met many violent men during his career with the Bureau and never felt any sense of fear. TallOne was an exception. He decided to play it straight. "Müller called me and asked me to come here to find some German war decoration, an Iron Cross."

Ronnie involuntarily stiffened at the mention of the medal.

"Herr Müller does not often ask someone to do something, he usually gives them an order," replied TallOne. "Where is this Iron Cross supposed to be? And what is so important about it?"

"Here, somewhere in this house. What significance it has, I have no idea."

TallOne motioned to the others. "The Iron Cross is a World War II medal." He took a pen from inside his jacket, picked up a newspaper from the table, and hastily drew a sketch of the award. "It is about two inches by two inches. It should have some sort of ribbon attached. Check every room and find it. Go!"

"You want me to look too," asked Anderson.

TallOne hesitated and then replied, "Of course. If you are working for Herr Müller, then work for him."

The five men scattered to search for the Iron Cross. One of the men that had arrived with TallOne quickly doubled back.

"That guy," he whispered to TallOne, "he is an FBI agent."

"Are you sure?"

"Positive! Two years ago, he busted my brother for selling some 'BC Bud' across the border."

TallOne looked at the man. "Go find the medal. Leave this FBI man to me."

Ronnie was awake. She heard the FBI reference but did not understand what it meant. She was careful not to move. She was terrified that Faust would catch her awake and hit her again. The cottage was quiet except for the odd sounds of the contents of a drawer emptying on to the floor, or a cupboard door slammed shut. Then she heard the footsteps coming towards her. She began to shake uncontrollably.

"I think it might be faster to ask the woman." It was Faust. He was grinning at the thought of using his fists to get the information from Ronnie. "Wake up, bitch," he yelled, pulling Ronnie's hair back to look at her face. Faust slapped Ronnie across the face. "The medal. Where is it?"

Ronnie knew she could not take the punishment Faust would enjoy inflicting on her. She raised her head, a small trickle of blood seeped from between her lips. She was about to speak when Anderson came from the kitchen area waving the courier receipt.

"Stop! The Iron Cross is in Vancouver. She sent it to," Anderson read the receipt, "a Professor Kingsmill. It left Sunday. It was to be delivered today."

Faust stepped back, obviously disappointed that he could not use force to extract the information from the woman.

Ronnie's head was still spinning from the force of Faust's attack. She closed her eyes, feeling stupid for having put 'World War II Medal' on the courier shipping form.

TallOne pulled out his cell phone and tried to call Germany to report the situation. The cell phone did not work. Anderson offered his. TallOne took the phone and stepped outside, closing the door behind him. He dialed a number and waited. Lüdden answered on the second ring.

"The Iron Cross is gone. It was couriered to Vancouver."

"Retrieve that medal at all costs. It is vital to our success."

"I will take care of it today. But, we have another problem."

"What?" Lüdden asked in an irritated voice.

"This person Müller sent with a message is an FBI agent."

There was a moment of silence before Lüdden spoke. "I know. He is Müller's contact. Take him with you. When you have recovered the Iron Cross, he will be of no further use to us. When it is appropriate, kill him."

TallOne smiled. "As you wish, Herr Lüdden," he replied, closing the flip phone as he returned to the cottage. "Faust, you stay here with these two." He nodded towards Anderson, "You come with me to this Professor Kingsmill's to get the Iron Cross."

"What about her?"

"Do nothing until I return."

MAYNE ISLAND   **1945 PDT**

The vibrant colours displayed on the foliage surrounding the Delta Airport signaled the impending end of summer. Flocks of Canadian Geese were forming in their usual 'V' patterns in preparation for their long journey south to escape the harsh Canadian winters. Normally, this was one of Dylan's favourite times of the year, but today he had other, more pressing issues to occupy his mind as the Pilatus PC-6 aircraft began to roll down the runway.

The turbo-charged 550 hp Pratt & Whitney engine easily lifted the aircraft from the asphalt surface in less than eight hundred feet. Tim Wilson initiated a slow bank to the right as the Pilatus began its climb out over the Georgia Strait. A fine haze hung over the islands.

"This thing really climbs well," shouted Dylan.

"Over 1,100 feet per minute," answered Wilson. "That's Mayne Island dead ahead, about eight miles."

Dylan adjusted his parachute rig, ensuring everything was secure. "What's the wind?"

"The direction is 290 degrees, at about 6 knots. You shouldn't have any problem getting in."

"The sky is perfect. It is just coming up to dusk. Fly one circuit to signal Ray to turn on the light." Dylan had called his neighbour to alert him that he would be arriving by parachute. He requested Ray shine a portable light skyward near the back of his cottage. Ray's house was far enough away from Dylan's cottage that he could use the light as a guide in order to land unobserved.

"There's the light, southeast corner," Wilson announced. "You want a jump run or are you just going out over the light?"

"Over the light is fine. With this 'chute, I can get in from there. Don't cut the engine; I don't want to draw attention to the plane."

Wilson held the aircraft steady, just easing off the throttle ever so slightly to reduce their speed. "We're at nine thousand feet, directly over the light," he shouted.

Dylan unlatched the door. He pushed it outwards and up out of the way. He gave the thumbs-up signal to Wilson and dove headlong out of the Pilatus.

At the exit altitude, Mayne Island had the appearance of a

large Amoeba drifting on the water. The sky was darkening and the lights on the island began to appear. The freefall portion of a jump from nine thousand feet above sea level is normally around forty-five seconds, which allowed for a safe opening at two thousand feet. Dylan reached terminal velocity in less than fifteen seconds as he passed through eight thousand feet. He knew that once he passed two thousand feet, he was less than ten seconds from the ground.

Dylan knew he did not want to be hanging in the evening sky any longer than necessary. He passed the two thousand foot level and continued downward. He wanted to open his parachute just below the one thousand foot level. That would give him a five-second margin of error. He checked his altimeter. He had three hundred feet to go. The trees on the island immediately started to appear very large. Dylan could easily identify the streetlights below. *"This would not be a good time for a malfunction,"* he thought, taking one last check of the altimeter. At eight hundred feet, Dylan pulled the release and the Spectra parachute opened instantly. He grabbed the steering toggles and did a cursory check of the canopy. Satisfied, Dylan scanned the ground, locating the light shining up from his neighbours' property.

He was only four hundred feet above the trees. In less than forty seconds, he turned on his final approach. The canopy handled perfectly as he maneuvered into position for a landing directly behind Ray Tilley's cottage. He touched down lightly, only twelve feet from his neighbour who was standing, looking up into the sky in the opposite direction. The parachute canopy floated to the ground beside Tilley, who jumped in surprise. "What the hell is going on?" he gasped.

"No time to explain Ray," replied Dylan taking off the parachute gear. "Keep this inside for me. I'll get it later." he said, handing the rig to Tilley. "Tell me again about the men who came by asking for me," he said making his way towards Ray's cottage.

"They were hard looking dudes. One was short and stocky man with a badly mashed nose. The other was a very tall, muscular guy. They came by asking where you lived. I haven't seen them since." Tilley paused, shaking his head. "You sure have some strange friends"

"These guys may be strange, but they are definitely not friends." Dylan paused for a second. "Do you have a gun in the house?" he asked.

"I've got an old single shot Colt revolver, but it hasn't been fired in years."

"It's better than nothing. Can I borrow it?"

Tilley jogged off into the house and returned a moment later carrying a bundle of cloth in his hand. "Here, you can have it," he said, as he opened the cloth to reveal the old Colt revolver. "It's loaded, but there's no guarantee it will fire."

Dylan looked at the old relic and shrugged. "Well, let's hope I don't have to use it," he said pensively, giving Tilley a friendly slap on the back. "Thanks." He quickly scanned the area. Daylight had almost disappeared and with it, the chance that someone would see him approach the cottage. Picking up the Colt, he turned and quickly disappeared through the trees.

Dylan paused beside a large fir tree, pulled out a pair of binoculars. The lights in his cottage were off and it was impossible to make out the figures. He had programmed Helen to cut all power inside the home in any situation involving intruders. She had done her job well. As he turned away, he noticed someone strike a match. At first, he thought it might be Ronnie, but a quick look through the binoculars dispelled that notion.

A second candle was lit and then a third. Dylan could easily make out the shape of the man with the matches. It was Faust. A second man appeared to be sleeping in a chair while a third was looking through the drawers. Dylan scanned the room again. On the second pass, he realized the figure in the chair was Ronnie. Her head was hanging forward. She was not moving. A surge of anger took hold of Dylan. He began to move towards the cottage, but immediately stepped back. He would have to have a plan before entering the lion's den. An ancient single shot pistol was not going to work against Faust and his accomplices. Even if he got Ronnie out of the cottage, he would have to have an escape route.

Dylan turned away from the cottage and stealthily moved down towards the water's edge where he kept his forty-one foot Morgan Islander Ketch 'Alcor' moored. He carefully avoided the path and negotiated his way down the rocky slope towards his private dock. He did not want to give Faust and company a chance to spot him. They would see him soon enough.

It only took Dylan twenty minutes to ready the Alcor for departure. He removed the laptop computer from the boat and made his way back towards the cottage. He stumbled several times as he negotiated the hill, almost dropping the laptop onto the rocks below.

Dylan approached the cottage from the East side. He could hear Faust talking as one of his accomplices left to meet the last Ferry from the mainland.

"Call me on my cell when you see him and follow him here. I want to take care of him and the woman personally."

Dylan could hear the vindictiveness emanating from the man as he spoke.

After Faust had returned inside, Dylan slowly crept up to the rear of the garage where the telephone junction box was located.

Three minutes later, he had connected his laptop into the cable feed. He booted up the portable computer and a few keystrokes later, he was in control of Helen's security functions.

It took only a moment for Dylan to reprogram Helen to use an on-screen chat system and not her usual voice response. He typed in a question. *"Who is in the house?"*

Helen responded immediately. *"There have been a total of six visitors in the last twenty-four hours. Sensors show three persons are currently in the house. One is Ronnie Patterson and there are two unknowns. A third unknown departed fifteen minutes ago and has not returned. Two additional unknowns departed the house two hours and ten minutes ago and have not returned."*

Dylan's mind was racing. How could he get Ronnie from the house without Faust shooting either or both of them? He looked at his watch, typed another message to Helen and waited for her confirmation. He closed his laptop, shoved the Colt into his pocket and made his way beneath the balcony. Dylan followed the slope of the property on the outside perimeter of the house until the balcony was almost out of reach. He carefully hoisted himself up and peered over the edge. He was directly opposite Ronnie.

Once again, he checked his watch. Twenty seconds to go. Dylan counted down the time. As he called out the final three seconds, he pulled himself up, swung over the railing and onto the balcony floor. At the very same instant, Helen's computerized program had turned on the power. The four high-intensity strobe lights at the front of the house were flashing wildly, accompanied by the sound of the security siren.

Faust and his accomplice panicked and raced from the house. "Smash those goddamned lights," Faust screamed. "And find that fucking siren and kill it."

Dylan was already into the living area and untying Ronnie before the first light went out. Ronnie could not believe her eyes. "Sean?" She tried to stand but her legs would not support her. "Where did you come from?"

The second light went out and then the third. Dylan picked Ronnie up and headed out the balcony door. "Don't talk. Just hang on." He followed the balcony to the back stairs leading to the dock.

As they reached the bottom of the stairs, the wailing of the siren suddenly ceased. The fourth light flashed once and then went out. The sky was black.

Dylan did not worry about being spotted and took the main pathway down to the waiting Alcor. He made the leap from the dock to the deck of the boat and with as much care as possible under the conditions, deposited Ronnie in the centre cockpit.

He could hear the voices booming back at the cottage. Faust and his accomplice had discovered Ronnie was missing. Faust was livid.

Dylan pulled the fan switch to clear any gas vapours and hopped off the boat. He immediately released the last two lines that secured the boat against the dock. He pushed the craft away from the dock and jumped back onboard. The adrenalin was coursing through his veins as he raced to get the boat started and moved out of range of Faust's guns. *"Don't fail me now, baby,"* pleaded Dylan as he turned the key to Alcor's engine. The small Volvo-Penta engine sputtered once and then sprang to life. Dylan engaged the engine into the forward position and pushed the throttle fully forward. Alcor began to make way just as Faust's accomplice came running along the dock, his gun firing wildly towards the boat.

Dylan hesitated for an instant, and then picked up Ray Tilley's old Colt.

"This thing had better work," he muttered to himself as he took aim at his adversary and pulled the trigger.

Dylan had not heard such an explosion from a pistol before. The gun fired with such velocity, the recoil knocked Dylan backwards onto the deck. He landed without incident and quickly pulled himself up to look for Faust's accomplice. The force of the bullet had propelled the man off the dock onto the rocks by the shoreline. The single shot had taken most of the man's upper body with it as it passed through him and slammed into the cliff face behind. *"Shit,"* said Dylan, as he gazed down at the gun. He shook his head in amazement. *"They don't make them like that anymore."*

Dylan made his way to the centre cockpit, eased the throttle back to mid-position and steered the 'Alcor' out into the Strait. He set a course for Sydney harbour on Vancouver Island. Once underway, he engaged the autopilot and assisted a dazed but grateful Ronnie down into the main salon area. She was recovering fast and wanted to talk, but Dylan insisted she stay quiet and remain calm. They would have time to talk later. He went topside and switched on the running lights. Dylan knew there would be no more Ferries leaving Mayne Island this night. Neither Faust nor his accomplice could get off the island.

Dylan returned below to tend to Ronnie. She was weak and had a few bruises, but otherwise awake and alert. He grabbed his cellular telephone and placed a call.

48

SEPTEMBER 26, 2007

MAYNE ISLAND   **0615 PDT**

Faust found the remains of the shattered body on the rocks near the dock as his other hired muscle returned from the Ferry docks. Faust wasted no time entering the vehicle. The two men quickly vacated Dylan's cottage and headed back to the landing.

When they arrived at the dock, it became obvious that they had nowhere to go until morning. It would prove to be a most uncomfortable and sleepless night as they waited for the first Ferry to arrive.

Faust spent the long hours cursing Dylan. As the sun appeared through the trees, he got out of the vehicle and walked up to the ticket booth. There was no one around. He spotted a tattered schedule posted on the ticket booth's window, wiped the morning dew from the glass and read the list of times for the daily sailings. The first scheduled departure from Mayne Island was at 0705. Faust kicked the side of the booth, turned and made his way back to the car. It was small consolation that they were the first in line to board the ship.

Faust watched a succession of Inter-Island ferries appearing from behind the surrounding islands and slowly making passage towards unknown destinations. He checked his watch. Still a half hour to go before the first ferry would arrive at Mayne Island. He would take the ship to Vancouver Island, where they would catch the main ferry back to the mainland. Faust's partner had remained silent during the entire night. He knew this man with the mashed face and huge meaty hands was a cold-blooded killer devoid of any compassion. He was content not to test Faust's disposition.

An open-decked ferry finally appeared around the point of the island and headed for the dock. For any other person, the scene would have been something out of a Norman Rockwell painting, full of the anticipation and excitement that came with traveling by boat.

The early morning weekday travelers were busily preparing to leave the ship. One mother was rounding up her two sons, trying to corral them into her SUV before the ship landed. The crew readied the lines to secure the ferry. The passengers who had arrived behind Faust were scurrying to their vehicles, eager to get onboard and continue their day's journey.

The atmosphere was in direct contrast to what was running through Faust's mind. He had called TallOne and told him what had happened. TallOne did not display any emotion, simply telling Faust to be on the ten-thirty ferry from Swartz Bay to Tsawwassen. He said he would meet him onboard the ship.

Faust knew that Lüdden and Müller would be pissed. He did not want to have to tell them that Dylan had rescued the girl. He thought it would be better if he told TallOne, but then, Faust knew that might only make things worse, if that were possible.

When the early morning passengers had departed from the ship, the attendant walked over and tapped on the roof of Faust's car. The sudden movement shocked Faust. He instinctively reached inside his jacket and grabbed his gun, but then quickly realized what was happening. He pulled his hand back out and waved to the attendant, started his vehicle and drove onto the ferry.

SYDNEY HARBOUR   0715 PDT

The early morning sun greeted a tired Dylan, bouncing off the surface like the sparkle of diamonds at a jeweler's convention. He checked over Alcor's hull for damage, and was amazed to find five of the shots from Faust's partner had actually hit the boat. All were within inches of the waterline.

Ronnie was awake but did not get up. They had a busy day in front of them and she needed all the energy she could get.

Dylan decided they would have an early breakfast at the Stonehouse Pub, a restaurant located just up the hill from the marina. It was a short walk from the Stonehouse Pub to the Ferry. They would catch the eleven o'clock ship back to the mainland. Sailing across to Vancouver in the Alcor would leave them too exposed to Faust and his men.

The water was calm. Dylan had tied Alcor to a temporary dock owned by a friend. Dylan was sitting at the chart table, turning Ray Tilley's old pistol over in his hands, when Ronnie appeared. "That thing really makes quite the noise," she said rubbing her eyes.

"That's nothing to what it did to that poor bastard who got in the way of its slug." He looked at Ronnie. Faust's attack had left bruises on her face, but nothing seemed to be broken. "How are you feeling?" he asked.

"Fine," she replied bravely. "Who were they, Sean?"

Dylan tried to explain everything that had happened over the past few weeks, but the more he talked, the more bizarre the events seemed.

"What about Jim?" she asked.

"He was moved out of the hospital and spent two weeks in a safe house. He was a very lucky man."

"Where is he now?"

"Jim has decided to leave the business world and enjoy life for a change," Dylan replied. "He has arranged to pack up whatever he thought was important and has moved over to Ireland."

The news shocked Ronnie. "What about the company? What about his home in Vancouver?"

"He has resigned from James T Walters and Company and instructed Bob Emerson to sell off everything and forward the funds to him." Dylan noticed the surprised look on Ronnie's face. "The man came close to dying. This will be a good change for him."

"What about the papers from the cylinder? Are you going to abandon the project?"

"To tell you the truth I'm ready to quit." Dylan said as he ran his fingers through Ronnie's hair, "but I want to end this on an even note. There are a couple of people out there I have to find."

Ronnie was still slightly dazed. She shook her head, trying hard to process all of the information. "Sean, I heard one of the men say he found your address through the company records. I even heard them mention the FBI."

"Nothing would surprise me. A lot of strange people have become involved in this project."

Ronnie suddenly clasped a hand to her mouth. "Sean. They've gone to Professor Kingsmill's home."

The news shocked Dylan. "What?"

"The tall man and the other man, the one who said he found your address. They have gone to get the Iron Cross."

"But how could they know about the Professor?"

"They found the courier receipt I got from Ray." Ronnie began to tremble. "I am so sorry," she cried, "I listed the Iron Cross in the description of the contents."

Dylan jumped up and grabbed his cell phone. "It's not your fault," he said as he punched in the Professor's number. "These people are professionals. They would have found it sooner or later."

The telephone rang several times before the Professor answered.

"Hello Sean, my boy. What a pleasant surprise."

"Professor, the game has gotten very rough. I have reason to believe that there are some very bad individuals on their way to visit you. They are looking for the Iron Cross. Get out of the house. Now!"

"But Sean," the professor objected, "I'm perfectly safe here in my own home."

"No. You are not safe against these people. Please, Professor Kingsmill, take the Iron Cross and get out of the house now!"

The professor started to answer when the telephone line went dead.

Dylan hit 'redial' and the telephone rang and rang. There was no answer.

He immediately dialed '911' and informed the dispatcher that someone had broken in to the Professor's home and that she was in danger. For the second time in two days, Dylan felt a sense of helplessness.

The next scheduled sailing time for the ferry to the mainland was not until 1100. Dylan placed another telephone call to the Marina office. He knew the owner quite well, having done some work for him in the past. He completed his call and set about getting Ronnie up and finding her some breakfast. First, he would help her find a change of clothes in the ship's locker. The selection was not that great, and when she emerged from the aft cabin, she looked like a recreational sailor after a hard night of partying.

"Sorry I don't carry much in the way of ladies wear on board," Dylan said apologetically. "But you do look a little better than yesterday."

Ronnie looked at him with a frown. "Well, at least its colour coordinated, even if it is four sizes too large."

"Nobody will care. Everyone around here is used to seeing boaters looking a little the worse for wear."

"Do they all have black eyes, too?" she asked, pointing to the dark bruise on the right side of her face.

"Well, sometimes. It depends on the quality of the party. Here, these might help," he said, handing her a pair of sunglasses.

Ronnie laughed as she climbed up into the centre cockpit to join Dylan. The two scruffy sailors climbed off the Alcor and made their way along the dock.

Dylan would check in at the marina office before heading up the main street to the Stonehouse Pub restaurant.

"Wait here and enjoy the sunshine. I will be back in a moment."

Ronnie nodded, taking a seat on an old wooden bench facing the sun as Dylan went inside.

"Hi Warren." Dylan greeted his friend. "Sorry to show up unannounced and all, but things were a little hectic last night. Did you manage to find that package for me?"

"Sean. Good to see you again," replied the owner. "Yes, I found it, but what's up. You in some kind of trouble or something?"

"No. I hope not. I just want to have a little insurance."

The owner handed Dylan a small shoebox. "Okay by me. Just bring it back when you're done. That is," he paused, "unless, you should happen to, or have to, lose it. I'll leave that decision with you."

Dylan opened the box and extracted a belt and shoulder holster, complete with a Smith & Wesson .38 Special. He removed his jacket and slipped on the harness. "Hopefully I won't need this," he said he turned to leave. "By the way, I put the Alcor in slip B-77. I should be back in a few weeks. Take care of her for me until then."

The Stonehouse Pub was a rustic jewel set amidst a fairy land display of flowers within a forest of majestic fir trees. The building was an old European-styled country home, constructed of the large stones from the surrounding area.

Ronnie fell in love with the place, but the events of the past few days and Dylan's concerns about the Professor, had diminished their appetites. As much as they would have liked to enjoy the fine food, they were not in the mood for a full breakfast and settled for some tea and muffins.

"We will have to come back here again," she commented, grasping Dylan's hand.

"We'll make a point of it when all this craziness has gone away." he promised. "Right now, we have a ferry to catch."

VANCOUVER 0915 PDT

The paramedic assisted the Professor onto the stretcher while Detective McCarthy hovered over her, asking questions.

"So, let me see if I have this right, Professor Kingsmill. A few minutes after eight o'clock this morning, while you are talking with this Sean Dylan fellow, two men cut your telephone line and then busted in your house. They claim you have something they want, and shoot you in the leg so you would tell them where it is. Then they get this call on their cell phone and rush out before we get here. Is that the gist of it?"

"You have it correct, Detective," Trudy Kingsmill answered. "Now can you please leave and let me get on with fixing this," she stated, pointing to her injured leg.

"Look, Grandma. I'm not going away until I get all of the details. What did Dylan want?"

"You should watch your manners, young man. I am not your Grandma. As for Mr. Dylan, Sean is my friend. We were talking and the line went dead. The rest you know. Now, that may be too much information for you to comprehend in such a short time, but I am leaving to get this unfortunate hole in my leg patched up. Good day, Detective."

Professor Kingsmill gave McCarthy her sternest look of disapproval and waved him away. The Detective was at a loss for words.

She immediately turned and addressed the ambulance driver. "Okay, my good man, let us get to your hospital, and patch up this old carcass. I have much work to do and I cannot afford to waste my day sitting here listening to all this gibberish."

The paramedic had to work hard to suppress his smile.

SWARTZ BAY   1022 PDT

The walk from the Stonehouse Pub to the Ferry Terminal took only eighteen minutes. Dylan knew Ronnie was still feeling the effects from the previous day's episodes. He did not want to rush her up the long walkway onto the ferry.

They purchased their tickets and made their way up the stairs to board the ferry via the gangplank that connected to the upper deck. They did not notice Faust sitting in the car directly below as they crossed the glass enclosed walkway to the ship.

Faust had started his car in preparation of driving on board the huge Ferry. He scanned the parking area, waiting for the attendant to wave him on. The attendant spoke into his lapel microphone and then motioned for Faust to proceed up the loading ramp. Faust slipped the gearshift into drive. As he passed under the glass-enclosed walkway, he looked up as Dylan and Ronnie passed by on the overhead pathway. He could not believe his eyes. "It's them," he shouted at his partner. "Goddamn it. I've got the bastard."

"Look out!" shouted his associate. Faust hit the brakes in time to avoid driving off the side of the ramp.

Seeing Dylan and the girl had excited Faust and in his rush to get aboard, he had a difficult time following the instructions of the ship's loading attendant. Faust parked the car on the starboard side of the vehicle deck, next to one of the large open windows. He turned to his partner. "Go up topside and find TallOne. Tell him I have some very important news. Have him meet me down here. Quick!"

His accomplice grunted in reply as he exited the car and headed for the stairs.

Faust wandered back over to the open window and watched as the other passengers and vehicles loaded onto the Ferry. He had a cruel, sadistic smile on his face as he pondered over how he would exact his revenge on Dylan.

ONBOARD THE FERRY   **1105 PDT**

The large ferry eased away from the dock and began making way towards Vancouver's main terminal at Tsawwassen. Dylan and Ronnie had settled in the comfortable seats on the Port side of the ship. This was where Ronnie would get the best view during the trip, especially in Active Pass when they passed the westbound ferry coming from the mainland. It would also keep Mayne Island on the opposite side of the ship. Dylan thought it would be better if she did not see the island and have to relive the memories of the past few days.

Faust was watching the water glide by when TallOne arrived with Anderson and the other hired accomplice close behind.

"Why did you have me come down here?" asked TallOne.

Faust was smiling. "They are here, onboard," he blurted out.

TallOne did not react. He moved around, opened the passenger door, and entered Faust's car. He motioned for Anderson to get in the driver's side. The move relegated Faust and the other man to the back seat. Faust was becoming very frustrated.

"Dylan and the woman." he stated again, waving his hands for emphasis. "They are onboard this ship."

The tall hitman smiled, "You are sure?"

"Positive. I saw them cross on the overhead walkway as we drove up the ramp."

"Then we shall have time to pay Mr. Dylan and his friend a little visit before we reach the Vancouver terminal." TallOne looked at Faust. "You are blessed with good luck, my friend. It will make you very happy to know that I have not spoken yet to Herr Lüdden about what happened last night. Perhaps I will have no need to report what happened and you will not have to suffer the consequences of your latest failings concerning the elusive Mr. Dylan."

"Thank you, TallOne," replied Faust with audible relief. "But it was not my fault."

TallOne smiled. "It never is," he mumbled under his breath.

Faust was eager to please TallOne. "I heard the news on the radio. The Professor was found shot in her home. Did you get the Iron Cross?"

"Of course, our friend here has it in his pocket," replied TallOne, nodding towards Anderson. "What else did they say about the Professor?"

"They think it was a home invasion. The Professor was taken to the hospital."

"To the hospital," queried TallOne. "But she is dead. No?"

"No," replied Faust, "the news report said she was shot in the leg. She is expected to recover."

TallOne looked over at Anderson. "You fool," he shouted. "You were supposed to kill the old woman. I never leave any traces. You have compromised my identity."

Anderson looked directly into TallOne's eyes. "I don't kill old women for no reason. Besides, the police were on their way. We didn't have time to mess around with the old bitch."

TallOne quickly regained his composure. He turned to the accomplice in the back seat. "Go upstairs and locate Dylan and the girl. Meet us at the elevator on deck number two as soon as you have confirmed their location. Be sure they do not see you." The man grunted an acknowledgment and left.

"You want me to go with him," asked Anderson.

"No, you stay here with me," TallOne replied. He looked at Faust. "You stay out of sight until we have located Dylan." He looked in the rearview mirror at Faust. "You will soon have your chance to get even with him," he said with an evil grin. "Now, please excuse us for a moment, I must talk with our new friend."

Anderson was not sure what the TallOne wanted, but his instincts told him it was not going to be good. He shifted uneasily in his seat to face TallOne. Faust had seen his partner play this exact scene on another occasion. He smiled to himself as he exited the car.

"So, what do you want to talk about?" asked Anderson as Faust disappeared between the lanes of parked vehicles. His eyes had only left TallOne for a split second, but when they shifted back, he was looking down the wrong end of a silencer connected to the business end of TallOne's handgun.

"What the hell is this about?" Anderson asked.

"You were supposed to shoot that old woman. I never leave anyone alive if there is a chance that they could identify me. You have jeopardized my presence in this country."

"We did not leave any traces at the Professor's home. She is an old woman who probably cannot even see properly. She will not be a problem."

"Perhaps," TallOne said flatly, "but that doesn't change the situation." TallOne looked at Anderson. "You have the Iron Cross. Give it to me."

The FBI man knew he was in trouble. "What situation are you talking about?" asked Anderson.

TallOne looked down the barrel of the gun he pointed at Anderson's head, "I do not know who you are, or what game you are playing, but I do know that you are connected to the FBI." He raised the gun closer to Anderson's face. "I am not in the habit of asking twice. The medal please."

"This is crazy, I am working for Müller. I am the same as you."

TallOne smiled. "You are hardly the same as me. I work for Herr Lüdden. Müller also works for Herr Lüdden. Apparently, you did do some work for them and now you have the Iron Cross. Please give it to me," he said in a cold-blooded tone, "Now!"

Anderson could feel the sweat forming on his hands. He had slowly dropped his left hand down to his side. "If it is the money, you can tell Müller and Lüdden to keep it." The single shot pistol strapped to his leg was now just inches from his reach.

"You Americans are such fools. You think you can deal your way out of anything. They have no reason to keep you on their payroll," said TallOne laughing aloud.

Anderson's hand made connect with his only chance for escape. He pulled the tiny pistol from its ankle holster and in one quick motion brought it up towards TallOne's body. The tiny pistol fired its single shot in concert with two muffled shots that blurted from the muzzle of TallOne's silenced MK-23 semi automatic handgun. Anderson's single shot had caught TallOne in the left side, but he did not flinch. Both of TallOne's shots hit under Anderson's chin, drilling upwards into his brain, before exploding through the top of his skull. A mix of blood, brain tissue and skull splattered against the window and onto the headliner above the driver's door.

TallOne calmly wiped the .45 caliber weapon clean and placed it into Anderson's hand, inserting the dead man's index finger against the trigger. He reached over and rolled down the passenger's window, cupped the gun in Anderson's hands and pointed it out towards the water. He pressed his thumb against Anderson's index finger. The silenced weapon burped again, firing a single shot through the open window into the Strait of Georgia.

"Now you have the residue to convince your FBI associates that it was a suicide," he said rolling up the window. TallOne carefully picked up one of the expended cartridges and backed out of the vehicle. He closed the door and made his way forward to find Faust. As he moved, TallOne could feel the effects of the single shot from Anderson's small .22 caliber pistol.

There was little blood, but he knew the wound was serious. He went looking for his partner. The hired killer Faust standing by an opening, watching fishing boats rock in the wake of the large Ferry.

"Your car is no longer available. We will depart as walk-on passengers when we arrive at the terminal," he said as they reached the elevator. He pushed the button and waited for the door to open. "Does your man have a gun?"

"Of course," the short man answered.

"Get it for me."

"Of course," replied Faust.

The elevator door opened and the two men entered. "Wait," shouted TallOne, "The medal. Go back to your car and get the Iron Cross from Anderson's pocket. Be sure you do not disturb the body or the gun. Meet me on the upper deck."

Faust spun around and headed back towards his car as the elevator door closed.

The sailing from Swartz Bay to Tsawwassen was just over an hour and a half in duration. Dylan studied Ronnie as she watched a small pleasure craft sail by on a westerly tack. "Now that's what we should be doing," she said innocently.

"When we get to the end of this strange adventure, we will find some time to go sailing in the Alcor and enjoy the open sea,' he promised. "How do you feel about some lunch?"

"That sounds divine. I am getting a little hungry."

"Good. Me too!" he said.

They had just placed their order with the young attendant when Dylan spotted TallOne's head sticking predominantly above other passengers on the other side of the room.

"*Shit!*" he hissed to himself. "Ronnie, we have a problem. Follow me."

"But what about our food?" she asked in bewilderment.

Dylan did not have time to explain. He grabbed her arm and forced her to move.

"Hey, you don't have to be rude. I'm coming," she protested.

"Sorry, but we have company."

"Who?"

"Not anyone you would want to meet in a dark alley or on a ferry boat," he replied. They made their way along the side corridor past the newsstand and coffee shop, turning into the stairwell that led to the next deck. Dylan was about to go outside when he saw one of the ship's officers come out of the purser's office. He quickly moved around the officer and caught the door before the door's hydraulic device pulled it shut. He pushed the door open. There was no one inside. "Quick, in here."

"But what if someone comes in?"

"Just tell them you are with someone from Transport Canada and you are waiting for me to return. I'll be back as soon as I can."

Dylan did not wait for Ronnie's agreement, exiting the Purser's office before she could reply. He had to find TallOne before the killer found him. A series of questions repeatedly flashed through his mind like a stuck record. *"How many others were with the killer? How could he ensure Ronnie's safety? How would they escape?"* Dylan took the stairs to the main deck.

TallOne had gone into the men's washroom where he found a cloth and some duct tape on the janitor's cart. He placed the cloth over his wound and taped it in place. Faust gave him the gun he took from his associate. "He was not pleased to give up his weapon."

"I should care?" he asked as they left the washroom. Faust's associate was waiting for them as they exited.

TallOne turned to Faust. "Did you get the medal?"

"Yes," replied Faust. As he reached for the medal, the two men ran headlong into a tour group of Japanese students. The throng of noisy tourists surrounded the three men. "Bloody hell," cursed Faust, as he lost sight of his associates. He jammed the medal into his pocket.

TallOne was not overly concerned, but Faust found himself in a panic as he was swallowed him up in the sea of humanity. TallOne smiled at his shorter friends' predicament.

Dylan appeared from the number two stairwell. TallOne spotted him immediately. "I have our quarry in sight," he casually announced. "But, he is alone."

"Where is he?" asked Faust, straining to free himself from the hoard of Japanese tourists.

"He is by stairwell number two. The one leading to the vehicle deck."

TallOne turned to Faust and his accomplice. "Proceed down the stairs. Check all of the decks. Find him. I want him dead."

Faust looked up at the tall man. "Where are you going?"

"The woman is still onboard this ship. I will find her." he grimaced, pressing one hand against the wound in his side.

Dylan made sure TallOne spotted him in order to draw them to him. He wanted to play out the chase on the vehicle deck where he would have a chance to eliminate them one at a time. He saw the sign for the lower vehicle deck and charged down the stairs, taking two steps at a time. He paused at the bottom and slid the automatic door to the upper level open, stopping just long enough to allow those following to catch a glimpse of him before he disappeared.

Dylan turned left through the doorway and ran along the deck. He paused at the door to the Engine Room. He pushed the door inward, then turned back around, dashing between the rows of cars.

He took up a vantage point several vehicles distant from the door, his hand firmly around the handle of the Smith and Wesson .38 Special. He did not have to wait long.

Faust and his partner burst through the doorway, immediately splitting up and moving in two separate directions. Dylan noticed the partner was carrying a knife, while Faust was carrying a small snub-nosed revolver. TallOne did not appear. The partner moved away in the opposite direction while Faust came directly towards him. Dylan was only seconds from taking him out with a shot to the body, when a young couple came through the doorway and made their way along behind Faust. "*Damned kids,*" he thought to himself, "*couldn't they pick some other time to make out?*"

He watched as Faust continued to approach his vantage point. One more car length and they would be in sight of each other. Faust scanned the area, spotting the open door to the Engine Room. He reversed his direction, quickly covering the distance to the door. He slowly pushed the door to a wide-open position and cautiously peered inside. Satisfied that he could see far enough ahead, Faust stepped through the doorway and descended into the Engine Room.

Dylan watched the man disappear. He focused his attention on Faust's partner who had gone forward. It did not take long to locate the man. He was moving slowly between the rows of cars. Dylan moved with the agility of a cat. In less than five seconds, he covered the distance between them. Coming up from behind, Dylan brought the butt of the Smith and Wesson down hard on the back of the man's head, producing a sound similar to a baseball bat hitting a coconut. The unconscious man slumped to the floor in a heap. Dylan looked around for somewhere to put the man so he would not draw attention. He spotted a pickup truck further down the lane. He pocketed the .38, grabbed the man's collar and dragged him along the deck. In the back of the pickup was some oilrig equipment, partially covered by an old tarp. Dylan pulled the tarp back. He reached down, hoisted the unconscious man up against the side of the truck and rolled him into the bed of the pickup. He quickly pulled the tarp over the body, repositioning a couple of pieces of loose equipment to keep it in place.

Dylan resumed his search for Faust, the .38 Special now firmly grasped in his hand. He moved catlike through the passageway towards the centre bulkhead of the ship. As he crossed through the opening and emerged on the other side, Dylan chose to look first to his left. Faust was waiting to the right. He heard the faintest sound of a snicker before he felt the blow from Faust that knocked him against the bulkhead causing him to drop the .38 to the floor. Stunned, he turned around to find Faust standing with his gun in one hand, the Iron Cross in the other.

"You are looking for this, no doubt," said Faust, waving the medal in front of Dylan. "Too bad, but this is of great importance to my superiors. You, however, are not." Faust slipped the Iron Cross into his jacket pocket and raised the gun towards Dylan. The Special Forces training kicked in as Dylan's left leg shot out towards the little man, connecting with Faust's hand, sending his weapon careening through the air. The gun landed between two vehicles and slid along the metal deck. The short man was quick to recover. He hit Dylan like a linebacker, sending him back against the hood of a Ford pickup truck. The force knocked the air from Dylan's lungs.

Dylan pushed Faust away and reached out to pick up the .38 revolver, but the stocky little man knocked it from his reach, sending it skittering under a car.

The two men grappled as they struggled to their feet.

"Now I am going to tear you apart," said Faust as he slammed his elbow against the side of Dylan's head with the force of a sledgehammer.

Stunned, Dylan wrapped his arm around Faust's, took a series of short breaths, trying to clear his head. "You are not fighting a defenseless woman this time," he replied, smashing his fist into the short man' face. "This time, you get hit back."

Faust staggered but kept upright. Again, he came towards Dylan like a crazed bull attacking the matador. Dylan sidestepped his charging adversary, pushing him against the rear of a small Honda. Using both hands together as one large fist, Dylan hit the man's back near his kidneys. Faust winced, but did not fall. He grabbed the fire hose that hung loose next to the window opening.

The hose played out, falling onto the deck. Faust had grabbed the end of the hose and started to swing the heavy brass nozzle in an arc over his head. He looked like some demented cowboy trying to lasso a horse.

Dylan timed his move perfectly to miss the deadly weight and dove low between the cars, hitting Faust in the mid-section. The brass nozzle flew off indiscriminately, smashing through the windshield of the Honda. The force of Dylan's hit drove his adversary back towards the railing. Dylan sustained the attack. Faust tripped over the loose hose and crashed into the railing below the open window. It was life or death struggle. Dylan grabbed the fire hose and attempted to wrap it around the killer's legs. Faust fought Dylan off and struggled to his feet, the hose still wrapped around his leg. Using all of his adrenalin-loaded muscle strength, Dylan pushed Faust against the wall, reaching into the pocket that held the Iron Cross. Faust grunted like a crazed animal, spun around and swung widely. The Iron Cross fell onto the deck. Dylan ducked to elude Faust's ensuing charge. The hitman's momentum carried him over the top of Dylan's body. Dylan stood up at precisely the right moment.

The move lifted Faust's body up high into the air and his forward motion carried the crazed killer through the window opening. Faust went headfirst into the Strait of Georgia with the fire hose still snagged around his one leg. The fire hose, with the full weight of Faust on its end, continued to play out. When it reached its full length, the hose snapped tight against the hull of the ferry, the sound echoing like a rifle shot and reverberated throughout the entire vehicle deck.

Dylan pulled himself up and looked out the window opening. The hose stretched tight down the side of the ship and disappeared into the water. There was no sign of Faust.

On the deck lay the Iron Cross. Dylan bent over, picked it up and stuffed it into his pocket. He moved slowly towards the open doors at the aft section of the ship, searching for any sign of the killer. As Dylan reached the rear of the ship, he heard the fire hose snap. He looked back to see there was only a small section of the hose still attached to the ship. It was waving unfettered in the breeze.

Dylan peered out of the aft doors and noticed a plume of reddish foam appear in the ship's wake. He realized immediately that the huge twin screws had chewed up Faust's body into tiny chunks of instant fish bait. The red foam quickly melded with the sea and disappeared as the ship continued on its path.

The effects of his battle with Faust had taken a toll on Dylan, but he knew his next opponent would be even more difficult. He struggled back to the stairs, pausing only to retrieve the two handguns. He put the .38 back into his holster and tossed Faust's snub-nosed revolver through the opening into the Strait of Georgia.

Dylan had no idea of the whereabouts of TallOne. He made his way up to the passenger deck to get Ronnie. The ship's recorded announcement confirmed the impending docking at the Tsawwassen terminal. Dylan had ten minutes to get Ronnie and make it back to the passenger departure deck.

Dylan took the back stairs up to the top deck. He wanted to avoid TallOne. He found the Purser's Office and knocked on the door. "Open up, Ronnie, it's me, Sean." It seemed like an eternity before he heard the door unlock.

The relief on Ronnie's face was obvious. "Thank God you spoke. I have had two others knock on the door since you left," she said nervously. "There was no way I was going to answer it."

"It's okay now, but we had best get moving," he replied. "The ship docks in less than five minutes."

They closed the office door and walked down the stairs to the departure area, passing the Ship's Purser on the way. Dylan was keeping a close watch for TallOne. The man was too big to disappear into thin air. They reached the bottom of the stairs as the ship gently nudged the dock. Dylan turned the corner and spotted the tall man on the opposite side of the ship. He was standing by the entrance to the stairs leading to the vehicle decks. He was holding his side. *"You will be hanging around for quite awhile if you're waiting for your short friend to appear,"* Dylan thought to himself as he moved Ronnie towards the passenger exit. TallOne looked up to see Dylan and Ronnie as they stepped onto the gangway leading from the ship, his face twisted in a mix of pain and hatred. He turned and pushed his way down through the crowd to the vehicle deck.

TallOne reached the vehicle deck. The scene was total chaos. Someone had discovered the body of the dead FBI man. Others were looking at a damaged windshield. He could not see either Faust or his associate anywhere on the vehicle deck. TallOne instinctively knew there was no reason to stay any longer. The pain in his side was getting worse and blood began to seep through the crude bandage. He slowly climbed back up the stairs to the passenger deck, made his way towards the gangway to leave the ship.

VANCOUVER **1310 PDT**

Dylan and Ronnie took a cab immediately after departing the ship. They stopped in the town of Tsawwassen, picked up a rental car and began the drive to Professor Kingsmill's home.

The traffic was normal for a Wednesday and they made good time going through the city. Ronnie was checking the radio for local news reports. As they crossed the Lion's Gate Bridge, the first report about a suicide aboard a BC Ferry hit the airwaves.

"What is that all about?" she asked.

Dylan was confused. "I'm not sure. Nothing to do with us."

Ronnie was about to ask what happened onboard the ferry when a second news story caught their attention. The report stated that Custom Officials had caught someone trying to gain entry into the United States in the back of a pickup. The man was a wanted fugitive. He had been hiding under a tarp. "Now that one," Dylan confessed with a half grin, "I might know something about."

Everything appeared normal when they finally reached the Professor's home just past two o'clock in the afternoon. There was no sign of any police presence. *"Maybe I was panicking for nothing,"* he cogitated.

Mrs. MacKenzie answered the door immediately. Maggie was barking in the background.

"Mr. Dylan. Come in, please. I know the Professor will see you."

"Is everything alright?"

"Well, we haven't had this much excitement around here since VE day," responded the housekeeper. "She's in her study."

Dylan and Ronnie made their way into the study and found the elderly woman sitting at her desk with one leg propped up on top of a pile of books.

"Sean, my boy," exclaimed the Professor. "How are you?"

"By the looks of you, it should be *'How are you, Professor?'* What happened?"

Trudy Kingsmill explained how the telephone line went dead while she was talking with Dylan and how the two men had barged into the house shortly afterwards. Her description of the two men was very precise and left no doubt in Dylan's mind that the taller of the two men was definitely TallOne. Dylan did not recognize the description of the other man.

"The tall one has the Iron Cross," the Professor announced grimly. "That's when I got this." She pointed to her bandaged leg. "It is just a flesh wound, though I dare say they might have got a bit rough though, if I hadn't given them the medal. They left when they heard the police sirens. Bloody impertinent fellows, they were."

"Did the police find anything?"

"Those incompetent fools," exclaimed Professor Kingsmill. "They are treating the event as an armed robbery, a home invasion of sorts. They seem to think this sort of thing happens all the time."

Dylan looked at the Professor. She did not look like someone who had survived an armed robbery, but Dylan knew it would hit her harder in a few hours when she finally realized of how close she had come to being a murder victim. "Professor, I know you have had a rough day and I don't want to overburden you with questions, but do you remember exactly what was written on the Iron Cross."

"Oh, I can do better than that," she beamed, "I had written down the coordinates earlier so I could send them to you," said the Professor reaching into the top drawer of her the desk. "Here."

Dylan looked at the writing and smiled. "I don't suppose you know where these coordinates will lead us," he said with a half grin.

"Oh yes," responded the diminutive Professor. "The Devil's Finger. It's a little piece of land jutting out from the southern coast of Foula, in the North Sea."

BERLIN   2215 GMT

Lüdden stood silently as he listened to TallOne's report on the apparent death of Faust and the other men. He did not react to the news that Faust had the Iron Cross with him when he disappeared.

"If Faust were alive, I would know. The only possibility is that Dylan may have taken the Iron Cross before killing Faust," said TallOne. "I will find Mr. Dylan. If he has the medal, I will secure it, and then kill him."

Lüdden thought for a moment. "Watch the girl. Dylan will want to protect her. If you can locate her, Dylan will be close. Find them, TallOne. Use any means you must, torture them if you have to, but bring me that medal."

"Yes," said the big man, with cold-blooded determination. "I will recover the Iron Cross and revenge Faust's death."

VANCOUVER   1550 PDT

Dylan swirled his Pinot Noir around in the large glass as he explained how an RAF Canso had attacked a German submarine during the war. "The cylinder contained papers linking two WWII submarines, the U-1220, which was known as a Milk Cow, a submarine that delivered supplies and ammunition to other submarines, and the U-112, a Type XI-B submarine that the Germans and the Allies alike claimed never existed. By deciphering the codes, we now know where the two submarines met and where they dropped off their mysterious cargo."

Ronnie stared at Dylan. "Do you know if there is any connection to the gold from the Priam Treasure and the escaping leaders of the Nazi regime?" she asked.

"We think so," replied Dylan. "However, there is no proof that there is any gold, or for that matter, any people involved. It was all so secret that it remains just conjecture at this point."

Professor Kingsmill opened a folder, extracting some documents. "I did a little research into the XI-B submarine. It was designed in the late thirties and was nearly twice the size of any other Second World War submarine."

The government awarded four contracts for this class of submarine, the U-112 thru U-115, to the AG Weser yard in Bremen on January 17, 1939, but then reported the cancellation of the order at the outbreak of the war in September of the same year."

Dylan pondered over her comments. "Did they never get built?" he asked.

"Many people claimed they were not only built, but at least one of the mysterious XI-B submarines sailed. The U-112. It was rumored to have been painted black and had a crew of about 110 men, almost double that of any wartime German U-boat. It was dubbed the Black Knight. However, there are no documents or pictures to prove it actually was built. The most popular saying in Germany was that it was somewhat hard to paint something black when it does not exist."

"Sounds like a fantasy to me," chipped in Ronnie.

"Maybe," the Professor continued, "however, it is a known fact that one of these so-called phantom submarines was sunk off the coast of the United States in 1944, although the US government will not confirm the location of the wreck and nothing has ever been recovered. At least that is their story. Funny thing is that the US Government refuses to allow any dives near the location."

"I am not sure about the U-112 submarine, but I do know that Schneider said the U-1220 could have taken the Priam gold to a location somewhere in the North Sea, to be recovered by the escaping Nazis."

Professor Kingsmill sat in her chair. "That is the hypothesis, and we now have the coordinates, all you have to do, my boy, is go there and have a look."

"It is kind of exciting," blurted Ronnie, "although I could do without all the violence."

Dylan looked at the two women. "I think we should be going and let the Professor get some rest. Tomorrow we can look into planning a trip to Foula Island."

Trudy Kingsmill looked up at Dylan and Ronnie. "The Devil's Finger. What a strange place to hide a treasure."

"Why is that, Professor?" they asked in unison.

"It is a small crock of land that juts out into the North Sea with high cliffs all around. There does not appear to be a good place to land a ship. It is all very strange. Very strange, indeed."

VANCOUVER   **1708 PDT**

Dylan parked the rental car and got out to assist Ronnie up to her apartment. The attendant greeted them at the door. "Good Evening, Ms. Patterson, Mr. Dylan."

"Good Evening, Grant."

"You have been away for awhile, Ms. Patterson. Were you on vacation?"

"Of sorts," laughed Ronnie. "It was a spur of the moment thing." She paused for a moment and then asked. "Where is David? This is usually his shift, isn't it?"

"He's had a bad cold lately. There is a lot of that going around. I'm just getting over mine."

Ronnie smiled at the door attendant as Dylan escorted her through the door towards the elevator. "Take care of yourself, Grant."

The ride to the sixteenth floor was quick. Dylan checked the hallway, unlocked the door to her apartment and entered first. He carefully inspected each room before allowing Ronnie to enter.

"You shouldn't have any trouble, but just keep the door locked. Under no circumstances do you let anyone in. No one, except for me, that is."

Ronnie looked disheartened. "Where are you going?"

"I have to see Stan Bennett," he replied. "There are a couple of issues I have to clear up regarding that business over on the island. I won't be long."

Dylan gave her a quick kiss on the cheek and exited the apartment, pulling the door closed firmly behind him. He stopped to listen for confirmation that Ronnie had slipped the deadbolt lock into place.

VANCOUVER   1755 PDT

The afternoon sun reflected off the glass towers in Vancouver as Dylan drove into town to meet Stan Bennett. The past forty-eight hours had produced a trail of carnage that had a number of official agencies working overtime. Dylan wanted to be sure that Bennett had taken care of the cleanup details, so no one would trace the events back to him.

He removed his sunglasses as he made his way into the underground parking in the building that housed Ashley Imports Inc.

Stan Bennett was surprised to see Dylan and quickly ushered him into a private office.

"You sure do cause things to happen, my friend. Do you know how many agencies want to talk to the person responsible for all the trouble?"

"It has been quite the ride," Dylan countered. "Did you find the parcel I left at my dock?"

"Yes," answered Bennett. "We picked it up within an hour of your call. It was quite the mess. What the hell did you use on him, an elephant gun?"

"An old single shot pistol I borrowed from my neighbour. The thing had a real nasty kick."

"I would say so from the damage it did."

"What about the cottage?" Dylan asked.

"It was all fixed before noon the same day. The only person around was Ray Tilley. A little nosey, but he does seems to be on your side. We just told him it was a special movie production and that you would explain it all to him later. He seemed to buy it."

"He'll be fine," Dylan stated, shifting in his chair. "What have you heard about some action on a BC Ferry?"

"I figured you might have been in on those too," Bennett said, shaking his head.

"What do you know so far," asked Dylan.

"Firstly, they found an FBI agent dead in a car. Shot twice in the head."

"Whoa," exclaimed Dylan. "I don't know anything about any FBI agent. I was involved with a whole other group."

Bennett detailed how they found Anderson's body on the ferry and explained the connection between the FBI agent and Dylan. "He wanted CSIS to have you followed. Apparently, at one time the US government was more interested in those papers than you know."

"The guys I was dealing with were the same ones who followed me in Germany and England. They were at the cottage. I don't know why or how the FBI agent was involved, but I know the Germans were certainly playing for keeps."

"The funny thing is that the FBI isn't screaming bloody murder about this Anderson guy. Normally they call out the troops and go after everybody. Makes me believe he may have been dirty. There was some talk about a call from his cell phone to somebody in Germany."

Dylan gestured with his hands raised up into the air. "I have never met this guy, but the German connection interests me. See if you can find out the telephone number he called."

Bennett made a notation on his pad. "Then we have some other guy being arrested at the US border for illegal entry, and there is a report of two missing passengers from BC Ferries," Bennett offered. "Quite the day."

Dylan laughed and explained how the man got into the back of the pickup truck. He also explained the demise of Faust.

"Sounds like the fish did alright today."

"I'm not sure, but I think they might have rejected the meal," Dylan joked. "He was one tough sonofabitch."

He got up and turned to leave, then paused. "Do you have a picture of this Anderson guy?" he asked.

"Not on hand, but I can get one. Why?"

"Two men broke into Professor Kingsmill's house yesterday and roughed her up. They were looking for a special item, the Iron Cross. I found it in the cylinder. I think this Anderson guy might have been one of those who paid a visit to the Professor."

"You think Anderson was working both sides?"

"I don't know. But I would like to find out."

VANCOUVER   2115 PDT

The buzzer startled Ronnie. She hesitated before getting up to answer the intercom. It was Grant, the door attendant.

"I have a package here for you Ms. Patterson. It's from a Mr. Jim Clark." His voice sounded a little strange, but Ronnie attributed it to the man's cold.

Ronnie's face brightened. "Send it up, Grant. Thank You."

It was only a matter of minutes before there was a knock on the door.

Ronnie was waiting and instantly unlocked the door. As she turned the handle to open the door, she remembered Dylan had told her Clark was in Ireland. Ronnie quickly tried to relock the door, but it was too late. The door opened with such force, it knocked her backwards over the chesterfield and onto the floor. TallOne stepped into the apartment and stood over the semi-conscious Ronnie. He had an evil smile on his face.

VANCOUVER 2235 PDT

Dylan pulled up in front of Ronnie's apartment building and exited the rental car. He scanned the area but did not see the door attendant. He walked towards the entrance, but stopped suddenly as his peripheral vision spotted a black shoe at the edge of the garden. A sense of dread came over him as he moved to examine the object. His worst fears were confirmed when he saw the black shoe was still attached to the foot of Grant, the door attendant.

Dylan did not waste time determining how the man met his fate. With lightening fast reactions, he rushed through the doorway to the elevator. He pushed the button and waited for what seemed like an eternity. The door finally opened. Dylan pushed the button for the Ronnie's floor. He knew he should be more careful, but he did not have any time to waste. Ronnie was in danger. His mind was racing with thoughts of what he would find. He was mad at himself for leaving her alone. As the elevator made its way up to Ronnie's floor, Dylan pulled his .38 revolver from his shoulder holster. The elevator door opened. Dylan eased out of the lift, checking the hallway for any signs of movement. He moved cautiously towards Ronnie's apartment. The door was slightly ajar. Dylan paused, took a deep breath, pushed the door wide open and dove headfirst into the apartment. He rolled up against the chesterfield, his eyes scanning the room as he tumbled. It was empty.

His Special Forces training was working at maximum efficiency as Dylan quickly checked each room in the apartment. There was no sign of Ronnie, but he did find a note on the table that read: *"Vancouver Terminal. Stewart Street Pier @ 2300".*

Sitting next to the note was the gold chain and charm with Ronnie's initials.

Dylan grasped the chain and thrust it into his pocket as he left the apartment. The drive from Ronnie's apartment to the pier was only about 12 minutes, and it was already 2250. There was no doubt in his mind that TallOne had taken Ronnie. He also knew the TallOne would not hesitate to kill her when it suited him. He felt a knot in the base of his stomach.

The rental car screeched around the final corner onto Stewart Street. Dylan slowed slightly. He did not need to attract any undue attention. More people would only complicate things. As he reached the entrance to the main pier, Dylan followed the road towards the waters of Burrard Inlet.

The terminal was working its normal night shift, loading containers onto the ships that would leave tomorrow for ports unknown. He scanned the area and quickly spotting a white car parked near the end of the pier, its lights shining out onto the water. Dylan noticed the exhaust emitting from the vehicle. The car's engine was still running. He turned the rental car's headlights off and slowly crept up behind the vehicle.

Dylan was less than fifty feet from the white car when he saw TallOne step out from between two containers. Overhead, the huge crane was moving another container towards a waiting ship. TallOne stood beside the vehicle with his arms folded on his chest, a gun held firmly in his right hand. He motioned for Dylan to stop.

Dylan slowed to a stop, put the rental car in park and exited the vehicle. He was just forty feet from TallOne. He surveyed the area for any sign of Ronnie. "Where is she?" he shouted.

TallOne pointed his gun inside the white car. "She is in here. You can have her back once you give me the Iron Cross."

Dylan had been part of hostage negotiations in the past. He knew there was no way this scenario was going to play out well.

TallOne was a sadistic killer. He wanted the Iron Cross and he did not intend to let either Dylan or Ronnie escape alive.

"Let her go," Dylan yelled as he reached into his jacket pocket and produced the medal. "Here. You can have it." Dylan tossed the Iron Cross towards TallOne, hoping to draw him away from the car.

TallOne looked at him with cold indifference. "You killed my friend."

Without hesitating, TallOne reached into the open window of the white car and pushed the gearshift lever downward, engaging the transmission. "You have caused me much trouble. First I take care of you, and then I take the medal," shouted TallOne. The car, and with its engine idling, was slowly edging forward towards the water.

TallOne had ended any possible negotiations. Dylan's hand reached inside his jacket, pulling out the .38 revolver. In one motion, he moved to his right and fired three quick shots, but TallOne had already dropped to the ground. Dylan's shots sailed harmlessly over his body, slamming into the metal siding.

TallOne moved faster than Dylan thought possible for such a big man. In seconds, he had covered the remaining distance to the shelter of the containers while Dylan, retreated behind the protection of his rental vehicle.

Dylan looked at the white car. It was starting to pick up speed as it carried Ronnie towards the end of the pier. He made a quick dash towards the car. Two shots rang out forcing him to duck for cover behind the leg of the giant overhead crane.

TallOne climbed on the top of the container, increasing his advantage over Dylan. "You had better hurry if you want to save your lady friend," TallOne called out with a vicious laugh. "She is not conscious. She will not be able to get out."

He had Dylan pinned down, forcing him to watch as the white car rolled towards the water, carrying Ronnie to certain death. Dylan looked around in a desperate search for a way to save Ronnie. Time had run out.

The white car slammed into the short guardrail, bouncing the front end up and over. The car skidded to a stop with its front wheel drive still turning in the air. The vehicle was teetering precariously over the edge of the pier. Ronnie still had a chance. Dylan had to reach her before the car tipped completely forward into the dark waters of Burrard Inlet. He looked skyward. The crane operator had just picked up a new container and was moving it towards the dock area. Dylan turned to confirm TallOne's position. The big man was still on top of the container. He was looking towards the white car.

Dylan did not hesitate. He began climbing the ladder towards the control box of the huge crane. Two shots rang out freezing Dylan on the ladder. Dylan looked over at TallOne and realized the killer was not shooting at him. TallOne was firing at the white car. Two more shots rang out and Dylan watched in horror as the rear of the car erupted in a massive ball of flame. The force of the explosion hurled the vehicle over the edge of the pier, landing on its roof in the water below. The flames quickly extinguished as the twisted wreckage of the car slipped under the surface.

The sound of TallOne's laugh reverberated throughout the terminal. "You have failed, Mr. Dylan. Now it is your turn."

Dylan was a man possessed with rage. He completed his climb to the control box, opened the small door and leaned in.

"What the hell?" the operator exclaimed.

Dylan brought his fist down hard on the back of the man's neck, rendering him unconscious. He pushed the operator to one side and entered the box.

"Where are you, my little friend," TallOne called. "You and I must settle this once and for all."

Dylan could see the big man was lying on top of the stack of containers below him. The cargo container hanging from the cables registered a gross weight of 65,000 pounds. Dylan made two small adjustments and aligned the container directly over top of TallOne. He did not hesitate.

"Consider it settled," said Dylan as he hit the release button and watched the thirty-three ton, fully loaded container release from its cables and plummet downward. TallOne had heard the distinct noise of the release mechanism. He turned his head, but only in time to recognize the corrugated metal imprint on the bottom of the container that sandwiched him against the lower container. The impact caused a thunderous explosion that rocked the giant crane.

It took Dylan less than two minutes to descend from the crane and reach the edge of the pier where the white car had disappeared. The area was in total confusion. A number of workers gathered around at the water's edge as a large portable crane maneuvered into position to drop a huge electro-magnet into the water. Dylan watched as the crane latched onto the remains of the white car and raised it out of Burrard Inlet. It seemed like an eternity. He joined the onlookers as the portable crane deposited the wreckage onto the dock. The car was empty. Dylan's mind was racing. He hurried back to the edge of the dock. The waters had calmed. There was no sign of any debris. There was no body. He had no way of confirming whether Ronnie had been inside or not.

The sounds of distant police sirens brought Dylan back to reality. He sprinted to his rental car, passing the dockworkers as they scrambled towards the twisted metal of the container he had dropped on TallOne. He picked up the Iron Cross and exited the terminal.

49

OCTOBER 2, 2007

VANCOUVER   **1015 PDT**

The harbour police found Ronnie's body the day after the events at the terminal. Her death was ruled an accident as a result of an automobile accident.

The police, for reasons known only to Dylan and Stan Bennett of CSIS, chose not to connect her death to the bloody remains they found between the two containers. With hardly enough left to identify as a human body parts, and no DNA identification matches in the police or FBI files, the City Coroner concluded that no identification would ever be possible. The police dismissed reports of gunfire as dock noise. They did not connect Dylan to the events.

The funeral service was small. Dylan had contacted Jim Clark in Ireland and told him about Ronnie's death. Clark said he would inform her sister.

The weather was a typical overcast fall day with a slight mist in the air. It would have been a perfect day to be alone, sitting beside a fire with a good book, or a good friend at your side.

For Dylan, it was the darkest day of his life. There were a handful of others gathered in the circle around Ronnie's casket. Most were from her office. Jim Clark did not attend.

The Minister adjusted his glasses and began to read a passage from the Bible. Dylan looked into each person's eyes. It was the darkest day of his life.

A black limousine arrived at the service. A tall woman dressed in black got out and made her way towards the group. A dark veil covered her face. She stopped opposite the end of the casket, next to Dylan. Although he could not see her face, Dylan knew this was Ronnie's sister.

It was an emotional experience and the woman appeared quite shaken. Dylan offered his arm to steady her.

The service was short, which was fine with Dylan. He had a host of demons playing handball inside his head. The sooner he got away from the cemetery, the better chance he would have to survive the day.

As the mourners began to leave the area, Dylan turned to the woman in black. "I am very sorry for your loss. She was a wonderful person." He reached into his pocket and extracted the gold chain with its unique locket. "She said that if anything ever happened, I was to give you this."

The woman, who had remained silent throughout the service, spoke. "She was a fantastic girl. She thought the world of you."

Dylan paused at the sound of the voice. "Excuse me?"

The woman in black lifted her veil. It was Bridgette. "We should go somewhere to talk," she murmured in a sad and distant voice.

The demons inside Dylan's head changed the game from handball to hockey as his thoughts crashed one into another, trying to make sense of what was happening. "What are you doing here?"

"You didn't know, did you?"

"Know what?" he asked incredulously.

Bridgette reached inside the top of her dress and extracted a gold chain with small gold box. It was identical to the golden box that Ronnie had worn, except for the initials, 'B.P'.

A missing link in the puzzle fell into place.

VANCOUVER   1535 PDT

Dylan had spent the entire several hours with Bridgette, being educated about the very different lives of the two sisters and the twists and turns each had taken since they left university.

Ronnie had gone to work for James T Walters & Company, while Bridgette went to Europe to work for a computer analysis company. "She never found out we were really an arm of the FBI. I was always working on classified documents so I could never tell her exactly what I did. She called me when she found out you were coming to Berlin."

"So that is why you were at the airport?" asked Dylan.

"Partly. I was given an assignment by our Seattle office to watch someone in Berlin. It was a coincidence that you were that assignment. I could not tell her or you what was going on. I should have opted out of the assignment, but I wanted to check out the person my sister was seeing. I wanted to make sure she was not going to get into a bad relationship." Her comment had hit Dylan hard. "She knew you were involved in something that might be dangerous." Bridgette said. "She would not blame you for what happened. It was not your fault."

"But it was. I should never have left her alone."

"You couldn't protect her every minute of every day, Sean. She would have rebelled and left if you had tried. She would want you to continue on with your life."

Dylan sat silently for a moment. "I can't do that until I find those responsible and avenge Ronnie's death."

"Do you know who they are?" asked Bridgette. "I would be only too happy to help you find them."

"That would jeopardize your career with the FBI. I can't ruin the lives of both sisters."

Bridgette looked at Dylan and smiled. "I am leaving the agency next month. I already filed my resignation papers."

"Why?"

"It's been enough. It is time to see some of the world as a tourist, not an FBI undercover agent. Someone killed Gary Anderson, my contact from our Seattle office last week. From what I hear, he apparently got himself into some serious debt. A couple of Germans who are involved in the underground Neo-Nazi Democratic Party were blackmailing him. I think you may have heard his name recently."

The news that Bridgette knew Anderson, hit Dylan like a Mohammad Ali uppercut. He paused to collect his thoughts, pulled out an envelope and handed it to Bridgette. "I just received this picture from a friend of mine. Is this Anderson?"

Bridgette looked at the face in the photo. "Yes, it is. But, this is an FBI ID photo. How did you get it?"

"You are not the only one with contacts. Anderson was the phony 'doctor' who did the attempted hit Jim Clark. Clark was Ronnie's boss and my best friend. Anderson came within an instant of killing him."

"It seems this underground Nazi group is more determined than anyone thought. What are you going to do next?"

Dylan's mind was starting to function again. "If you are still interested, I could use a little help in Berlin."

50

OCTOBER 5, 2007

BERLIN   **1115 GMT**

Bridgette entered the building that housed the underground Neo-Nazi Democratic Party dressed in a very sexy black outfit featuring a short skirt that highlighted her beautiful long legs. She wore a long dark wig that contrasted the unusually heavy facial makeup. The interior of the building was drab, void of any bright colours. She approached the plain wooden door to the office of the underground Neo-Nazi Democratic Party. She knocked and entered. Bridgette had not yet fully entered into the office before Hans Müller had intercepted her. "May I help you?" he asked tersely.

"Herr Lüdden, please."

"What business do you have with Herr Lüdden, please?" asked Müller, giving Bridgette a more than cursory glance.

"That is between Herr Lüdden and me. But you may tell him that it concerns a certain Iron Cross he has been searching for," she stated with an air of domination.

The mention of the Iron Cross shocked Müller. He resented a woman putting him down and did nothing to hide his contempt, but he knew better than to send her away. "I will see if Herr Lüdden is in."

Bridgette was enjoying herself, but she was also very cognizant of the dangers surrounding these men. She would not take any unnecessary chances. Dylan had instructed her to advise Lüdden that the Iron Cross with the co-ordinates for the location of the Priam gold, was for sale.

"Herr Lüdden will see you now," announced Müller on his return. "Please follow me."

Müller led Bridgette into Lüdden's office. "This is the woman who says she knows something about an Iron Cross."

"So," said Lüdden with great innocence, "you know something about an Iron Cross. Is this supposed to mean something to me?"

Bridgette sized him up quickly. This man was responsible for her sister's death. She felt total repulsion towards the man, but outwardly managed to remain calm. "Only if you want to find the missing Priam gold."

"I see. And where is this information, Miss …"

"Names are not important. At least, not mine. Sean Dylan on the other hand, is a name that should be of great importance to you."

Lüdden looked at the woman before him. He manufactured a sinister smile. "So what does Mr. Dylan want in exchange for this information?"

Bridgette took a short breath. "He wants ten million dollars in United States currency together with the use of a private jet to fly from here to a destination of his choice."

"That is a lot of money, and he wants the use of a jet plane. How does Mr. Dylan think I can come up with such things?"

"That is totally up to you. You have twenty-four hours to confirm the deal or he will give the Iron Cross to the British Government."

Lüdden looked over at Müller who immediately moved behind Bridgette, effectively blocking any retreat.

"But what if I decide to keep you here until I get the information," he asked as Müller moved to block her path to the door.

Bridgette had noticed Müller's move, but remained composed. "If I do not return on schedule, Mr. Dylan has documents from the TallOne and others that implicate you in several murders. He is prepared to release these documents to the German Government." She placed her cellular telephone on Lüdden's desk, pushed the speakerphone button and spoke, "Is that correct, Mr. Dylan?"

Dylan's voice emanated from cellular, "Precisely."

Bridgette flipped the cell phone shut. "Twenty-four hours, Herr Lüdden. That would be at noon tomorrow. You can reach me at this number." She placed a card on the desk, turned on her heel and walked out of the office, closing the door as she went.

Lüdden was stunned. Bridgette had caught him totally off guard. "Müller, we must play this carefully. Call the Pakistan Consul and find Rashim Abul. He has the ability to get the money and the plane. Inform him I have the location of the missing gold from the Great Priam Treasure. Tell him that I will double his investment within one week. By this time next week, I will have the gold returned to Germany. When it is all done, I will also see that Mr. Dylan and that woman are quite dead."

"Are you sure this is a wise approach, Herr Lüdden?"

Lüdden answered with a menacing glance at Müller. "Never question my judgment, my friend. You might end up like our dearly departed Otto von Schlippenbach."

51

OCTOBER 6, 2007

BERLIN 0805 GMT

Dylan, Bridgette, and Ozzy were in a suite in the Grand Hyatt Hotel on Marlene-Dietrich-Platz, waiting for the call from Lüdden. They had gone over Dylan's plan repeatedly, until each person knew each other's role as well as their own. There could be no glitches.

"Do you think he will come up with the funds?" asked Ozzy. "It's a hell of a lot of money."

Dylan looked at the others. "Greed is a powerful motivator, and Lüdden has displayed nothing but greed since the beginning. He is driven to find the Priam gold and will do whatever he has to in order to get his hands on it for the underground Nazi Party."

"But we don't even know if the treasure is at the coordinates that are written on the Iron Cross."

"No, but I am sure Herr Lüdden is convinced that it is. For him, finding the treasure and resurrecting Nazi Party to its former glory would be a dream come true for him. The realization that such an event may be possible will cloud his judgment big time."

"We could just go get the treasure for ourselves," suggested Bridgette. "If it is that big a deal, why take the chance that might see Lüdden getting his hands on it?"

Dylan got up from his chair and walked over to the table

where several maps lay spread. He pulled out the map of Foula Island and placed it on top. "If the Priam gold is here," he said, making a circle around a small outcrop of land on the southern tip of the island, "we would first have to get it out without alerting the local government, and second, we would have to find a way to sell it off in order to make a profit. Remember that Heinrich Schliemann, the man who found the Priam Treasure, could never sell it because he had no official proof of its origin."

Bridgette nodded her head in agreement. "So, the treasure would be next to impossible to sell to any museum."

"Actually, it would be completely impossible unless it is melted down into small ingots. As part of the Priam Treasure, Perhaps when this is all over, the treasure will get returned to those who rightfully own it."

Ozzy looked at his watch. "Carol should have secured our transportation by now. Bridgette is meeting her tonight to get everything set for our arrival. How does that fit with our schedule?"

"Our departure time is set for eighteen hundred hours, six o'clock for you non air force types. We arrive around twenty-one hundred hours," replied Dylan. He looked over at his friend, "Ozzy, you will have to move fast in order to file the flight plan to the first destination. You also need a little extra time to pick up our documents. Make sure they are correct. We can't afford mistakes."

Ozzy gave Dylan a thumbs-up signal.

Bridgette made her way over to Dylan to review her list of tasks. "I am to wait at Lüdden's office until Müller calls to confirm you have given him the Iron Cross. When Lüdden transfers the funds to the master account, I go directly to the bank, here," she said, pointing to an intersection on a map of Berlin, "and re-transfer the funds to the sub-accounts. Correct?"

"Right," Dylan confirmed. "Don't forget to withdraw the interim spending cash and put it into the black satchel. I will make sure no one follows you when you are leaving the bank. We will meet on the departure levels at the EasyJet check-in area. Ozzy and I just need enough for our trip to the final destination. You can then proceed to your flight and rendezvous with Carol. Baring any unforeseen problems, Ozzy and I will join you within twenty-four hours."

Ozzy looked around at the others. "Well, everything seems to have been arranged at our end; all we need now is the call."

The morning passed slowly. Dylan and Ozzy were looking at a map, discussing details of the plan when Bridgette emerged from the bedroom and joined them. She had changed her hairstyle and makeup. Dylan was awestruck by her resemblance to Ronnie.

"Would you gentlemen like some coffee?"

Ozzy was about to answer when the telephone rang. Dylan picked up the receiver on the second ring. It was Lüdden.

"Mr. Dylan, you have the Iron Cross?"

"Yes. Do you have the money?"

"I have the money. But first I must be sure it is the real Iron Cross and that it contains the information we seek."

"That is not a problem. You can have someone check it out before you transfer the funds."

"Very well. Where shall we meet you?"

Dylan paused for a moment. "There is no 'we' Lüdden. Send one person, alone, to meet me at the New Synagogue Museum in Oranienburgerstrasse, at 1500 hours. When he has confirmed the Iron Cross is real and has the information you seek, you can transfer the funds to our account. I will have another associate come to your office to witness and verify the bank transfer. Once the funds are confirmed in our account, I will give the Iron Cross to your representative."

There was a short silence. "A very strange place for a meeting, do you not think," the Nazi leader quizzed.

"Strange maybe, but it is safe, Lüdden," Dylan answered. "In light of what has happened over the past couple of months, I prefer not to take any chances."

"Very well, then. Hans Müller will be at the New Synagogue Museum in Oranienburgerstrasse at exactly 1500 hours."

"How will I identify him?" asked Dylan.

"He is wearing a blue suit with a red handkerchief in the jacket pocket."

"I trust you have the use of a private jet for us."

"Yes. As you demanded," said Lüdden. "A private pilot is standing by at Hanger number 17."

"To be sure we arrive at our destination; I will file the flight plan only when I arrive at the airport. You will instruct your pilots to fly exactly as I direct. Only the pilots and my people are to be on the plane. Understood?"

"But," stammered Lüdden, "I can't just let you take off with a jet plane without some guarantee I will get it back."

"This is not negotiable, Lüdden. Your pilot has control of the aircraft. If you play by the rules no one will get hurt and you will get your aircraft back." Dylan paused for a moment. "Do we have an agreement?"

There was an awkward moment as the German considered the terms. "Very well," he said reluctantly, "but nothing happens until we have verified the authenticity of the Iron Cross."

"Of course," acknowledged a smiling Dylan as he replaced the receiver onto the telephone.

BERLIN 1205 GMT

The offices of the underground Neo-Nazi Democratic Party contained a diverse group of people. Rashim Abul, a large black man dressed in army fatigues, joined Hans Lüdden and Müller. He carried a pearl handled Colt .45 pistol in a holster on his belt and looked like a bad imitation of General Patton. Four members of the Pakistan National guard stood behind him.

"Hans, are you positive you will be able to find the treasure once you have the Iron Cross?" asked Abul.

"There is no question. The Priam gold will be ours within the week."

"I do hope so," said Rashim Abul, "for your sake." He walked around behind Lüdden and placed his hand on the German's back. "You should be very careful. This Dylan person does not seem to be a fool and you would not want to lose my money or my jet, Hans. That would be a big mistake."

"They are all fools," Lüdden stated emphatically. "We will get the Iron Cross, retrieve the Priam gold and bring it back to Berlin," he boasted with a ruthless grin. "The recovery of the gold will restore our party to its rightful place as the leader of Germany."

Abul removed his hand from Lüdden's back and placed it on the Colt revolver as he made his way around to the front of the desk. "You are very sure of yourself, Herr Lüdden," he said with a cold indifference. "One should always temper such confidence with a high degree of reason."

Lüdden noticed Abul's hand resting on the Colt. "Have your men ready to track Dylan and the money. Once we have the Iron Cross, it will lead us to the gold. You will soon have all of your money returned. You have my word," he stated with great flair.

"I am not concerned. Our pilots are trained mercenaries. Once they land, they will keep Dylan and his associates under surveillance until we have recovered the treasure. Then they will recover the money and dispose of the lot."

He turned to the party's number two man. "Müller, you will meet with this Dylan person. Take this special lamp. Pass it over the front of the Iron Cross. It will expose the Commanding Officer's name. The name you should see is *Helmet Mohr 099893*. He was a fine officer in the Third Reich's Navy. His name will confirm the medal came from the right submarine. Once you confirm the name, pass the light over the back of the cross. If the Iron Cross is real, the black light will reveal the coordinates we need on the arms of the medal. Once you have verified the information, bring the Iron Cross straight back here."

"I understand," said Müller, taking the light from Lüdden.

Lüdden slowly turned to face Müller. "If the information on the Iron Cross is different in any way, abort the meeting and leave. Once you are outside the synagogue, make sure you point out Dylan to Rashim. He and his men will be standing by to make sure he is eliminated."

Rashim Abul folded his arms across his chest, as a sinister look came over his face. "It would be our pleasure."

BERLIN   **1255 GMT**

The New Synagogue Museum in Oranienburgerstrasse was crowded this Saturday. Dylan arrived early driving an old pickup truck that Ozzy had arranged for him. He was wearing casual blue jeans with a sweatshirt, runners, and an old baseball cap. He would be another face in the crowd of foreign visitors.

Given the players in the game, Dylan thought the choice of the synagogue was quite appropriate. The security was as strict as always and Dylan wanted to be inside when Müller arrived.

At exactly 1500 hours, Müller appeared at the door to the synagogue. The security officers searched his small bag, put it through a scanning device and then ushered him into a separate scanning booth. Two minutes later, he was in the building.

Dylan waited for a moment to be sure there were no others following Müller and then slowly moved in behind him. "Herr Müller, I presume," he whispered. "Move straight ahead into the next room, please."

Müller proceeded as directed. The room was less crowded than the lobby area, but there were sufficient people around to give Dylan a good degree of comfort. Müller had no way of knowing if any of the people in the room were friends or foes. Dylan shepherded Müller towards the far corner of the room.

"You must be Dylan," said a nervous Müller. "You are not what I expected."

"Don't judge a book by its cover," replied Dylan. "You want to inspect the Iron Cross?"

"Yes, with this," said Müller, pulling the portable black light from his bag.

"You brought a portable black lamp with you?"

"Yes, it is the only way we can confirm the authenticity of the medal.

Dylan acted surprised at the news of the black lamp. "You will have one pass on the front of the Iron Cross, and one pass on the back. That is all. Understand?"

Müller grunted affirmatively.

"Turn it on," said Dylan as he slipped his hand into his jacket pocket, withdrew the medal, and held it out.

Müller switched on the lamp and hesitantly lifted it towards the Iron Cross. Beads of sweat began to form on his forehead. Dylan did not take his eyes off the man. The lamp moved in a shaking motion across the face of the medal, exposing the hidden name written years before. *"Helmet Mohr 099893".*

Müller was perspiring even more as Dylan flipped the Iron Cross over in his hand. There were two small pieces of tape covering a portion of arms of the medal.

"Why is the tape there?" Müller asked apprehensively.

"It covers the first part of the co-ordinates. You do not think I would show you the full co-ordinates, did you?"

"I suppose not," replied Müller nervously as he prepared to scan the backside of the medal. The light reflected back from the surface to show a portion of the hidden co-ordinates. *"08'30.38" N, 03'42.00" W"*

Dylan reached over and flipped the power switch to 'Off'. He handed Müller a cellular telephone. "Place your call to Lüdden. Tell him what you saw."

Müller looked at the telephone number on the device's screen. "But this is not his number," he protested.

"I know. It is the private number of my associate. She is with Lüdden. Just hit the 'Send' button to place the call, and then the speaker-phone button."

The short German man looked at Dylan's eyes. They were totally devoid of emotion. He pressed the Send button. The cellular telephone made the connection and began to ring. Bridgette answered.

"I would like to speak with Herr Lüdden," said Müller with a slight quiver in his voice.

"I will put our phone on to speaker mode so everyone can hear what is said," Bridgette announced with finality.

Müller detailed the results of the scanning process he had just completed, confirming the name and serial number that were on the front of the Iron Cross, and the co-ordinates written on the back. "I have seen the co-ordinates," he stammered into the telephone.

Dylan plucked the cellular from his hand and spoke to Lüdden. "Your man has confirmed the information as required," he stated candidly. "You can start the bank transfer. I am going to call my associate to verify the jet waits as promised. If all is well, we can conclude our agreement."

"Are you sure it was the correct information, Karl?"

"Yes, Herr Lüdden," confirmed Müller nervously. "I am very sure."

BERLIN   **1308 GMT**

Bridgette opened her laptop and punched a series of keys to bring up a connection to her bank. She watched as Lüdden placed a telephone call to his bank to authorize the transfer. He spoke into the telephone. "That is correct. Please proceed. Thank You."

The screen on Bridgette's laptop remained passive. She looked at Lüdden.

"Nothing has moved yet," she reported. "Are you sure the bank understood your directions?"

"It takes a few minutes for the transfer to be completed," Lüdden responded.

Bridgette watched the screen. Slowly the numbers on the LED screen began to change, as the bank transfer became reality. The full ten million US dollars was now showing in her account.

Her cellular phone rang again. It was Dylan.

"What is the status?" he asked.

"The transfer is complete," Bridgette responded.

"Good," said Dylan. "I will escort Herr Müller and the Iron Cross back to his office. I would not want him to lose such a valuable item on his way. Ciao."

Bridgette flipped the cell phone shut, turned towards the door and left without a word.

Lüdden pressed an intercom button. "Follow her. I want to know her every move." He paused for a moment, *"How convenient of Mr. Dylan to escort Müller,"* he stated to himself. *"Abul's men are waiting outside the synagogue to seize him as soon as they leave. With luck, we will retrieve the Iron Cross and Abul's money without before the day is over."*

BERLIN   **1325 GMT**

Dylan escorted a frightened Müller, the Iron Cross grasped firmly in his hand, towards the exit. As they passed the entrance to the washrooms, he motioned for Müller to turn and enter. Dylan reached into his pocket and extracted a small piece of rope. He grabbed Müller's arm and pulled it around behind his back.

"If you call out, it will be the last thing you do. The other arm please," Dylan demanded.

Müller complied, as his eyes grew to saucer-like proportions. "What is this about?"

"Do not try anything stupid," Dylan warned as he finished tying the man's hands behind his back. "I just want to make sure I am able to leave here without your friend Rashim Abul and his cronies causing me any delays."

Müller began to protest. "But, I don't know ..."

Dylan cut him off. "We rigged the cellular telephone my friend took into Lüdden's office to continue transmitting after she left. I heard Lüdden instruct you to point me out to your friend Abul and his men so they could give me a personal greeting after the exchange."

Müller looked terrified. He was on the verge of panic

"I don't know what you mean, I ...." his voice trailed off as Dylan moved him towards the last stall.

"In here," he said, giving Müller a little push to encourage his cooperation. "Sit down on the seat."

Müller did as instructed. Dylan moved around back and tied the cord around the connection at the back of the toilet.

"There. That will keep you for a moment. If you are good and do not make any noise for five minutes, my associate standing outside the door will not have to come back and kill you. Do you understand?"

The German nodded in the affirmative. "What are you going to do?" he asked tentatively.

"We have kept our end of the deal. Now, I am going to leave as planned," said Dylan. He looked down at the man sitting on the toilet and smiled. "I am sure there will be someone in here to help you in a few minutes." He turned and left the washroom.

Dylan exited the synagogue and casually walked towards the old pickup truck, glancing about the area as he walked. He did not see any sign of Abul or his men, but he knew they were there. He started the pickup truck and drove out of the parking lot towards the centre of town. The first part of the plan had worked without a hitch. It was now time to check on Bridgette's progress.

It took ten minutes for Dylan to reach the bank. He parked

the pickup truck on the opposite side of the street, punched in a number on the cellular telephone, let it ring once and hung up. He waited for Bridgette's signal confirming everything was proceeding as planned. In less than a minute his cell phone range twice and then stopped. Dylan relaxed. Everything was progressing as planned.

The cell phone rang again. This time it was a single ring that told Dylan that Bridgette was about to leave the bank. He started the truck and slipped it into gear at the exact moment Bridgette departed by way of the bank's revolving door. She was carrying her purse and the black bag. Dylan watched as she got into her car, started the engine and pulled away from the curb. Seconds later, he noticed an older Mercedes pulling out directly behind her. *"Here we go again,"* thought Dylan. *"Another Mercedes."* He eased the pickup truck into a gentle U-turn and slipped in behind the black Mercedes. The procession continued through six traffic lights before Dylan saw an opening. He floored the accelerator and pulled in ahead of the Mercedes. The driver of the Mercedes gave a blast on his horn. Dylan raised his arms as if it were not his fault. The driver shook his fist as the traffic light ahead changed. Bridgette continued through the intersection feigned a stall of the truck's engine. Again, the driver leaned on the horn to show his displeasure. Dylan opened the door of the pickup, got out, pointed to the light and made an obscene gesture towards the Mercedes. The Mercedes driver sat helplessly as he watched Bridgette vanished into the traffic.

BERLIN   **1415 GMT**

Lüdden was furious when Müller finally arrived at the office and explained how Dylan evaded Rashim Abul and his men. The sight of the Iron Cross however, seemed to calm his anger. The men huddled over Lüdden's desk with the black light, rescanning the medal to confirm the coordinates. Lüdden had connected his computer to the internet, was using the Google Earth feature to establish the exact location of the Priam Treasure gold.

Müller read out the coordinates. "Sixty degrees, eight minutes, thirty point three eight seconds North, two degrees, six minutes, forty-two point zero seconds West."

He watched as Lüdden maneuvered the image of the globe the LED screen of his laptop, zoomed in to the corresponding area. "It appears the gold from the Priam Treasure was taken to a small peninsula on Foula Island known as 'the Devil's Finger'. Once we have confirmed the death of Dylan and his friends, we will recover our money and then visit the Devil's Finger to recover our prize."

"Herr Müller," said Lüdden. "Rashim's pilots are waiting for Dylan. Take Abul's men to the airport and make sure they have eliminated Dylan and his group. Report to me as soon as it is done."

BERLIN AIRPORT 1733 GMT

Bridgette returned her rental car to the car park and made her way through the airport security. As she walked along the concourse, Dylan appeared at her side, slipping his arm into hers.

"You have your traveling funds?" he asked.

"Yes," she replied. "The balance of the hundred thousand is in here." She handed a black bag to Dylan.

"Okay. We are heading out in less than an hour. See you tomorrow". The exchange took less than fifteen seconds as Dylan, the black bag in hand, slipped off to the side to take an elevator down to the lower level where he would catch a shuttle bus to hanger number seventeen.

Ten minutes later, Dylan was standing in front of a sleek Gulfstream G100 corporate jet. There were no visible markings other than the normal aircraft registration numbers. He approached the plane cautiously. The planes folding staircase hung down from the rear door. The aircraft's interior was totally dark. Dylan scanned the area. There was no one in sight. He began to climb the stairs to enter. As he stepped into the aircraft, he came face to face with a pilot. Dylan reacted with a quick swing of the black bag that grazed the pilot's head. He reached inside his jacket and withdrew his gun.

"Christ, Sean," the man yelled, "It's me. Ozzy."

Dylan recognized his friend's voice and apologized. "Sorry, Oz. I didn't recognize you in the pilot's uniform," he said with a laugh, "you look so damned official."

"Very funny," he replied, rubbing the side of his head. "I'm just glad you were slow on the draw and didn't actually shoot me."

"Probably would have missed you anyway." he joked, putting the gun away. "How did you make out with our fly boys?"

"They are not nice fellows. They had guns and I think they were seriously considering doing us harm," said Ozzy, mimicking shock at the thought. "Right now, they are doing penance in the First Class section of another jet inside the hanger," replied Ozzy with a laugh.

"What about the transponder?" Dylan asked.

"Did a quick hack into the system and altered the response code. No problem, we are now a registered private jet belonging to Avionics Inc. in Geneva, Switzerland."

"Fantastic," beamed Dylan. "And our flight plan?"

"Filed and confirmed. We have a full load of fuel. We formally registered this journey as an equipment test flight. We are due to land at 2120, provided we don't get lost."

Dylan reached around and in one motion, grabbed the railing to raise the stairs, and swung the door shut. "You really do know how to fly this crate, don't you?" Dylan questioned his friend with a slight hint of fake nervousness in his voice.

"Actually, yes," replied Ozzy. "It's been awhile, but I think I still remember how."

Dylan dropped the black bag into one of the plush seats and moved forward to join his friend in the cockpit. "It has been awhile," he said as he went over the pre-flight checks with his partner. "I forgot how much fun this was."

"Juice truck is here." The airport service truck had arrived and assisted in starting the two jet engines. Ozzy contacted Ground Control and received immediate clearance to proceed to the taxi strip. Dylan instinctively looked back towards the hanger as Ozzy received final clearance for takeoff. A van had arrived at the hanger gate. Two men carrying automatic assault rifles were motioning towards the jet. "I think we have some angry folks back at the hanger. You best get this bird up soon or we might end up on the wrong end of some target practice.

"On our way," replied Ozzy, easing the throttles forward. The twin Honeywell 731-40R Turbofan engines increased their thrust, gently starting the Gulfstream G100 on its roll down the runway. The armed men returned to the van, backed up a short distance and drove into the centre of the locked entrance gate, snapping the two sections from their hinges. The force hurled gate to one side in a heap of twisted metal. Ozzy pushed the throttles fully forward, sending jet fuel rushing to the two engines, converting each into 4,250 pounds of thrust. The van screeched to a halt. Abul's men jumped out of the van, but they were too late to interfere as the sleek corporate jet lifted clear of the runway and into the night sky.

LIVERPOOL 2128 GMT

After a smooth, non-eventful flight that lasted almost four hours, most of it circling over the Atlantic, the Gulfstream G100 glided in over the estuary of the River Mersey and touched down on runway 09 at the John Lennon Airport in Liverpool, England.

Dylan was out of his co-pilot's seat and making ready for a quick exit. Ozzy was relaxed as they rolled off the main runway, taking the last taxiway. He shut down the port side engine and listened to ground control as they issued instructions directing the aircraft to a special parking area reserved for test flights. Ozzy acknowledged the instructions and continued along the taxiway, making a sharp left into a parking area normally reserved for local aircraft, shut down the starboard engine and killed all power to the lights. The parking area was in total darkness.

"Carol has done a good job of knocking the lights out," Ozzy stated with a hint of pride. "That girl never ceases to impress me with her talents."

The Gulfstream rolled to a stop alongside the small private aircraft. Dylan unlatched the door and pushed it outwards, walking down the steps before it had completely unfolded. Ozzy followed close behind.

Dylan and Ozzy scrambled across to the far end of the parking area towards a small English sports car. When they reached the vehicle, Dylan dropped onto one knee and felt along the top surface of the rear tire. His fingers quickly found the key Carol had left for them. Seconds later they had entered started the vehicle and began to make their way out of the airport.

"Shit," exclaimed Ozzy. "I forgot the bag with our new documents. We have to go back."

Dylan slammed the car back into low gear and spun it around, heading back towards the Gulfstream. He put the car into a slide, bringing it to a stop alongside the jet. Ozzy jumped out and darted into the plane. He returned seconds later carrying a small red bag, hitting the door switch on the way. As he entered the car, the door on the aircraft closed tightly.

"That ought to hold them for a bit," Ozzy panted.

The car resumed its path out of the parking area, turning left on Dungeon Street and then left again on Hale Road past the entrance to the airport. Dylan spotted the huge yellow submarine mounted in the centre of the traffic circle in recognition of the Beatles. He laughed as Ozzy started to sing the Fab Four's tune.

"We all live in a yellow submarine…"

"Now that is a fitting tribute," he announced, smiling as he checked his mirrors. No one seemed to be following them, but he avoided turning on the vehicle's lights until they had reached the M56 motorway heading for Manchester.

BERLIN   **2250 GMT**

The glass clock smashed into the wall beside Müller, exploding into a mess of glass and mechanical parts on impact.

"What do you mean, the jet disappeared?" Lüdden screamed. "A jet cannot just disappear."

"They must have altered the transponder call sign or perhaps we were given the wrong information by Rashim. In any case, we were unable to track the aircraft on radar," said Müller.

The Pakistani rebel turned in his chair to face Müller. "You had the correct call sign for my aircraft," he hissed. Abul placed his hand on the Colt revolver. "You should be very careful of who you accuse of giving wrong information." Müller seemed to shrink in size. He knew the Pakistani would not hesitate to kill anyone who got in his way.

Although Lüdden was livid, he realized he could not appear to lose control in front of Abul. "Perhaps Herr Müller is correct. This Dylan person or his associate may have altered the transponder code. However, the plane must still be in Europe and one does not hide a Gulfstream jet too easily. We will find it, Rashim."

Rashim Abul slowly raised himself from the wide leather chair. "What bothers me Herr Lüdden is that if this Dylan person could alter an aircraft transponder, what else is he capable of doing?" The Pakistan rebel paused. He made direct eye contact with Lüdden. "Now I question if you really do have the real information for the location of the Priam gold?"

"Yes, of course I do, Rashim," Lüdden countered positively. "The information is exact and matches what I know to be true. There is no doubt we have the correct information to locate the gold."

Abul stepped towards the door. "Then perhaps we should visit the location and verify what you claim to know." Rashim's four armed guards moved in unison to flank Lüdden. The surreptitious movement of Abul's guards made the German very uncomfortable.

"But we were planning to visit the location early next week, as soon as we had recovered your aircraft and your money."

"Apparently the aircraft will take longer than expected to recover, and your men have lost contact with the woman so we may never find the money," hissed Abul. "My men will personally escort you to the location of the gold tomorrow.." It was not a suggestion. Abul had taking over. "When I find the treasure, I will deduct my costs. You can have the rest, "Abul stated with finality. "Of course, if we do not find any gold, then you will have another problem."

Lüdden was enraged. He reached into the top drawer of his desk, but stopped cold when two of the guards swung their rifles around, pointing them at his head. "Let us not be too hasty, Rashim. The treasure is there. We will cover all of your expenses. That is without question. If you wish to visit the location tomorrow, then so it will be." He withdrew his hand from the desk drawer and motioned to Müller. "See that we have a plane is ready to fly us to Foula tomorrow morning. We shall scout the location and verify the location of the treasure and ease our friend's concerns."

Müller let out a sigh of relief. "Yes, Herr Lüdden, "I will arrange it at once."

Abul looked at the two Germans. "You had better hope we are successful," he said with a menacing grin. "It would not appear good to my superiors if you lost both their plane and their money."

"Not to fear, Rashim," Lüdden declared, "the Priam gold is there. We will find it."

"I am sure that you will, my friend. However, it would be better for all concerned if my guards escort you and Herr Müller."

Lüdden shrugged as he turned to the door. "As you wish."

MANCHESTER   2330 GMT

Dylan and Ozzy arrived at the Manchester International Airport and left the rental car in the short-term parking lot. Carol had rented it under an assumed identity and there was no need to check in at the rental desk.

Dylan purchased two tickets on the late flight to Madeira Island, off the coast of West Africa.

It was an ideal place for Dylan and his friends to begin new chapters in their lives.

52

OCTOBER 12, 2007

MADEIRA ISLAND   **1030 GMT**

The warm soothing colours invaded their senses with different shades of green set against an azure sea as Dylan moved the SeaSearcher out of the harbour into the sea off Madeira. The weather was the hallmark of the subtropics. There was a hint of rain in the air. The unique beauty of the island was one of its many charms. Its serenity a product of a narrow ribbon of black sand separating a landscape painted with the green of the mountains and the crystal blue of the sea. It was a world of tranquility.

Carol and Bridgette had arranged for the charter of a 62-foot Flybridge yacht complete with provisioning for two weeks. The SeaSearcher provided a private cabin for each person, and although they had been cruising around Madeira Island for six days, Dylan was still feeling a little awkward about having Ronnie's sister onboard. His cabin was adjacent to Bridgette's, but he had kept his distance. Ozzy and Carol, however, preferred to share the comfort of the private double berth in the forward section. It seemed to be the perfect way to relax after the events in Germany.

Dylan eased the throttle forward on the twin 790 hp motors, until they pushed the yacht along at a comfortable sixteen knots while Bridgette took in the sights from a lounge chair on the rear deck. She enjoyed taking in the sun as Dylan maneuvered the yacht.

After checking the GPS and autopilot from the upper helm station, Dylan plotting a course that would take them on a cruise around to the western side of the island. At 1300, he reduced speed and slowed to a stop. Ozzy came topside in time to assist him drop the anchor just off the bay of Funchal. The highest peaks on the island protected the area, but it still enjoyed the best of the sunshine.

Bridgette and Carol went below to slip into their bikinis before preparing lunch.

"Well, my friend," announced Ozzy, "it just doesn't get much better than this."

Dylan nodded his head. "I wonder what our friends are up to today."

"They are probably still looking for their plane," replied Ozzy with a grin. "I did manage to trace the owner through the original transponder code. The plane belongs to a company in Pakistan. Does the name Ali Bawaraf mean anything to you?"

Dylan looked over to his friend. "The 'Tiger of Waziristan'. He is one ruthless rebel leader. He is a former mercenary soldier who kills first and asks later. We want to avoid dealing with his kind."

"Great," exclaimed Ozzy, "According to my sources, he's listed as the owner of the Gulfstream we borrowed."

"Well, that is not entirely great news, Oz," said Dylan dryly. "Rashim Abul must have been working with Lüdden."

"You think they would come after us?"

Dylan seemed lost in his thoughts. "No, he doesn't have enough to trace anything back to us."

"That's good. However, just in case, Carol and I are going to stay here for a little while. Get something a little smaller than this rig, and just enjoy the island. What about you and Bridgette? What are you two going to do?"

"As far as I know, Bridgette is going back to Berlin. I am going to head over to St. Maarten in the Caribbean," replied Dylan. "By the way, if you and Carol are staying, I would be tempted to continue using the new identification packages we picked up. That way no one will tie you to any of the wild events of the past."

"That probably would be best," agreed Ozzy. "She is quite the lady and we are planning to enjoy life."

Dylan smiled as Carol and Bridgette arrived on deck with a plate full of sandwiches and some cold Coral beer.

"Did I hear you say you were going to St. Maarten's?" asked Bridgette.

Dylan looked up at the tall statuesque woman. "Yes, I want to follow up on the last page I found in the cylinder. I was not able to get it decoded. The Germans used a different group of settings on the Enigma transmission."

"What do you think it is?"

"I am not entirely sure, but the Germans never coded any numbers. The paper contains a reference that could be latitude and longitude coordinates. It's just a hunch, but I want to check it out."

"You want some help?" asked Ozzy.

"No. You people have been through enough. Stay and enjoy yourselves."

"Well, just call if you need us."

Dylan looked at his friends. "I will keep in touch."

53

OCTOBER 13, 2007

FOULA ISLAND   **1440 GMT**

"It looks like Mr. Dylan has put one over on you, Herr Lüdden."

"That is impossible," bellowed the leader of the underground Neo-Nazi Democratic Party. "The treasure is here, somewhere. We just have to keep searching."

"The accuracy of the war-time instruments was not as exact as what we are dealing with today, Abul," said Müller, somewhat hopefully. "The topography has changed much over sixty years. Herr Lüdden is correct. We must keep looking."

Rashim Abul observed the two Germans moving about with their handheld GPS units. The coordinates they retrieved from the Iron Cross put their search area on top of a small peninsula overlooking the North Sea. The ground was a completely flat area that dropped off a sharp cliff three hundred feet down into frigid waters below. "There is no way anyone would have brought any treasure up that cliff. This location is a ruse." Abul was getting angrier by the moment. "I am beginning to believe the whole treasure idea was nothing but a scam you concocted to steal from me, Lüdden." Abul advanced towards the German leader. The Pakistan guards closed ranks behind. "This whole story about the treasure and Hitler escaping was all a trick."

"That's absurd, Rashim," Lüdden protested, backing towards the edge of the cliff. "You know I would not do anything against you."

"You have failed me. You have lost ten million US dollars and my corporate jet. How do you propose to repay me?"

Lüdden paused for a moment. He knew he did not have an answer. "I can't at this moment. I must find the treasure first."

Abul kept advancing towards Lüdden. The German was only a few feet from the edge of the cliff. He turned his head and could see the vast stretch of cliff face running along the coast, the waves breaking over the rocks below and dragging back into the sea. It was a tranquil, but deadly scene. Lüdden was starting to panic. "Müller, do something." he screamed.

"Müller can do nothing. He is as guilty as you."

"You must give me more time," the German leader pleaded. "I will find the treasure. I will repay you twice what you have lost." He reached into his jacket pocket and pulled out a piece of paper. "Look, I have more proof of our great leader's escape. It has the coordinates of the island where he escaped. This is worth millions."

Abul stood stone-faced. "No," he said coldly. "You are finished."

In a desperate move to escape, Lüdden lunged toward Abul. A hail of bullets from the Pakistani guard's rifles stopped his forward progress before he reached the Pakistan rebel. Lüdden stood motionless for a moment and then slowly stumbled back to the edge of the cliff. Abul took two steps towards the body that tottered before him. Lüdden was on the edge of the cliff. Abul reached out and removed the paper from the dying man's hand. His eyes locked with Lüdden's as he gave the German a gentle push, sending him backwards over the cliff. The leader of the underground Neo-Nazi

Democratic Party fell downwards in a slow spiral onto the rocks below. The rebel leader watched as the waves quickly swallowed him up and pulled him into the sea.

Rashim Abul showed no emotion. He scanned the paper he took from Lüdden, smiled and stuffed it into his shirt pocket. He looked over at Müller who had wet himself. "Throw this coward over the cliff too," he said ruthlessly.

Abul's men moved towards Müller. The smaller German suddenly stood erect in defiance of the advancing guards. They were almost within reach of him when Müller reached into his jacket and extracted the Luger pistol that Lüdden had used to kill von Schlippenbach only months before. He took dead aim at Rashim Abul and fired, hitting the Pakistan rebel in the right eye. The bullet exited the back of Abul's head, taking most of his brain with it as it completed its trajectory. The guards were dumbfounded. Müller fired off three more rounds. Two of the shots hit Abul's body. The third missed. The Pakistani guards recovered from the shock at Müller's uncharacteristic move and emptied their rifles into his body.

EPILOGUE

NOVEMBER 29, 2007

ST. MARTEN   **1434 GMT**

A fit and tanned Sean Dylan sat in the cockpit of a forty-four foot Morgan Cutter, sipping on a warm cup of tea as he read the daily paper. He spotted the name 'Foula" within an article on the previous page. He paused, turned back to the page and scanned the article. The story was about three bodies found off the coast of Foula. *"All three bodies had apparently been shot. There was no apparent motive. Locals remembered some foreigners coming to the island back in October, but no one saw them again, nor could anyone remember them leaving."*

"Do you always sit around reading the paper?"

The sound of the voice caught Dylan by surprise. He looked up to see the shape of a beautiful woman standing in the sunlight.

"May I come aboard?"

The shock of seeing Bridgette rendered Dylan immobile for a moment. He was speechless. He nodded his head.

"I'll take that as a 'Yes'," she said with a smile as she climbed aboard the yacht.

Dylan quickly recovered from the shock. "What on earth are you doing here?" he asked.

"I was just in the neighbourhood and thought I would drop by to see how you were doing."

Dylan gave her a hug. He was very pleased to see her.

The two friends spent the afternoon reminiscing over a bottle of Pinot Noir. When they discussed the events surrounding Ronnie's death, Bridgette reached into her small travel bag and handed Dylan some letters. "These will help explain some of what went on."

Dylan read the letters. The first was from Ronnie. She wrote to Bridgette about the relationship between Jim Clark and Captain Neil Evans, the pilot of the "Irene". Clark's mother was Evan's daughter, the one the RAF pilot never had a chance to see.

The second letter was from Schneider's Granddaughter. Schneider had received the pocket watch Dylan had recovered from the wreck of the U-1220. It had made his last days very happy. Schneider had passed away in November.

Dylan showed Bridgette an article from the newspaper. "I'm thinking I might go to Foula in a couple of years too, when everything has become very quiet."

"But why would you want to go there?" she asked in total amazement.

"Well, Lüdden and his pals really did not have a snowball's chance in hell of finding the gold. You see, the Professor and I exchanged the real Iron Cross with a replica with false latitude and longitude coordinates."

"You naughty boy." she exclaimed with a laugh. "That explains the bodies. They must have been absolutely ticked."

"At the very least," Dylan replied with a grin.

"What are you going to do now?"

"I thought it might be interesting to check out the real location someday," he replied. "Right now though, I am heading down the coast of South America to Ilha Fernando de Noronha, a tiny island whose location that matches the coordinates in the last encrypted message. I think it might have been the final destination of the passengers transported by the U-1220. If nothing else, it would be interesting to poke around and see what I can find." Dylan paused and looked at the attractive woman sitting across from him. "It would definitely be more enjoyable if I could make the trip with a friend."

Bridgette smiled that beautiful smile.

THE END

ISBN 142514059-9